I HEART VEGAS

Lindsey Kelk is the author of *I Heart New York*, *I Heart Hollywood*, *I Heart Paris*, *I Heart London* and *The Single Girl's To-Do List*. When she isn't writing, reading, listening to music or watching more TV than is healthy, Lindsey likes to wear shoes, shop for shoes and judge the shoes of others. She loves living in New York but misses Sherbet Fountains, London and drinking Gin & Elderflower cocktails with her friends. Not necessarily in that order.

To find out more about the *I Heart* series, sign up for the newsletter, read exclusive extracts and much much more, visit www.iheartvegas.co.uk

Follow Lindsey on Twitter @LindseyKelk

By the same author

I Heart New York
I Heart Hollywood
I Heart Paris
I Heart London

The Single Girl's To-Do List

Jenny Lopez Has a Bad Week
(novella only available on ebook)

LINDSEY KELK

I Heart Vegas

HARPER

Harper
An imprint of HarperCollins*Publishers*
77–85 Fulham Palace Road,
Hammersmith, London W6 8JB

www.harpercollins.co.uk

A Paperback Original 2011
7

A catalogue record for this book
is available from the British Library

ISBN: 978 0 00 734562 5

Set in Melior by Palimpsest Book Production Limited,
Falkirk, Stirlingshire

Printed and bound in Great Britain by
Clays Ltd, St Ives plc

MIX
Paper from
responsible sources
FSC™ C007454

Faster, faster on your feet . . .

For Ryan

Acknowledgements

Top of my Christmas card list this year is . . . Rowan Lawton, the best agent & tour buddy a gal could wish for. Everyone at HCUK, especially Lynne, Thalia and Hana. I'm sorry I've taken so many years off your lives. Thanks to everyone at *Marie Claire* for the amazing opportunities you've given me this year, especially Charlotte, Andrea and my twinsie, Kasie. And of course, a special thank you to Holly Patrick and Elinor Fewster – fag and a mag, anyone?

Without Sarah Donovan, I would never have made it through Vegas alive and without Jackie Dunning, Emma Ingram, Della Bolat, Sarah Benton, Kari Torson, Janet Bunde, Beth Ziemacki and Rachael Wright, I wouldn't make it through every day alive.

So, you know, thanks kids.

CHAPTER ONE

Hands on hips, I stood in the middle of the living room and surveyed my work. Excellent. The Christmas tree was up, champagne was chilling in the ice bucket and the apartment was, hmm, passable. As long as no one turned the big lights on. Alex would be impressed. Almost as impressed as the random man on Kent Avenue staring up into our window, surveying my pants. Shit. If I was going to insist on walking around the house in my knickers, we were going to have to get curtains. I staggered backwards, trying not to trip over in my borrowed high heels and hit the light switch. Another bright idea, Angela, I mentally slapped myself as I stumbled straight into the kitchen counter, banging my knee hard as I went. Because nothing went as well with black lace lingerie as a purple throbbing bruise, did it? Surely most twenty-eight-year-olds had grown out of being such an incredibly clumsy cow. Surely most twenty-eight-year-olds didn't wander around in the pitch black wearing four-inch heels. Surely most twenty-eight-year-olds weren't like me.

There was a reason for my playing peep show.

Alex, my lovely boyfriend and quintessential rock god, had been away touring the Far East for exactly forty-three days, and he was due home any minute. Having had far too long to think about how I would welcome him back, I'd let Jenny, my best friend and quintessential sex kitten, talk me into a sultry seduction scenario over one too many afternoon cocktails. Although now I was here, trussed up like a chicken, I couldn't help but feel he'd have been as happy with beer and a pizza. Served me right for meeting her at the bar at Hotel Delmano on a Wednesday afternoon. I was so weak in the face of peer pressure. And Pinot grigio.

'Alex gets back tonight, right?' she had asked.

'Yep,' I had replied.

'Big plans?'

'Beer. Pizza. Lovely sit down. He'll have been on a plane for a billion hours.'

'Really?'

'Yes.' Pause. 'Why?'

'Dude, if my guy had kept his pants on for an entire month while he was on tour in Japan, where all the groupies live, well, I kinda think he'd be expecting a more exciting welcome home.'

At which point she removed her spike-heeled, black patent leather Louboutins, forced them onto my feet and a plan was born.

'Too late now, Clark,' I whispered to myself, rubbing my knee and hobbling over to the sofa to arrange myself in what I hoped would be a sultry fashion. Sexpot was not my natural setting. Not that I wasn't excited to see him. My 'ladyboner', as Jenny would call it, was at Thumper levels. I was twitterpated out of season. Seriously, I was just about ready to knock

2

Alex right off his feet the second he walked through the door, but I still wasn't convinced spending twenty minutes trying to fasten a pair of suspenders onto seamed stockings (after spending twenty minutes trying to get the seams straight in the first place) was a good use of my time. Not least of all because for most of that twenty minutes, I looked less like Dita Von Teese and more like a very slutty dog chasing its own tail. Why were these things so hard to put on? How was putting your neck out fastening the bastards supposed to put you in the mood? There was also the fact that there were a lot of other things I probably should have been doing with my time. Like Christmas shopping. Like looking for work. Like cleaning the bathroom for the first time in three weeks instead of going in, pulling a face and shutting the door. Lots of things, really.

But now wasn't the time to worry about that, I told myself as I lowered my arse onto the couch, trying to fan my dark blonde hair out around my head and position myself so as to avoid any and all exposure of cellulite. Which was basically impossible. The clock on the DVD player flashed nine p.m. Alex's flight was due into JFK at seven-twenty. He would be walking through the door any second. I yawned and tried not to fall off the sofa. It had been a long hard day of procrastination. Any second now he'd be home. Any second . . .

'Dude, hit lights?'

Keys jangled in the door. I rubbed my eyes, leaving big black smudges on my fists. Keys? Burglars? Burglars with keys? I noticed the champagne bobbing around in a bucket full of water. What time was it? And why was I semi-naked?

'Where do you want this?' The voice again, this time definitely inside the front door. With very little time to make a decision, I decided to stay on the couch and hide. I really wasn't dressed for vigilantism. Batman hardly ever wore heels, after all.

'Uh, just drop it anywhere. Angela?'

Angela? That was me! And that voice belonged to Alex! It wasn't burglars, it was . . .

'Woah, dude!'

The living-room lights flickered into life, revealing me on the couch in all my sultry glory. If looking like a very confused, cut-price hooker with messed up eye make-up and a little bit of drool on her pillow was in fact sultry. Judging by the expressions on Alex, Graham and Craig's faces, it wasn't. Of course he'd come home with his band mates. And a four-way with my boyfriend, his gay drummer and super slutty guitarist, who I was almost certain must have at least one STD at any given time, really wasn't in my plans for the evening.

'Oh, Angela.' Graham, gay as the wind, turned away immediately. Craig, straight as a die, grinned from ear to ear. 'Nice rack.'

'Craig!' I couldn't even look at the giggling guitarist. 'If you want to keep your balls, just stop bloody laughing.'

I pushed myself up, performing a very clumsy fan dance using the sofa cushions before tripping over my own shoes and landing in a graceless pile at the foot of the Christmas tree.

'Alex?' I called, face in the floor.

'Angela?' he replied. I could tell he was trying not to laugh. Twat.

'Could you turn the lights out, please?'

'Absolutely.'

The living-room lights dimmed, and somewhere inside my shame I heard him herding the others out of the apartment. Much to Craig's dismay. A healthy combination of humiliation and the throbbing pain in my knee kept me face down on the hardwood floor while I waited for the click of the lock. At least my Christmas tree smelled nice. That was something.

'Hey.'

I opened my eyes to see a pair of knackered Converse by my side, followed by a pair of bright green eyes covered by a floppy black fringe that was considerably longer than the last time I had seen it.

'Hi.'

'Nice outfit.'

'Thanks.'

'The flight was delayed,' he explained. 'I thought you'd be asleep.'

'Well, I was . . .'

Lying side by side on the cold floor wasn't quite how I'd envisaged this welcome working out. Well, sometimes it was, but mostly I'd hoped we'd make it to the bedroom. Or at least stick to the sofa. Alex reached out a hand and wiped away some of my smudged mascara.

'I missed you,' he said.

'I missed you too.' I really was going to need to ice my knee. 'Probably should have stuck with the beer-and-pizza welcome-back, shouldn't I?'

Alex hopped up and reached down to grab my hand. Wobbling to my feet, I let him wrap my arms around his neck before draping his own around my waist, hands resting on my hips. Staring up at him, I couldn't quite catch my breath. Even after dating him for more than a year, even after living with him for the last few months, it never failed to delight me just how bloody hot Alex Reid actually was. His hair was messy, his bright eyes a little bloodshot from his long flight, but he was still so beautiful. High cheek-bones, full lips, pale skin. I wanted to lick him. Sometimes in public. But I didn't. Mostly. And he was mine.

He leaned forward and rested those lips gently against mine and I felt a shiver all over my body that had nothing to do with standing around in my pants. Well, maybe it was tangentially related, but it didn't have anything to do with being cold.

'Now, you know I love pizza,' he whispered into my ear. 'But it can wait until tomorrow. I really, really missed you.'

Wrapping me up in another kiss, we staggered towards the bedroom door, Alex shedding clothing as we went, me trying not to let my knee give out. So the evening hadn't gone quite according to plan, but as long as I was getting the result I was after, who was I to complain?

A few hours later, I was rudely awoken by a throbbing pain in my left kneecap. I bent my leg slowly, wincing through the pain but too tired to get up and take painkillers. When I wasn't in agony, this was my favourite way to be: not quite awake, not quite asleep, watching Alex dream away on his pillow. It was like watching an extremely attractive puppy take a nap. He stirred in his sleep, turning towards me, hair post-coitally mussed up, and his foot brushed against my bare leg while he made tiny sleeping noises. I'd got so used to having the bed to myself, the thrill of waking to find Alex beside me wouldn't let me go back to sleep. Instead, I lay and looked at him, fighting the urge to wake him up just so I could see him smile.

These few months had been amazing. At first, the idea of moving in with him terrified me. I'd lived with someone before and that had not gone well, but touch wood, I'd been here for a while now and we were still in a good place: Alex was still putting the toilet seat down and I was still shaving my legs every day. Domestic bliss. I snuggled up against him and sighed happily when he draped a hand over my hip, his warm legs curling up under mine, his bare chest pressed against my back. This was how it was supposed to be. This was how it would be. For ever.

Alex Reid was a heavy sleeper at the best of times, but adding jet lag into the mix? He was going to be out for at least twelve hours. Which gave me almost enough time to clean the apartment. Obviously, my charms had kept him distracted the night before, but in the cold (below freezing, in fact) light of day, I saw my hovel through new eyes. It was amazing what sort of a sty you were prepared to live in when it was just you. When Alex did finally surface, I wanted him to be happy about coming home, not trip up over the pair of tights I'd taken off on the sofa three nights before during a mega Harry Potter movie marathon that ended when I passed out on the sofa at two a.m., too tired to crawl to bed.

I managed to clean the bathroom, sweep the living room and scrub the kitchen before I accepted I was going to have to brave the frigid outdoors. My constant need to have the heating on full blast all of the time meant that leaving bin bags full of rubbish in the apartment was not a possibility. The word 'fester' had been bandied about once before, and there was very little a bottle of Febreze could do when you had four-day-old sushi going manky in the corner.

Wrapping Alex's giant Brooklyn Industries parka over my shorts, T-shirt and ancient cardigan Uggs, I shuffled out of the door and down the hallway with two giant bin bags, trying not to breathe in as I went. Fucking hell it was chilly. I cracked open the front door, chucked the rubbish as close as I could to the kerb without hitting the great big man walking his teeny dog and slammed it shut on the frosty clouds that had been my huffs and puffs. And then opened it again on a very angry-looking postman.

'Sorry,' I said, holding my hand out for either the mail or a slap on the wrists. 'Cold.'

'You think?' he said with chattering teeth and a filthy look.

I'd dismissed the idea before, but maybe I *could* be a postman. I watched him hop back on his bike and pedal furiously away. Obviously I would have a super-cute vintage fixie instead of the regulation red road bike. And possibly a nicer outfit. But it could be good: I'd get some exercise and be a vital member of the community. As long as no one wanted their post delivered between November and March. Or before midday. But as I was holding three envelopes in my hand at ten a.m. in December, that seemed unlikely. I reluctantly added 'postman' to the list of unsuitable jobs along with accountant, physicist and barista. Nine times out of ten I couldn't remember what I'd gone into the kitchen for, let alone how three thousand people a day wanted their Starbucks.

The need for work was becoming pressing. I still

had my column in the UK edition of *The Look*, but that really wasn't enough to live on and my savings were running dry. I really needed more work here in the States, but I was struggling. At first I'd put it down to a slow summer. And then a hectic autumn. And no one hired at Christmas. Fingers crossed January would bring something exciting, otherwise I was going to be finding out the difference between a venti wet latte and a grande Americano very soon. But still, at least I had post.

Everyone alive knows there is nothing more exciting than post, especially at Christmas. Two of the envelopes had a distinctive Christmas-card vibe to them, one with British stamps. Too impatient-slash-lazy to go back upstairs to open them, I perched on the step, knees pulled up under Alex's coat, and tore into them. Ahhh, merry Christmas from Louisa, Tim and the Bump. The second was a Christmas card from Bloomingdale's. What lovely people, I thought happily; must pay them a visit as soon as I find the credit card I begged Alex to hide from me before he went away and have since spent weeks tearing the place apart to find. The third envelope was distinctly less seasonal – white oblong, too thin to bear goodwill – but while I was there, I figured I may as well open it.

And immediately wished I hadn't.

I scanned the letter quickly, feeling sicker and sicker by the second.

Dear Ms Clark,
    We have been informed that your employment status has changed . . . As such your L-1 visa has been revoked with immediate effect . . . Thirty days to leave the United States . . . Please

contact the following department with any
questions . . .

Your visa has been revoked.
Thirty days to leave.
Standing up, I floated back up the stairs, my fingers
skimming the wall as I went. Was the plaster always
this bumpy? Were there always so many steps?
Fumbling with my key in the lock, I let myself back
into the clean, sparkly apartment. It seemed smaller.
The Christmas cards slipped from my hand and clat-
tered lightly onto the hardwood floor as I moved
through the rooms. Eventually I came to a standstill
in the bathroom before a sharp stabbing pain in my
stomach brought me to my knees and, without really
knowing what was happening, I threw up, INS letter
still in hand. Thirty days to leave.
Minutes or hours could have passed, I wasn't sure,
but eventually the trance subsided and I was left
sweaty, tear-stained and broken on the bathroom floor.
I read the letter once more, looking for something I
hadn't seen before – a side note, a postscript, anything
that didn't say I had to leave the country in a month's
time. But it wasn't there. How could such an important,
life-changing message be so brief? America was the
land of opportunity, of 'How can I help you?' and
'Have a nice day', not 'It's been fun, now piss off'.
This wasn't possible. I left the letter on the cold tiles
and pulled myself up, gripping the sink with my
clammy hands. A few splashes of water to the face
later, I was able to look in the mirror. I did not like
what I saw. And apparently neither did America.
    'OK,' I told myself. 'This is going to be OK. We'll
sort this.'
Even my reflection didn't look convinced.

There was only one thing to do. I engaged my last three working brain cells to remember where I'd put my phone and pressed my speed-dial.

'Angie?'

'Jenny,' I whispered. 'I need you.'

CHAPTER TWO

Jenny Lopez was, as far as I was concerned, the luckiest girl who ever did live. Now, she would tell you that everyone makes their own luck, but after you had nodded sagely and agreed, she would then go on to tell you how she was dating a Swedish male model whom she had initially offended on an epic level by assuming he was gay (I might have suggested it first, to be fair), was living with a female model who shared her shoe size, was never there and was stupid enough to pay three-quarters of the rent, and, if that wasn't enough, she had lucked into an amazing job organizing events for one of our best friend's PR firm. I was very proud of her. I was also, on occasion, ever so slightly jealous. A feeling that didn't exactly go away as the lift doors opened into Erin White PR to display a life-sized black and white photo of a half-naked Sigge, Jenny's boyfriend, advertising a very scanty pair of pants. English usage. There were some things you never needed to know about your friend's boyfriend, and as far as I was concerned, the contents of his Calvins was one of them. But it was a bit late for that. Jenny was an oversharer.

I blinked four times at the receptionist, who acknowledged me with a raised eyebrow, then skulked directly
over to Jenny's office, trying not to make eye contact
with any of the girls on the floor. I'd never quizzed
Erin on her hiring policy, but I was prepared to bet
none of these girls had ever seen the inside of a
McDonald's. Everyone was so bright and perky. Why
they were called public relations when they bore no
relation to the public whatsoever was a mystery to me.

Luckily, I was soon safely inside Jenny's office, hidden
from the judgemental, overly made-up eyes of the office
minions. That is to say, Jenny's corner office. Jenny's
huge, airy, floor-to-ceiling-windows corner office. Ever
so slightly mad, accidentally ended up living with a
high-class hooker in LA, borderline alcoholic Jenny had
it together. Forget earthquakes, hurricanes and the
advent of Justin Bieber; if Jenny being a grown-up wasn't
a sign of the apocalypse, I didn't know what was.

'Hey.' I knocked lightly on the door and stuck my
head in cautiously. 'It's me.'

Jenny leapt up from behind her desk, resplendent
in her sexy secretary skyscraper heels, pencil skirt and
pussy-bow blouse, masses of hair levered away from
her face by several thousand kirby grips. She made
Joan from *Mad Men* look like the office frump.

'Hey!' She skittered around her desk to give me a
huge hug before holding up her hand for silence and
pressing a button on her Star Trek phone. 'Melissa,
could you bring me two Diet Cokes, please?'

She paused, biting her bottom lip with eyes as wide
as saucers and pointing at the phone with pantoesque
enthusiasm. Like I said, I was so proud.

'Sure, Ms Lopez,' a voice chirped over the intercom.
'Can I get you anything else at all?'

'That'll be fine, Melissa,' Jenny replied. 'And please stop calling me Ms Lopez – you're making me feel like I'm your homeroom teacher.'

'You love being called Ms Lopez, don't you?' I asked as she took her finger off the button.

'First time the bitch calls me Jenny, she's fired,' she confirmed, settling back into her chair as a tiny blonde bounced through the door and deposited two icy cans of Coke on the desk in front of us before vanishing in silence. 'God, I love having an assistant. Now, tell me everything.'

'I'm getting kicked out.' I picked up my drink to see it had already been opened. Melissa wouldn't want Ms Lopez to break a nail. Melissa was a genius. 'I don't have a job, which means I don't have a visa, which means I'm getting kicked out.'

'You do have a job. You're my therapist and personal shopper,' Jenny acknowledged. 'Actually, scratch that, I'm yours. What is it you do for me?'

'Generally make you feel better about your life?' I suggested. 'Oh, and I get your shoes reheeled.' I passed her a shoe bag containing the borrowed Louboutins, freshly heeled and shined to perfection by the lovely man on the corner of North Eleventh and Berry.

'Thanks,' she said, stashing the shoes under her desk. 'What did Alex say?'

'He's sleeping.' I shook my head hard, trying to shake away the black and white lines of the letter that had imprinted themselves on my eyelids. 'I didn't want to wake him.'

'Pretty sure he'd want to be woken for this,' she said, holding her hand out. 'You must have really rocked his world last night, huh? Give me the letter.'

'I flashed his friends, fell over, knackered my knee and then rocked his world,' I said, ticking the order of events off on my hands before pulling the offending piece of paper out of my MJ bag with my thumb and forefinger. I just didn't even want to touch it. 'Enjoy.'

'As long as worlds were rocked,' she said, eyes trained on the letter. 'Shit, Angie.'

It was never a good sign when Jenny reacted to something badly. The queen of positive thinking, I'd sort of been hoping she would laugh, ball it up and throw the letter in the bin. Instead, she was putting on her reading glasses.

'This doesn't look great. Did Mary tell you they were going to do this?'

'Nope.'

Mary Stein had been my editor and ally at Spencer Media, but since we'd parted ways, I hadn't heard a peep out of her. Not totally shocking: Mary was all business and, well, we weren't in business together any more, but even so, I couldn't believe she hadn't given me a heads-up on this. I mean, it wasn't a slap on the wrists, it was a deportation notice.

'So, no luck with anything new?' Jenny gave me her concerned face. 'You email any other editors?'

'I've emailed everyone I've ever met,' I said. When Alex was first away, I'd spent days contacting every single editor I'd ever met in New York City. People from newspapers, websites, blogs – everything but high-school newsletters. And they were next. I'd even tried setting up my own blog with my fingers crossed for enough ad revenue to keep me in the style to which I had become accustomed, but to date I wasn't even making enough to keep a gerbil in the style to which it had become accustomed. Those spinning-wheel things are not cheap.

'But there's nothing. Not even rejection emails. It doesn't make any sense. I know I'm not exactly the world's most renowned journalist, but after the whole James Jacobs thing, I thought I'd definitely be able to find something.'

'The whole James Jacobs thing' being the time I accidentally outed an actor when I was just supposed to be interviewing him. Still, as my dad always said, better out than in.

'OK, I'm scheduling you an appointment with our lawyer,' Jenny said, tapping away at her keyboard while I pushed my Diet Coke back and forth, leaving a wet trail across her desk. 'He definitely works on employment visas and stuff. We have an Australian girl here, and he helped with that. You have to go and see him. Can you do this afternoon?'

'What else do I have to do?' I asked. This woman was truly a goddess. 'I'll be there.'

'He's hot.'

'It won't help.'

'It always helps.'

'Fair enough,' I accepted. 'Bad news does sound better coming from a pretty man. I don't know, I just hate not knowing what's going to happen.'

'That's because I turned you into a super-awesome take-control-of-your-own-destiny proactive ass-kicking wonder-woman,' Jenny explained before taking a deep breath and a deep draught from her Coke. 'But now there's some stuff that's out of your control and that's hard to accept. Unless you take the control back.'

'But how do I do that, oh genius?'

I genuinely couldn't see a way. Granted, I was still wallowing deep in the mire of imminent deportation, but how was I going to turn it around in thirty days? No one would give me a job, and I was fairly certain the US government wasn't going to make a special exception for me to stay here just because I asked nicely. There wasn't even time to sleep on it: thirty days was too soon.

'I want to take it back,' I said, trying to sound determined. 'In fact, I demand it back. Control, I summon thee.' I slapped the table, making my can jump. 'I do want to be in control, but I don't know what to do.'

'Honey, I am the queen of solving the unsolvable. It's what I do, it's what I live for.' Jenny pulled her thinking face while I thanked my lucky stars for my wonderful friends. She was very good at putting problems into perspective. 'To help poor unfortunate souls like yourself.'

'Please don't quote *The Little Mermaid* in my time of need,' I begged. 'Although, if you can strike a deal to swap my voice for a visa, I'd consider it.'

'And the world's karaoke bars would rejoice,' she murmured. 'OK, am I right in thinking if you get a job, you can get a visa, or do you need a visa to get a job?'

'Both.'

'That's not going to work, Ange.' Jenny shook her head. 'Visa or job? Which comes first?'

'The chicken?'

'That doesn't even make sense . . .'

Before Jenny could get up out of her chair and throttle me, the door flew open and Erin sailed in. That sealed it: I could never work in PR. Here I was, sitting in this sparkly, shiny office with dirty hair and jeans that hadn't been washed for so long that they had started cleaning themselves, while Erin's hair was so shiny, I could actually see how disgusting mine was in its reflective surface. For shame.

'Angie's being deported,' Jenny answered for me. As was the way amongst our people. 'Her visa got revoked.'

'Shit.'

We all nodded. It was pretty much the only viable response.

We sat in silence for a moment, Erin pursing her lips in concentration, Jenny staring at her shoes, me thinking that I really should have taken my coat off before now. I was not going to feel the benefit when I got back outside. Massive concern. As was the fact that I had apparently become my mother.

'You know what?' Erin kicked off her high, high heels and leaned back in her chair. 'That's the easiest problem I've had to solve all day. I can't believe it took me a whole minute to work it out.'

It was?

'It is?'

'Sure.' She looked at me and shrugged. 'Just marry Alex.'

Huh.

For a moment I felt sick. Then hot. Then cold. Then hot again because I still had my coat on.

Just marry Alex.

Ooh.

'Oh my God, that makes so much freaking sense,' Jenny shrieked. It was as though Erin had walked in, put two and two together and miraculously come up with a four when all we'd been getting were fives and threes. 'You can just marry Alex! Why didn't I think of that?'

'Because it's stupid?' I suggested.

Because it was. Wasn't it?

'Do you think he'd say no?' Jenny gave me her best sympathetic eyes.

What a bitch. And the second she said it, I was terrified he might.

'I don't know what he'd say and I don't want to know,' I said quickly, curtly. 'Next idea, please.'

My brain was completely overloaded. Half of me had heard the words 'marry Alex' and already run off down the aisle, drowning out my worries with the 'Wedding March'. The other half had caught the 'for a visa' part and was not happy. It just felt a bit grubby. In that slightly grubby, slightly exciting, but almost definitely it's-a-bad-idea way. The idea of getting married to stay in the country hadn't even occurred to me. And now it had been floated, it did not make me feel good about myself. In fact, it made me feel a bit sick. Not because I didn't want to marry Alex – locking that boy down legally was absolutely on my to-do list; but not like this. A marriage of convenience was not a marriage I was interested in.

'He would totally do it.' Erin raised her eyebrows, a picture of innocence. 'And that would solve all your problems, right? I mean, even if they want to investigate you guys, you get to stay here while they do it. And you're a real couple – you'd pass.'

'It's not like you're not already living together,' Jenny added in a hurry. 'And we'd all give testimonials. I can totally verify Alex's sex noises.'

'Thank you.' I wished all the lucky stars I'd thanked earlier into an early supernova. 'But seriously. Not happening.'

They looked at me with very different expressions on their faces. Jenny's was somewhere between pride and optimism with just a dash of 'what the fuck is she thinking'. Erin clearly thought I was insane.

'Jenny – ' I decided to take a different tack – 'how would you feel if Sigge asked you to marry him for a visa?'

'I would have that shit on lockdown before you could sing "Here comes the bride",' she replied, her face completely straight. 'Have you seen him? The dude is ridonkulous.'

'You're probably the wrong person to have this conversation with,' I said, shaking off my coat. Too little, too late. 'What I mean is, if he asked you to marry you just for a visa and you said yes, you'd never really know if he loved you, would you? Whether or not he would have asked you to marry him even if there wasn't a visa involved. Even if you loved the arse off him, you'd never really know whether or not it would have happened out of love. It would always be hanging over you, the reason you got married. It's like when people meet online, it's always there. Even if they say it's not, it is. A marriage of convenience is not a marriage.'

'Oh, honey.' Erin laid a perfectly manicured hand on my knee. 'I keep forgetting this is your first. A marriage of convenience is the perfect starter marriage.'

America was a very strange place sometimes.

'I know this is going to sound very old-fashioned,' I said – I was going to give it one last try – 'but I'm really hoping to just stick to one marriage. I know it's against the odds, but I really am hoping.'

'Angie, we're all hoping.' Erin held up The Letter. 'But for real, if it's the difference between staying in the country or not staying in the country, wouldn't you rather marry a man you love than hightail it back to the UK?'

Hmm.

'Back to your old life?' Jenny added.

Gulp.

'Back to your mom?'

Shit.

'Fair point.' I dropped my head backwards and stared at the ceiling. 'I really can't go back.'

'Oh, Angie.' Jenny leaned right across her desk, arms outstretched. 'Please ask him. He'll totally say yes – the dude still gives you puppy eyes every time you walk into a room. I'll organize everything, all you'd have to do is show. It's not really a visa wedding if you're in love, if we do it properly. Please?'

'Actually, it could be kind of awesome,' Erin chipped in. 'We could get you a venue super easy, dress shouldn't be a problem, and we'd get an awesome deal on a caterer. How long do you think it would take to put together, operations director?'

I took a Twizzler from the candy dish on Jenny's desk. Two hours ago I was fishing hair out of a plughole and looking forward to watching a repeat of *Elf* on the settee. Now I was organizing a quickie wedding to ensure I wouldn't be dragged kicking and screaming from the country in four weeks' time.

'Like, two weeks?' Jenny stuck out her bottom lip. 'Ten days if we really pushed things. And if we could get her into a sample-size gown with no alterations, which we totally could if she puts that Twizzler down.'

She put the Twizzler down.

'Brooklyn's gonna be the easiest place to get a venue, but we could maybe pull some strings in Manhattan if we could do a Friday. We'd never get a weekend, though. How about the Bell House? Music venue, nice tie-in to the groom's day job? Or I could pull some strings back at the Union?'

'I could call the PR at the W,' Erin mused. 'Or the Hudson. That's a little too midtown, though.'

I sat in silence, staring at The Letter, listening to my friends planning my wedding, imagining myself in some super swanky hotel, clad in a ridiculous designer dress, hobbling down the aisle in borrowed shoes. Despite the ridiculousness of the whole thing, the only real problem I had was simple. I couldn't see Alex in any of it. This wasn't us.

Just imagining asking him to do this for me made my eyes well up and my heart beat faster, and not in a good way. What if he did say yes? What if we did get married, then he freaked out about being stuck with me because of the visa? I didn't want my marriage to be an obligation. Even worse, what if I asked and he said no? Maybe he wasn't ready. He'd ask when he was ready. We'd had this conversation; I didn't want to push him. He meant too much. He meant everything.

'Flowers might be tricky.' Jenny was still planning out loud. 'We'd need to call in some favours.'

'We've got favours to spare, doll,' Erin commented. 'I'm more worried about the lighting design.'

'Um, ladies?' My interrupting their creative process was not particularly well received. 'What if we put all our creative brain-power into working out another way for me to stay in the country? I'm not being difficult, honestly – I just really, really don't want to do this.'

They both deflated before my eyes. I felt quite bad. There was nothing Jenny loved more than threatening people to get what she wanted. I felt like I'd taken her best toy away.

'Aside from the fact that I don't want to bully my boyfriend down the aisle, I want to be here because I deserve to be here.'

Now this is where I was prepared to accept I was being naïve.

'If I can't get a visa without getting married, then what's the point? That will just mean I haven't achieved anything since I got here. I'll be right back where I started. I might as well go home, get myself at least seven cats and start referring to myself in the third person while paying for the bus with exact change. And that's not happening. So can we please apply our not inconsiderable talents to finding another way for me to stay?'

Jenny wiped away a fake tear. 'My baby is all grown up.'

'So you can't get a job without a visa?' Erin said, accepting defeat and chomping a Twizzler. How come she was allowed one and I wasn't? I hated the naturally skinny.

'And I can't get a visa without a job,' I confirmed. 'Basically, I think I'll need someone to sponsor me like Spencer Media did.'

'Can we do it?' She chewed, swallowed and stared at Jenny. 'You might as well work here. Seems like I'll take in any damn waif or stray.'

'I'm the best damn employee you have,' Jenny cried, slapping her hand on the desk. 'Kinda. But, yes! You could totally work here. As my bitch.'

'Thanks.' Bless her. 'But you have already got a bitch, and I'm not sure the government will let me stay in the country to be your general dogsbody. I'll totally ask the lawyer, though. I could always be someone else's bitch.'

'So what do you actually need to do?' she asked. 'Is there, like, a list? Something we can tick off?'

'Another question for the lawyer,' I replied. 'There must be loads of different visas, right? Loads. I must be eligible for at least one.'

Jenny picked herself up off the desk and bounced back into her chair. 'Well, I'm not worried,' she announced. 'Not at all.'

I was glad someone wasn't. Erin certainly looked concerned.

'No, really. You're super-smart, you're super-talented,' she said, ticking off my fantastic attributes on her fingers. 'You're ambitious, you're cute, and it's not like

23

you're claiming welfare or anything. You're a lock. Angela Clark, you are the American dream. There's just no reason not to give you a visa.'

Well, when you put it like that, what on earth was I worrying about?

CHAPTER THREE

'Basically, there's just no reason to give you a visa.'

Oh.

Erin's lawyer, Lawrence, was indeed hot. Tall, dark, handsome. Looked like he spent all day in the courtroom defending sick orphans before going to the gym to bench-press murderers and sweat out all the injustice in the world before rescuing a puppy on his way home. But it turned out that didn't make the news any easier to take. In fact, it made me a little bit angry. He looked like he ought to be selling me aftershave, not telling me I'm a pointless mooch who shouldn't be allowed outside the M25, let alone into America. Possibly I was paraphrasing.

'I'm a writer,' I ventured. 'I only want to stay here and write.'

'So you say,' he said, templing his big hands under his chin and giving me a level stare. 'And if you're a successful writer, you could apply for an 0-1, which means you're an alien of extraordinary ability. Are you a successful writer?'

'Define successful.'

'The 0–1 visa is a non-immigrant visa available to foreign nationals with extraordinary ability in the field of arts, science, education, business or athletics. The applicant must be experienced in their field and indicate that she or he is among the few individuals who have risen to the very top in their field of endeavour.'

'You didn't even need to look in a book,' I breathed. And there were loads of books in his office. Loads.

Lawrence the Lawyer did not crack a smile. 'So, are you successful?'

'It's possible I might not quite meet that definition.'

'So, next.' He didn't even blink. 'You're a journalist, that's correct?'

'Sort of.' I didn't feel entirely right confirming or denying. I hadn't done any journalisting for a while. Possibly because I was calling it journalisting.

'I'll take that as a yes,' Lawrence replied. 'Which means you could apply for a media visa. That's actually a considerably simpler process.'

Oh! Things were looking up!

'Yes,' I nodded, excited. 'How do I get that one?'

'You go back to London, find a media outlet prepared to give you a contract that says they will be paying you to work in America for between one and five years, and then apply at your embassy.'

'I have a column for a magazine,' I offered. 'Would that be enough?'

'Perhaps.' He considered his reply. 'It would need to be enough to financially support you. And you would need to put together a portfolio of work and get several letters of recommendation from peers in your field.'

I was suddenly less excited. What *The Look* paid me was not enough to financially support a chimp.

'And then you would need to go back to the UK,

interview at the embassy and stay in your home country while your application is processed.'

'For how long?' I hoped they had Ferrero Rocher at the embassy.

'Upwards of ninety days.'

Shit. Three months in the same country as my mother. Not happening.

'There's no way of getting it without going back to London?'

'No.'

'And I'd have to get all that other stuff?'

'Yes. The contract, the financial evidence, the letters of recommendation and the portfolio of work.'

I thought for a moment. Maybe I was extraordinary. I'd interviewed a proper celebrity, I'd had a column in a magazine, been sent to Paris for a magazine and managed to get a boy in a band to stop shagging other women. If that wasn't extraordinary, what was?

'Tell me about the O-1 again?'

Lawrence the Lawyer gave me a stern look. 'Quite honestly, Miss Clark, if you're questioning your ability to get a media visa, I really wouldn't even consider wasting your money on applying for the O-1. An example question from the application would be "have you ever won an Academy Award or equivalent".'

Damn it, I knew I'd regret not taking drama A level one day.

'Is a Blue Peter badge an equivalent?'

'A what?'

'Never mind.' I didn't have a Blue Peter badge anyway. 'So there are no other relevant visas I could apply for? My friend said I could work at her PR company.'

I looked at the lawyer. The lawyer looked at me. I gave him my best 'Please don't kick me out the country' look. He gave me his best 'Are you really going to make me say it?' face.

'I wouldn't pursue "the friend" option,' he said. 'Obviously, one other option would be if you were to marry a resident, then you could start the spousal application process, but there's no guarantee it would be granted. The INS don't look kindly on fraudulent marriages.'

'INS?' The bastards who wrote The Letter.

'Immigration and Naturalization Services,' he sighed. We were fast approaching 'wasting my time' territory. 'Look, Miss Clark, if I were you, I'd go back to the UK and do some research. And some serious thinking. Maybe now isn't the right time for you to be applying for a US visa. Maybe you should be concentrating on your career. Working on a reason as to why the US government should want to have you here.'

'I'm very nice,' I offered.

'I'm sure you are.' Lawrence the Lawyer stood up and gestured towards the door. 'Unfortunately nice isn't an extraordinary ability.'

'Really?' Bloody well felt like it was at that exact moment.

'Thank you, Miss Clark,' he said, sitting back down before I'd even left the office. 'I hope to see you again soon.'

'That's because I just paid two hundred dollars to be told I'm a pointless sack of shit,' I muttered under my breath on the way to the lift. The next time I wanted to pay to feel horrible about myself, I'd just go to Abercrombie & Fitch to try on jeans.

By the time I got back to Williamsburg, it was already dark and my Christmas tree was all lit up, sparkling happily in a corner. Illuminating the shithole we lived in. My cleaning spree hadn't been that thorough and it had been cut somewhat short by the whole INS-trying-to-ruin-my-life thing. Besides, there was no point trying to keep the place tidy now – Alex was home. In the space of time it had taken me to go out, meet the girls and see the lawyer, he'd taken over the apartment again. Record sleeves, empty cans of root beer and various items of discarded clothing strewn all over the apartment declared Alex was in the building. The queen put up a flag to let people know she was home; Alex Reid left a half-empty pizza box on the coffee table and a pair of skinny jeans over the back of the settee. But not even knowing he was here could cheer me up. The sight of Alex sparked out on the settee in his pants almost raised a smile, but the thought of having to go back to a country that didn't have Alex in it, pants or no pants – particularly no pants – wiped that smile right off my face.

'There's a way around this,' I told myself quietly, opening and closing kitchen cupboard doors. Food. Food would make it better. 'I just don't know what it is yet.'

'Don't know what what is?' a sleepy voice asked from the other side of the room.

'What's for dinner,' I fudged, not really knowing why. 'What do you fancy?'

'Whatever.' Alex's head popped up over the back of the sofa. 'You wanna go out?'

I leaned backwards against the kitchen counter. His hair was pushed all over one side of his face and his eyes were still half closed. No one wore jet lag better. In that moment, everything just became very real. What if I couldn't get a new visa? What if I had to leave in four weeks? All of a sudden, getting down on my hands and knees and begging the boy to marry

29

me didn't seem so bad. Definitely better than the alternative. A lifetime of looking at that face, hearing that voice, or fifty-plus years of Dairylea Lunchables, paying the TV licence and arguing with the council over how often they came to empty the wheelie bin.

'Whatever you want to do,' I said, turning back to the cupboards and feigning interest in an outdated packet of tortillas to hide the fact that I was this close to bursting into tears. Oh my God, what was I doing? Why was I risking this? Alex was the most amazing man I had ever met. I loved him, and the thought of spending a single day without him made me want to punch a kitten. And I loved kittens.

'Maybe we should just get a pizza,' he pondered. 'I missed pizza. And I missed you. Where have you been hiding all day?'

'Hmm?' My voice was too thick and unreliable to answer with actual words. This was ridiculous. The more I thought about leaving, the more I wanted to marry Alex. And it had nothing to do with needing a visa and everything to do with the fact that I loved the arse off that man. Except that now there was a visa issue, any discussion of a wedding would be visa-related. If I asked him, even if he asked me, it would be about the visa, regardless of how I felt. There was no way around this. If I had finished reading *Catch-22*, I would absolutely without doubt know for sure that this was a catch-22 situation. Cock. 'I was just doing visa stuff.'

'Visa stuff?'

''S complicated,' I replied, drifting out of the kitchen and into the bathroom. I ran the cold tap and held my wrists under the water. 'I, uh, my visa expired so I had to see a lawyer.'

'But you're getting the new visa, right?' He sounded slightly concerned. 'There's no problem?'

I took a deep breath in and pushed it out slowly through pursed lips. Crying wasn't going to help. 'There are a few different ones I could apply for, but, well, it's not going to be as easy as I'd hoped it might be.'

'Oh.' He appeared at the bathroom door. Half naked and half asleep. Just the way I liked him. 'Anything I can do?'

Marry me, marry me, marry me, marry me, marry me.

I leaned over to give him a light kiss, then turned back to the sink. There was no way I was leaving New York. Just no way.

'What could you do?' I asked.

Marry me, marry me, marry me, marry me, marry me.

'I don't know,' he said, pushing my hair out of my face and giving it a tug. 'There was this guy on our lighting crew once and he needed, like, letters of recommendation? I could write a letter.'

'Recommending me for what exactly?'

He raised an eyebrow and gave me a heart-stopping smile.

'Pretty sure that won't count towards me being an "extraordinary alien",' I replied. 'As far as I know.'

'I think you're extraordinary.' Alex took my hand out from under the cold tap. I'd been so preoccupied with looking at his face, I'd forgotten it was there. 'That's got to count for something.'

Only if you marry me, marry me, marry me, marry me, marry me.

'Counts for everything with me,' I replied. 'Not so much with the INS.'

'Those sons of bitches.'

For a moment everything froze. Alex looked at me with his big green eyes, suddenly serious. I stared back with my baby blues, hoping they weren't bloodshot or panda-like. He held my hand tightly and cleared his throat. I held my breath. Oh. My. God.

'Angela,' he started slowly. 'I don't want you to leave. You know that, don't you?'

'I do now,' I squeezed his hand. 'And you know I don't want to leave.'

'I do now,' he said. 'I want you here. With me.'

I nodded, a giant lump in my throat stopping any words from actually escaping. Probably my subconscious trying to stop me cocking this up. Clever subconscious.

'I love you.'

'Mm-hmm.'

'This is it for me. You and me, this is it. Everything's going to be OK, right? With the visa?'

This *was* it. This was my chance to show him the letter, to tell him I only had four weeks to find a way to stay. Simple as that. Except it wasn't. My blood pressure soared and then crashed. It was too much pressure. It wasn't fair. Basically, I was still too scared that he'd run for the hills. Brilliant.

'Mmm-hmm.'

'It'll all be fine.' He let go of my hand and pulled me into a hug. 'You'll find a way.'

I breathed out, gasping for air. He broke the hug and kissed me on the forehead.

'Now, let me find some pants and we'll go eat. Sound good?'

'Sounds bloody brilliant,' I replied. 'Pants. Dinner. Done.'

He gave me a self-satisfied smile and sauntered off towards the bedroom.

Bloody hell.

*   *   *

'And so we had to drag his ass out of there before her dad took his head off with a sword.' Alex shook his head and inhaled another taco. 'Seriously, the guy had a sword. After that, Graham didn't let him out of his sight the whole trip. He was like, grounded for a month.'

'Oh, Craig.' I stirred my drink with my fourth straw. I'd already dropped two and snapped one. It was safe to say I was distracted. 'He really shouldn't be allowed out on his own, ever.'

'Yeah, we should have known better than to take him to Japan. The groupies were insane.' Alex expertly inhaled half a taco in one mouthful.

'Wow.'

'And since Graham is gay, I had to deal with all of them,' he went on. 'So many groupies. Seriously. I thought it was gonna kill me.'

'Yeah?' I stared out of the window of La Esquina, watching Williamsburg walk by, trying to commit it all to memory.

'Yeah, sometimes there were a hundred a night.'

'Wow.'

'You're just not listening, are you?'

'What? With the what?' It was possible that my inability to string a sentence together was going to damage my plan to get a visa based on my talent as a writer.

'I thought I was the one who was supposed to be out of it,' Alex said, looking towards my plate and giving me a hopeful look. 'You gonna eat that?'

I pushed it towards him and leaned back in my chair. Jet lag made him into a complete pig. It was ridiculously cute. But no matter how happy I was to have him home and to be consuming my own body weight in Mexican food, I was distracted. I stuck my hand in my knackered MJ bag to check the time on my phone but instead found a text from Jenny.

'911, call me!'

I looked over at Alex, who was happily truffling up my leftover fajitas. I had time to make a call.

'Jenny wants me to ring her – I'll just be a sec.' I stood up as Alex nodded, merrily piling as much food as humanly possible into a flour tortilla. Happy as a clam. Not that I could see why stupid clams were so happy. Plucked out of the ocean where they *were* perfectly happy and dropped in some pasta sauce. Stupid saying. Stupid clams. Anyway, Jenny . . .

'Hi, are you OK?' I stepped outside into the chill night air and watched my breath appear in a bright white puff. 'Is everything OK?'

'It's fine,' she answered immediately. 'Jesus, calm down.'

'You said 911.' I hugged my arms around myself. Jesus Christ, it was cold. I could actually hear my mum in my head asking where my coat was. Inside. On the back of my chair. As opposed to when I was sweating like a bastard wearing it in Jenny's office. Sigh. 'What's wrong?'

'Yeah, the house isn't burning down, I just need a favour,' she said, yawning. 'I'm running an event tomorrow night, just like a cocktail party for one of our fashion clients, and we're down a waitress. Bitch I hired quit to go to some shitty audition.'

I pursed my lips. 'I don't see how this relates to me.'

'Because you're broke as shit?'

I was broke as shit.

'You want me to waitress for you?' Was this a brilliant friend doing me a brilliant favour or a new low? I wasn't sure. 'At a cocktail party?'

'Yeah,' Jenny confirmed. 'It'll be great. It's super-low

34

key, just a couple of hours in an awesome apartment in Tribeca. It won't even be like work. You'll just be hanging out with super-cool people including *moi* for a couple of hours and leaving with a couple of hundred dollars in your back pocket.'

Brilliant favour?

'And it's a Christmas party. You love Christmas, right?'

OK, brilliant favour.

'It's just handing out champagne when people come in. Literally. That's it.'

Still a favour, though.

'And, uh, I have something I need you to wear.'

Ah-ha.

'It's cute, though.'

'What is it, Jenny?'

'It's super-cute. Just say you'll do it. You'll be saving my life.'

I tried to think back to when I'd seen waitresses in super-cute outfits but kept coming up with blanks. Mostly because I'd never seen a waitress in a super-cute outfit. But Jenny needed my help and I needed the money – there really was no other answer.

'Of course I'll do it,' I said, ignoring her slightly too loud expression of surprise. 'Just text me the address and I'll be there.'

'You're my favourite,' she sang down the phone. 'Tomorrow at six – I'll send you all the deets. I love you, Angie. Fuck it all, I'll marry you. After the cocktail party.'

'Thanks.' I rubbed my semi-bare arm and stared in through the window of the restaurant. Alex was still chomping away as though he hadn't seen food in a month. He wasn't a big sushi fan, and God knows how long he'd lived on ramen before the band made money.

Japan must have been a little bit tricky for him. 'Have you talked to him yet? Has he proposed? Can I book the venue?'

'Jenny.' I used my stern voice. 'Leave it.'

'I still think it's worth talking about. How many times are we going to discuss your issues with communication?'

'How many times are we going to discuss your issues with keeping your nose out?'

Jenny laughed in response. It was almost impossible to piss her off when she was getting her own way, which was always, and therefore massively annoying. 'OK, lover, we'll talk tomorrow. I have to go ravish my Viking.'

'Sigge is from Sweden, not Norway,' I pointed out. Given that she'd been shagging him for almost four months, you'd think she'd have basics like geography down.

'There's a difference?' she asked. 'Anyway, got to go. Sigge wants to make dinner. It had better not be freaking fondue.'

'And that's Swiss,' I sighed. 'Talk tomorrow.'

'Everything OK?' Alex asked as I shivered back into my seat. 'Did she burn the place down yet?'

'Not yet.' I pulled my coat around my shoulders. This was my punishment for wearing a T-shirt just because it made my boobs look nice. 'She wants me to waitress at a party tomorrow night.'

'Do they make a waitress visa?' He rubbed his denim clad leg against mine under the table. 'I'd leave you really great tips.'

'I don't think so.' Wow, I'd managed to go a whole thirty seconds without thinking about the V-word. I bit my lip for a moment, watched him shove in another mouthful of chicken, and then went for it. 'Jenny says she's going to marry me. For the visa.'

'I'll buy you soundproof headphones as a wedding gift.' He speared a red pepper and popped it into his mouth. 'But if it's the only way for you to stay, I could totally get behind you two hooking up. You marry Jenny? Hilarious.'

I threw back a mouthful of icy water and tried to ignore the brain freeze.

'So I should marry Jenny, then?' I asked.

'Angela, I would drive you down to City Hall myself,' he replied.

Well, at least I could ride the elephant in the room all the way back to the apartment.

CHAPTER FOUR

'Are you shitting me?'

Jenny stood in front of me with a hopeful smile on her face and a PVC French maid's costume in her hand.

'I thought this was supposed to be a fashion party?' My arms were folded tightly, hugging my satchel to my chest, hoping the holy presence of Marc Jacobs would protect me from the ensemble Jenny was waving at me. 'Have you got a fluffy tail and a pair of ears to go with that?'

She cocked her head to one side and looked at the outfit as though it were entirely defensible. 'Would you believe it's a last minute demand from the designer?'

'Is this why the other waitress quit?' I asked, gingerly rubbing the wipe-clean fabric between my thumb and forefinger. As soon as I touched it, Jenny let go. Great. Now it was all mine. My precious.

'No.'

'Jenny, I know when you're lying to me.'

'Fine. Yes. She said she was an actress, not a whore.' She flicked her smooth, straightened blow-out over one shoulder. Without her trademark curls, Jenny didn't look herself, but she did look intensely polished and professional. Something that would be difficult to pull off in a French maid's costume. A red PVC French maid's costume. 'I did try to explain that she's a waitress, not an actress, but that just seemed to make her even more pissy. It's the designer – he's kind of a, um, enormous sleaze. Angie, you have to do this for me. I'll make it up to you. Please.'

I gave her the look.

'For Erin?'

I closed my eyes.

'For Christmas?'

Now that was a low blow. That was practically 'If you loved me you'd wear it', and I had no defence against that.

'If you loved me—'

'Fine.' I held out my hands to stop her from talking and looked to the heavens for strength as Jenny wrapped me up in a giant hug. She really was very strong for such a slim girl. And I was very stupid for such a British girl. 'I cannot believe I'm going to do this. Alex is going to laugh himself sick.'

'I don't think there's a single straight guy in the universe whose initial reaction to seeing their girl-friend wearing this is to laugh,' Jenny clucked, pulling my bag from my shoulder and hurrying me into getting changed. 'They'd strike him off the hetero register.'

Shedding my New York winter layers in the bath-room of someone else's swanky Tribeca duplex, I slithered into the outfit and thanked the Lord that I was wearing decent knickers since everyone and their mother was going to be able to see them for the next three hours. With a gleeful grin, Jenny held out her black patent Louboutins and a pair of fishnet hold-ups.

'None of the other girls are wearing Louboutins,' she said as I baulked. 'Loubous totally class this shit up.'

'It's not the shoes so much as the stockings,' I grumbled, snatching them and sitting on the edge of the bath to put them on. 'In for a penny . . . Classy my arse.'

Ooh, bugger me that bath was cold.

'Who's actually going to be at this thing?' I asked. I just needed reassuring that it wasn't going to be my mum, my ex-boyfriend, every boss I'd ever had and my year nine maths teacher. Because in my head . . .

'Just fashion assholes,' she said, flipping her hand dismissively. 'Erin is trying to get this guy to give us his account. He runs some online boutique or something, and he said if we pull off his Christmas party, we'll get his PR business. Between you and me, I think he's kind of a pervert.'

'You don't say.' I looked down at my outfit. Low at the top, short at the bottom, tight in the everywhere. I wanted to take a photo and text it to Lawrence the Lawyer with the caption 'extraordinary enough for you?'. Except he'd probably just reply 'no'.

'You should wear it home and then ask Alex what he thinks about marrying you,' Jenny said, carefully rolling my non-hooker wear and stashing it in a garment bag. 'Pretty sure you'd get the answer you're looking for.'

'I thought you were going to marry me?' I asked, taking a regrettable look in the bathroom mirror. The black eyeliner and cherry-tinted lip gloss I'd put on at home had seemed simple and classic with my jeans. Now I looked like a shop-worn Playboy bunny. Hef would take one look and banish me from the Mansion. Could there be anything more damaging to your self-esteem than being dismissed by a jilted octogenarian?

'I'd totally hit that,' Jenny said, leaning her chin on my shoulder and smiling at our reflections. It wasn't a picture I was comfortable with, Louboutins or no Louboutins.

'Good, because I'm officially taking the whole visa marriage thing off the table.' I rested my head on hers. 'I'm going to find another way. But I'm staying, don't worry.'

'I think you need to convince yourself, not me,' she said, kissing me on the cheek and slapping me on the arse. 'I believe you.'

It was a good thing one of us did.

With a brave face and a bare arse, I crept out of the bathroom and into the party. People were already starting to arrive, giving me very little time to scoot into the kitchen and surreptitiously neck a glass of champagne. How was I supposed to walk around the room wearing this? Catching a glimpse of my backside in the microwave window only made me feel worse. Not only because it wasn't the most flattering angle, but also because the only thing reflected in my microwave was the cheese from last night's pizza. For a split second I considered legging it for the lift before any more people arrived, but I didn't. Because Jenny actually looked very nervous. Because I'd made a promise. And because I didn't know where she'd hidden my coat. So instead of dashing for the streets, I picked up a tray of champagne, tried to forget the fact that my mum still served me a half-full cup of tea because 'I couldn't be trusted' and headed for the living room. While I wasn't quite so keen for them to get a look at me, I was looking forward to seeing what a 'fashion asshole' looked like.

'Oh. My. God.'

One step into the party.

One step straight back into the kitchen.

Apparently 'fashion assholes' looked like Cici Spencer.

Tall, blonde and the devil incarnate, this was not good. The last time I'd set eyes on Cici, she was howling with rage and drenched in iced coffee. Because I'd thrown it at her. Cici was the assistant of my former editor at *The Look* magazine and had made ruining my life her pet project. She hadn't quite managed total destruction at the time, but she did successfully destroy my entire wardrobe. Oh, and made sure I lost my job, since she was the godforsaken hell spawn of the magazine's owner. It was ironic that a more appropriate name for Cici also started with a 'C', but my mother would never forgive me if I used it in public.

'Oh my God, Angela.' Cici tottered over, holding one very skinny hand to her flat chest, laughing with delight as though we were old sorority sisters. 'Look at you!'

I was frozen to the spot. Yes. Look at me. There she was in a floor-length, one-shouldered red gown, her hair sweeping down the other shoulder in an icy cascade of blonde curls with a slash of dress-matching lipstick on her perfectly porcelain face. And there I was, in my cheap, shiny, wished-it-was-Ann-Summers French maid's costume with air-dried hair and a dab of L'Oréal lip gloss. Sigh. I really didn't have anything to say to her.

Luckily, Cici had lots to say to me.

'This is amazing.' I felt a very light, very evil hand on my shoulder. 'I was just thinking about you the other day. I was updating Mary's holiday card list.'

'Oh.'

'I cut you.'

'Right.'

I assumed she was saying I wasn't getting a Christmas card, but if she'd meant an actual physical slashing, I wouldn't have been surprised.

'Figured you would have left by now. Like, run away back to England or something?'

'Um-hmm.'

'Because you don't have a job?'

'Gotcha.'

'Because we fired you?'

Not running away five minutes ago was turning out to be a really bad idea. 'But look at you,' Cici gushed. A small crowd of her cronies had gathered around to watch the entertainment. 'You are working. As a wait-ress. Dressed like a hooker.'

The best part was, it was all true.

But I wasn't going to give her the satisfaction of me going the full Charlie Sheen, even if the idea of throwing an entire tray of Cristal in her face before beating her to death with the tray was very tempting. It was Christmas, after all, and I really didn't want Jenny to get fired. Or to go to prison. I wasn't sure if New York had the death penalty or not, let alone whether they served Christmas dinner inside. That said, I would have a good defence. 'But your honour, she was a massive bitch' would work, surely? No, I had to take the high ground. I had to be the bigger person. And I hated that.

'Hi.' I reset my expression and smiled. If looks could kill, it wouldn't have even tickled. Butter would've actually chilled while I looked at it. 'Champagne?'

'What did you do to it?' She reluctantly took one of my glasses, sniffing it with suspicion.

'Oh, Cici.' I attempted to laugh, but it may or may

43

not have come out slightly more like a sob. 'It's just champagne. Enjoy your evening.'

Feeling my restraint starting to waver, I turned carefully on my borrowed heel, making sure not to twist my knackered knee, and headed back towards the kitchen, passing another French maid on the way out. She gave me a supportive grimace and I nodded in return. Solidarity, sister.

Once the door was closed and I was safely away from Cici and all of Satan's little helpers, I let out what I hoped was a relatively controlled screech of rage, kicked a cardboard box across the room and slammed a cupboard door. It actually felt quite good. Not as good as throwing a drink over her, but OK. Just not OK enough. I'd only been moved to violence twice in my life, but I was more than a little bit worried we'd hit the magic number if I went back out there. Fisticuffs were becoming my natural setting.

'Hey, are you OK?' Jenny snuck into the kitchen and pushed the innocent cardboard box back into position under the counter. 'You motored back in here kinda fast.'

'Remember my friend Cici? From *The Look*?' I asked.

'Cici?' Jenny's smooth forehead creased with concern. 'Your friend? Wasn't she the one who gave you all that bullshit in Paris?'

'Yep,' I confirmed. 'And had my luggage blown up.'

'The Balmain . . .' Jenny pressed a hand to her heart. It had been a difficult time for both of us.

'She's outside. In the red.'

Jenny Lopez was someone who wore her emotions on her face and wasn't terribly good at camouflaging the way she felt. In the following thirty seconds she was completely silent, but we managed to get through confusion, shock and sadness (for the dearly departed

Balmain) before finally settling on intense rage. She stuck her head back through the door and peered outside before turning back even angrier, if possible, than before.

'Halston?' she asked. 'The one in the Halston?'

'I don't know, do I?' I loved fashion, but if I couldn't see the label, I didn't have a clue. Identifying shoes, on the other hand, was my secret super-power. 'It's long and red and one-shouldered.'

'The Halston,' Jenny confirmed. 'Shit, it's gonna be so hard to do this to a dress like that.'

Alarm bells.

'Do what?' I reached out to hold my friend back, but she was quicker than me. 'Jenny, where are you going?' I hissed as she slipped back into the party with a wicked grin on her pretty face.

For a moment I stood stock still, frozen to the spot in the kitchen. What on earth was she going to do? I grabbed a small tray of snacks, mostly so that I had something to defend myself with when things got nasty, and went once more into the fray.

Jenny was right in the middle of Cici's circle and, unlike me, she looked like she belonged there. As much as I hated the world's most jumped-up secretary, it was hard to deny that her overall presentation was amazing. A product of several generations of excellent Upper East Side breeding, she was tall, slender, blonde and born to wear designer clothing. Unfortunately, that sort of heritage often came both with a flat chest and a chip on the shoulder. Cici's chip was so big, she'd have struggled to cart it around in an Hermès Birkin. But Jenny . . . Jenny was a goddess. Blessed with the legs of a prized pony, gorgeous glowing skin and the ability to set absolutely anyone at ease, if I'd had her natural gifts I would have (a) been a complete bitch and (b) married a billionaire at the age of eighteen. But Jenny always used her powers for good. Well, good was relative, wasn't it? As far as I was concerned she was a white knight, but I had a feeling Cici was about to see what happened when you incurred the wrath of Jennifer Lopez. And I didn't care whether or not the other Jennifer Lopez was one of the most famous divas on earth, she didn't have a patch on my girl. I was almost too scared to watch. Almost.

'We're so pleased you could come, Cecelia,' Jenny cooed, her arm wrapped through Cici's skinny limb. 'Tonight is such a special night for the designer.'

'Thomas is one of my favourites,' Cici crooned, batting her eyelashes in the general direction of a short, very skinny, entirely repellent man with over-dyed black hair in the middle of the room. Thomas, pronounced 'Toe-Mah' of course, wasn't wearing one of his own designs. He was wearing a red PVC Santa costume. With the arse cheeks cut out. I believe trousers such as his are more commonly known in the business as chaps. Father Christmas does not wear chaps; they are not practical in his line of business. I hadn't laid eyes on him before this moment, but at least I now realized why I was dressed like a very cheap prostitute. And at least I wasn't the worst-dressed person in the room. Never before had Christmas made me so sad.

'I'm so glad I could be here – the holidays are just crazy,' Cici was saying, rolling her eyes at Jenny. 'All the parties, all the travelling, the shopping – it's just chaos.'

'Isn't it though?' Jenny nodded sympathetically. 'The shopping is just the worst.'

'It sure is. I hate shopping when it's not for me!'

No one enjoyed Cici as much as Cici enjoyed Cici. 'I hate Christmas.'

So it was true, she *was* the devil. I softened the shock of this news with a handful of snack mix from my tray.

'You're not supposed to eat those,' one of the other dead-eyed waitresses said as she sailed by with champagne. I shrugged and went back in for seconds. I had a feeling this job wasn't going to be a big tipper for me anyway; might as well get my money's worth.

'Yeah, it's just so . . .' Jenny waved her hands around to agree as emphatically as possible. And accidentally spilled a glass of red wine right down the front of Cici's dress. 'Oh. My. God.'

The shriek that came from Cici's throat would have sent the virgin Mary into an early labour. There wouldn't have even been time to get to the stable. The little donkey would have had to act as midwife. I couldn't believe Jenny Lopez had sacrificed couture to the great girl-vengeance gods. I nibbled on a wasabi pea. This was better than the cinema.

'This is archive Halston,' she hissed. 'I have to return this to the PR.'

'Sabrina?' Jenny waved away her concerns. 'One of my best friends. I'll call her. Don't sweat it. In fact, let me make it up to you. I've got one of Thomas's designs from his new collection in the back. I was going to have a model come out in it later, but I don't suppose I could beg you to wear it for me? I know Thomas would love it. You've got such a perfect figure.'

Cici gaped like a guppy. Lovely teeth. And I had to admit, this was a curveball I did not see coming. How exactly was letting Cici wear a beautiful, exclusive designer dress revenge of any kind?

'Me? Wear a brand new Thomas design?' She actually gasped. 'Where do I change?'

Confused-dot-com, I watched as Jenny pointed Cici in the direction of one of the bedrooms, but just before she vanished behind the heavy white door, she flashed me a wicked smile and raised her eyebrows in a silent promise. She would have made a great Bond villain. What was her wicked plan? Maybe she was holding Cici's head down the toilet and flushing repeatedly while I stood there watching a closed door. I wondered whether or not it was too late to retract my Christmas list and ask for a sopping wet Cici from Father Christmas this year. I wanted it even more than a Mulberry Alexa. No, really.

'Part of me is convinced she's going to come out of that door naked,' a very familiar voice groaned over my shoulder. 'She'd set a dog on fire for attention if she thought it would work.'

I turned and almost dropped my tray. Right in front of me was Cici's double. The same long limbs, the same blonde hair, even the same icy blue eyes, but instead of knocking me on my arse with the evil equivalent of a Care Bear stare, her baby blues just looked tired and bored. On closer inspection, this Cici was altogether less frightening. The elaborate hair pleat had been replaced by loose waves, and the show-stopping red gown had given way to a classic black sheath. Still stunning, but in a 'wow, you look great' way, not 'wow, please don't steal my soul'. It was a subtle difference.

'I'm Delia.' She held out her hand and I couldn't help notice the lack of manicure. Was it possible that this Cici clone actually *worked* for a living? 'The living Barbie doll is my sister. Twin sister. For my sins.'

And suddenly it all made sense. Cici's sister. Why

did I know Cici had a sister? Clearly it wasn't from our cocktail hour heart-to-hearts . . .

'I'm Angela.' I took her hand and shook it, as was traditional amongst humans. 'Cici and I actually used to work together. Sort of. Because, you know, she doesn't really work.'

Delia's eyes flashed with recognition and I readied myself for a slap. It was one thing to slag off your own sibling, but it was quite another to have Krystal the Call Girl-cum-Waitress do it for you. She raised her arm, but before I could duck I was pulled into a huge hug and her dry voice gave way to a glorious laugh.

'Angela Clark!' She pushed me away then grabbed my arms. I dropped my tray but managed to stay upright, so I took it as a win. 'Ohmygod, I love you!'

I froze, wide-eyed, and took the hug.

'Thank you?'

'No, really.' Delia had quite the firm grip. 'I love you. I used to read your blog all the time. I told Grandpa I was never going to speak to him again when he killed it.'

Grandpa. Delia's grandpa was Cici's grandpa. Who was Bob Spencer, the owner of my previous employer, Spencer Media. Who had fired me after reading a particular email that was somewhat peppered with expletives and other colourful expressions describing his little princess. Every single one of which was justified, but still, I imagined very few people would enjoy seeing their pride and joy described as a 'raving psycho that should be beaten to death with a spoon', even if it was true.

'Thank you?'

And again.

'And I know it probably doesn't help, but I'm so sorry – I know what a bitch she can be.' Delia finally

49

let go of my arms. Funnily enough, I still couldn't really relax. 'One time, when we were in high school, she pretended to be me to get a date with this guy. I was super-excited to get to school on Monday morning and find out I'd lost my virginity when I thought I'd been in the Hamptons studying.'

'Woah, really?' That was genuinely evil. Maybe Jenny had competition in the Bond villain stakes. 'Who is that evil that young?'

Delia shrugged. 'She didn't want to get a reputation, so she gave me one instead. Not the best birthday present I've ever gotten. Happy sweet sixteen, Delia. I bought her a Tiffany charm.'

'And you didn't kick her arse?' I would have actually killed her. Actually murdered her.

'Living well is the best revenge,' she replied. 'Or something. And with Cici, that means just ignoring her. There's no point going to war with someone like that, sister or not. I'd rather just not deal with her.'

'You're my hero.' I pressed my hand against her shoulder. 'I've been having some trouble controlling my rage lately, and I won't lie, I'm a bit worried about being in the same room with her.'

'Oh, please, feel free to punch her in the face.' Delia gave me a beatific smile. 'After what she did to you? She totally deserves it. So what are you doing now?'

I looked down at my outfit and back at Delia.

'Right.'

'Yeah.'

We stood in awkward silence for a moment while I tried to think of something to say that didn't involve how much I hated her sister. This was the season of goodwill, after all.

'Christmas, eh?' I nodded at the black PVC tree in the corner of the room. Obviously Thomas's tastes ran to the more exotic, but I was always excited by the presence of a Christmas tree. The mini dildo baubles made me blush a little, but still, 'twas the season. Each to his own. 'Any exciting plans?'

'Just to actually have Christmas.' Delia gave me a tired smile. 'I just can't believe another year has gone by already. I swore I was going to get myself together before New Year's, and here I am again. Still working for Granddaddy, still under the thumb.'

'You work for Bob – I mean, Mr Spencer?' I corrected myself quickly. We probably weren't still on 'Bob and Angie' terms any more. 'You're at Spencer Media too?'

'Bob, yes,' she replied. 'Spender Media, no. He runs a bunch of real estate businesses too – I've been there for a few years. I'm overseeing an apartment complex in Brooklyn right now.'

'I live in Brooklyn!' I exclaimed. Probably wasn't any need for me to sound quite so excited about having something so minor in common, but still, common ground. Nice. 'Do you like it? The real estate thing?'

'I actually always wanted to work in publishing,' she admitted. 'But of course, Cici got there first. Cecelia always gets there first. Once she had a foot in the door, there was no way I could follow, and I wanted to stay on at school, get my masters. She went straight into the office.'

'If it helps, she's not there all that often.' I thought back to all the times I'd got her answering machine when I was calling Mary, our boss. 'I don't think Anna Wintour needs to worry about her position.'

'I know, I just hate competing with her. This is the problem with being the good twin. She's always going to play dirty to get what she wants, and I can never win.'

'Oh, I don't know about that.' I tapped her on the

51

arm and pointed towards the bedroom door. 'This should be good.'

Jenny emerged first, a smile stretched all the way across her face. She looked like she'd just been for a quickie with Bradley Cooper. But this was much, much better. This was something we could all enjoy. Following her out of the bedroom and into the party was a very proud, very smug, very almost naked Cici Spencer.

'For the love of God,' Delia groaned as she made her full entrance.

Once she had worked her way into the middle of the room, I could see that Cici was actually wearing something, and as soon as I laid eyes on it, despite never having seen any of his work before, I knew it was a Thomas. The bum-skimming white silk shift dress draped artfully off one shoulder, rendering a bra unwearable, and the sheer nature of the silk meant that it was a flesh-coloured thong or nothing. Cici had opted for nothing. It was the modern sartorial equivalent of the Emperor's new clothes, and Cici looked every inch the Empress.

But that wasn't enough for her. Under Jenny's instruction, she gave us all a spin, allowing me to spot the real *coup de grâce* of the ensemble. On the front of the dress was a black and white screen print of a great big cock. Seriously. Cici was wearing, to all intents and purposes, a see-through T-shirt with a picture of a knob on it. Thomas, you are a master. Jenny, you are a genius.

'Is it me,' Delia started, 'or . . .'

'It's not you,' I stopped her. 'It's really not you.'

'Delia!' Cici trotted over, proud as punch and not even drunk. 'You came? You never come.'

'Thomas is buying one of my condos,' Delia explained,

ignoring the fact that her sister was standing in the middle of a very glamorous Christmas party ninety-nine per cent naked. 'I thought I'd show my face. Good of you to show everything else.'

I couldn't help but think it must be something of a strange sensation to see your twin, your identical twin, parading around a formal cocktail party more or less in the buff. It must have been like taking a really annoying funhouse mirror with you everywhere you went. And tonight, it was a bit of a pervy mirror as well. I didn't want to be staring at her tits, but I had very little choice in the matter. Jenny stood behind her looking like the cat who got the cream. Then spiked the cream with acid and served it to Cici.

'I know my dress is amazing,' she said to me. 'But you could be less obvious while you're checking me out. What's wrong? Get bored of turning other people gay?'

'It's a very lovely dress,' I said, trying not to giggle, but half a cackle managed to escape as a squeak. 'You look charming.'

'Right.' She pursed her lips and raised an eyebrow. 'So, that guy you were seeing? Alan?'

'Alex.' I took a couple of deep breaths. It really didn't matter what she said, this was too good. She was this close to being stark bollock naked and still giving me attitude. There was something faintly admirable about it. Or at least there would be if she weren't Satan.

'Yeah, Alex. Did he dump your ass yet or are you still his charity fuck?'

Jenny physically recoiled as though she'd been hit, but before she could strike, I stepped in. I had this.

'You can't dump charity at Christmas,' I said, smiling politely. 'We're still together, thanks.'

'I'm sure he's going to get tired of you soon enough,' she shrugged. 'You should give me his number. I still work in the media. I could help his band.'

'His band doesn't need help, and actually, I still work in the media,' Admittedly it was just barely, but still. Semantics schemantics.

'Only because I couldn't get the UK office to fire your ass.' She looked me up and down. 'It's actually kind of amazing how easy it was to get you blocked. Maybe because you suck? I figure it will take me longer to get you banned from whatever this is – ' she paused to wave a horrified hand at my 'wait-ressing' outfit – 'because I don't usually hire the help, but give me a couple of days and you'll be out on your ass. Again.'

'Blocked?' I blinked.

'Maybe it wasn't me,' Cici mused. 'Maybe every publisher in New York canned your ass because you don't understand simple words.'

So that was the reason no one at Spencer would hire me. Not because I sucked, but because Cici did.

'Are you for real?' Her sister spoke up before I regained the power of speech. 'Seriously, what is wrong with you? Why do you always have to have an enemy?'

'Eff you, Deals. She threw a coffee at me!'

'You got me fired!' I shouted. Inside voices, Angela, inside voices. 'And blew up my shoes! And you're a massive cow!'

'Uh, I'm a massive cow?' she scoffed. 'I didn't know they made fetish outfits in a plus size.'

'I wasn't calling you fat, I was . . .' A red mist settled over my ability to form a sentence. It was impossible to enjoy shouting at someone if they were too stupid to understand exactly how you were slagging them off. 'You're an idiot.'

I looked at Delia. She looked at me. I looked at Jenny. She looked at Cici. Cici looked far too happy with herself. As I saw it, there were two ways this could go. I could be the bigger man, turn around and walk out of the party with my head held high. Or I could slap the mare silly.

'Sorry, Jenny, I have to go.' Apologizing, I stepped out of my borrowed shoes and picked them up. There was no such thing as a speedy exit in Louboutins. 'I'm really sorry to let you down.'

Before Jenny could reply, Cici let out a tiny wicked cackle. 'Are you sure you can afford to pass up work? And dude, those shoes are clearly not yours. Christian Louboutin would set them on fire before he let you walk around in his shoes.'

Now that was a mistake. Insult me, fire me, but never insult my shoes. Even if they were actually borrowed. Besides, I was never more dangerous than when I had a pair of Louboutins in my mitts, but GBH by way of shoe had been done before and so instead I grabbed a glass of red wine from a passing tray and took aim.

'Not the dress!' Jenny yelled, dashing to stand in between me and Cici. 'Kick her ass, but don't hurt the dress!'

I paused. On one hand, I really did want to throw the wine at her. On the other, I didn't want Jenny to get fired.

'Angela, give me the wine,' Delia said, taking the glass out of my hand. 'Just hit her. We all know she deserves it.'

'Please, she couldn't hit for shit,' Cici said, smug

and safe behind the outspread arms of Jenny Lopez. 'No one cares what you think, Delia.'

'Oi, Cici.' I waited for Jenny to move, for Delia to stop blushing, for the entire assembled mass of the party to be watching. 'No one cares about you, full stop.'

And then I punched her in the face.

CHAPTER FIVE

'And then Jenny had to fire me but it was OK and she said it was OK and then she called me a cab and I don't think it really hurt that much because her nose didn't bleed or anything but ohmygod, Alex . . .' Pause for breath. 'I *hit* her.'

More to make me feel like a big man than anything else, I was seated on our sofa with a freshly purchased bag of frozen peas on my fist, relaying to Alex the tale of how I slayed my second dragon.

'This punching people thing – ' He held the peas against my knuckles with one hand and stroked the hair back from my forehead with the other. 'Is this something I should be worried about?'

'Apparently I'm only into girl-on-girl fighting,' I replied, flexing my fingers. They didn't really hurt, but I ouched for good measure. 'I don't think you need to be concerned about domestic violence. Yet.'

'I love that you're a feminist.' He planted a kiss on my forehead then went to the fridge to get more beer. Because I needed more beer. 'And you met her sister? And she wasn't a bitch?'

'She wasn't.' I shook my head. 'She was nice, actually. I might friend her on Facebook.'

'You are a strange girl.' He stood in front of me, bearing a Corona and staring into my glittering, fevered eyes. 'And just so it's clear in my mind, Cici the Satanist was naked during the foxy boxing, and you were wearing . . . this?'

Of course I was still resplendent in PVC.

'She wasn't naked,' I tutted. 'Honestly.'

Trust a man to actually find this sexy. If someone had goaded Craig into punching them hard in the face, Alex would have fist-bumped him and then got beers. I suppose I did have a beer.

'And you're missing the key points here. Not only did she get me fired, she's stopping me from getting any other work. Cici is the reason I have to renew my visa. She's the reason all this shit is happening. She's the reason there's a problem.'

'I thought there wasn't a problem,' he said. 'With the visa.'

'Oh, yeah,' I pouted. Now really wasn't the time, was it? 'Well, just . . . I suppose . . . worst-case scenario stuff . . .'

'You're such a pessimist,' he said, dropping back down on the sofa and folding me into a very big, very careful hug, avoiding my injuries. 'Chill. Just wait until after Christmas and then we'll work it out. No one can deal with stuff like this close to the holidays – their brains are already on vacation.'

I knew all I needed to do was to sit down with my boyfriend and explain exactly what was happening, tell him exactly what the INS had said and have a simple, grown-up conversation. But I was so tired and so mad at Cici and, well, making excuses. I also felt I lacked some integrity in the outfit I was currently wearing, so instead of having an adult conversation with my adult partner about my adult situation, I let him give me a hug and sulked quietly instead. I would talk to him tomorrow. I would start researching options for the visa. I would make everything right. Immediately after I had burned the French maid's costume.

After a long and involved Saturday of research, googling, watching *True Blood* and thinking about pizza, I managed to rouse myself to prepare for Jenny's Christmas party. Or to be more culturally sensitive, holiday party. But I have never been much for cultural sensitivity when it involves a fat man in a red furry suit, so I was getting ready to get my Christmas on. I added Jenny's borrowed shoes (one more wear couldn't hurt?) to my red silk Marc by Marc Jacobs dress and attacked my face with blusher. The two-seasons-old (aka ancient) frock was one of the few survivors from my pre-Paris wardrobe, but happily it was perfect for a Christmas party. Ruby red, little puff sleeves and a fitted waist that still allowed for the over-consumption of mince pies. I had made mince pies.

I had also absolutely, one hundred per cent planned to talk to Alex about my visa sitch. I'd even got The Letter out of my handbag to show him, but he'd run out early in the morning (for him) and hadn't resurfaced until it was time to get ready for the party. Plan scuppered. Now I was going to have to build my nerve all over again tomorrow. And by build my nerve, I meant knock back a couple of white wine spritzers. As much as we'd been through, as much as I knew he loved me, there was still that little voice in my head whispering that he was pleased I was going home. That he was pleased I would leave and he would be free. And that little voice could only be silenced by two things – kissing and booze. And it was very difficult to talk during the kissing.

It was the same voice that said, yes, you do look fat in those jeans and no, wearing red lipstick doesn't brighten up your face, it makes you look like a tart. I hated that voice. Part your mother, part your year nine Biology teacher and part Jeremy Kyle. Living with Jenny had really helped me put The Voice back in its box where it belonged, but right now it was coming through loud and clear. So I did what any good English girl would do and ignored it completely, pushing it down, down, down until it was just a bad feeling in my stomach instead of a bellowing in my ear. Jenny would tell me the only way to silence it was to address the issues. Jenny was American. I chose to quietly hope it would go away on its own, like a medium-sized spider or a funny rash in a special place. Since there was sod all I could do about the visa on a Saturday night, I decided to stash those concerns all together. May as well give myself an ulcer for lots of problems rather than just one, surely? I would not worry about things for the next twelve hours. There. Done. Sort of.

'Ready?' Alex had gone all out for the party. Not only had he washed and brushed his hair, he was wearing a suit, shirt and tie. I had forgotten he owned a suit, shirt and tie. It was silly how good he looked. The suit and tie were black and skinny, the shirt was white and shiny. If he'd been a girl, he would have been doing a spin in his high heels to show off, but since he was a manly man, he was just pushing his feet into his black Converse. Which should not have worked with the outfit, but, irritatingly for someone with her trotters rammed into very pinchy pumps, he looked great.

'So who's going to be there tonight?' Alex asked as

we shut the door behind us and I felt the icy sting of the New York winter on my bare cheeks. At least tonight it was just the cheeks on my face. Living by the water was wonderful. We had a beautiful view of Manhattan, and in the summer, sitting on the rooftop with a cold glass of wine and a gentle breeze, it was perfection. But in winter, that gentle breeze became razor blades on your skin with a nice after-splash of TCP to really freshen things up.

'Big crowd? Intimate gathering?' He took my hand and squeezed it, pretending he wasn't terrified of either.

'It's Jenny,' I squeezed back, trying to get the feeling back into my fingers. 'She'll have invited everyone she's ever met. Hopefully they won't all come at once.'

'Cool, whatever,' he replied, fumbling in his pocket for a MetroCard. 'I haven't seen her in forever.'

It was cute of him to pretend that wasn't a relief. I knew full well he was terrified of my best friend, and of crowds in general. Alex could happily entertain thousands of people from the safety of a stage, but parties made him uncomfortable. He would go along, smile, nod, laugh when appropriate, shake his head when required and everyone would love him, but I could tell. Once a high-school music nerd, always a high-school music nerd. Despite everything he'd accomplished by the age of thirty-one, he was always waiting for the popular kids to kick him out of their kegger. He had explained to me what a kegger was. I wouldn't have been invited to one either. It was funny when you found out that men were exactly like women sometimes.

After scrabbling down the stairs and dodging a platform full of parkas, I managed to throw myself onto the L train and squeeze myself into a seat as soon as the doors opened. Alex stood in front of me, half shouting over the rumble of our journey about the trains he'd taken in Tokyo. Opposite, I could see two girls checking out his backside. I wanted to be offended, but it really was a great arse.

'See how easy it would be for him to replace you?' The Voice interrupted Alex's story to remind me how very attractive my boyfriend was in our neighbourhood. Clearly, he was hot wherever he went, but in Brooklyn, he was like hipster catnip. And I was prepared to bet anything that the two girls in their denim cut-offs over black fishnets finished with scuffed-up DMs hadn't sat around all afternoon watching gay vampires with tooth-paste on their spots. They had probably been making jewellery out of electrical equipment or painting pictures of something very deep and meaningful with hummus.

'You have to come with me next time,' Alex said as I tuned out the bad-news bears in my own head. 'You can't leave me with Craig and Graham again. You're gonna love Japan – honestly, everywhere we went I was like, Angie would go crazy for this. I think the guys were kinda sick of me by the end.'

'Next time,' I smiled. Hurrah, I had kept my promise not to mention my lack of visa.

'When you've got your visa, we'll go everywhere.' He nudged my knee with his and I forced myself not to kick him in the balls.

'Yep.' I looked back at the hipster girls behind him. They didn't need toothpaste spot cream or visas. They did need to learn some manners, though.

The party was wall to wall with people, just as I'd predicted, and most of them were hatefully beautiful. I hadn't even taken my coat off before Alex had to give me a not-particularly-gentle punch in the shoulder to get me to stop staring at the three perfectly muscled men wearing nothing but red fur-trimmed Speedos.

'I – it's Christmas . . .?' I said, defending myself. While having another look.

'Yeah, Santa's been working out,' he replied, openly miffed. I kissed him on the cheek and steered my eyes away, but really, it never hurt to see him a little jealous. I was trying to be a grown-up, but I was still a girl.

'Angie!' Jenny squealed and jumped up from the sofa as though I was the only suitable kidney donor in all the world and I'd just walked into the hospital to save her life. From the glazed look in her eyes, she'd more likely be looking for a new liver under her tree. She was hammered. 'You look adorable. Are those my shoes?'

'They are your shoes,' I confirmed. 'I didn't think you'd mind since you made me wear a PVC maid's outfit last night.'

'Did you burn it?'

'I did.'

'Good.'

It was nice to be considered adorable, but I couldn't help but think that sometimes it might be nice to be considered a stone-cold fox like Jenny. If I'd known she was going to be wrapped up in a red Herve Leger bandage dress, I might have worn a different colour, but, like Delia and Cici, though with considerably less vitriol, there was no point in competing with Jenny.

'There are so many people here.' I waved a hand at my face, fanning warm air right back at myself. Last winter, I'd spent more than one day wearing a scarf and mittens indoors. Our building suffered from a severe case of knackered boileritis, but the sheer number of bodies in the room was keeping things nice and toasty. And speaking of bodies, I peered around her hair to look for Jenny's very beautiful boyfriend. 'Is Sigge around?'

'Over there.' Jenny pointed at the trifecta of half-naked men by the window as she gave Alex a kiss on each cheek and a perfunctory hug. He was scared of her for a reason. She insisted on keeping what she referred to as a professional distance with regards to their being friends. According to Jenny, it was her job to keep Alex on his toes, a fact that wasn't lost on him. He was on his tiptoes whenever Jenny was around. He always tried his best with her, but I could feel he was on edge, hence the suit *and* tie. I was under no illusion that the dress-up was for me, but the two of them getting along so well gave me a happy.

'I didn't recognize his abs,' I said, trying to be as nonchalant as possible. I wasn't terribly good at it. 'It's so different seeing them in person.'

'Right?' Jenny sipped her champagne. It looked like love in her eyes, but it could just have been booze. 'He thought it would be funny. I tried to explain to him it was a little *Zoolander*, but that just made it worse. Now they keep flashing each other Blue Steels and giggling like women.'

The three of us looked over at the model playpen across the room. Such sharp cheekbones.

'That's my boyfriend,' Jenny sighed. 'Can you believe it?'

'I'd totally date that dude,' Alex replied. 'And I know Angela would.'

'I'm not going to lie – if you weren't here I would be sitting on Santa's lap right now,' I admitted, eventually dragging my eyes away to begin the search for booze. There was no way I would be able to stay at this party for more than fifteen minutes unless I got very drunk, very quickly. I'd been on a bit of a non-drinking kick while Alex had been on tour, but not drinking at one of Jenny's parties was basically self-harm. It would have been a good idea to have had a couple of drinks at home to take the edge off, but I wasn't that bright.

'The apartment looks nice,' I told Jenny, sending Alex off to the bedroom with our coats and a clear message not to come back without two glasses of something cold and bubbly. As well as whatever he wanted. 'You've painted?'

'Sadie painted,' Jenny corrected. 'I told her we were gonna have a holiday party, and she said she'd get someone in to tidy up a little. I figured she meant a cleaning service, but then I get home from the office and the whole damn place has been covered in White Out. In a day. She couldn't run the vacuum around?'

'I can't imagine someone who gets paid thousands of dollars to stand around in their pants is particularly big on domestic chores,' I said, ignoring the fact that I wasn't either. 'Does she know what a vacuum is?'

'Sigge changes light bulbs,' Jenny said, looking doubtful. 'But he's not so good with actual appliances. I guess that's why the house always ends up so gross on *America's Next Top Model*.'

'Tyra isn't very handy with a can of Pledge,' I nodded. My feet were starting to hurt. 'But given how you two met, I'm not too shocked. Where is Sadie, anyway?'

If I had met Sadie the way Jenny had met Sadie, I would have had a restraining order issued, not invited her to move in. Jenny had landed the lucky role of Sadie's 'handler' at one of Erin's events, and now she was living that role. As far as I was concerned it sounded like a living nightmare, but Jenny thrived on a project. She loved a challenge; she always wanted to fix something. And man alive, was Sadie broken. I'd always laughed when people said models were like racehorses, but she was the most highly-strung racehorse of the modelling world; except that instead of refusing hurdles, she refused common courtesy and basic human compassion. The first time we met, she looked me up and down, asked where I lived, then asked if I knew Agyness Deyn, and then actually answered for me with a massive laugh and 'of course you don't'. She was a charmer.

'She forgot she had an event tonight.' Jenny made tired-looking air quotes around the 'forgot'. 'VS, I think. It's fine – it's not like the modelling industry is under-represented.'

She was right. For an at-home Christmas do, there was a disproportionately large number of very pretty people in Jenny's front room. Not that I would ever describe any of our friends as dogs, but these were the kinds of girls and boys that you wanted to stare at until you could work out exactly what it was that made them so transcendentally beautiful. And then maybe poke them a bit.

'So did you talk to Alex?' Jenny asked, pushing some random off the sofa so we could sit down. It was still weird to me that there was someone I'd never laid eyes on sitting on what was very recently *my* sofa. I didn't like it.

'No, I didn't talk to Alex, and I distinctly remember banning you from mentioning that subject,' I said, slipping the balls of my feet out of my shoes. Oh, sweet baby Jesus in the manger, that felt good. 'So shut up. I'm working on it. This time next week, it'll all be sorted out.'

Jenny leaned her head to one side. 'How so?'

'Because I'm due a Christmas miracle,' I replied with

confidence. 'And I'm cashing in my voucher. Everyone gets one, don't they?'

'Angie, honey – ' She gently rested a hand on my knee in a very clear 'you're blatantly a little bit mad' move. 'I know you're super into this whole "I need to get the visa on my own merits" thing, and you know I think that's awesome, right?'

'Right.'

It was awesome. I was awesome. Take that, Lawrence.

'And I know you don't want Alex to ask you to marry him just to get the visa, right?'

'Right.'

At least we were clear on that.

'But you do love this dude?'

'Correct. I do love the dude.'

'And he loves you.'

'I believe that to be the truth.'

'So just ask him. People don't meet in the rain trying to jump in the same cab these days, they meet online, they get engaged on reality TV. They hook up with their friends and they get knocked up. They get married because they need a visa. When and where he puts a ring on your finger isn't important, as long as he loves you.'

'That is the most depressing thing I've ever heard,' I said, slapping her hand off my leg. 'You will never have bedtime story privileges with my kids.'

'Be real hard to tell a bedtime story to kids in England.' She raised an eyebrow then looked away. 'No one's arguing with the fact that you could get a visa another way, but there's no need to make it harder for yourself. You don't have anything to prove. Just ask Alex.'

'Just ask Alex what?'

Two glasses of champagne appeared in front of me.

Since he didn't seem to be carrying anything else, I only took one. Begrudgingly.

'Your beloved Angela Clark and I were just talking.' Jenny beamed up at my boyfriend as she spoke.

'About Christmas dinner,' I squeaked. 'I was saying Jenny and Sigge should come over to our place for Christmas dinner.'

'Sure.' Alex aimed his champagne glass in the giant Swede's direction. 'I will totally get into an eating contest with that guy.'

'Dude, your waist is skinnier than one of his thighs,' Jenny scoffed. 'Are you kidding me?'

'Oh, Jenny, Jenny, Jenny, you have no idea,' I said, proudly wrapping an arm around Alex's waist. 'He's got hollow legs. Honestly, it's disgusting the amount he can eat and stay this thin.'

'Don't worry, I'll get real fat when I'm old,' he replied, kissing me on the top of the head. 'Good and fat.'

'Awesome.' I leaned into him and tried to envisage a porky Alex on a porch swing playing a banjo.

Totally hot.

Some hours and several glasses of champagne later, I wandered out of the front room, leaving Alex to protect my lovely friend Vanessa from the advances of his disgusting friend Craig, who had somehow found his way into the party. Facebook had so much to answer for. After a liberal application of lip balm and a tipsy spritz of Jenny's Gucci perfume, I checked my phone. It was admittedly a slim possibility that anyone would have called to offer me a job at half-past eleven on a Saturday night, but you never knew. Shit. Three missed calls. All from my mum. I did a quick calculation on the time difference: the last call was an hour ago, making it three-thirty in the UK. I sobered up in a heartbeat and pressed redial. Cooling my warm forehead against the window, I stared out at the Chrysler Building, all lit up, well, like Christmas, and wished on every star I could see that everything was OK.

'Hello? Angela?'

'It's me, Mum. What's wrong?' I closed my eyes and wished harder.

'It's your dad,' she replied. 'He's been taken poorly.'

I closed my eyes as I tried to strike a deal to change my Christmas miracle.

'What's wrong?' A million different scenarios were running through my head. Heart attack? Stroke? Had he fallen downstairs? Dad was fit and active for a man in his sixties, but you could never be certain. What if it was some horrible illness? I'd give him a kidney. A kidney for Christmas. Anything for my dad.

'I don't want you to panic – the doctor says he's probably going to be all right,' she went on, her voice pale and grey. 'But basically he had a bit of a funny turn at Auntie Sheila's Christmas do, so we had to take him into hospital.'

'A bit of a funny turn? Are they the words the doctor used?'

'Not exactly,' she hedged. 'But I thought you'd want to know. So you could come home.'

Home.

Before I could reply, I heard Dad's voice in the background demanding to be given the phone. After what sounded like a relatively non-violent altercation, my dad's voice came on the line.

'Angela, I told her not to call you, I'm fine.' Aside from sounding a bit tired and rough around the edges, he did sound like himself. I relaxed by one-eighteenth of a degree. 'I'm just in overnight for observation. There's nothing wrong.'

'But what happened? What sort of funny turn? Do I need to come home?' I wiped the tears away before they could ruin my mascara and tried to work out how I could manage to squeeze a flight back to the UK out of my meagre bank account. Flight prices in December were obscene. I had a better chance of someone lending me a private jet. Actually, Erin's husband had a private jet. Maybe if I got really drunk, I could forget I was English and ask for a quick borrow.

'You don't need to come back for this – I'll see you when I see you,' he replied. 'Really, I had something I shouldn't have and, like your mum said, I had a funny turn. I'm fine.'

'You're allergic to something? Might I be allergic to something?' Obviously, I was very concerned for his well-being. And a little bit about mine. 'What was it?'

'I don't think you need to worry, really. You're fine, love. Now, when are you coming to see us? Your mother is still insisting on buying the world's biggest bloody turkey in case you decide to grace us with your presence for Christmas dinner.'

Hmm. Was it me or was he being weird?

'Dad?'

'Angela?'

'What did you eat at Auntie Sheila's that put you in hospital?'

'We were just having a nice night in with Sheila and George and your Uncle John and Aunt Maureen came over,' he explained slowly. 'And, well, your Aunt Maureen had made some special cakes. For a laugh.'

'Special cakes?'

'Yes.'

'For a laugh?'

'Yes.'

'Dad . . .' It took a very long time for me to understand

70

what he was saying. And then just as long again for me to accept it. 'Were you and Mum doing space cakes?'

'Yes.'

'Oh dear God.'

The desire to go home and nurse my poor old dad to health transformed into a desire to go home and slap my stupid old dad around the head whilst tutting at my mother and shaking my head in disappointment.

When I was seventeen, my mum marched into Gareth Altman's eighteenth birthday party, saw me standing next to Briony Jones, who was holding an unlit hand-rolled cigarette, and shrieked, 'Angela Clark, I will not have a drug user in my house!', then dragged me out by my borrowed Radiohead T-shirt. Which was subsequently thrown out because they were a 'druggy band'. Explaining this to my then boyfriend was a bit tricky, but we were seventeen and the promise of a hand-job cured all. If only life was still so simple: I'd have a green card by now.

'So let me get this straight. You're in hospital because you ate too many space cakes and overdosed on marijuana?' I just wanted to be clear.

'I know, I know,' he giggled. Brilliant. He was still high. 'You'd think it was the Seventies.'

'Dad, you know we don't discuss anything that happened before I was born,' I reminded him. As far as I was concerned, my parents came into existence in the early Eighties, my mother already pregnant with me and my father just a lovely, middle-aged Ken doll. They didn't have sex and they certainly didn't do drugs. He was really killing my champagne buzz. I was not beyond seeing the irony in that. 'Just get lots of rest and I'll call you tomorrow. When we will discuss the concept of "Just Say No".'

71

'Your mother wants to say goodnight,' he said, giving me a huge yawn and ignoring my sanctimonious tone. It was a shame, really, because if I was being honest, I was quite enjoying it. 'Call tomorrow, love.'

Even though my mum couldn't see me, I took a moment to put on my best 'Would you like to explain yourself to me, young lady' face.

'So, I've got to let your Auntie Sheila know if you're going to be back for Boxing Day dinner at hers, because she's buying the beef next week and needs to know.'

I was actually quite impressed at her attempt to get on with business as usual.

'And obviously she'll want to know how much weed to score,' I added. 'For dessert.'

'Oh, very funny, Angela.'

'Or will we be going straight on to the crack, what with it being Christmas?'

'Angela, are you coming home or not? I'm sick of asking.'

'I can't.' I tried to say it without whining, but it was difficult. 'The flights are so expensive. Next year, I promise.'

I didn't feel like explaining that next year I could be back for good. She didn't deserve a shot of *Schadenfreude*: she would just love to hear all about my general failure as a human. I hadn't been entirely honest with my parents about my professional status for the last few months, and by 'not entirely honest', I mean I'd been flat-out lying.

'Oh, Angela Clark, you worry me sick,' she moaned. 'All the way out there, no money, spending Christmas on your own.'

'I'm not on my own,' I replied. 'And I'm not broke.' Only half of that was a lie. Pretty good going for a conversation with my mother.

'Of course, this boyfriend of yours. When are we going to be meeting him? Is he back from gallivanting around the world without you?'

'He was on tour, and you'll meet him when you meet him,' I said. The sound of Jenny shrieking in the other room reminded me I wasn't in the middle of a very odd Nineties anti-drug after-school special but actually at a party. 'I've got to go, I'm at Jenny's – we're having a Christmas party. Without any drugs.'

There was no way I could know that statement was true.

'Fine, you go off and have your party and I'll sit in the hospital with your father. Don't worry about us.'

I paused and counted to ten before I spoke. 'He's not dying, Mother, he's as high as a kite.'

'No, it's fine. I'll speak to you tomorrow. Love to Jenny.'

And she hung up.

I looked out at the busy Manhattan street below me. How was it that my father was in hospital after having an adverse reaction to a vast quantity of an illegal substance of which my mother had also partaken, and yet I was the one being made to feel like the irresponsible teenager? I watched someone come out of Scottie's diner across the street and my stomach rumbled. Brilliant. I had sympathy munchies.

Only ten minutes in real time had passed since I'd left the room, but that equated to about three hours in party time. There were at least another dozen people squished into the front room, perching on windowsills and poking their heads into the fridge, and no one was where I had left them. Instead of finding my lovely friend, my wonderful boyfriend and his regrettable band mate on the sofa, it was populated by some very

73

drunk male models and the man who swept the lobby every other morning. He seemed to be enjoying the male models. Who knew? The apartment wasn't big enough for me to lose anyone, so if they weren't in the front room and they weren't in the kitchen, that left the bathroom or my old bedroom. Sure enough, while the rest of the flat was overrun with beautiful strangers, my old bedroom was populated with all of my friends. Erin and her husband, Thomas, Vanessa, Sigge, Alex and Jenny were all draped across the bed, laughing like loons. It was a fairly wonderful sight.

'What did I miss?' I asked, forcing my way into the throng. Everyone shuffled up and rolled around until we all had our own bit of bed. 'Why are we in here?'

'Because I just remembered I hate everyone I invited,' Jenny said with delight in her eyes. 'So we're hiding.'

'In that case, I propose we go over the road and get some chips – I'm starving,' I said, resting my head against Alex's chest and trying not to purr as he ran his hand through my hair. 'I just talked to my mum and dad. Booze won't be enough – it's time to bring out the big guns.'

'Ooh, I want a chilli dog.' Jenny kicked me from across the bed. 'Are they good? Are they coming over?'

'Dear God no.' Perish the thought. 'My dad is in hospital because they went to a party and he got stoned and had a "funny turn", and my mum is my mum. Apparently weed has absolutely no effect on her whatsoever.'

'Your parents are awesome,' Vanessa said to the ceiling.

'My parents are dickheads,' I replied.

'Is he going to be OK?' Alex asked.

'He is.' I was suddenly sober and shattered. There was only one cure.

'Let's get you something greasy,' he said, sliding off the bed and holding out a hand.

'I love you.' I let him pull me off the bed. I wanted chips. I wanted chips so badly.

'Angela?' Sigge's tone was innocent. 'Were your parents at a swingers' party?'

His question was not.

I turned to Alex with pursed lips and a glare that meant business. 'I need to be eating right now.'

'We have to do gifts before we leave.' Jenny bounced up off the bed, bumping Thomas onto the floor and Erin onto her face. 'Wait right here.'

'Presents?' I looked at Erin and Vanessa, alarmed. 'We're doing presents?'

Quite aside from the fact that I hadn't bought any presents yet, it wasn't Christmas, and I had very strict rules about opening presents before the twenty-fifth. This was only acceptable if the gift giver was going to be either out of the country or dead by Christmas morning. Clearly Jenny didn't fall into either of those categories. In theory.

'You and I aren't doing gifts,' Erin yawned. 'If that helps. I didn't get you shit.'

'Appreciated.' I mentally took her Marc by Marc Jacobs scarf out from under the tree and put it back on the shelf. And then mentally took it off again and put it back under the tree with my name on it.

Jenny sailed back into the room carrying a small blue chequebook-shaped box wrapped in silver ribbon. Since a chequebook would be a fairly odd gift, I assumed it was something small and wonderful. Possibly shiny. I immediately forgot my rules and snatched it out of her hands. Christmas could do terrible things to a girl's manners.

'So, I know you've been super-stressed lately,' Jenny

started explaining as I tussled with the tightly tied ribbon. 'And I was like, what would totally chill Angie out?'

Massage vouchers? A weekend away in the mountains? Lots and lots of drugs? No, that would be from my mum.

'And I thought about the things that help me when I'm freaking out. The places that make me feel like Jenny again.'

Uh-oh. Pole-dancing lessons? Tickets to Vegas? Lots and lots of drugs?

'And I came up with this. It's going to be the shit, doll.'

I wasn't sure about 'the shit', but the fevered look in Jenny's eyes scared me. Everyone was silent while they watched me give up and rip the ribbon from the box with my teeth, because I'm so classy, and tear into the box.

Meep.

Inside the box was a copy of *Gambling for Dummies* and three plane tickets.

'Vegas, baby!' Jenny bounced up and down on the bed. 'Me, you and Erin. Girls' weekend away, just a total, awesome blow-out. We're going to go crazy. No over-thinking, no panicking, no worrying. Just fun. It's exactly what you need.'

'It is?'

It was?

'Totally,' she said, landing on her arse right next to Vanessa's face. 'We'll get drunk, we'll dance, hang out by the pool, go to the spa. It'll be awesome. No one needs to get on the pole like you do, honey.'

'Yeah, Ange,' Alex contributed. 'You do need to get on the pole.'

I could have punched him, but I was all Rocky'd

out for one week. Instead, I took a spectator's stance and watched as Vanessa pushed Jenny off the bed and onto the floor, right on her backside. She did have it coming.

'And when Jenny's finished trying to kill us all, I have a client opening a store in the Crystals, so there is going to be some intense window shopping going on,' Erin said. 'And don't worry, I won't let her make you pole dance.'

After a moment of fear had passed, I started to smile. I was more concerned that it wouldn't be a case of 'making me' so much as 'stopping me'. I'd always wanted to go to Vegas, always. It just sounded so fabulous: all girls in feathered headdresses serving elaborate cocktails to shady blackjack players while Frank Sinatra belted out 'Strangers in the Night' on stage. Somewhere, I was semi-aware that these days, Vegas was more Kim Kardashian knocking back jello shots while P. Diddy set his iPod to shuffle in the DJ booth, but still. Surely there was still a good old glamorous time to be had somewhere on the Strip?

'So.' I held up the tickets. 'When do we leave?'

CHAPTER SIX

When Monday rolled around, I was all business. Being the lovely, loyal girlfriend that I was, I waited until midday for Alex to wake up before I callously abandoned him and headed out to Bedford Avenue for a bagel. I wasn't entirely heartless; I did leave a note.

After I'd woken up, cleaned up and successfully dressed myself, I'd decided today would be the day when I put everything right. So what if my parents were car-key-party-throwing junkies? So what if my visa was about to expire? So what if I hadn't got a proper job? As long as my dad stayed off the meow meow and out of hospital, I could cope with their extracurriculars. And as for the visa-slash-job drama, I was on top of it. So on top of it that I'd cracked open a brand new notebook, bought a new pen and set up shop in the living room. I was going to work out what made me an extraordinary alien if it killed me. Just as soon as I'd finished writing my Christmas list. And my Christmas shopping list. I looked around my work-space – it was missing something. In fact, it was missing everything. I needed to go out and buy vast quantities of food and some magazines to motivate me. And pad out my wish lists. Nothing incentivized me like the allure of the latest It bag or a massive packet of Haribo.

Joy of joys, the terrible weather had broken and it was a clear, cold, beautiful day in Brooklyn. The hipsters of Williamsburg were still as colourful and ridiculously dressed as ever, swathed in neon scarves, Moon boots and giant furry hats. Their heavy black-framed glasses were a constant. It was reassuring. I dug my hands deep into my pockets, trying not to look into shop windows; each one was more tempting than the last. But I was strong. And, more to the point, hungry. I powered down the uneven sidewalks, past the Music Hall where I'd seen Alex play one time, past The Cove where Alex had seen me sing drunken karaoke lots and lots and lots of times. Oh, memories.

The guy behind the counter of the magazine store sighed as I walked in. I nodded curtly and walked quickly down the aisle to hide behind the Popchips. Every time I came here, I was expecting a 'this is not a library' sign to have appeared. Shopkeep enjoyed my work even less than the editors of Spencer Media, but it didn't matter. I was here on an urgent journalistic mission. Yes, I'd emailed everyone I knew in publishing, but there had to be millions of people I didn't know, and what better time to get in touch than in this season of goodwill? I had a plan. Now I just needed names. But if I was going to take New York's magazine world by storm, I was going to have to know the magazines. What a chore – an afternoon poring over fashion mags. My eyes darted around the shelves and my breath caught in my chest. Every single cover looked magical. Dark reds, forest greens, gold and silver everywhere. Covers with foil. Covers with glitter. Ahh, all the underage mothers from MTV's *Teen Mom* standing next to each other under the tree. Christmas brought everyone together. While I covetously fingered the current issue of *Vogue*, my eyes started to stray. Oooh. Wedding magazines.

Checking my blind spot over both shoulders, I grabbed a copy of *The Knot: New York*. It was heavy. It made my heart pound. I opened up on a random page, landing on a super-cute bride and groom and their Christmas wedding at New York's Rainbow Rooms. Ohh. The bride wore Romona Keveza, the groom wore YSL, and the rings were from Cartier. Immediately, I started to tailor the details to a more Angela-friendly ceremony. Tiffany bands, for a start. And Alex would probably wear vintage. I'd want something I designed myself. And then threw away only to replace it with something I couldn't possibly afford at the last minute. And also some Valium, I thought, slamming the magazine shut. It really was weighty. Satisfying. It would definitely cause a very serious injury if hurled at someone.

'You getting married, miss?' The man behind the counter suddenly appeared over my shoulder, eyeing my wedding porn.

I replied with a perfectly justified shrill cackle.

'Me? No.' And yet for some reason, I was entirely incapable of putting the magazines back. 'Not right now.'

'Right.' He started to back away slowly and hid behind the counter again. Clearly any goodwill I'd earned from my potential betrothed status was ebbing away fast. 'But you like to read the wedding magazines?'

Who was he, the publishing police? I'd been treating this shop like a library for months and not had a peep out of him, but today was the day he wanted a natter?

'I'm a journalist, it's research,' I announced, dumping

all the magazines on the counter. 'I'm a very important journalist. Extraordinary.'

He was buying it as much as Lawrence the Lawyer.

'OK.' He rang up the mags with eyebrows raised. 'Some ladies, they just like to read the magazines. That'll be thirty-nine dollars.'

'Fucking hell.' I pulled almost every penny I had out of my pocket and handed it over. Clearly I needed to get into the wedding magazine business. Wasn't *Heat* like a quid or something? 'I mean, thanks.'

'Thank you.' He gave me my change and slid my purchases into the slightly seedy brown paper bag in which they belonged. I'd be less embarrassed walking around this neighbourhood with a copy of *Juggs*.

Deviant mags in hand and head held high, I walked confidently out of the shop. And then practically ran into Bagelsmith, heart pounding, hands sweating, desperate to get another look at that artisan sterling silver favour box. I wanted to see some red hot nuptials.

'Angela.' Ronnie the Bagel Boy raised a hand from behind the counter. 'Usual?'

'Usual,' I waved back, hopping straight onto one of the bar stools in the window and pulling out my stash. This was one of my favourite places to sit in the winter. Come summer, I'd be outside the ice-cream store up the street. Spring and autumn saw me sitting beside the East River, watching the ferry sweep back and forth between Brooklyn and Manhattan. But inside Bagelsmith, peering out of its steamy window, was my favourite place when the weather turned against me.

I watched every kind of person walk by while I panted over wedding dresses, chair coverings and place cards. We had models, musicians, delivery men, students, yummy mummies, ancient locals bemoaning the influx of yuppies and hipsters alike. There was always something new, but never anything surprising. Until today. An unmistakeable mop of curly brown hair, clad in a scarlet trench coat, standing across the street, staring directly at me. Jenny. I waved madly in the window while pulling my phone out of my bag to dial in case she was blind. But my excitement at seeing her shifted from a simmer to a boil and I started to panic. Why was she here? Why hadn't she called first? What was wrong? Her apartment had definitely burned down. After a moment, she waved back and started across the street. I looked down at my magazine. Shit. She could not see this. Panicked, I rammed it into my MJ satchel as fast as the fraying seams would let me.

'Hey!' She rushed in, rosy-cheeked and wide-eyed. 'Hi.'

'Hi.' I gave her a quick hug and moved onto the second stool, bearing the brunt of a filthy look from the Mexican guy now squished into the corner. 'What are you doing out here? Is everything OK?'

'Everything's fine,' she said, grabbing a bottle of water from the open fridge and whipping off the top. 'Why wouldn't it be fine?'

'Because you're in Williamsburg in the middle of the afternoon on a Monday,' I said. No reaction. 'And you work on Mondays. And you hate coming to Williamsburg.'

'I like coming to see you,' she replied with a bright Jenny smile. 'And I like bagels. What's good?'

'You came to see me?' Now I was confused. 'Why didn't you call?'

'Jesus – chill, Miss Ego.' She necked half her bottle of water in one gulp. 'As much as I love you, I am prepared to cross water for other reasons than to see your sweet ass.'

My ass was not sweet. And by January it would be

even less sweet following my annual Christmas pig-out. 'Such as?'

'That nail place.' She waved an unpolished hand in the general direction of 'over there'. 'It's supposed to be awesome. I took a long lunch, figured I'd drop in on you on the way and talk Vegas.'

'Which nail place?' There were a million nail places in Williamsburg and I couldn't have named one of them. 'I don't have a nail place.'

'And again, I do know people other than yourself.' She grabbed half my bagel as soon as Ronnie put it down in front of me. 'One of the girls in the office swears by it. She won't go anywhere else and, you know, I want to look extra awesome for fabulous Las Vegas.'

Brilliant. Something else to add to the list, which already had on it buy a swimsuit in the dead of winter, steal all the quarters from the laundry jar and endure the horror of a bikini wax. The last time Jenny and I had entered bikini territory, she had put me through a DIY waxing horror and made me wear one of her Brazilian beauties. This time I was hoping for a professional wax and a bikini that covered more than fifteen per cent of my arse. It was a big ask, but I was confident it could be achieved.

'Ew, tuna fish.' Jenny made a face at the first bite of my bagel but, curiously, kept on eating. 'I told myself no carbs before Thursday. What are you doing to me, Clark?'

'Expanding your horizons,' I said, snatching the second half before it disappeared. 'So, viva las Vegas. Did you talk to the hotel?'

Jenny, a former hotel concierge, had fingers in all kinds of hospitality industry pies and had promised to arrange the whole thing during the after-party party at Scottie's Diner on Saturday night. Obviously she was aware that I was on a clock with regards to travel plans inside the US of A despite my very confident (if baseless) declarations that everything was going to be fine.

'I did talk to the hotel, and I talked to the airline, and I talked to Erin, and I have news,' she nodded, picking apart her half of the bagel. 'We're going on Thursday.'

'This Thursday?'

'Uh-huh. We're staying at the De Lujo, we're flying in the morning and we'll be back by Sunday night. Monday you recover, and Tuesday we get our asses into gear. I made you another appointment with the lawyer and this time I told him you don't leave the office until he has sorted his shit out. So, *viva la visa*. I hope you're feeling lucky, Angie.'

I pushed the rest of my bagel towards my friend. I'd love to know what I'd done in a former life to deserve a friend like Jenny. Lucky wasn't the word for it.

'You're going to Vegas?'

'Yes, Louisa,'

'Without me?'

'Yes, Louisa.'

'I'm so jealous. It's not fair. You're going to Las Vegas and I'm stuck here.'

I made a face into my webcam.

'You're stuck in your beautiful home, with your wonderful husband, pregnant with your first, no doubt glorious, child,' I replied. 'I reckon it's a fair trade that I get three nights in what is essentially a debauched Alton Towers.'

She made a face right back. This was the problem with Skype. Having people able to see your expressions

84

made it really hard to pretend not to be pissed off with the person you were talking to. Not that Louisa was trying. She never had before; why start with the civilities now, just because technology demanded it? My oldest friend and I tried to get a good Skype chat/bitch in once a fortnight, at least. Ever since she had got knocked up, we were up to a weekly date. I had a morbid fascination with the bump. Louisa had always been the skinny one, and I was damned if I was going to miss this. And so, on Monday night, I lay on my belly in front of the Christmas tree, looking at the truly hideous sleety shitty weather through the window and happily scarfed a carton of Goldfish crackers for my lunch while we chatted. At home, Christmas meant bag upon bag of Mini Cheddars, and this was the closest I could get. Plus they were shaped like fish and no one loved a novelty snack like I did.

'I really thought you were going to come home this year,' she sulked. 'Being pregnant is shit. I'm fat, I'm miserable and I can't bloody drink. Imagine Christmas without being able to have a drink. My mum and dad. Tim's mum and dad! Jesus, I'm probably going to have to see your mum and dad. And without so much as a Baileys.'

'While that does sound like the best argument I ever heard for sterilization,' I replied, 'I'm still going to Vegas. And you're still going to be knocked up whether I come home or not, aren't you?'

'Maybe I'll just have a drink anyway,' she said, poking her bump. 'See how she likes a couple of sweet sherries. My breast milk is going to be ninety per cent Sauvignon anyway.'

'My mum will probably sort you out with a nice bit of crack,' I suggested. 'Or a lovely drop of meth. Since it's Christmas.'

'Don't!' She physically pulled away from the screen. 'I cannot believe your mum and dad smoke weed. The baby cannot believe your mum and dad smoke weed, and she doesn't even have a consciousness yet.'

Wait, she? I leapt up – it was a she now? How had I missed that memo?

'She?' I wanted to rap on the screen to get her attention. Sometimes I forgot that using Skype wasn't the same as when I saw the neighbour's cat licking its arse on the other side of a window; this was actually a human woman, thousands of miles away. 'It's a she? You know it's a she?'

'She's never been an it. Only you call her "it",' she said tartly. 'And no, we don't know. We're not finding out. I just, you know, have a feeling.'

Well, that was disappointing.

And until it was on Facebook, it was an 'it', wasn't it?

'Do you get lots of feelings?' I asked. 'Baby feelings?'

Pregnancy genuinely terrified me, and I was fascinated with Louisa's experience. I considered it to be a condition somewhere between a nine-month-long debilitating hangover – the vomming, the cravings, the need for a nice sleep and a lovely sit-down – and being attacked by the face-hugger in *Aliens*. It was a living thing! Inside you! That you didn't ask for! Well, I accept that bit is debatable, but you get the idea. No one wakes up and thinks, 'I'd love to have a nine-pound screaming beast yanked out of my vagina today and then latched onto my boob for two years, cheers,' do they? They think 'Ooh, lovely babies'. They think they want to glow. They think they want the last seat on the tube. They don't consider the middle part. At least not as much as I did. As far as I was concerned, my period was a monthly blessing, not a curse.

'I do.' Louisa scrunched up her nose. 'Mostly horrible ones like sore boobs and haemorrhoids. But I'm excited, you know? In four months, I'll have an actual baby.'

'Christ.'

'I know.'

We sat and stared at each other in silence for a moment. I didn't know what Louisa was thinking about, but I was prepared to bet quite a lot of money that it wasn't the time she wrapped the school guinea pig up in a blanket, pretended it was her baby and pushed it around in a pram for an entire afternoon before dropping it in the pond while nursing it to sleep.

'So when are you coming back, anyway?' She broke the silence first as always. It was clinically impossible for Louisa to be speechless for more than one minute. Unless you were making a 'bit of a scene' at her wedding and breaking the groom's hand. And in my defence, I only did that the once. 'I really miss you, babe.'

'If I don't get the visa sorted, I'll be back very soon for a very long time,' I said, wrapping my hair into a ponytail, a sure sign it needed cutting, and then letting it droop around my shoulders. We'd already covered my least favourite topic and I just couldn't bear to go over it again. 'I know there's nothing anyone can do, and I know no one wants me to leave, but I just . . . I don't know – I feel like maybe they're not taking it as seriously as they could be.'

Louisa did her best to look sympathetic to my cause instead of excited at the prospect of a cheap babysitter. Not that anyone would ever leave me alone with an infant. Or a toddler. Or anything really precious, like their Sky Plus box or iPhone.

'When you say they, do you mean Alex?' she asked.

I pouted. She nodded. 'And have you actually talked to him?'

My bottom lip was out so far she could have sat on it.

'Angela.' Louisa gave me a very stern stare. 'You have to talk to him. As in actually tell him what thoughts are going through your tiny mind and not just make passing comments and hope he'll pick up on them. What have you told him?'

'That I need to get a new visa.' This was true.

'And what haven't you told him?'

'That I'm not technically eligible for any of them and if I don't get one, they're going to kick me out.'

'So you haven't talked at all?' Annoyingly, this was also sort of true.

'Yes, we have,' I lied merrily. 'We talk all the time.'

Of course we hadn't bloody talked. I'd thought about talking. I'd tried talking. But ever since Jenny's party he'd been out or asleep, and I could hardly pop my head around the bedroom door, give him a cheery grin and a quick 'Ooh, I'm off to Vegas, love, but when I get back we need to have a wee chat about how I'm going to be deported in four weeks' could I? Or at least that's what I'd convinced myself.

'Alex doesn't deal well with pressure.' I tried to talk the look off Louisa's face. 'He just wants to know it's going to be OK. Which it is. All he'll say is "we'll work it out after Christmas". So there's no point in worrying him. He doesn't need to know.'

'I think you mean you don't deal well with pressure,' she replied. 'And just what happens if you don't get a new visa?'

'Then I'm screwed.'

'Oh, Angela.' She shook her head sadly. 'Screwed?

You've gone all American. You'll be *buggered*. Maybe you should come back.'

'I'm bilingual, you cow.' Sticking my tongue out was a perfectly mature response, yes? 'But yes. I'll be buggered. I know Alex is always getting visas to play gigs in other countries, so maybe he doesn't think it's a big deal. And to be fair, I wasn't that worried before he went to Japan. I was sure a job would come up before there was a problem, but now . . .'

I felt my stomach drop hard and fast. Probably a bit like Kylie, the year five guinea pig.

'It might not feel like it helps, but I do believe you'll be all right, honey,' she said, flashing me a smile that had been getting me through tough situations for twenty-eight years. 'This is you we're talking about. Angela who up and moved to New York all on her own. Angela who met all these amazing friends that I'm insanely jealous of. Angela whose handbag I would swap my husband for. You can do anything you want if you put your mind to it.'

'You wouldn't trade me Tim for that handbag if you could see it now,' I said, looking mournfully at the battered bag sitting sadly on the sofa. 'And besides, a Marc Jacobs handbag isn't going to help you with the three a.m. feed, is it?'

'And Tim is?' she asked.

'Good point,' I acknowledged. 'Good point, well made.'

On my computer screen, gorgeous, glowing Louisa bit an already ragged nail.

'Ange?' She pressed her hand against her mouth.

'Lou?'

'I'm really scared about having the baby.'

'Oh shut up.' I wanted to reach out and slap her.

'You're going to be the best mum ever. What's brought this on?'

'It's just . . .' She looked behind her to check the coast was clear and leaned into the camera. 'Do you remember when I dropped that guinea pig in the pond at school?'

'Talking to Louisa?' Alex wandered into the living room, elegantly attired in his boxers and an old Led Zeppelin T-shirt, hair rumpled from another afternoon nap. The jet lag was making his sleep patterns even more erratic than usual, and he paused for a moment, trying to work out his path through the epic pile of magazines, Post-it notes and highlighters I had spread out on the floor. The more mess I made, the more confident I was about securing my new visa and, man alive, there was a lot of mess. Torn-out mastheads, scribbled headline ideas and, well, quite a few circled shoes that weren't going to get me a job per se, but were going to motivate me to do well.

After a couple of seconds, he gave up, kissed me on the top of the head and made a beeline for the tree. Sigh. He'd only been home a couple of days and already nearly all my candy canes were gone. I had tried to explain that tree candy was not for eating until after Christmas day, but he argued a very strong case against me. Primarily because he'd found two empty Cadbury's advent calendars and a whole pack of chocolate tree ornaments hidden in the recycling. I was just going to have to buy more candy canes. That was $1.99 coming straight out of his Christmas present fund.

'Yeah,' I said, snapping shut my MacBook. 'I can't believe she's going to have a baby. She is a bloody baby.'

'People do keep on doing that.' He tore the wrapping from the sugary goodness with his teeth, tiptoed through my 'office' and sat down beside me. It was so good to have him home. So good, the little 'I Love You' butterflies fluttered into existence in my belly. Better butterflies than candy canes – less fattening. 'She's all good, though?'

'All good,' I nodded. It was still weird to me that two such important people in my life had never met. 'Jealous of me going to Vegas without her. I think it's fair; she's having a baby without me.'

'That's not really something you could have helped with,' he said, leaning his head back against the sofa and giving me a look. 'Your mom didn't tell you about the birds and the bees?'

'No, of course she didn't. At the time I thought she was being a prude, but now I'm thinking maybe she was too high to actually know herself.'

He nodded thoughtfully, sucking on his candy cane. 'Well, when two people really love each other . . .'

It only took one bash with a cushion to shut him up.

'About Vegas.' He snatched the cushion from my weak and feeble hand and threw it across the room. 'When are you going?'

'Allegedly this weekend. On Thursday.' I looked doubtful. 'Jenny claims it's all organized, but it's just so last-minute. At least Erin's coming. I'm sure she'll keep us in line.'

'Right.' Alex sighed and turned to face me. 'So, I saw Jeff in the elevator this morning.'

Uh-oh. Any story that involved Jeff ended badly. The former love of Jenny's life, current fiancé of a girl named Shannon and our next-door neighbour. Stories involving Jeff often ended in tears or at least drunken recriminations. Unless I bumped into him while I was taking the recycling out, in which case it all ended very well for me. I'd read everything by Germaine Greer (well, skimmed it at uni and seen her on *Newsnight*), and I had decided there was nothing anti-feminist about letting men carry heavy things. Especially heavy dirty things.

'So yeah, we went to grab coffee and he got to talking about his bachelor party and how they had someone drop out at the last minute and, yeah, he kinda ended up inviting me along.' He crunched off a piece of candy cane and chewed for a moment.

I did not have a good feeling about this.

'It's in Vegas.'

Oh no.

'This weekend.'

Oh, good God, no.

I really wanted to believe that Jenny had no idea her ex-boyfriend was going to be in Vegas at the exact time we were going to be there. I really wanted to believe that she was genuinely over him and moving on with Sigge. But then, I also still believed that if you went to sleep naked the house would burn down, and if you wore mismatched socks, you were guaranteed to get run over. Sometimes I was stupid. And sometimes I was not.

'You think she knows?' Alex asked.

'You think she doesn't?' I asked. 'I don't know what I'm going to do with her. She'll only deny it if I ask her, but there's just no way it's a coincidence. Someone is going to die on this trip, aren't they? Someone's going to die, and I'm going to prison.'

'Right?' Alex agreed. 'Good thing I told Jeff I'd go, so you've got back-up.'

'You did?' I couldn't remember a time I'd actually

been happier in my entire life. Maybe when I found a Cadbury's Creme Egg in my knicker drawer a month after Easter and I thought I'd eaten them all. Maybe.

'You're coming to Vegas?'

'I did and I am,' he nodded, and carried on crunching. 'I haven't been in the longest time. Vegas is the best.'

Vegas is the best? I sat back and observed my boyfriend. He was the last person on earth I'd have had pegged as a Las Vegas fanboy. What other secret passions did he have hidden away? Was he buying porcelain dolls from QVC every night after I went to sleep?

'What do you do in Vegas?' The words were out of my mouth with way too much emphasis on the 'you' before I could stop them. It was all I could do not to add 'please don't say hookers'.

'Hookers?' he shrugged. 'And, you know, poker. I like to play sometimes.'

'I don't know which I'm more shocked about,' I said. 'Probably the poker.'

'Thanks,' he replied. 'I haven't played in a while but I'm pretty good. Maybe I'll win big and buy you something pretty.'

'I won't hold my breath.' It was a lie. I was holding my breath while I said it and I would be holding my breath all the way to Nevada.

'How about a beer for now?' He clambered over the back of the sofa to avoid my magazine madness. 'Looks like you've been working hard.'

'Very hard,' I confirmed, tearing out an article on how to make your own Christmas crackers. 'Some of us can't hibernate through winter.'

I turned back to my pile of magazines and waited to be inspired. And waited. And waited.

'Angela?'

'Alex?'

Hmm. Was I interested in a feature on transforming your life through fish ownership? Maybe not.

'What the fuck is this?'

I froze. Tongue sticking out. Sharpie in hand.

'What the fuck is what?'

Ohhhhhh shiiiiit.

I'd left my handbag on the kitchen top. My handbag full of wedding magazines.

'This?'

I turned slowly, ready to launch into my 'they're research!' speech, but instead of finding Alex with a fistful of bridal porn and eyes full of fear, all he had in his hand was a white sheet of paper. Oh. The Letter. I really had to stop carrying that around with me.

'Right.' I uncrossed my legs and crossed them again. 'That.'

'This.' He waved The Letter at me. Unnecessary, really – I was already very aware of what it said. 'What the fuck is this?'

'It's a letter,' I replied. 'From the INS. It's not a big deal.'

It was quite amazing how I was able to utter those words given my initial reaction to The Letter, but as I said them now, I almost believed them. I was very, very good at deluding myself.

'Not a big deal? It says here they're gonna kick you out,' Alex reread as he yelled. Quite the multitasker, my boyfriend. 'In a month. In less than a month. That's your idea of not a big deal?'

'Well, it has the potential to become a big deal,' I replied calmly. 'But it's going to be fine.'

'How? How is it going to be fine?'

I couldn't remember a time I'd seen him this angry. The edge was taken off his rage by the fact that he was still only wearing a T-shirt and boxers, but still, he was not a happy bunny, and that fact was weaving a very unpleasant knot in my stomach.

'I just have to get another visa,' I whispered. The louder Alex was, the quieter my voice became.

'And I'm gonna guess there's more you haven't told me about that too?' He couldn't seem to tear his eyes off the piece of paper in his hand. Well, it was that or he was just too mad to look at me, and that didn't make me feel any better. 'Do you want to tell me what's going on, or should I hope some more pieces of paper fall out of your purse when I walk by?'

Fall out my arse. I knew he'd been rooting around in there for sweets. Hopefully, he hadn't found them. I had a feeling I would want them later.

'Well, maybe the lawyer wasn't quite as enthusiastic about me getting a new visa as I might have suggested,' I said slowly. 'But it's not like he said it was impossible. I just need to put together a case. Or get a contract from a UK magazine. And some references. And a portfolio. And some other stuff. But it's not impossible.'

'It isn't? Because it sounds pretty tricky.'

He had a point. When I put it like that, it did sound quite impossible. Or at the very least, a bit difficult.

'What the fuck, Angela? Why didn't you tell me about this?' He was really very mad. This close to naptime, Alex was usually as mild-mannered as a man could be. Between his sleepy demeanour and floppy indie-boy fringe, the most he could manage was crossing the street without getting run over, but right now his eyes were bright and sparky with rage. He looked like he could quite easily go Godzilla on the street.

'OK, please calm down,' I said. Stupid. I was waving

a metaphorical red rag at the metaphorical bull. 'I just haven't had a chance to tell you yet, that's all. I was going to. Honestly, it's not going to be a problem.'

'Bullshit you haven't had a chance. And how is it not going to be a problem?' He threw The Letter back into my bag and his hands into the air. 'How is you getting your ass thrown out of the US not going to be a problem?'

'This really isn't helping,' I pointed out. 'Shouting at me isn't going to get us anywhere.'

'I have to shout because you don't talk,' he shot back. 'I'm not helping? You're not helping. You not dealing with things like an adult, as usual, isn't helping. You not telling me shit again. Again, Angela! That's what's not helping. Jesus Christ.'

It was everything I could do not to cry. I hated to row, but he was right. I'd brought this entirely on myself.

'Alex, don't,' I sniffed. 'It's not like I wasn't telling you for fun. I really thought I could work it out on my own.'

He opened the fridge calmly, took out a beer, popped the cap and then slammed it shut again. Inside, everything rattled.

'Because that's worked out so well for us in the past?'

Ouch.

'Alex – ' I started, but he just took a deep swig from his bottle and held out a hand to keep me away.

'I'm going to take a bath.' He shook his head to shut me up. 'You didn't want to talk to me, and I can't talk to you right now.'

I turned back to my piles and piles of paper, my heart sinking down into the pit of my stomach. Every second that passed made it more and more difficult to try to speak. Instead of saying sorry, I sat with my mouth open, guppy-like, second-guessing myself into silence.

Looking around at the chaos I'd created, my confidence started to ebb away. I wasn't extraordinary. I wasn't even really a journalist. I was just a chancer who got lucky and my luck had run out. Also, I was a petulant brat who thought kicking the stack of magazines to the floor would make her feel better. It didn't, it hurt my knee and gave me a paper cut on my big toe. See, this was why I shouldn't have moved in with a boy. Jenny would have had at least two inspirational spreadsheets, an action plan and a flip-chart displaying my progress on the go by now. Alex was sulking in the bath with a beer. Admittedly I would much rather have been moping in the tub, but as I had learned, that didn't get you anywhere in life. Baths were for wallowing like a grumpy hippo, and I did not have time to be a grumpy hippo. I didn't have time to sit here and fret over Alex's really quite extreme reaction. And I certainly didn't have time to keep being distracted by the new YSL bag in *Marie Claire*. Adopting the tried and tested 'What Would Jenny Lopez Do' approach to life, I wiped away a stray tear, banished Alex's angry words from my memory and opened my notebook to a blank page. And pushed *Marie Claire* right under the sofa with my foot. I was going to do this. I was going to get my visa. And then I was going to punch Alex in the arm for being such a tit.

I looked at the blank page. It looked right back at me. OK, maybe he wasn't being a complete tit. He was angry because he was scared I was going to have to leave, right? And not because I had accidentally forgotten to tell him about my getting deported, although I was prepared to accept that might be a possibility. A slight possibility. Well, maybe it was a bit of both. I took the lid off my pen. I looked at my pen. I wondered how people got over writer's block when all they were trying to write was a list. I pulled *Marie Claire* back out from under the sofa to inspire me.

Angela's Action Plan

1. Identify relevant magazines
2. Write proposals
3. Contact editors
4. Write my blog
5. Pray to all known deities

There. That was enough to prove I was serious, wasn't it? And I could definitely accomplish something within the next four weeks, give or take a weekend in Vegas. But that still didn't resolve the problem of the angry boyfriend. Naturally, my reaction to our first proper argument was to stay on the sofa, bottom lip out and wait for him to surface, hopefully pretend it had never happened and let it stew until one of us threw it in the other's face during a completely unrelated row in seven years' time. That was the British way, after all. But if I was going to be a big girl, I figured I might as well start acting like one sooner rather than later. First time for everything.

'Alex?' I knocked lightly on the bathroom door, knees pulled up under my chin, back against the wall. Better get comfy for this.

No answer. Time to pull out the big guns.

'Alex, I'm sorry.'

Cue the sound of water sploshing around the bath and a rather loud sigh.

'Can I come in so I can talk to you, please?'

'Door's locked.'

'You could unlock it?'

'I'm not getting out of the tub to let you in.'

I was so glad he bothered to clarify his reasons.

'Fine, I'll talk out here,' I started. 'I'm sorry I didn't tell you about the letter. I'm not making excuses – I should have told you right away, but it only came the other day and you'd only just got home. Then we had such a busy weekend and you've been so jet-lagged, I didn't want to stress you out with it. I really did think I could sort it all out. I really do think I can sort it all out. There is a plan, you know.'

'There's always a plan,' he replied. 'But your plans suck.'

'They don't all suck,' I frowned, trying to come up with a plan that was unsucky. Just because I couldn't think of one off the top of my head didn't mean there wasn't one.

'Tell me a plan of yours that didn't involve either violence or leaving the country,' he retaliated. 'And every single time you're in this situation it's because you don't talk to people.'

To be fair, he wasn't wrong. The last eighteen months or so had been heavy on the air travel and slapping people about a bit. First I hit my best friend's husband with a shoe and ran away to New York because no one had bothered to tell me my ex was a cheating scumbag and I had chosen not to notice. Then I went to LA and accidentally outed a gay actor. Didn't hit anyone that time but I really had thought quite hard about it. And then there was the trip to Paris where I slapped one girl around the chops, took a train back to England, raided M&S Simply Food and went straight back to Paris to have an out-and-out brawl with another girl live on stage at a festival. That had been a high point. Oh. And my recent Cici-slapping situation. But if ever there was a deserved decking, it was that one. So perhaps my plans hadn't been terribly well laid out to date, but this time I had a real live actual action plan. And a notebook! How could I fail?

'I'm talking to you now?'

'Nice try.'

'If I promise to discuss all important decisions with you from now on, not leave the country, hit anyone with a shoe, buy any shoes or throw drinks at anyone, will you please open the door so I can come in and talk to you properly?' I asked.

There was a moment of splishy quiet while he considered my offer.

'It's open,' he said finally. 'I lied about locking it.'

'Arsehole,' I muttered, pushing the door open and crawling along the bathroom floor to lean against the side of the tub. Alex was a picture. Bubbles up to his chin, hair wet through, mardy look on his face and beer in his hand. On the upside, it was impossible to be mad or upset at him. Unfortunately, it was also very hard to make puppy-dog eyes at someone when (a) all you wanted to do was laugh and (b) the recipient of said expression was refusing to look at you.

'Nice bath?' I asked, flicking a handful of bubbles into the air.

'Yes.' He readjusted his bubble blanket. He had achieved excellent coverage. 'Thanks.'

'The beer really makes it very macho.'

'Screw you.'

'Charming.'

We sat in a semi-comfortable silence for a moment, Alex drinking his beer, me resting my chin on the side of the bath. I would have let it play out longer but the bathroom floor was not a comfortable place to hang out and his bubbles were disappearing at a rate of knots. I had a feeling I'd struggle to keep up my end of a serious conversation once I could see the goods.

'Are you really mad at me?'

'Yes,' Alex said, pushing his wet hair off his face. 'I am really mad at you. But I'm sorry I lost my shit. I shouldn't have shouted. What is it going to take for you to actually start telling me stuff?'

I shrugged and wiped a drop of water from his forehead before it fell into his eye.

'There's nothing you don't know now,' I said quietly. 'And I promise this won't happen again. I'll tell you everything. You'll be so sick of hearing about my every thought, you'll want a mute button for my mouth.'

He took my hand in his, all warm and wet from his bath, and squeezed it tightly.

'I'm not joking,' he said, his eyes all serious. 'I know you're on this. And I'm pretty sure Jenny's on this too, right?'

I nodded.

'And as we all know, Jenny always gets what she wants. But I need to know about these things. It's important, Angela. How do you think I feel, finding out you could get thrown out of the country and you didn't even bother to tell me even though all your friends know about it?'

'Not brilliant?' I suggested.

'Not brilliant,' he confirmed. 'You're my girlfriend.

We live together. We're supposed to deal with this stuff together.'

'I know.' I was trying not to whine but it was quite hard. 'I've just got used to sorting things out for myself over the last year, and I suppose I'm not good at asking boys for help. And I really didn't want you to worry.'

'I'm not boys,' he reminded me. 'I'm your boyfriend. I want to help. I want to worry. I worry about you breaking your neck in some dumb pair of shoes, I worry about you choking on a pizza crust because you inhale your food so damn fast, I worry about you dying of exposure because you won't wear a proper winter coat. At least this would have given me something real to worry about.'

I was quite touched. Mildly offended but mostly touched. And I wanted to tell him I worried about him too, but mostly I worried that some gorgeous, super-cool, super-skinny blonde girl was going to steal him away in the night, and that didn't have the same sweet sentiment as his concerns, did it? I didn't need to read *Cosmo* (again) to know that rabid paranoia and groundless jealousy were not attractive qualities in a girlfriend.

'Your winter coats make me look like the Michelin Man,' I said, giving his hand a gentle return squeeze.

'That's because it's minus ten outside, you idiot.' The frustration in his face broke into a reluctant smile and he stretched over to place a very light kiss on my lips. 'Now get out so I can take my bath in peace, and go get a job before I kick your ass out of the country.'

'You girl!' I snatched the beer bottle out of his hand, jumped up and legged it out of the bathroom. 'Do you want a candle lighting or something?'

'We didn't have any,' he shouted back as I closed the door to.

Sipping what was left of his warm beer, I gazed at my very professional pile of shit in the living room. I had survived our first proper shouty row; arguing my way to a work visa would be easy. Provided I could survive Vegas.

CHAPTER SEVEN

Bright and early on Thursday morning, I kissed Alex goodbye and skipped out of the front door into a shiny black town car, impervious to the bitter cold.

I'd had a great week. After our motivational tiff, I'd put together dozens of proposals for editors all over the place, offering myself up as their eyes and ears on the ground in New York. I was a great choice, I told them. Connected to the city's cultural under-ground, Hollywood celebs, totally in the fashionable know and situated smack bang in hipster central. There was no better US correspondent than Angela Clark. So what if I was a bit biased? If you tell your-self something often enough, it starts to sound true, good or bad, and I was genuinely feeling so much better about things. A quick call to Lawrence the Lawyer confirmed that the media visa was all but in the bag if I could get a contract with a 'recognized media outlet', and what with all the phone hacking scandals, I was pretty sure loads of newspapers and magazines were looking for bright, upstanding young go-getters with their integrity intact. Who were perfectly happy to out celebrities for a living. An honest day's wage for an honest day's work. It was probably a plus that I couldn't work out Twitter, let alone break into Hugh Grant's voicemail.

Plus things with Alex were great. From the moment he had dragged himself out of the bath on Sunday, he'd been the perfect boyfriend. Winter walks in the park, playing teaboy, suggesting features for my proposals, bringing M&M's back from Duane Reade unbidden. It was wonderful. My wedding mags were still stashed under the mattress, spines broken, corners folded over, automatically opening at the dirtiest pages (the dresses), but I'd put it out of my head. Yes, I wanted him to put a ring on it. Yes, I wanted to lock it down. But I wanted it done right. I'd been engaged before after all, but that time, when presented with a modest ring on the back of a horse-drawn carriage in Seville, my reaction had been sort of 'Oh. Yes, I suppose so.' When I thought about Alex proposing, I actually held my breath. And people needed to breathe, generally speaking. I wanted to share the rest of my life with him. The spectre of deportation had confirmed that for me, but what about Alex? I knew he wanted me with him – he'd said that over and over – but there was no mention of making it official. We shared an apartment. We shared a love of pineapple on pizza. We shared a razor, even though he didn't know that. But did he want to share the rest of his life with me?

The more I tried not to think about it, the more it plagued me. All I could think about was weddings. A trip around the supermarket turned into a trial for the aisle. Every song on my iPod was a contender for the first dance. Every time Alex reached into his coat pocket, my heart stopped – phone or ring? Phone or ring? Quite often, it was ChapStick. What a girl.

*   *   *

I hadn't seen Jenny since our tuna bagel liaison. I'd called, I'd texted, I'd offered to come over for lunch, for drinks, for coffee, but she was 'way too busy'. Apparently taking two days out of the office at this time of year was 'insanity' and she just didn't have the time. The fact that I didn't point out to her that she'd only been working full time in said office for two months was evidence, to me at least, of how I was growing as a person. Not having had time to chat, of course, meant that we had not had the chance to discuss the Jeff situation. Namely whether or not Jenny knew about his bachelor weekend and whether or not the timing of our impulsive getaway was in any way related. I'd told her Alex was going to be in Vegas, I'd told her he was going with Jeff, I'd sighed with frustration when she just replied by reminding me this weekend was about 'bros before hos'. She was giving me nothing.

'Yo-yo-yo.' Jenny utched across the back seat of the car to make room for me and my massively over-stuffed satchel. There was nothing I could need that I did not have in this bag. Blanket, snacks, socks, plasters, headache tablets, Berocca, kitchen sink. 'Are you excited? I'm excited. Vegas, baby!'

'I'm excited,' I confirmed with a businesslike nod and pulled out my phone, refreshing the emails and not really giving Jenny the enthusiasm I knew she was looking for. 'Vegas, yeah.'

'That was the weakest "yeah" I've ever heard.' Jenny reached across and snatched the phone out of my hand. 'I'm turning this off. It's girl time. No emailing Alex, no texting Sigge – see?'

She pressed the power button on my phone first, then hers, and tossed them deep into her beautiful YSL Muse. It was so beautiful.

'I was actually checking to see if I had heard back from any of the magazines overnight. But thanks.'

'Any time,' she replied, missing my point entirely. 'So, we fly at eleven, we land at two, we need to be at the pool by three, and I want to be drunk by four. It's been a bitch of a week.'

'There's a chance I'm being a bit stupid,' I acknowledged before I asked my question, 'but isn't December in Vegas the same as December anywhere else? Won't it be a bit cold for the pool?'

'Why, I'm glad you asked Angela,' Jenny said in her best concierge voice. 'The average winter temperatures in Nevada rarely drop below sixty degrees in the daytime, and this week, the city of Las Vegas has been enjoying an unseasonable heat wave of temperatures up to eighty degrees. Should the weather let us down, Hotel De Lujo has a state-of-the-art climate system in their pool area, guaranteeing a balmy eighty-five-degree year-round summertime.'

'Excellent work.' I was genuinely impressed. 'You are very good.'

'That's why they pay me the big bucks,' she said, pulling epic amounts of long, curly hair out from behind her back and flicking it over her shoulders.

'Do they?'

'Not really.'

'Right.'

We sat quietly for a moment, both holding our breath as the car swerved up the ramp and onto the BQE. Once we were sure we'd survived joining the freeway, I breathed out (my jeans wishing I hadn't) and turned to ask Jenny the question she'd been dodging all week.

'So.' I turned on my serious face. 'Jeff.'

'Jeff?' she asked, applying lip gloss. 'What about him?'

'He's in Vegas. This weekend. On his bachelor weekend.'

'Yeah?'

'Are you going to tell me you didn't know that when you booked this?'

'Angie.' She dropped the Juicy Tube back in her bag and gave me a smile that was so close to being patronizing, I thought I might slap her. 'Sure I know he's going to be there. We've still got mutual friends. But I didn't know until after I booked the trip, honestly.'

'You didn't?' I believed her about as far as I could throw her. Probably not as much as that, to be honest. She was very slim at the moment.

'No, I didn't. But even if I did, it wouldn't have changed my plans. Jeff and I live in the same city. I'm not about to move back to LA to avoid him, am I? So what if we're in the same town for a weekend? Vegas is a big place, we're not gonna run into him unless we go looking for him. It's way less likely that we'll see him between now and Monday than it would be if I was, oh, I don't know – visiting you? Since you live in the same building?'

I could tell she was annoyed because she was doing the fun thing where she went up at the end of every sentence, and she only did that if she was drunk or pissed off. Her very best Valley Girl accent. It was a fair point. New York was a small town; you saw the same people every day. I had any number of friends I nodded to on a regular basis – Chihuahua Man, Pink Coat Lady, Sir Coughs-A-Lot. OK, so I hadn't slept with any of them, but I ran into them endlessly. She was a lot more likely to have to deal with Jeff on her home turf (or rather mine) than she was in the wild and wacky world of Las Vegas. But still.

'Fine. If you say you didn't know, you didn't know,' I said, softening my stern face slightly. But only slightly; I still wasn't utterly convinced. 'Just, is there a contingency plan for what happens if we do run into them?'

'No. There isn't a plan. I don't do anything,' Jenny replied, a little bit sad. 'He's getting married. I'm with Sigge. How many times have you and Erin and Vanessa and Gina and my therapist and my doorman and that guy in the bodega told me? I need to move on. I'm moving. If we see them, I'll be polite, I'll probably need to do a shot, and then I'll cry myself to sleep later on.'

'Oh, Jenny.' I launched myself across the back seat, aided by a very cavalier swing into the next lane by the driver, and gave my friend a huge hug. 'I'm sorry. I know it's still shit. I didn't mean to be an arsehole.'

'It's always shit, no matter how happy you are,' she sniffled. 'You're kinda lucky you don't have a big heartbreak in your past.'

'Don't tempt fate,' I warned. 'Nothing is official, is it?'

'Hmm.' Jenny checked her manicure. 'There's every chance I might veto an engagement anyhow.'

She didn't look like she was joking. I raised an eyebrow.

'What does he think he's doing at my ex's bachelor party?' she said, starting on a semi-rant. 'What happened to Team Lopez? You're my best friend, he's your boyfriend. Doesn't he realize his loyalty is automatically with me? He's being an asshole.'

'Ahh.' Gotcha. 'Yeah, apparently he just really loves Vegas. And I suppose he and Jeff are kind of friends?'

I shrank back from whatever form her rage would take. They were kind of friends. Admittedly they weren't giving each other makeovers and having sleepovers every weekend, but they went for a drink occasionally.

'Friends my ass,' Jenny said quietly, calmly. 'If I see him out there, he'd better be careful. That's all I'm saying.'

And it was all that needed to be said.

'Where is she?'

Jenny was well into her second Starbucks and starting to curse Erin White's name. 'If she makes me miss this flight, I will kick her tiny ass.'

'She'd have called you if there was a problem, wouldn't she?' I looked at my watch again. We only had twenty minutes until boarding and I had no idea where in LaGuardia we needed to get to make the flight. Plus I was wearing heels; there would be no running in heels. In an attempt to avoid checking my suitcase, I'd packed as light as possible, but that meant I was hobbling around the airport in six-inch tassled Giuseppe shoeboots that Jenny insisted were 'totally Vegas' when she'd brought them home from the sample cupboard. At the time I'd agreed: they were totally Vegas. But they were not totally running around an airport in Queens. I looked like a tit. A tit with tassles on. So yes, totally Vegas.

'Hey!'

Across the airport, we saw a tiny blonde hurtling towards us. I couldn't help but notice she was not in any way, shape or form packed for a trip. Hmm.

'Jenny! Angie!' Erin raced over, her cheeks red, her perfectly coiffed blonde bob fluffy from the cold. 'Why the fuck aren't you answering your phones?'

'We're answering if someone's calling.' Jenny scrabbled in her handbag to pull out her phone and wave it in Erin's face. 'See? No missed calls.'

'It's turned off, genius,' she said, tapping at the blank glass. 'Oh my God, I thought you were both dead.'

'Oh, yeah . . .' Jenny had the decency to blush and handed me my phone. I took it back and apologized effusively.

'Don't worry about it.' Erin waved away our words and beamed. 'I only came to tell you I'm not coming.'

'Huh?' Jenny was genuinely flummoxed. 'Shut your face, White, and get on the plane. We'll buy you new shit when we get there.'

'I can't.' She pulled what looked like a slim white pen from her pocket and held it out to Jenny. 'I'm pregnant.'

'Jesus Christ.' Jenny immediately dropped the pregnancy test on the floor. 'Did you pee on that? You gave me something you've peed on?'

Erin stared her down.

'I mean, congratulations!'

We wrapped the tiny lady up in a big hug and bounced around for a moment. As much as the shoe-boots would allow. Erin was older than Jenny and me, and we both knew she'd been trying to get pregnant for a while. This was big news. It was also my first stateside friend to get on the baby wagon. Scary. I could happily convince myself Louisa was doing nothing more than waiting for Amazon to deliver a Tiny Tears doll because she was a whole ocean away, but Erin? I saw her all the time. I would see her getting fat. I would see her in those amazing-looking jeans with the big elasticated pouch. This one would be real. A real baby. Eeep. I hoped she wouldn't give it to me or Jenny to hold; one of us would definitely break it.

'Yeah, I just did the test this morning.' Was it possible that she was glowing already? 'I'd been kinda sick for a few days, but I just put it down to a bug or something. Then, I don't know – I just decided to do a test before I left this morning, and there it was. Positive. We're having a baby.'

'And we're going to be awesome at it,' Jenny said, giving her one last squeeze.

'I did mean me and Thomas, but sure, why not?' Erin smiled. 'It just sucks that I can't come with you guys. I don't want to be an asshole, but there's no way I'm going to be able to deal with the partying and everything. I'm exhausted already.'

'We completely understand,' I answered on both our behalves before Jenny could argue. 'Go home, rest, paint a room yellow.'

'You guys are the best.' Erin, my most composed and sophisticated friend bounced from foot to foot, pressing both hands against her stomach. 'I can't even tell you. I won't be that mom, I won't, I swear. I just . . . I'm so happy.'

With one last flurry of kisses, Erin bounced out of the airport and back into her glossy black town car. As we passed through security at last, I thought about how much things would change. Erin was tiny and perfect and terribly glossy. Soon she'd be massive and messy and terribly stressed. Goodbye Bottega Veneta handbag, hello nappy mat. Louisa was having a baby, Erin was having a baby, Jenny was behaving like an adult. Sort of. The world had officially gone topsy-turvy.

After we had taken our squishy leather seats and I had prepped my seat-back pocket with all the magazines on earth, I slipped on my flight socks, wrapped myself up in my blanket and readied myself for a lovely, lovely nap. The flight from New York to Las Vegas took six hours. That was a decent four-hour kip with an hour either side to read my Las Vegas guidebook and make my list of ultimate Vegas to-dos. I already had quite the list as a starting point: I wanted to see a real-life showgirl show at Crazy Horse, I wanted to ride the rollercoasters at the Stratosphere, I wanted to take photos of myself with every single Elvis impersonator that crossed my path, I wanted to put everything on red 36, I wanted to take photos of myself outside the Little White Wedding Chapel and give my mother a heart attack. It would serve her right for thinking it was appropriate for us to be Facebook friends. There were so many things: everyone had a recommendation for me.

But on the plane, I wanted to rest. Possibly watch *Captain America* without Alex around to make me skip through those scenes where Chris Evans took his shirt off. This was not meant to be. I managed about seven minutes of reading and listening to my iPod post-take-off when Jenny tapped me on the shoulder.

'Angela, we are so lucky,' she declared.

'And why's that?' I asked, suspiciously eyeing the six burly men seated in front of, behind and across from us, and staring at Jenny as though it were feeding time at the zoo.

'Because Brad here is a world-class poker champion and he's headed to the De Lujo for a tournament,' she gestured towards a very large, very smug-looking man who resembled a strongly medicated game-show host. 'He's going to teach us how to play poker.'

For every ounce of mania in Jenny's grin, I mustered

up an equivalent lack of enthusiasm. Really? We hadn't even crossed the state line yet and she was already encouraging attention from men who, as far as I was able to ascertain, loved nothing as much as poker, double denim and Subway sandwiches. There wasn't a single one of them who wasn't clutching a foot-long sandwich. A meatball sub at eight a.m.? Ick. If Brad Pitt wanted to reprise his *Ocean's Eleven* role and show me the way around a game of five-card stud, I'd consider it. Until then, I was out of any and all card games.

'I'm all right, thanks,' I said, popping my earbud back in, only to have it yanked back out.

'Angela!' Jenny wasn't having any of it. 'Brad and his friends would like to show us a few basics. Isn't that nice of them?'

I gave Brad and his friends a courtesy smile and an acknowledging, but not encouraging, nod. One of the friends giggled. Good grief.

'Jenny . . .' I was as polite as I possibly could be for someone who had woken up at five a.m. 'I can't even play snap without getting confused. Why don't you take point on the cards, and I'll look after the slots.'

'I would totally look after their slots,' Brad stage-whispered to the giggler.

'Excuse me?' I pulled out the second earbud and sat up straight.

'Angie.' Jenny placed a calming hand on my arm. 'Don't mind the boys. They're excited. They don't get out much.'

'So we're on for drinks tonight, hot stuff?' Brad leaned over out of his seat to give Jenny the full force of his drunk-in-the-morning leer. 'Play some cards? Or some slots?'

'No.' Jenny sighed and leaned back in her seat. 'I'll look after my own slots.'

Like all good gamblers, Brad knew when he was beaten. He slunk back into his seat, ignoring the jibes and jeers from his friends. Swing and a miss for the big guy.

'What was that all about?' I hissed at my seat buddy. 'Has dating Sigge messed you up? Are you incapable of registering the relative attractiveness of any other man alive? Because Brad is not attractive.'

'I know. Shut up,' she sulked, waving down a stewardess. 'Two margaritas, please.'

'I don't want a margarita,' I told her. 'It's eight in the bloody morning.'

'Who said it was for you?' Jenny pulled down her tray table. 'But actually, yeah, you are having one. Better make it three.'

The stewardess gave me a quizzical look but headed back off to the galley, under orders.

'Is everything OK?' I wrapped the earphones around my iPod and put it away. Clearly my services were needed. 'What's going on?'

'Vegas, baby.' She played out a feeble drum roll on the table. 'Can we please agree that we're going to have an awesome, awesome time?'

'Can we please agree that we won't speak to Brad ever again?'

'Yes, we can,' Jenny nodded, taking her drinks from the returning stewardess. 'If you drink this.'

'I hate drinking on planes,' I whined, sniffing the marg. Nothing like a tequila-based cocktail before midday. 'It makes me sick.'

'Vegas insists you drink this,' she said, waving it around under my nose. 'If you don't drink this, you'll make Vegas sad. Do you want Vegas to be sad?'

'Do you want me to be sick?' I asked.

'If you puke, I'll buy you a steak dinner,' she promised, handing me the glass and clapping with glee.

'If I puke I won't want a steak dinner,' I pointed out, taking a sip. Actually, it wasn't so bad. There was hardly any tequila in there. I would be fine. And I needed to do something to distract myself from Brad picking his nose across the aisle. Ewww.

'How're you feeling?' an irritatingly fresh-looking Lopez asked as we joined the line for taxis in fabulous, freezing Las Vegas several hours later. So much for a heat wave: the sun was blazing, but it was definitely on the chilly side. My in-flight jeans and jumper combo were not nearly enough.

'Not brilliant,' I replied, fumbling for my sunglasses and trying not to hiccup. There really hadn't been a lot of tequila in my margaritas, but if you drank enough of them, it turned out there was just enough. Mid-air drinking was even worse than midday drinking. And I'd been drinking in mid-air at midday. And now I felt like I was going to die.

'You'll be fine.' She punched me in the arm and flashed the guy behind me a huge smile.

A lot of people say best friends usually share a similar level of attractiveness or earn a comparable salary. I believe the most important thing to have in common with someone for a friendship to work out is a comparable alcohol tolerance. It's impossible for a monster drinker to be BFF with someone who is on their arse after a sniff of the barmaid's apron. Usually, Jenny and I went at an even three-martini maximum, but the lack of breakfast combined with drinking at altitude meant I was very much on the back foot. In fact, I felt very much like a back foot. The back foot of a badger.

'Honestly, honey, you'll be fine.' She gave me a side hug, cleverly avoiding the risk of being puked on. 'It's going to be the best weekend. Lots of rest. Helicopter ride over the Grand Canyon, hanging out in the spa, a few drinks, a little dancing. Maybe some Christmas shopping? Doesn't that sound good?'

'It sounds good.'

It sounded all right. Not as good as an hour in bed in a darkened room with an ice pack on my forehead and a bin on the floor beside me, but still. Pretty good.

'And, oh! Awesome!' Jenny scrolled down her iPhone happily. 'Sadie's going to come meet us.'

Oh. Awesome.

Vegas had managed to give me a headache before we'd even landed, and now we were going to be joined by the biggest arsehole I'd ever had the pleasure of calling a friend. Well, a Facebook friend. I wasn't sure of the girl rules on best friend's room-mates, but Sadie seemed to think paying rent to Jenny gave her automatic rights to get involved in anything and everything in her life. And if I was in her general vicinity, that included me. From the look on Jenny's face, simultaneously managing my throbbing head-ache and waves of nausea had stripped me of the ability to control my facial expressions.

'Because we have a spare bed now Erin's not coming,' she explained. 'You're not mad? Don't be mad. She emailed to say she was gonna be home for the weekend and it's so close to Christmas and she's on her own and I said we were here and she said she'd come out and I said she should stay with us and she said—'

'Jenny – ' I held up my hand and swallowed back something unpleasant – 'it's fine. Can we just get to the hotel?'

She nodded and took my suitcase from me. I nodded back and let her take it before turning around and puking in a bin.

'I owe you a steak dinner,' Jenny said quietly.

CHAPTER EIGHT

And then things went from bad to worse.

Whatever I had been hoping for from Vegas, it wasn't this. I hadn't been dreaming of a below-standard-issue beige bedroom with a mini flatscreen TV bolted to the wall. And bars on the windows. Admittedly, I'd been spoiled by some beautiful hotel rooms in my time, but this was . . . this was just awful. So awful.

'We'll hardly even be in the room,' Jenny said confidently, dropping her handbag on the scratchy sheets of the bed. 'We're just sleeping in here. It totally doesn't matter.'

'That it's shit?' I peeped out of the window to get a beautiful view of the room directly opposite. A very fat man was passed out on his very own scratchy sheets. Naked. Beautiful.

'Yeah, I, uh, hmm.' Jenny bit her lip. 'Maybe we can switch rooms. This isn't really what I was expecting. I'm pretty sure we're supposed to be in a superior room, and this isn't that superior.'

I stared down at a dark red stain on the carpet and looked up at my friend with wide eyes.

'Jenny, someone died in this room.'

'It's wine,' she said, rubbing a delicate hand firmly over her face. 'I'm sure it's just red wine. Why don't you go down to the pool and I'll go see if I can talk to someone.'

'I'm too scared to go in the bathroom,' I said, clutching my satchel to my chest. 'What if there's a body?'

'Just get changed, OK?' Jenny shoved her room key into the ass pocket of her spray-on James Jeans and strode back out into the great unknown. 'I'll see you down at the pool.'

The pool. The pool would make me feel better. As long as it wasn't a skip with a hose pipe in it and judging by the state of the bedroom, that was quite possible. With great effort, I managed to slip out of my clothes without stepping on a single extra inch of carpet and put my Fifties-inspired one-piece on without even taking off my underwear. I knew wriggling in and out of my knickers in swimming class would come in useful one day. I pulled a pair of flip-flops out of my suitcase, slid them onto my feet, pulled a Victoria's Secret cover-up over my bathing beauty ensemble and practically ran for the door.

It was with no small amount of joy that I discovered the pool was absolutely bloody beautiful. As soon as I stepped out of the lift, I felt myself smile. Calling what lay in front of me a pool was like calling the Atlantic Ocean a pond. There was sand, sun and more deep blue sea than I could shake a stick at. And in the true tradition of Vegas, none of it was real. It really put the art into artifice.

'Can I help you, miss?'

A tiny but beautiful boy with thick brown hair and chocolate-drop eyes appeared at my side, alerting me to the fact that my mouth was opening and closing of its own accord.

'Cabana? Cocktail?' He gestured towards a bank of luxy looking banquettes lining the beach. Soft, squishy sofas were shielded from the sun by jewel-coloured fabrics, while lots of very happy-looking people lounged around drinking neon drinks through matching straws. Scratch 'happy' – on closer inspection, what I meant was very *drunk* people. They didn't look like they were concerned about whether or not someone's throat had been slit in their bedroom, and yet we were all staying in the same hotel. There was only one possible explanation . . . booze.

'Cabana, please,' I told the beautiful boy.

From the outside, De Lujo really was a beautiful hotel. Shining bright white in the sunshine, stretching up high into the sky, it was incredible – exactly what Jenny had promised. It was just a shame that the rooms inside looked like something from *CSI*. Checking in hadn't been awful, but I'd been trying so hard not to throw up, all I could really remember was the shiny marble floor of the lobby reflecting my headache right back up at me, followed by the not nearly smooth enough lift. After that, it was just the shabby carpet of the sixth floor and then the crime scene of a bedroom. But this? This was magical. A light breeze passed over the water, and while the sky looked bright, blue and entirely as nature intended, I just knew there was nothing natural about the heat that warmed my skin but I couldn't see a heater anywhere. Whether it was wind machine or witch-craft, I did not care to know. It was wonderful. I was a world away from my problems, a world away from my worries, and only ever two minutes away from a margarita. There was a lot to be said for that, hangover or no hangover.

After a quick jaunt down the shoreline, white sand

seeping in between my toes, I was shown to my own private beachside booth. I smiled politely and ducked inside, collapsing onto the fluffy pillows that lined my cabana. Within seconds, I felt my shoulders relax for the first time since I'd boarded the plane. Was it really December? Had I really left a sub-zero New York City only hours earlier? I felt like I was in the Caribbean. If the Caribbean had the odd ten-foot, fully decorated Christmas tree placed in between the palm trees. Not weird at all.

The waiter took my room number and vamoosed, leaving me alone to pop two Advil and pull my laptop out of my bag. I settled into the giant sofa and waited for it to flicker into life. It couldn't hurt just to check a couple of emails before I succumbed to a wanton weekend full of fun and frolics, could it? Well, regardless, I had to. I was riding high on the proposals I'd sent out earlier in the week and just wanted to see if I'd had any feedback. And I was desperately trying to ignore the topless sunbathing taking place in the cabana opposite, primarily because I had total boob envy. I logged into the interwebs. It was, of course, a mistake.

Dear Ms Clark,
   Thank you for your interest in our magazine. At present we are not commissioning new writers . . .

Dear Miss Clark,
   Many thanks for your pitch. However, we do not feel this idea is right for our publication.

Dear Angela, thank you so much! We loved your idea but we have already published something similar recently.

Well. At least they had all spelled my name right.

I silenced The Voice before it could start to speak. This didn't mean anything. If anything, it was good when rejections came back quickly; that meant editors were reading your pitches and taking you seriously. There were still five other proposals out there and they were good proposals. This wasn't anything to worry about. I was sure of it.

Opening a new tab, I flicked over to my new website. The Adventures of Angela-dot-com. Since *The Look* had 'retired' my blog, I figured I might as well keep the same name. Make it easier for all my fans to find me. I only realized I had snorted out loud when the topless ladies opposite lowered their sunglasses to look at me. I waved and gave them a big smile. They looked away. Didn't they know who I was? Here I was, eighteen months into my adventures, and I was right back to the beginning. Writing an online diary dealing with the ins and outs of daily life. But it had worked once, it could work again. Positive mental attitude would get me everywhere.

The Adventures of Angela: Viva Las Vegas

So here I am in fabulous Las Vegas, poolside in December. Across the street, I can see people walking around in parkas, I'm in a swimsuit. Clearly something isn't right with this place.

When my BFF surprised me with a girls' weekend away, I had no idea what to expect but I was excited. I dreamed of a glamorous world filled with sequins and showgirls, built around stories of the rat pack, Elvis movies and Siegfried & Roy fantasies. But I was very aware of the other side of Vegas. Facebook photos of debauched hen nights – pink cowboy hats and all. E! Entertainment specials starring assorted Kardashians and twenty-four-seven debauchery. In all honesty, I had never recovered from watching Jessie from Saved by the Bell wearing pasties and I doubt I ever will. But I need my Vegas experience to be more Dita Von Teese than Showgirls.

In the interests of investigative journalism, I thought I would keep you updated on our adventures (if only because it's the name of the blog), so here are the main players. Me, a twenty-something Vegas virgin, already hungover and petrified of the boob implants staring at me across the pool. Jenny, my best friend and glamour junkie, who is going to have to be kept in kiddie reins if I want to get back to NYC alive. And finally, Sadie the supermodel, aka Trouble with a capital T. I won't lie. I'm worried.

So far we're fifty-fifty with our hotel. The pool looks like a movie set but our bedroom looks like a crime scene. I'll check in later when I've made my first million on the blackjack tables, lost it all again and married a stripper.

I paused, I perused and I posted. If we were going to be stuck in the Bates motel room of Las Vegas hotel rooms, I was likely to be spending a lot of time by this pool. I popped on my sunglasses so I could have a good stare at what was going on around me, but my view was suddenly blocked by a huge, bright green glass of frozen yumminess.

'Your complimentary De Lujo cocktail, Ms Clark,' said the beautiful boy who had shown me to my cabana, presenting the drink with a flourish.

'Oh, I just wanted a Coke,' I stammered, trying not

to make eye contact with temptation. I didn't need it and I didn't want it.

'The mini-fridge is fully stocked with sodas.' He nodded towards a shiny silver box in the corner of the cabana. 'This is on the house. Let me know if there's anything else I can get you.'

I wondered if it was possible to sleep in the cabana instead of my room.

Since my mother had taught me never to look a gift horse in the mouth, and my father had taught me never to turn down a free drink, I took a cautious sip of the cocktail. Well, bugger me backwards, Bob, it was delicious. On closer inspection, the concoction inside the glass was a frozen medley of red and white stripes, and unless I was greatly mistaken, there was a lot of mint schnapps going on. It was like frozen candy cane. My dream cocktail.

Snapping the laptop shut, I rolled onto my back and smiled up at the red silk that lined my cabin. Alex would be in the air, winging his way over with the bachelor party. Jenny was somewhere, doing something that I hoped would result in a better bedroom. And, for the moment at least, I had no idea what Sadie was doing or where she was doing it. Thankfully. Very aware that these might be the last ten minutes I had to myself for the next three days, I sat up to take one more sip from my drink and let the schnapps wash away the remnants of my hangover before closing my eyes and letting it all go. Nothing better than a little nap with the lapping of the ocean in your ears. The fact that it was a fake ocean was neither here nor there.

Because it wasn't confusing enough to wake up wearing a swimsuit face down on a chaise longue that was not my own, the first thing I saw when I opened my eyes, not a foot away from my nose, was an inch of pure white snowy snow. I blinked once, twice. Nope, it was still there. And yet when I looked up, all I could see was beautiful clear blue sky, and across the way there were dozens of people splashing around in a swimming pool. Sunshine. Swimming pool. Snow. Oh, right. I was in Vegas. After marvelling at the madness for a moment longer, I gathered up my things and decided it was time to go on a Jenny-hunt. The battery on my mobile had died while I was napping and she hadn't surfaced, which meant either she'd been murdered in our room or she just couldn't find me. Taking my life into my own hands, I packed up my laptop, took a big slurp from my now melted but still delicious cocktail and ventured back inside to hunt her down. I was like Columbo but without the mac. And the cigars. And the catchy theme tune. But aside from that, just like Columbo.

My heart sank as I tiptoed out of the opulent lift and into the 1980s Travelodgeness of the sixth floor, but it soon speeded up again as I inserted my key card into the door of room six-nineteen. Nothing. I rubbed it on the arse of my cover-up and tried again. Nothing. Just a rude blinking red light refusing to give me access to my things. What was going on? Had I been roofied? Already? I'd assumed I'd at least make it to day two before I woke up *sans* tooth and *avec* tiger. Maybe even day three.

'Oh, bloody hell,' I muttered, knocking as subtly as possible on the door. 'Jenny? Are you in there?'

Suddenly consumed with fear that whoever had offed the previous tenant of our room had come back for Jenny, I started banging harder. You might have even called it hammering. 'It's not like I even really want to go in,' I shouted at the crappy wood veneered door. 'You big wooden bastard.'

'Excuse me, Ms Clark?'

A slightly scared-looking woman wearing the same outfit as the beautiful boy at the pool reluctantly interrupted my rant. It was times like these I was glad Alex wasn't around me all the time.

I smoothed down my cover-up and cleared my throat. 'Yes?'

'Would you please follow me?' The woman tried not to look alarmed as she led me to the lift. I wouldn't want to be locked in a metal box with the crazy lady who was battering down a door while shouting abuse at it either.

Naturally, I assumed I was being chucked out, so I was a little confused when she reached across me in the lift to press the button for the twenty-sixth floor. And after the most awkward seventeen seconds of my entire life, when the doors opened into a plush white vision of a hallway with one grand golden door at the end of the corridor, I was very confused. And when she opened that grand golden door onto what can only be described as the most amazing room I had ever seen in my entire life, she had lost me completely. Or she wished she had. With a gentle shove, she kicked me into the thick, white carpeting of the suite. Not a single bloodstain to be seen.

'Jesus, Angie, there you are!'

Jenny had not been murdered. Jenny had been upgraded. Significantly upgraded.

'You have to teach me how to make a complaint,' I whispered, almost too scared to take another step. Maybe I was still dreaming. Maybe this was *Inception*. Hopefully Leonardo DiCaprio would pop out in a second to confirm it. Or Joseph Gordon-Levitt. Or Tom Hardy. I didn't mind really. Jenny was perfectly poised by a giant floor-to-ceiling window overlooking the

Strip. It wasn't really fair to call it a window as I couldn't actually see any exterior walls that weren't transparent. It looked like the whole suite was made of glass. Glass and peonies, my favourite flowers, were almost all I could see. I gave myself five minutes before I broke something, stained something or just started crying. It took twenty-five steps to cross the room to Jenny. Twenty-five steps down into a sunken lounging area full of overstuffed sofas, more peonies and low, crystal-clear coffee tables and back up again, past the bar, past the movie-screen-sized TV, past the DJ booth – the DJ booth! – and over to the window.

'It's a pretty nice view, right?' She sipped from her glass of champagne and grinned with an undeniable smugness.

The sun was setting and a dark orange glow cast shadows over the Strip. As I stood and watched, utterly silent, it sprang into life. All the world seemed to be crammed into this little stretch of desert. To one side of us, I saw Venice and Rome. Appropriately close together. Paris lay opposite, the Eiffel tower sparkling in the sunset. I made a mental note to avoid it. Paris, France or Paris, USA, I wasn't taking any chances. Following the Strip down, I spotted home sweet home. The Empire State Building and Statue of Liberty, wrapped up by a rollercoaster, winked at me as their lights came to life. I watched as, beyond them, a tower of light leapt from the point of a giant black pyramid and King Arthur's castle offered Disneyfied japes and jaunts around merrie olde England. I made another mental note to avoid that bad boy. I hadn't come all the way to Las Vegas to eat dodgy shepherd's pie and giggle at spotted dick. Overhead, planes delivered fresh meat to be sacrificed on the Strip, and as the sun dipped low behind us, floor-level lighting illuminated the inside of the suite as the sky got darker. Outside, Vegas yawned, shook herself down, and, with a couple of blinks and one big yawn, was wide awake and ready for another night.

'Wow, right?'

'It's a hell of an upgrade,' I agreed, my fingertips pressing lightly against the glass. Everything was just too *Alice in Wonderland* – I was sure I was about to fall down the rabbit hole. But the glass didn't melt away, it stayed hard and cold under my hands, holding me back from what could be.

'Technically it's not an upgrade.' Jenny coughed and handed me a glass of champagne. I took it, looked at it and set it down on the counter. There were a remarkable number of surfaces at just the right height to set down drinks in this suite. 'Technically we're kinda couch surfing.'

'Technically I don't give a shit,' I replied. 'This is amazing.'

'Of course it is. I only do amazing.'

Silhouetted in a glowing doorway, Sadie gave me a triumphant look.

'So there you are. You win after all, Jen.'

'What do you win?' I hated it when she called her Jen. No one called Jenny Jen. It was proprietary and annoying and, well, I was jealous.

'Nothing.' Jenny knocked back her champers and refilled quickly. 'Go take a shower. I need to eat.'

'I said you'd decided Vegas wasn't for you and you'd gone back to New York,' Sadie explained, slithering into the room in bare feet and a bikini so tiny, her gynaecologist would have been embarrassed by it. 'And Jen said you'd probably just got lost.'

'Sorry to disappoint you both.' I cast Jenny a quick, narrowed-eye glare to which she rolled her eyes in an awkward apology. 'I was just by the pool and I didn't know we'd switched rooms.'

'I tried to call you,' Jenny said hurriedly. 'It went to voicemail.'

'Yeah, I always stay here.' Sadie flung her long legs onto one of the coffee tables, knocking a silver box of tissues onto the floor. 'I like space.'

'But you could fit your entire apartment onto that sofa,' I replied, desperately fighting the urge to go and pick up the tissue box. This room was not supposed to be untidy. It was supposed to be clean and neat and not have me in it.

'But that's home.' Sadie stretched out, showing us all just how thorough her waxing technician had been. 'Home should be cosy. Hotels should be so big you can lose a horse in them.'

It was fair to say Sadie had a lot more experience of hotels than I did. She was the one running around the world, letting men take photos of her in her pants. And you know, all the other stuff a model did that I didn't want to think about because it made me insanely jealous. Maybe you did need a lot of space to unwind properly. Maybe Red Rum was somewhere in here. Had anyone ever thought to check?

'I need to charge my phone,' I said to Jenny, ignoring Sadie's yoga stretches on the couch. I had no great desire to see her vagina before dinner. Or after. 'Where did you stash my stuff?'

'It's in your room.' She pointed down the corridor Sadie had emerged from. 'Second on the right. I gave you the view.'

Happily skipping by the sofas, eyes avoiding Sadie's downward dog, I marched into the second room on the right and burst out laughing. When Jenny said I had the view, I sort of assumed she was taking the piss. At best I'd imagined a billboard of the *Thunder from Down Under* male revue, but no, she wasn't joking. From the windows of the lounge, we had an unparalleled view of man's devotion to Having a Good Time. The windows from my super swanky bedroom showed something so far away from the fluorescent fantasy of the Strip that it took my breath away. Behind the casinos and clubs, I was finally able to see where the sun had run away to hide, and I didn't blame him one bit. Who wanted to see a bunch of drunken tourists walk up and down what now looked like a ponced-up bit of Blackpool in comparison with my bedroom view, miles and miles of desert stretched out in front of me, painted orange and red with broad strokes. The nearby mountains were silhouetted against the twilight sky – dark grey highlighted with orange flecks and purple shadows. They almost passed for far-off thunder clouds threatening a soft, golden, glowing sky that bled into a pale blue and promised to turn midnight any second. I'd never seen the desert before. Now I couldn't imagine I would ever forget it. If this was how Nevada looked at the end of the day, I couldn't wait to watch the sunrise. I wished Alex was there to see it too.

Turning my back to the window, I found the room almost as stunning a sight as the scenery. An enormous bed was angled into one corner, all thick white quilts and giant, cloud-like pillows, while a purple velvet chaise longue was placed right by the window, perfectly positioned for daydreaming into the desert. Across the room, separated by a frosted glass partition was a walk-in shower, just the right size for, ooh, seven people? And if that didn't take your fancy, in the middle of the room was a rolltop bath so big, I started looking for the Ark. No wonder Nevada was so dry; it would take an ocean to fill up that bad boy.

CHAPTER NINE

'Oh, honey, what are you wearing?'

I stopped dead in the middle of the lounge and felt my jaw drop. I thought I'd done quite well; my outfit was very classic. It was a vintage, floor-length midnight-blue silk gown with a deep V in the back and what I thought was a terribly seductive keyhole cut-out in the front. Together with my little gold clutch and gold vintage strappy sandals, I was the vision of sophistication. Very Julia Roberts in *Ocean's Eleven*. Apparently I had missed a memo. Jenny and Sadie were also channelling Julia Roberts; however, they had taken their inspiration from the *Pretty Woman* era. Sadie had been poured into a pair of leather leggings that gave the impression she'd been dipped in oil from the waist down and was topping off the ensemble with a hot pink scooped-back tank top. Jenny was in the same red Leger bandage dress she'd worn to her Christmas party, but somehow it seemed short and tighter. It could have been the spiked bondage heels she was wearing. They really didn't look that Christmassy.

'You look like you're going to a funeral,' Sadie commented, lining her lips with a bright red bullet bedazzled with Swarovski crystals. 'Only, don't wear that to my funeral, you won't get in.'

'Do you have a date in mind so I can clear my diary?' I asked brightly.

'Angie, honey, it's beautiful.' Jenny pushed me back towards the bedroom. 'It's just, you brought a knife to a gunfight, honey. This is Las Vegas. You need to go a little wild.'

'This is very low in the back,' I pointed out.

'It is,' she agreed, patting my shoulder. 'It is. Now, what else did you bring with you?'

I looked towards my wardrobe and pulled a face. 'I'm not sure you're going to find anything "more Vegas" in there.'

Jenny took a deep breath and opened the wardrobe door.

'I blame myself,' she muttered. 'I should have helped you pack.'

'What's wrong with my clothes?'

I'd been studying shopping under Jenny's tutelage for almost eighteen months and I thought I was doing well. I hardly ever called her before I bought something these days, and she'd only sent me home to change once in the last twelve months – and that wasn't my fault. Fancy dress means something very different in New York. Jenny wanted me in a cocktail dress. She got me dressed as Dorothy from *The Wizard of Oz*. We had words. But my wardrobe for this weekend was impeccable. I'd put together a capsule collection of vintage glamour, lots of long skirts with seductive slits (I'd read enough magazines to know they were in), silk blouses, a sparkly little capelet I found in Beacon's Closet and some very pretty strappy sandals.

'They're not tight enough, they're not glam enough

and they're not cool enough,' Sadie declared without even looking. 'They're kind of like you.'

No. Words.

'No offence,' she shrugged, leaving the room.

'Oh, none taken,' I called after her with forced ease.

'It just . . . maybe it needs Vegas-ing up a little.' Jenny was back, trying to be diplomatic, but I was still disappointed. I didn't want my Vegas experience to be tequila shots off frat boys. I wanted it to be martinis with the rat pack. Possibly my problem was I also wanted to travel back in time.

Before she could even make a suggestion, Sadie sailed into my bedroom brandishing a giant pair of shiny silver shears and stopped in front of me. A giant shiny smile on her beautiful face.

'Problem solved,' she announced, lunging at me with the blades.

Oh dear God, she was going to kill me. I closed my eyes and raised my hands over my face. I couldn't believe this was how I was going out. Slaughtered by a supermodel for crimes against fashion. But instead of slashing at me, she dropped to her knees and hacked three feet off the bottom of my dress.

'Hey!' I swatted at the top of her head like an angry cat, but she just ducked and carried on chopping. By the time she stood up, triumphantly displaying yards of silk, I could feel a distinct breeze around my nether regions.

'Better.' Sadie stepped back to examine her handiwork. 'Not great, but better. Now, can we eat?'

'I hate to admit it, Angie,' Jenny said, taking a step back until she was side by side with the emerging designer. 'It looks pretty awesome.'

Folding my arms in disgust, I reluctantly went over to the giant freestanding mirror in the corner of my room to review the damage.

Shit. It looked pretty awesome.

'I'm always telling you to show off your legs.' Jenny was trying to sell Sadie's handiwork hard. And while I knew that the dress did look good, it physically pained me to be too enthusiastic. She'd ruined my beautiful dress. I could have just got changed, for God's sake. What sort of mental slashes someone's dress to shreds while they're wearing it? What sort of mental slashes someone's dress to shreds without asking? The kind of mental who was now fashioning the bottom of my dress into something akin to a boob tube.

'You're welcome,' she overenunciated while wrestling her arms through a complicated series of knots, turning two feet of discarded skirt into a skin-tight halter top. Annoyingly, it looked really, really good. 'Come on, Jen, let's jet.'

'You look so great,' Jenny whispered, taking my arm and moving me towards the door. 'And now I can see your amazing shoes.'

'Your amazing shoes,' I replied, trying not to stare daggers into the back of Sadie's head. 'That you're this close to never getting back, *Jen*.'

When Jenny said we had dinner plans, I had figured we were off to some nice little restaurant inside the hotel, so I was a little concerned when Sadie swept out of the lift and into a waiting limo as though it was second nature. Which it probably was.

'Where are we going?' I asked Jenny as she folded herself into the leather seats like she did this every day, while Sadie shouted into a shiny silver iPhone. I didn't know they made silver iPhones.

'Dinner,' she repeated. 'Just try to relax, honey. I know Sadie can be a little . . . off plan, but she's fun. Once you get past the attitude.'

136

'She has an attitude? I wouldn't have known.'

'She just needs some real people around her,' Jenny said, standing firm. 'She's always difficult when she comes back from a job. Imagine being surrounded by assholes pushing and pulling you into place, telling you what you can and can't do. I'd be ten times worse than she is.'

Good friend that I was, my first reaction was to shout her down, tell her she couldn't ever be that way. But it wasn't true. She'd be a right bell-end.

'You'd be a monster,' I translated out loud.

'Damn straight,' Jenny said, leaning back against the leather bench and nodding. 'Damn. Straight.'

As soon as we pulled out onto the Strip, I was too distracted to carry on arguing. Looking at the bright lights of Las Vegas from a hotel-room window was one thing; to be slap-bang in the middle of them was another. It was like driving through the middle of a neon snow globe that was constantly moving, constantly being shaken up by an unseen hand. I felt almost seasick from the undulating lights, flashing billboards and promises of what could be.

'Isn't it amazing?' Jenny whispered, pressing her nose against the darkened glass beside me. 'Don't you love it?'

'I do,' I said, my eye catching its first wedding chapel as I uttered the words. 'I actually do.'

'It's like, nothing bad could happen while you're in Vegas. Like, real life is suspended,' she said with an excited intake of breath. 'We're going to have a great weekend, Angie. Everything is going to be OK. Like, life and everything.'

I couldn't decide if she was making a promise or a threat, but either way . . .

'Who are you trying to convince?'

'Why would anyone need convincing?' Her tone was light and Jenny-like, but her expression, reflected in the black glass of the window, was tight and tense. 'Everything is A-OK in Jenny-world. Work, good. Stud of a man, good. Keeping off the carbs, getting there. A-OK.'

Right. Because that was the sort of thing you said if it was true.

'Is everything all right? At work?'

'Mm-hmm.' Her eyes stayed locked on something I couldn't quite catch in the middle distance.

'And with Sigge?'

'Yeah. What are you going to have for dinner?'

Ahh. Attempting to distract me with the promise of food. So there was something wrong. It might have worked before, but it would not work again.

'Jenny, what's going on?'

She turned to me with a bright smile, shaking the troubles from her face.

'Vegas, baby!' She barrelled me over with a very aggressive hug and knocked me onto my back. Legs in the air, knickers on display, right on my back.

'Angela!' Sadie was off her phone call. 'I think my mom wears the same underwear as you.'

It wasn't a compliment.

Dinner in the Palms was a relatively tense affair. I ate everything put in front of me. Jenny ate and drank everything put in front of her. Sadie just concentrated on the drinking. The restaurant was amazing – everything in the room was shiny, from the shining walls to the stainless-steel surfaces; even the fabric on our chairs was a slippery silver leather. Platinum, I thought more accurately. Everything was platinum. Sadie and Jenny fitted in perfectly. Even in my 'customized' dress, I felt like my nan. Clearly I needed to try harder tomorrow. If I'd been going out in NYC, I'd have been perfectly happy with my look, but here I needed to up my game. It looked like I was living through fear of clothing in Las Vegas, rather than fear and loathing.

'I wish I could eat like you,' Sadie commented as I speared my second mouthful of perfectly cooked steak. 'I'd love to just pig out whenever I wanted.'

'I can't even begin to imagine how you would cope with solids,' I replied. 'If you had to keep them down, I mean.'

'You have to make sacrifices for your dreams.' Sadie stretched her arms over her head and arched her slender back. And then without missing a beat, added, 'Jen tells me you're gonna get kicked out the country for sucking. What's going on with that?'

'Jen' spat her cocktail across the table and exploded into a coughing fit.

'Angela's got it all under control,' she spluttered, pressing a napkin to her glossy lips. 'Dontcha, Ange?'

'All under control,' I lied, ready to put all my gambling monies (all thirty-six dollars) on Cici Spencer and Sadie Nixon being BFF.

'And did I tell you Erin's having a baby?' Ever the diplomat, Jenny steered the conversation in the opposite direction as quickly as possible. But it was too late. Sadie had her foot down for a head-on collision.

'Wow, Erin's having a baby?' Her eyes never left mine. 'So exciting. And you're being promoted. And you've got that delicious man. Everyone has so much going on right now. So, Angela, how is it that you're not going to get your ass-hand delivered back to England?'

139

She snapped a breadstick in two and leaned back in her chair.

The cow.

'I have to use the loo.' I threw my napkin down on the table and pushed my chair backwards in a hurry. I would not cry at the table; I wasn't a child. We were about as far removed from a youth hostel in the Peak District as it was possible to be, and Sadie was not Karen Thompson, my year nine nemesis. I would not rise to her heckling.

Safely locked in a stall, I let a couple of frustrated tears escape. What was wrong with some girls? Why did they have to make you feel like shit to give themselves a happy? And I hated myself for knowing that the prettier and more successful they were, the more it stung. Now there was a throwback from Robinstone Comprehensive. It was all Fuzzy Peach perfume, Boots 17 lipstick and tears before bedtime. I distinctly remember my sixteen-year-old self swearing it would all be different when I was older, but here I was, all Chanel perfume, MAC lipstick and Christian Louboutins, snivelling in the toilets. And this time Louisa wasn't here to talk me down. Because Louisa was at home, with her husband, having a baby. Just like Erin. And supersuccessful Jenny was too busy talking to her new best friend. I'd seen *Mean Girls* (loads of times). I knew how this worked.

Not ready to go back out to the table, I went through the crying-girl-in-the-toilet motions. I carefully wiped away any mascara smudges with a tissue, reapplied my lip gloss, powdered my nose and scrolled through my phone. Nothing from Alex yet. An email from my dad telling me to have fun on holiday. Thank God it didn't say 'don't do anything I wouldn't do'. A text from Louisa to say the baby had just kicked her awake.

More reminders that life went on without me. If I had to leave New York, how long would it take my friends here to forget me? It had only taken eighteen months for everything I knew in England to change completely. Louisa was married and pregnant, my parents were crack-head swingers. My ex hadn't even waited for me to leave to replace me. How long would it take Alex?

'Angela, are you in here?'

I heard Jenny's hooker heels click-clack across the bathroom tiles before she spoke, which gave me just enough time for the ol' flush and blow. I waved my hand in front of the sensor, waited for the toilet to flush and gave my nose a good old honk so she wouldn't know I'd been crying. The perfect crime.

'Oh my God, are you crying in there?'

Damn it.

'No,' I replied, putting down the lid and sitting back down. 'I'm just . . . thinking.'

'In the restroom of a restaurant?'

'Shut up.'

'Angie, Sadie wants to apologize. She's tired, she's been working a lot, she didn't mean to be a bitch.'

'Then where is she?' I asked. 'How come you're in here and she isn't?'

'Uh, she has a phobia of public bathrooms,' Jenny replied. 'I know, I know. Just come on out, OK?'

'I don't want to.' Sometimes I could be incredibly mature.

'Don't make me come in there, because I will do it.'

'Course you will.' I looked at the gap under the toilet door. Plenty of room for someone as skinny as Jenny, but there was no way she was going to crawl around on the floor of a lav in Herve Leger. 'I won't hold my breath.'

'Wait no more, bitches.'

Silly me. Of course Jenny wouldn't get down on the floor of a toilet (sober, by choice). But she would climb over the stall. In six-inch heels.

'How are you doing that?' I marvelled as she threw one leg over the partition, then the other, hooked her hands to the top and dropped down onto the floor.

'Clearly you never had to leave a date via the bathroom window,' she replied, shimmying her dress back down over her arse. Thank God she was wearing underwear. 'You'd be amazed at what I can do, Clark.'

'All bets are off with you, Lopez.' I shuffled across the toilet seat to make room for her tiny bottom. 'Now what's this about you getting promoted?'

'Aww, it's nothing.' She screwed up her face. 'It's not really a promotion. I'm just taking on more work, really. That's practically a demotion, right?'

'Um, no.' It was hard to hug someone sitting on a toilet, but I found a way. 'New title? Pay rise? Tell me!'

'Basically, Erin emailed me to say she wants me to take on more stuff while she's away on her baby vacay, like running a few of the accounts as well as organizing the events,' she said, trying to play it down, but I could see she was excited. 'I'll be managing a few people. It's probably gonna be a nightmare.'

'It will be amazing. You know it will.'

'Yeah.' She rested her head on my shoulder. 'I kinda kick ass at this job thing, don't I?'

'You kind of do,' I confirmed. 'But you always do. You were a kick-ass concierge, you were a kick-ass stylist. I bet you were a kick-ass babysitter at some point, weren't you?'

She nodded decisively. 'Four years' professional babysitting and not one fatality.'

'I'll take that as a yes.'

'So, are you going to get your ass out of the bathroom

142

and come join the party? We're gonna hit up Ghostbar.' She stood up and held out a hand. 'Or are you going to stay in here and be a Debbie Downer.'

'Debbie Downer,' I grumbled.

Jenny slapped me around the top of my head. 'How about tomorrow we do something, just me and you?'

'I don't want to be a knob, but I would love that,' I said, taking the hand and leaving the toilet stall behind. 'Do I really have to go back out there and deal with her?'

'Not if you don't want to,' Jenny said. 'It's your vacation. Do you want to go back to the hotel? Shall I call the car?'

I considered my options. Super-swanky club with super-swanky girls, doing shots, dancing until dawn in a dress that made me feel like my RE teacher, or finding out how long it took to fill up that tub in the middle of my room and go to bed. I spent a good three seconds trying to convince myself I wanted to go to the club before answering.

'There will be another club tomorrow, won't there?'

'There will.'

'Hotel, then, please.'

'Your wish is my command.' Jenny waved me towards the door with a flourish. 'We are living in a fairytale, and I am your fairy godmother, lady.'

'Jenny. How drunk are you?'

'Angela. Very?'

'Thought so.'

Twenty minutes later, I was back in my room, truffling through the mini bar and running the world's most exciting bath. So, my first day in Vegas had been a bit of a let-down. It always took a little bit of time to unwind on holiday, didn't it? And I had a lot to be wound up about. Visa worries safely locked up in an emotional box that could give me an ulcer another day, I thought I was safe and sound. Cast your cares away, worries for another day. But now, joy of joys, I had to share my holiday with Sadie, and I couldn't cast her nearly as far away as I would have liked.

Slipping off my butchered dress and wriggling out of Sadie's mum's underwear, I stepped into the bath, feeling appropriately decadent. All I was missing was a Flake. Stupid American chocolate. It was strange, the things I missed about England. Obviously, I missed my family and I missed Louisa. I missed *X Factor* Saturdays. I missed mooching around Boots to kill ten minutes. I missed Percy Pigs, Wotsits and proper lemonade. Why didn't America have lemonade? Sprite was not lemonade. But that wasn't a patch on what I'd miss about America. Three hours of *Come Dine with Me* on a Sunday was not a fair trade for the love of your life. Speaking of whom, my phone buzzed into life on the cleverly placed table right by the bathtub.

'Hello?'

'Hey, it's me.'

Talking to Alex on the phone always put me on high alert. I hated using the phone in general, a throwback to calling my mum and lying through my back teeth about where I was spending the night as a teenager, I was sure. It just set me on edge; but at least when it was with Alex, it was a good edge.

'Are you here? Are you in Vegas?'

'Yeah, we're at the Wynn,' he yawned. 'It's nice. And Jeff's friends seem pretty cool. We're gonna hit the tables.'

'I couldn't convince you to come over and tuck me in, then?' It had to be worth a try. 'There's a mini bar and an amazing view and all of the TV channels. All of them.'

Alex replied with a low laugh. 'I don't think that fits in with the "guys only" theme of the weekend, but I could probably get away tomorrow?'

'I'm supposed to do something with Jenny.' I dangled my leg over the side of the bath. If I smoked, I'd be having a cigar right now. 'But I really want to see you.'

'We'll work it out,' he promised. 'Where are you? Can I hear water?'

'I'm in the bath.' I splished and splashed for maximum effect. 'It's amazing.'

'You're calling me from the bath, but you tried to convince me to come over by way of mini bar and cable TV?'

'Yes?' There was a chance I was not the world's premier seductress.

'I love you, Angela Clark.'

Cue warm, fuzzy feeling that was nothing to do with the bath.

'I love you,' I whispered back. Sometimes I was still scared to say it. Like I had a finite number of uses and one day I'd run out and it would all be over.

'So you get back to your bath, I'll go make our millions, and we'll see each other tomorrow.'

'What are you wearing?' I asked quickly, desperate to keep him on the phone.

'A leather harness and a banana skin,' he replied without pause. 'This is boys' night. You can try to seduce me all you like, but I am made of steel. But only because I know I'm going to see you tomorrow.'

'Go on then,' I relented, placated by his qualifier. 'Have fun. But not too much fun. And no strippers. Or lap dancers. Or lap-dancing strippers.'

'Just straight-up hookers then, I got it. Get some sleep.'

'OK.' I wished I hadn't come back to the hotel. I was

sure I wouldn't be missing him half as much if I was dancing on a bar in my underwear somewhere while The Situation did body shots of my friends. 'I'll see you tomorrow. No hookers.'

'No hookers.'

Forget you, William Shakespeare. Had there ever been a sweeter goodnight between lovers? I think not.

CHAPTER TEN

The next morning I woke up bright and early at nine a.m. Technically the middle of the night by Vegas standards. After a good ten minutes spent staring out of the bedroom window (I opened the drapes from my bed with a remote control. This room had everything), I dragged myself into the lounge and gazed down upon my kingdom. In reality, if I were the King of Vegas, I probably wouldn't be wearing a Star Wars T-shirt and giant pink cotton pants, let alone be wide awake and staring at an almost completely abandoned Strip before ten in the morning, but I was.

These were the benefits of being an early riser, I told myself smugly – you got time and you got space. Not that I'd normally know; I hardly ever saw anything outside of my eyelids before ten, but my brain was still on New York time, making it twelve and a perfectly reasonable time for me to be vertical. At least when I stood half-naked in this window, no one could see. Well, if they could see, more power to them. That would have to be one very powerful telescope and one very committed pervert. We were ever so high up.

A trail of handbags, high heels and empty packets

of crisps suggested Jenny and Sadie had made it home at some point before sunrise, but their doors were firmly closed. Pouting, I paced the giant room, sitting on a sofa, getting up to look at the view, peering in a cupboard, flicking on the TV. A good night's sleep had left me restless, and I didn't quite know what to do. I could go for a swim, but I was hungry. I could order room service, but then I'd still be in the same place. Only one thing for it. I was going to have to go on an adventure.

Suitably stuffed into a pair of skinny J Brand jeans and one of Jenny's cast-off Splendid T-shirts, I grabbed my satchel, tossed in my phone and room key and called for the lift. There was something a little bit heartbreaking about leaving the room – it was so beautiful; but my stomach was rumbling in a big way. It was going to be tough to go back to my apartment on Sunday night. *Probably a good thing*, The Voice popped up out of nowhere; *good idea to get used to saying goodbye to things.*

Ooh, you bastard, I thought in response, how dare you have a go before I've even had a cup of tea?

Given the state of the street outside, I was expecting the casino floor to be quiet at the very least, if not empty. I was wrong. All traces of the early morning sunshine were erased and replaced with the most unnatural light known to man. Even though the casino looked just as shiny and exciting as it had when I'd passed through the night before, something was off. Slot machines clunked and rang with sirens of success, crowds huddled around the roulette tables, crumpled and tired, with no idea of the time. The card tables were even more frightening. Aching, bloodshot eyes stared at bored-looking dealers, just waiting, waiting for that one card they knew was the next out of the deck. All I would have to do was touch them, just a gentle tap with one finger, and they would shatter into a million pieces. It was intense. And it didn't look like fun.

'Hey, it's that girl from the plane,' someone shouted from one of the card tables.

Surely most people qualified as 'you from the plane'?

'The one with the stick up her ass, with the super hot friend.'

That sounded a little bit more like me. I turned to see Brad and his gambling buddies two tables away. They looked like they hadn't had an awful lot of sleep since they arrived. Or fresh air. Or non-alcoholic drinks.

'Hey, blondie, what's going on?' Brad yelped over a very unpleasant-sounding cough. 'You win a million yet?'

'Not yet,' I replied politely. 'Give me time.'

'I'd give you something,' he snarked. 'What room you in?'

'Not yours.' I had to eat before I could come up with a better comeback. 'Good luck, Brad.'

'Dude, she totally remembered your name.' His friend sounded shocked. It made me sad.

Morning gamblers weren't glamorous; there were no hot girls in cocktail dresses, no laughing, no glasses of champagne. Just hard liquor and occasional shouting. Even the sexy cocktail waitresses weren't sexy. The outfit the De Lujo had them trussed up in made my recent waitressing uniform look more modest than K-Midd's wedding dress. All I could think was, either they've been in those heels and that bum floss ensemble for hours, or they had to put them on at about six o'clock this morning and come to work. It was impossible to decide which was more depressing. At least they weren't having to strip, I told myself, but then, they'd probably be in bed now if they were strippers. And at that point I realized there was almost definitely a morning shift for Las Vegas strippers, and that almost took away my appetite. Almost.

'Table for one, madam?'

Words that should strike fear into the heart of any unmarried woman faced with enough food to put Comic Relief out of business for at least a decade.

I have always been a girl who likes her food. But nothing could have prepared me for what lay before me. There was not a sausage roll to be seen, and for the first time in my twenty-eight years, I could say this was a Good Thing. Led to my table, I passed a station full of seafood. Another full of cheeses. A salad bar that put every Pizza Hut in England to shame. There couldn't be a cuisine that was not represented in that room, and when all the world's foods come together, all the world's foods smell good.

Two-thirds of the way through my second plate of deliciousness, my former roommate collapsed into the chair next to me and lay her face down on the table. The air conditioning made the hotel a bit chillier than I might have liked, but there was absolutely no need for Jenny's giant mohair sweater teamed with what looked like the same leather leggings Sadie had been wearing the night before. Her lips were stained with day-old pink lipstick, and the rest of her face was hiding behind huge sunglasses. Her standard hangover hairdo was to bind it all out of the way in an enormous bun or ponytail to stop it irritating her, but today it seemed like she needed the extra camouflage. That or she didn't have the energy to try to tame all the curls that bounced excitedly around her head. It was the only thing about her that seemed even faintly energetic.

'Morning.' I raised my cup of tea in solidarity. 'Fun night, then?'

'I don't know yet.' She waved over a waiter and begged for coffee. 'What the fuck are you eating?'

'Everything.' I began to push a croissant towards her, but pulled it back hastily when she retched at the table. 'Looks like a good night. Why are you awake?'

'Because I said we would do something today,' she reminded me, seemingly entirely against her will. 'And we're doing something.'

'As much as I really want to hang out with you, I don't really want you to puke on me, so do feel free to go back to bed.'

'Two things.' Jenny thanked the waiter for her coffee, then stared into the cup in silence for a few seconds. Then pushed it away. Too soon. 'Firstly, I'm so hungover that when I lie down, the room spins and I puke. Secondly, I made an appointment for us with this stylist guy I met in LA. He's going to give us a Vegas-over. I'm going to glitz the shit out of you.'

'Two things,' I replied. 'Firstly, your Vegas-over looks to be complete already, my love, and secondly, if the room is spinning, it means you're still drunk, not hungover.'

'Yeah,' Jenny nodded, taking a very slow sip of coffee. 'Yeah, it does.'

I gave her a very judgemental look. It felt good.

'Shopping should be fun, then.'

'Shopping drunk is super fun. If I hadn't ever stopped into Urban Outfitters tipsy, I wouldn't have red jeans in my closet,' she responded.

'And I don't know how the world would cope,' I replied. 'Where's Sadie?'

'Don't know. I do know we switched outfits in the club, and I know there was dancing, and I'm pretty sure there was some dude from that show about those guys, but then she wasn't there any more and I came home. Without the guy from that show, before you ask.'

'Well, who can resist some dude from that show about those guys?' I asked. 'And I absolutely wasn't going to ask. I know you're all smitten kitten for the Sigster.'

'Don't call him that,' she said, pushing herself up from the table and trying to focus on the food while keeping her coffee down. 'Which way to the toast?'

'Right over there.' I pointed towards the bakery station and paused. No. Shopping. Must not be full of bagel. Am already full of Everything Else.

I was very excited. Not working regularly had limited my shopping excursions, and I'd been very, very sensible with my last few pay cheques. Meaning I was probably about to be very unsensible with whatever was left in my bank account. I still had a ton of Christmas shopping to do, but I told myself this was vital research. How was I going to write for fashion magazines if I didn't set foot inside a department store? You can't write about clothes you haven't seen. Or touched. Or tried on. Or murdered your credit limit for.

'The limo's waiting,' Jenny said as we attempted to navigate the casino floor without bumping into Brad. 'I am so not going to want to get on the subway on Monday morning.'

'I think I probably do prefer the limo,' I agreed. 'Although if it was a toss-up between the limo and Sadie or taking the bus and no Sadie, I'd be on a double-decker by now.'

'I don't know what you're talking about.' Jenny pressed a hand to her forehead as she clambered into the big black car with significantly less elegance than she had displayed the night before. 'But I would guess you're right.'

The limo slid away from the hotel, leaving a towering white palace behind us, glittering in the crisp winter sunshine. Shame I knew Jenny had puked in the toilet just before we left. Took the shine right off it.

The Strip was still pretty quiet as we swept along past the casinos. Some of them looked magnificent in the daylight. The Wynn stood tall, commanding respect by refusing to subscribe to a silly theme, but then the Venetian actually took my breath away. I'd never been to Venice, and while I was quite aware that this wasn't the same thing, I couldn't wait to get inside that hotel. Plus there were huge billboards for *Phantom*, and oh to the em to the gee, I loved me a musical. It was no *Les Mis*, but still. I wondered if I would be able to sneak away for a matinee, knowing full well I'd be on my own for it and not caring in the slightest.

A couple of minutes later we were pulling into what looked like giant chunks of glass sprouting up from the ground. It was as though Superman had fallen on hard times and flogged the Fortress of Solitude to a Las Vegas developer and said developer had filled the fortress with everything that was great and good in the world. And by that, I meant shops. Wonderful, wonderful shops.

'So this is the Crystals,' Jenny explained, taking my hand and patting it reassuringly. 'You should prepare yourself. Shit's about to get real.'

'How did you know about this?' I asked, trying not to give myself whiplash as we entered the complex. Gucci, Lanvin, Tom Ford, Marni. 'This is insane.'

'I came here a couple of times when I was in LA. Heaps of styling work in Vegas.' Bulgari, Dior, Versace, Bottega Veneta. 'Damn city is full of reality TV girls who don't know how to dress themselves. And Erin is talking to some guy who is opening a boutique here, so really we're working today.'

'Amazing.' I held my battered Marc Jacobs satchel close to my body to shield its eyes from all the pretty things in the windows. At least I didn't need to worry about my credit limit. There wasn't a single thing in a single store I could afford. 'Only, I daren't touch anything.'

'And that's why we have a personal shopper.' She took my arm and led me through the beautiful, beautiful window displays and through a frosted glass door until the Beautiful Things were safely behind us.

And in front of us was a man. A man so pretty I had to wipe my palms on the arse of my jeans before I even stepped towards him. It was impossible to process how beautiful he actually was without looking away to clear out your eyes and then looking back, just to confirm it. Easily over six foot, broad shoulders, thick sandy blond hair styled into the perfect Don Draper and clad in an exquisite suit I assumed he had sold his soul for, he did a double-take and sparked into life. His perfect features broke into a wide crooked smile and his suit ruched up as he opened his arms into what would become an all-consuming hug. For Jenny.

'Jenny Lopez! I saw your name in the diary and I thought it was the other one! Why didn't you tell me you were coming? What the hell?'

Apparently, Jenny knew this gentleman.

'It was all kind of last minute.' Jenny untangled herself from the hug and took several steps back until she was parallel with my jaw. Which was on the floor. She wrapped her own slender arms around herself and gave him her biggest, fakest smile.

Huh.

'This is my friend, Angie.' She cocked her head towards me. 'And she needs the full Vegas.'

'The famous Angie.' He was on me in one stride. Jenny leapt away and coiled up on a couch quicker than a scalded cat. Double-huh. 'I'm Ben, and it looks like I am your stylist for the day.'

'Hello, Ben.' I reciprocated his double kisses. It wouldn't do to be impolite, would it? 'So, you know Jenny?'

'We worked together,' she explained before he could, although I could tell by his raised eyebrow that 'worked together' was apparently a fun new euphemism Jenny was using for 'we shagged each other senseless on at least one occasion'.

'We did,' he confirmed, hands on my shoulders. 'Now, let me take a look at you.'

I was perfectly happy for him to look all day long. And if he needed to touch a little bit, that was fine. Alex would completely understand. This man was so beautiful, I dare say he might even want a quick touch himself. He could make any man alive ask himself some questions. I actually couldn't think of a man straight enough to turn him down.

'And I get to give you a Vegas makeover? Oh, this is going to be fun,' he promised. 'Let's go into the dressing room.'

I followed him happily while Jenny lagged behind. I wasn't too carried away to notice the moment between the two of them when she passed by as Ben held the door open. It was exciting to see sexual tension between pretty people. Like watching a live action movie. As long as it didn't turn into a live action porno, we were good. Although I did have a credit card and some time to kill if Ben ever decided to go into adult entertainment.

The dressing room was, like everything else, super-plush. Giant cream couches, champagne on ice, fizzy pop, olives, cheese, everything. A giant TV showed E! entertainment, there was a Mac connected to Facebook in one corner of the room, and in the other corner a frosted-glass shower stall. Clearly some people were spending a lot of time in here.

'So, I have my brief, I have your measurements, you ladies relax in your dressing room and I'm gonna go pick out some pieces. You know the drill, Lopez. Don't cause me any trouble.' Ben gave us a stern look that elicited the girliest giggle I have ever had the shame to produce. I coughed, blushed and looked at my feet.

I waited the requisite fifteen seconds after the door had closed before spinning around to demand answers. Plus details.

'Before you even start – ' Jenny pushed the sunglasses she had been wearing throughout onto the top of her head and glared at me – 'Yes, we did. But it was for like five seconds when I was out here one weekend, and then nothing happened.'

I pressed my lips into a thin line and tried to ratchet my eyebrows back down my forehead.

'We're not even Facebook friends.'

So she was serious.

'Jenny, he's beautiful.' I picked up a silver cocktail ring and twisted it onto my right hand.

'And he's effed every girl in Vegas. This is not something I'm proud of. Let's just not, OK?'

I would have been proud. I would have put it on a T-shirt.

'How does he have my sizes?' I asked. 'Is he sure he doesn't need to measure me?'

'He has your measurements because he's effed every

girl in Vegas,' Jenny repeated. 'That's his party piece, guessing bra sizes. He's pretty good.'

'Fine, I believe you, he's an arsehole.' I plopped onto the sofa beside her. 'Besides, he's still not as good looking as Sigge. Or as nice.'

'No.' She stretched her arms over her head, shaking the last of her hangover away. 'He's not. It's all surface. All smoke and mirrors.'

I stretched my legs and shook off the thought of smoke and mirrored ceilings. 'But he's such a good stylist, we had to come and see him?'

'He's good,' she said. 'But the other girl who works here is a bitch. And you know, he's super-hot. So, happy Christmas.'

'I love you.'

'I know.'

'It's very nice.' I stood on a raised dais in the middle of a room of mirrors, examining myself from every angle in a very, very tight black Bottega Veneta leather shift dress. I was regretting eating all of the food now. 'I just don't know if it's me?'

'It's so you.' Ben ran his hands down my silhouette. 'It's the autumn-winter—eleven-fetish you. It's the high-fashion you.'

Hmm. I was far more comfortable with the Forever 21 me. And much more comfortable when he didn't have his hands on me. Turns out Jenny was right, Ben was a bit of a sleaze. And no matter how pretty a man was, if he couldn't keep his hands off your arse when they hadn't been invited, it was off-putting.

'I can see you don't love it.' He turned away with a flourish and headed back into a rail of outfits. 'Take it off.'

Since he'd come behind the screen and seen me in

my knickers twice already, I didn't see a lot of point in bothering again and so I struggled out of the sticky leather right there in the middle of the room. Jenny, nose deep in a copy of *Us Weekly* and sipping a champagne flute full of the finest hair of the dog, did not comment.

'This one next.' He held out a gorgeous sapphire-blue gown that looked much more workable. 'Alice and Olivia. Cute but still sexy. I'll find some shoes.'

I slipped into the one-shouldered minidress, rolling down its Grecian ruching until everything was approximately where it was supposed to go.

'Jenny?' I liked this one. The careful pleating and folds hid my bagel bloating, but the single shoulder and super-short skirt made it look appropriately festive. As in, just the right side of slutty.

Jenny looked up from her magazine, gave me the once-over and then gave it a thumbs-up. 'Shout me when he's got the shoes,' she commented.

Yay. She liked it! I hadn't picked it and couldn't really take any credit, but she liked it! Ben reappeared clutching a pair of silver strappy sandals and a pair of chunky suede black and silver peep-toe booties.

'What does your heart say?' he asked. Melodramatic? A bit. But my heart did have an answer. I'd seen a pair of strappy silver sandals like that once before and they'd been wrapped around my ex-boyfriend's waist. I had no interest in taking them out for a spin.

'Pass me the boots.' I held out a hand and ignored the bile in my throat. Stupid Gina and their stupid core collection. I'd thought how versatile they were at the time. Wonderful taste in shoes, terrible taste in men, that girl.

'Miu Miu,' Ben said as I slipped my foot into the gorgeous stacked suede boot, my hot pink pedicure peeping out at the front. The silver sparkle lifted the look, and the weight of the boot against the lightness of the dress created the perfect clash. I knew I'd done well. 'Gorgeous. There's just a couple more things I want you to try.'

'Wow, Angie.' Jenny actually put her magazine down. 'You look so good. When I've done your make-up . . .'

It was a compliment. In a way.

'Wait until Alex sees you in that shit.'

'Actually, can you check my phone and see if he's called?' I reluctantly slipped off the booties and unzipped the dress. Come hell or high water, it was coming home with me. 'I said I'd check in.'

'Boyfriend think you've run off to the Little Chapel without him?' Ben asked, passing me a sliver of spangly black fabric. I looked at it, puzzled as to how I was supposed to put it on, for two seconds too long before he grabbed it back and signalled for me to hold my hands above my head.

'Probably more worried that Jenny's got me working in a strip club.' I blew a strand of hair out of my face while this grown man dressed me. 'Or that I'm locked in the boot of someone's car in the desert somewhere.'

'She means trunk,' Jenny translated automatically. 'Is that Dolce?'

This time the magazine was on the couch. The champagne was on the counter. We had her full attention.

'Yes. And I want you in these boots.'

He handed me two giant slivers of buttery soft black leather.

'Are they Zanotti?'

Jenny was giving it the full meerkat on the sofa.

I did as I was told.

'Holy shit.' Jenny stood up.

'And we're done.' Ben took two steps back.

I stared into the mirror and gulped. The dress was a second skin of spider-like black lace, scattered with bright silver stars. Long sleeves and a high neckline were counteracted by a delicate hemline that barely covered my knickers, its brevity emphasized by the fact that the high-heeled boots Ben was zipping up stopped only three inches short of meeting it. The effect was arresting. In that it would get me arrested.

'What's wrong?' Jenny asked, reading my face. 'Too tight? Too short?'

'A little from column A, a little from column B,' I stuttered. 'I can't go out looking like this. Besides, I can't afford it.'

'There's no way I'm letting you leave this room without this outfit.' Ben folded his arms and went to stand next to Jenny. They formed a wall of agreement. 'And all this stuff is on loan. Don't sweat it.'

'Don't sweat it or don't sweat in it?' I frowned and looked back in the mirror. It was amazing and shockingly flattering. I just wouldn't be able to bend down. Or sit down. Or stand up for too long.

'So we're doing this and we're doing the Alice and Olivia with the Miu Miu?' Ben asked Jenny. Clearly my opinion was no longer required. 'And I have something for you too.'

With an almost shy smile, he handed Jenny a garment bag. She took it, looking a little shocked, and unzipped it carefully, facing away from me.

'What is it?' I whined like a little girl. Damn these heels, I couldn't move fast enough to get a good look.

'Ben . . .' Jenny turned back towards us, her hand pressed against her heart. 'This is insane.'

'It never looked better on anyone than it did on you,' he told the floor. 'Take it, OK?'

'Thank you.' She reached out and touched his hand.

I stood in the middle of the two of them, the world's most overdressed gooseberry.

'I'll leave you two ladies alone . . .' Ben coughed and backed out of the room, leaving Jenny standing holding the garment bag, me holding my breath.

'Oh my God. Drama?'

I turned to see Jenny still clutching the dress, her face completely impassive.

'You OK?' I asked. 'Is there actually a horse's head in there? Is it the prom dress from *Carrie*?'

'It's just something I wore one time, is all,' she said, throwing it down on the sofa as though it were nothing at all. 'The dude is an asshat.'

'Asshat,' I agreed merrily. 'Going around giving girls free clothes. Who does he think he is? Can I see it?'

'Whatever.' She could pretend all she liked, but I knew there was something amazing in that bag. And if it was big enough, I was borrowing it.

'Holy Mary, Mother of God.'

There were feathers. There were ruffles. There was a black leather obi belt. It was strapless, it fell to the floor and it was gold. And there was no way on Earth it would fit me.

'Did you suddenly become religious?' Jenny asked. 'Or is it just Christmas that's bringing on the blasphemy?'

'Christmas,' I nodded, unable to take my eyes off the dress. 'I am a devout believer in Christmas. And Easter, because, you know, the bunny. Jenny, this is amazing.'

'Lhuillier,' she replied, a little sadness in her voice. 'It's the most beautiful thing I ever wore.'

'And when did we wear this? I don't remember seeing you at the Oscars.'

'Just on a date.' She pulled the dress gently out of my hands. 'The dress is beautiful, Ben is an asshat. That's really all there is to it.'

'I would be prepared to accept quite a lot of asshattery for a dress like that.'

'Women like you are holding us back as a gender,' Jenny replied sternly. 'You are the glass ceiling.'

'Yep,' I said, eyes still full of feathers. 'I'd give back the vote for that dress. Chain me to the sink, fill me full of babies, just let me wear that bad boy while I'm cooking you dinner.'

'You're hilarious.' Jenny zipped the garment bag with a sharp pull, breaking the gown's spell, and passed me my phone. 'You have a text from your boyfriend-slash-proponent of the patriarchal agenda.'

My boyfriend! I had one of those! The dress had almost made me forget. The Lhuillier was the kind of dress that could make you forget everything. I clicked on the text; he was spoken for until the evening, when they were going to some club in their hotel and could I meet him there? Hmm. I was fairly certain I wasn't going to get away as lightly as I had the night before, but surely there was some way to get a quick fix without having to expose Jenny to the Jeffstravaganza.

I clicked over to my email quickly while Jenny was distracted with her own text messages. At least she was smiling now. I assumed Sigge and asked no questions. Sex texts were only ever meant to be shared between two people, contrary to what Jenny thought. The last time we'd been out for drinks I'd been shown a picture text that really put the cock into cocktail (the tail as well, really, if we're being fair), and I hadn't been able to look at Sigge the same way ever since.

My inbox was heaving, in no small part due to the fact I had subscribed to every single Christmas-related newsletter in the United States of America. I knew where every market, Santa's grotto, pop-up ice rink and seasonal peppermint hot chocolate could be found within a fifteen-mile radius of wherever I was. But in between the e-shots from DailyCandy, *Time Out New York* and UrbanDaddy, there were assorted Facebook messages, e-cards (evil, lazy people) and then several more emails from editors. Every single one of them was a rejection. And then the real kicker.

Hi Angela,
   Hope you're feeling festive, ho-ho-ho!
   Anyway, we need to talk about your column. Having a rejig of the mag in the new year and we're thinking it's time to go in another direction. Give me a call when you get this. Maybe I can help you find something else?
   Sara x

Not only had every single one of my ideas been rejected by every single editor I'd written to, my UK column had been killed. That was it. I was buggered. I would give her ho-ho-fucking-ho. On the upside, it turned out I could sit down in the crazy short dress, a fact I became aware of when I realized I was cross-legged on the floor and no longer standing up.

'Dollface, what's wrong?' Jenny took the phone I held out to her and scrolled quickly. 'So? It's just a few. You've got loads of these out there, right?'

'That's all of them,' I said, feeling simultaneously very sick and completely empty. 'That's every single one.'

'So we go to plan B.' Jenny crouched down beside me. 'Don't do this, Angela. Don't. We will figure this out.'

'Yeah.' I sniffed hard, looking Jenny in her fiercely determined eyes. 'We will. I know.'

'We will. Now, dress off, jeans on and, man alive, we deserve a drink.'

I did not point out that it was only two in the afternoon and she'd already had three glasses of champagne. Didn't seem worth it. Instead, I yanked off the dress, kicked out of the boots and got my clothes on in record time.

'So – ' I peered through my jumper – 'what exactly were you drinking last night?'

'Jagerbombs?' Jenny winced. 'Tequila? Whiskey? All of the above?'

'Sounds perfect,' I said. 'Make mine a double.'

CHAPTER ELEVEN

'It's my own fault,' I slurred into my cocktail. 'I should have thought about this earlier. I should have thought about this before.'

'Noooo.' Jenny rubbed my hair vigorously. 'No, because, like, when things are going good, you know, you, like, don't think about, you know, bad stuff. You know?'

'I totally know.' I held my glass up for an enthusiastic toast. 'And things were going good. Things were awesome. Things were the bestest ever things. And now it's all gone to shit.'

'Ever ever,' Jenny agreed.

'With work and with boys and with you and just with me and everything.' I sipped my martini and tried not to slurp. It was delicious. Even more delicious than the first three. 'And now it's all shit. It's just shit.'

'It is not!' Jenny signalled for the bartender to refill our glasses. He nodded and passed two fresh drinks across the bar. What a pro. We'd been propping up the bar in the Bellagio for some time, and while I wasn't feeling any better about my situation, I was finding it harder to remember precisely what that situation was, so that was a plus.

'Things are awesome, Angie, they are. You've got Alex. You've got me. We haven't gone to shit.'

'Well, even if I have to leave, you've still got Sadie,' I sniffed, missing my mouth with an olive. Probably best.

'Whaa?' Jenny slapped my shoulder. 'Don't be a dumbass.'

The bartender smiled.

'It's true. You've got Sadie, and let's face it, she's going to be a lot more fun than me. When was the last time I did a jagerbomb? I don't even know what a jagerbomb is. And she's, you know, younger. And prettier. And cooler. And blah blah blah.'

'Blah blah yourself, dumbass.' She slammed her empty glass down on the bar. 'You're jealous of Sadie?'

'I'm jealous of everyone,' I wailed. It was all coming out now. 'I'm jealous of Sadie because she has you. I'm jealous of you because you have an amazing job and an amazing boyfriend. I'm jealous of Erin because she's having a baby. I'm jealous of Louisa because she's having a baby and I'm not there. Everyone's life is moving on except mine. All I have is a martini.' I looked up at the bartender and tried to give him my best smile. 'And it is an excellent martini, sir. Just, very good.'

'Aw, Angie, that's such bull.' Jenny shoved her hand in between my glass and my face, leaving me with a mouthful of cocktail ring. 'You're just freaking out because of this visa shit, and we're gonna make that OK. Your life is totally moving forward.'

'How? How is it moving forward?'

'You're living with your boyfriend, you know what you want out of life, and you're trying to get it. That's moving forward.'

'I'm living with my boyfriend, I don't have a job,

I'm writing a blog no one is reading and I don't know what country I'm going to be living in this time next month. I've literally gone back in time eighteen months.'

'Except now your boyfriend is awesome and not a cheating asshole,' Jenny rallied. 'And you've achieved so much. We just have to work out how to put that experience into practice. And we will. Just, dude, not today.'

'I know.' I leaned over the bar and rested my head on my arms. 'I know. And I'm not really jealous, honest. I'm just feeling a bit lost. I'm really happy for you.'

Jenny pinched at the latex covering on her legs and gave me a half-smile. 'Thanks, doll.'

'And you deserve it. You work so hard. And after the whole Jeff thing – ' I held her hands and pulled a face – 'you deserve to be happy. So happy. So, so, so happy.'

'Thanks, doll.'

'Sigge's so awesome. And yes, I know I thought he was gay when you met him, but yeah. He's not.'

The bartender laughed.

'He's really lovely. And hot. And funny. And is he clever? I bet he's clever. I know he's a model, but I bet he's clever. And he's not gay.'

'Angie, honey, you're rambling.'

I was rambling.

Jenny had adopted the same expression I'd seen when Ben had given her the garment bag.

'Not gay.' I waved an imaginary flag in the air. 'Yay.'

'Yay.' She finally gave me a smile. 'Total yay.'

'You are happy, aren't you? Because you should be. Your life is so sorted, I . . . God, what do I want to say?' I mined my limited vocabulary for the words I needed. 'I admire you. You're my hero.'

'Oh, Angie.' Jenny rested her hand on top of mine. 'I am not a good hero.'

'Shut up.' I wasn't having any of it. 'They should put you on T-shirts and give them to little girls. They should want to be you. I want to be you.'

'With my ass?' She gave me a wry smile. 'You wouldn't last a day. I know for a fact you wouldn't survive my morning run. And then you wouldn't be able to eat. Or drink. And then you would have to throw yourself in the East River.'

I gazed into the drink in front of me.

'Fair point. But honestly, I just . . . I love you, Jenny Lopez. You are my best friend. Sometimes I feel so guilty because, you know, Louisa has always, you know, been my best friend. But you're just as important as she is. More. I can tell you anything and I know you'll never judge me or have a go, you'll just understand. That's amazing.'

Jenny looked at me with her big brown eyes, which were considerably less bloodshot than they were the last time I'd looked into them but just as hazy. Afternoon drinking was the worst. Slash best.

'You mean that?' Her bloodshot eyes started to tear up.

'Yes.' I nodded once to confirm. 'I do. Totally. You are so my go-to human for any and all things. Happy things, sad things, difficult things. You know that bit in *Sex and the City*? Where Carrie gets her diaphragm stuck and Sam has to help her – you know?'

'I do know.' Jenny wrinkled her little nose.

'If you got your diaphragm stuck and you absolutely could not go to a hospital or Sigge for help and had tried loads of times, I would absolutely help you.'

'Angela.' She pressed her hands against her mouth. 'That is the nicest thing anyone has ever said to me.'

'Any time,' I said, raising my glass and waiting for Jenny to do the same.

'And I would totally remove your birth control,' she replied with a clink. 'Any day of the week.'

The bartender looked uncomfortable.

'If I couldn't get it out,' I explained. 'Of my vagina.'

'Shots, ladies?' he offered. 'On the house?'

What a lovely man. I accepted my shot with a nod, a smile and a shiver as the tequila coursed its way down my throat. Well. Tonight was going to be interesting.

'We should get a cab,' I mumbled as we staggered down the Strip an hour later. We were late to meet Sadie back at the hotel, and I for one did not want to deal with her sour-puss if we were any later. Jenny was not fast on her feet, and I wasn't entirely sure where we were going. The lovely, ever-present limo had chosen now to go AWOL, and so we were stranded in the middle of Las Vegas, ambling towards a big white building in the near distance. 'I feel like we've been walking for ever.'

'We're still outside the Bellagio,' Jenny pointed out. 'Everything looks closer because it's so huge. The De Lujo is only next door, it's just that next door is, like, it's far.' She held her hands apart to indicate distance, in case far was too foreign a concept for me to grasp. It was fair – I was a bit drunk. The fresh air had happily had a sobering effect on me, so I was able to hold it together. Unfortunately it had gone the other way for Ms Lopez; she was looking greener by the second.

'Let's watch the fountains,' she suggested, grabbing at the wall by the lake and sitting down before I could give her a yay or nay. We were watching the fountains, then.

I pulled out my phone to text Alex, but it was still open on my inbox. The orgy of rejection made me suck my breath in sharply. Jenny was right. There was another way. I just had no idea what it was. Unless it really was time to talk to Alex.

'What're you doing?' Jenny pawed at my phone, grabbing it away. 'Dude, do not look at these emails. You will bring us down. You will kill my buzz.'

'Your buzz is already sickly.' I held my hand out for my phone. 'Give.'

'So you can throw a pity party all the way back to the hotel? Nuh-uh.' She opened her handbag on her knee, looked up at me with her best 'I dare you to stop me' face, and tossed the phone into the bottom of her bag. Except she missed. And I watched as my phone sailed merrily through the air and splashed into the Bellagio fountains, its landing dwarfed by an enormous geyser, synchronized perfectly to 'It's the Most Wonderful Time of the Year'.

'Oh crap.'

It was the second phone I'd lost to a body of water, but this was the first one I hadn't hurled myself. This time, it was not nearly as satisfying.

'It's OK.' Jenny kicked off her boots and thrust her bag at me. 'I'll get it.'

'Jenny, no!' I reached out to grab her, but I was far too slow. Or maybe I didn't want to stop her enough. Before I could even get to my feet, she was waist-deep in lake Bellagio, eyes down, looking for my phone.

'Ew, this shit's nasty,' she called. 'I can't see a thing.'

'Jenny, get out.' I didn't know whether to laugh or cry. 'You'll get arrested.'

'Fuck that, I'm looking for your phone,' she shouted back. 'They can't arrest me for being awesome.'

They might not have been able to arrest her, but she

was certainly drawing a crowd. The admirable fountains stayed true to the old showbiz adage and the show went on while Jenny fished for a phone to the tune of 'White Christmas'.

'Ha,' she called, holding it up triumphantly. I was actually quite impressed. 'I totally found it. That is way better than taking out your diaphragm, right?'

'Theoretical diaphragm,' I explained to a baseball-cap and bum-bag-wearing couple beside me. 'No need to look so scared. She's my best friend.'

I leaned over the wall and held out my hand. 'Come here,' I said, grabbing her wrist as she attempted to cock a leg over the wall and haul herself out of the water. 'You climbed over a seven-foot toilet partition last night, and now you can't get over a three-foot wall?'

'I'm wet,' she stated unnecessarily.

'I noticed,' I replied, trying to get a firmer grip. It was impossible – she was too slippery.

'Here, I'll get a hold of you,' she said, taking hold of a wrist with each hand. 'Now you pull.'

But before I could yank her out, I felt her slip, all of her bodyweight shifting backwards. Every sodden inch of her collapsing into the water and dragging me over the wall and into the water with her.

My first instinct was purely survival oriented. Must save the Marc Jacobs. I held my bag aloft, trying desperately to keep it out of the water while I kicked and splashed around trying to stay upright. In the fountain. Outside the Bellagio. While Christmas carols belted out in the background and fountains performed an elegant, synchronized display. It was official. Geysers were more graceful than me.

'Well, I think I'm sober now.'

Beside me, the drowned rat formerly known as Jenny

Lopez wiped at the giant panda patches that had taken over her face. I picked up her sunglasses as they sailed past and handed them over.

'Thanks.' She slid them on and nodded. 'Much better. Shall we?'

'Let's.'

With great effort, we waded through the fountain towards the growing crowds on the pavement.

'OK, people, nothing to see here,' Jenny shouted as she heaved her sodden self over the wall and collapsed onto the floor. She was the world's skinniest beached whale. I hoisted myself up and over, dropping my dripping bag on the floor beside me. Ruined. It was ruined. I'd process the fact that I'd just dived head first into a fountain in public in my clothes later. *La Dolce Vita* this was not.

'Hey, Angela.' I turned my head to see Jenny, still spread-eagled on the sidewalk, face covered in mascara, holding something out to me. 'Your phone.'

I took it, slipped it into my handbag and stared up at the sky.

'Thanks. Appreciate it.'

'Don't say I never do anything for you.'

After a very sorry, sodden walk back to the hotel, we finally made it into the lift along with a very confused-looking family. Mum and Dad did their best not to look at us, but their two sons weren't so constrained by the rules of polite society.

'What?' Jenny asked the oldest, really quite loudly, after fifteen floors of straight staring. 'Yeah, that's right. I'll give you something to cry for,' she shouted as they made a hasty exit two floor later.

'Jenny – ' I said, trying not to smile.

'Fuck 'em,' she replied.

I couldn't really argue with her.

Back in the suite, we found a huge rack of clothing from Ben, a bottle of chilled champagne and a note from Sadie telling us to meet her at Tryst by midnight, our names were on the guest list. I didn't think I'd ever been so relieved. There was no way I could have coped with watching her perky arse bounce around the room when all I wanted to do was collapse in the bath and have a nap. Almost drowning in a fountain really put things into perspective. After briefly perusing the racks, reading the note and silently retching at the sight of the champagne, Jenny nodded silently and headed straight into her room. I followed suit, locking my door behind me.

As I ran my bath I thought hard. Based on this afternoon's emails, I was not going to be able to apply for a media visa. Realistically, I was not going to become an alien of extraordinary ability within the next three weeks. I needed a plan B. The thought of losing Alex, of going back home with my tail between my legs, hurt my heart more than looking at my poor, poor bag. And that hurt a lot. I stretched my arms up high above my head, feeling the last few trickles of cold water run down my back, peeled off my wet clothes like layers of skin and settled myself in the bath while the warm water rose all around me. A much more pleasant aquatic experience.

Maybe Jenny had been right all along. Maybe I was being stupid about this. I should just sit Alex down and explain. It was just paperwork. We would go to city hall, sign something, go home and not even think about it again. And if the time came when we decided we wanted to do it properly, and it had bloody well better, we would. We'd just have a proper wedding and not mention to anyone that, technically, we were already husband and wife. It wasn't a big deal. It didn't have to be a big deal.

Except it was. But did it have to be? I was a girl. I was having girl emotions. Alex was a man, he would be practical and reasonable. And it couldn't hurt to talk about it, could it? I let out a long, slow sigh and dipped my hair under the water, the cold fighting against the heat for just a second before I was glowing from the top of my head to the tip of my toes. But inside, my bones still felt cold.

CHAPTER TWELVE

Without a working phone, I hadn't heard from Alex, but I did know he was going to be at the Wynn and, happily, so were we. Jenny had informed me, while backcombing her hair until it was big enough to warrant its own orbit, that Tryst at the Wynn was the only club to be seen at on a Friday night. Other than LAX, Pure or Moon. Or Marquee. And to a lesser extent XS and Jet. But since Sadie had us on the guest list for Tryst, there was only one winner.

After a bath-nap-shower combo, I was feeling almost human again, and I had nervous energy to spare when I thought about seeing Alex. Or, more to the point, when I thought about Alex seeing me in my outfit. Jenny had insisted I wear the Dolce star-spangled Band-Aid and over-the-knee boots, and I had given in. My hair had been forced into loose, bed-head waves, and in case people didn't assume slut as soon as they saw my outfit, I was wearing more MAC Blacktrack eyeliner than I knew existed. Obviously Jenny had been in charge of my make-up, so it managed to somehow err just on the right side of RuPaul. Light pinkish gloss and flawless foundation balanced out the eye make-up, so I didn't quite look like Alice Cooper. Not quite. Maybe by morning.

Jenny, of course, looked like a cosmetics commercial. Instead of my uncompromising black, her chocolate eyes were lined with various shades of bronze and brown, specs of gold lighting up her whole face. Sheer peach cheeks and matching gloss only heightened the luminous effect. It was as though she had her own lighting person constantly diffusing any harsh rays that might stumble across her face. One day, one day, I would manage that effect myself. Until then, it was racoon eyes for me. At least it covered up the real dark circles.

'Ready?' Jenny asked, shuffling the hem of her dress around under her bottom.

'Ready,' I confirmed. 'Are you sure about going to Tryst?'

'Um, yes?' She looked up. 'The dress isn't too much?

'I would wear that everywhere, every day if I looked like you right now,' I replied. The more I stared at her, the more incredible she looked. From one side, the dress looked like nothing more than a fitted black mini, long sleeves, high neck cut to hug every curve. But when she turned to give me the full frontal, the solid black fabric drew across her waist in a point, whittling it away to nothing. The rest of the dress was made of beautiful, delicate lace lined with silk the exact shade of Jenny's honeyed skin. 'But really, Tryst? Should we absolutely positively be going to the hotel Jeff is staying at?'

'So it's a thumbs-up?' She gave me a spin, picked up her purse and ignored my question. 'Let's go.'

'Jenny – ' I blocked her path to the lift. 'Jeff?'

'Angela – ' she gave me a terrifying look. 'Let it go.'

I let her push past me and call the elevator, while

wondering how I could rearrange Alex. Just because we were both going to be in the Wynn didn't mean he would definitely be in Tryst. Alex wasn't a dance club kind of a guy, and I didn't think Jeff was either. I could probably sneak off early and meet him in the casino. Or in his room. I really was missing him. I knew there were a million reasons Jenny didn't want to deal with this, the most likely one being that she was still a little bit heartbroken. I tried to push it out of my mind and concentrate on having a great time. Shouldn't be too hard.

Leaving the lift and walking side by side with someone who was dressed to ruin the life of every man she met gave me enough borrowed confidence to hold my head up high and work my own ensemble. We were almost through the lobby when I spotted the same family we'd met earlier in the lift. The boy Jenny had scared so effectively did a double-take. This time he looked terrified. Jenny threw him a wink. He paled visibly, and I was fairly certain we had witnessed his transition from boy to man. Someone would be having funny feelings in the night tonight.

'Glad you got dressed up?' Jenny asked quietly as we arrived at the Wynn. I nodded. Glad was an understatement.

Immediately I understood Jenny's commitment to turning out. This was the only place on earth where it was impossible to be overdressed. Every lily was gilded. And then studded with diamonds. And then gilded again. Velvet ropes vanished from view as we made our way into Tryst, and in mere moments we were seated at a table and supplied with a bottle of Grey Goose and various mixers. I sat back and tried to take everything in. Without flashing my knickers.

At least tonight they weren't giant, pink or cotton. I had totally committed to my outfit and gone the full Agent Provocateur. Sadie would be proud.

'Oh my God, you actually look, like, good.'

Speak of the devil and see his horns.

The look of surprise on Sadie's face was softened slightly by the level of drunk in her eyes. Someone had been pre-partying. For some time.

She pulled me upright, span me around and cackled with laughter.

'Is that D&G? Jesus, Angela, who dressed you?'

'I did.' An arm swept around my waist and dipped me backwards into a theatrical welcome. I didn't get a chance to stop him before I felt Ben's lips graze mine. Before I knew what was happening, I was upright again and he was repeating his hello on Sadie. Well, that wasn't unpleasant. Jenny, on the other hand, looked like someone was about to slap her around the face with a kipper. Ben swooped in on her before she could run, but this time, instead of a peck on the lips, Jenny was on the receiving end of a smacker of old Hollywood proportions. I stood goldfishing as Sadie clapped her hands together in delight.

'Right.' Jenny wiped her mouth with the back of her hand as soon as she was upright and turned her back on Ben. 'Shots?'

'I'll be right back,' Ben whispered. A promise and a threat, according to the look on Jenny's face.

'I didn't know you knew Ben?' Sadie cried, turning to our table and popping a bottle of bubbly. A bottle that hadn't been there two minutes earlier. I scanned the room for the booze fairy but couldn't see anyone. Shit, this was a classy joint.

'Just from when I was styling,' Jenny said. 'You guys worked together?'

'When he used to shoot, yeah.' Sadie handed me a glass of champagne without actually looking at me. Still. Baby steps. 'And he's just one of those guys who is always out in Vegas, you know?'

I did not know.

'Anyway, you guys look smoking.' Sadie looked back at me again, the shock melting into approval. 'We should dance.'

'We should dance,' Jenny agreed, pouring out generous shots of vodka. 'Here. To Vegas.'

'To Vegas,' Sadie and I repeated together.

The afternoon's martinifest was a distant memory, and so with a glass of champagne in one hand and a vodka in the other, I did the shot and promised myself a night worthy of my outfit.

It is a truth universally acknowledged that a club full of drunken women must have many and plentiful toilets. But as soon as I started looking for them, there was of course no loo to be found. At least not a ladies'. After three laps of the club and no better option in sight, I knocked on the door of the gents, poked my head around and bolted inside. This was a classy joint – surely I'd be safe using the gents just this once? As soon as I was safely in a stall, I really didn't care. But Sod's Law was applicable even in Vegas, and the second I started to relax, the door to my stall swung wide open and two bodies fell directly into my lap.

'Shit-shit-shit, haven't you heard of locking the door?'

In the scrum of pushing two men off my lap while simultaneously trying to pull up my pants, I recognized that voice. British accent, snogging another man in a public bathroom, causing me physical and emotional injuries? It could only be one man.

'James?'

'Angela?'

Dress up around my waist, pants on full display and eyes wide open, I threw my arms around James Jacobs' neck as though he was my long-lost fairy godfather. Well, it had been almost a year and he most certainly was a fairy, if you didn't mind the most politically incorrect 1980s' term-your-nan-might-use definition of the word.

'Shagging in the toilets again? Jesus, was George Michael a lesson to no one?'

'I'm not ram-raiding Snappy Snaps, am I?'

To the best of my knowledge, he wasn't.

'Cover yourself up, woman – don't you read the papers?' James hugged me back with the strength of someone who worked out by lifting combine harvesters for shits and giggles. 'I'm a total homo. Flashing your vajayjay this way won't help you in the slightest.'

'Really?' I gave him one last squeeze and pushed him away.

'Absolutely. They frighten the life out of me.'

'I forget what a good actor you used to be.'

'Not loving the use of the past tense there.'

James Jacobs was an actor I'd interviewed back in the heady days of actually having a job. And when I say interviewed, I do mean accidentally dragged kicking and screaming out of the closet. Something that apparently wasn't a problem now. I looked at his friend, aka the dark-haired, dark-eyed man standing staring at the floor and trying to surreptitiously fasten his fly. I couldn't help but notice it wasn't his beloved boyfriend Blake. Which I was fine with, because Blake hated me and, to be fair, I wasn't that keen either.

'What are you doing in Vegas? Reporting? Are you following me?' He shoved his shirt back into the waistband of his trousers with none of the subterfuge of his friend. 'Because I'm not a very exciting story any more, I'm afraid.'

'Not quite.' I held a hand out to the fly fiddler. It was always nice to be nice. 'Hi, I'm Angela.'

'Are you a man?'

And sometimes it wasn't necessary to be nice at all.

'No, I am not a man,' I spluttered, pointing directly at my boobs. And then remembering my knickers were still on public display. Bugger, I'd almost kept them covered for a whole day. Ish. 'Jesus.'

'Just . . . because you're in the men's bathroom, and, you know . . .' He shrugged and looked away again. This one was not the sharpest pencil in the box. 'You could be a man.'

'Do you want to wait outside for a minute?' James interrupted before I broke my duck on decking a man. 'I won't be long. Get me a drink?'

My new least favourite man on the planet exited the bathroom with a sulky expression. At least he didn't have a black eye to go with it.

'I can't believe you're here.' I gave him another big hug. Cliché or not, gay-friend hugs were the best. He was like a big, camp bear. Except not a bear. Too well groomed. 'How are you here?'

'I'm here all the time,' he said. 'Which you would know if you ever checked your Facebook messages. I've been telling you to get your arse out here for months. I thought you were ignoring me.'

'Oh, yeah,' I clucked. 'I don't do that. Like, ever. I can't cope with people posting about buying a new hoover. That and the fact that my mum friended me. Not OK. But what's with the new model? Where's Blake?'

'Blake dumped me.' He hopped up onto the sink

unit and pouted. 'Last month. Hence the "I'm here all the time".'

'Shit, I'm sorry.' I scrabbled up to sit beside him. 'I didn't know.'

'But you would,' he said, 'if you ever checked your Facebook messages.'

He made a good point.

'I did email,' I said feebly, trying to defend myself. 'But you were far more interested in talking to my boyfriend than to me.'

'I did mention I'm gay?' he replied. 'Anyway, I'm fine. It's fine. I've been busy, you've been busy. And to tell the truth, it was just too much, the Blake stuff. He wanted to stay in every night and stroke kittens and knit. I missed my life.'

'Is stroking kittens a new euphemism I don't know about?' Trust me to sit on the bit of the sink that was piss-wet. The dress might not show a damp spot, but it is never fun feeling like you've pissed yourself. 'Anyway, I'm sorry. And next time, call me.'

'There won't be a next time for a very long time.' He shook his curly head slowly. 'No more boyfriends for me for a while.'

'Does the offer to be your beard still stand then?' I hopped down from the vanity. As much as anyone can hop in three-inch-heeled thigh-high boots. 'It might work out for me about now, but we'd have to upgrade to marriage.'

He pretended to weigh up the option for a moment. 'Have you seen *Indecent Proposal*? How about I marry you if I can have a night with your bloke?'

'To play video games and eat pizza?'

'Let's say yes.'

'Done.' I leaned in for another, shorter hug. 'Speaking of whom, I'm supposed to be meeting him.'

'How long are you in Vegas for?' He dropped to the floor with far more grace than I would ever achieve. 'Can we hang out tomorrow?'

'Yes,' I promised, without having a clue what we were supposed to be doing tomorrow. 'Let's get a drink tomorrow night. I'm at the De Lujo – shall we meet in the bar?'

'Very fancy,' James said approvingly. 'Bar it is. Midnight?'

'Midnight?' I baulked. 'Bit late? I'm very lazy.'

'Angela, it's after two now,' he replied. 'And the night is very young.'

I looked at my watch. Bloody hell, it was. No wonder I was tired. And hungry. What time did the breakfast buffet open again?

'Midnight, then. I'll text you if anything changes. And you should come and have a drink with me now, save me from my friends.'

'I think I'm going to head out to Marquee,' James replied with a firm slap on my arse. 'Bloody hell, did you piss yourself?'

'Couldn't help myself,' I shrugged. 'I just met *the* James Jacobs.'

'Shut up, you cow.' He headed into one of the stalls. Alone for a change. 'See you tomorrow. Give Alex a big filthy snog for me.'

'Oh, I will,' I promised. 'In fact, I'll give him two.'

Tryst was beautiful. After one more glass of champagne and an hour of dancing with Jenny and Sadie, I decided to sit one out and take in the scenery. Half of the club was out in the open, and a huge golden waterfall tumbled down by the dance floor, backing the beat of the DJ with a rush of water. Aside from making me constantly need a wee, I thought it was amazing. I leaned back in my booth, curling my boots up underneath me, the leather soft and supple against my skin.

Despite Sadie's presence, we were having a great night. When the music was loud and her mouth was shut, she was almost fun to have around. Ben's concept of 'be right back' was apparently very different from everyone else's – he hadn't been seen since we walked in. His absence meant that Jenny relaxed a little, and relaxed Jenny was fun Jenny. I watched her throwing herself around the dance floor, busting out moves that Lady Gaga might think were crossing the line, and smiled. She needed to cut loose. I needed to cut loose.

I sipped what I promised myself was my last glass of champagne and waited for the buzz. I was already tippish, but was really pitching for pleasantly pissed. Much more pleasantly than I had been earlier in the day. Thank God I'd pigged myself stupid on the buffet: my stomach was adequately lined, even if my dress wasn't. It was hard trying to reach the perfect level of drunkenness in a noisy nightclub; far too easy to slip over the edge.

'Angie, get your ass up here,' Jenny yelled from across the dance floor. 'I want to dance with you.'

It seemed like a perfectly reasonable request so I uncurled and made my way towards her, but before I could reach my destination, I felt someone grab me under the arms and sweep me up off the floor. Was I being abducted? Was this an alien-themed hotel and I didn't know? Was the Wynn owned by Scientologists? I had seen someone who looked a bit like Tom Cruise earlier on. But no, once set safely on a firm surface, I turned to see that my abductor was just a very big man surrounded by several other very big men.

'Dance, honey.' Very Big Man Number One pointed

at something behind me. That something was a pole. Oh. 'Come on, you don't got no moves?'

'Wuh?' I seemed to be ever so high up off the floor.

'Your girl ain't got no moves!' Very Big Man Number Two slapped Number One on the back and laughed. 'My girl, she's gonna dance your girl into the ground.'

I spun quickly, too quickly, to see just who this allegedly stellar pole dancer was. Of course it was Sadie. Of course it was.

'Oh, Angela, just get down.' She reached one hand towards the pole and kicked her leg up high above her head to a hollering crowd down below. 'Just don't do it.'

'If I could get down, I would get down,' I said, dipping a toe over the edge of the platform to try and find the floor. Nope. No floor. Here I was, four feet up in the air on a six-foot-square platform being cackled at by fifteen hundred stag parties and a snarky super-model. Who wasn't that super. Supermodels didn't advertise sanitary towels as far as I knew.

'Oh my God.' She could barely stay on the pole for laughing. 'Oh my God, you can't even get down.'

'Do it, Angie!' Jenny bellowed, pushing her way to the front of the crowd. 'Do it!'

Now, it was true that I did not know how to do this, but that did not mean I was not going to do it. I had seen *Striptease* and what had been seen could not be unseen. And who said I didn't know how? I didn't know how to do a lot of things, but I'd learned how to do them. Admittedly sometimes I learned by falling flat on my face. I hoped and prayed this wasn't going to be one of those times.

'Angela, don't embarrass yourself,' Sadie laughed, spinning gracefully around the pole, landing on her toes and pushing her backside up into the air to the whoops of a very receptive audience. 'I know I make it look easy.'

'You mean slutty,' I called back. 'You make it look slutty.'

And with the same determination that had seen me carried out of Sing Sing when I refused to give the microphone back halfway through the entire score of *Les Mis*, I grabbed hold of the pole, reminded myself I would never see any of these people ever again as long as I lived, and danced. Danced like my life, the life of my child, ailing parent or whatever other plot device my movie needed depended on it. And it was sort of fun. Until Jenny started taking photos. But it was too late to back out now.

Soon enough, we had half the club watching us spin and twirl around. It was like the world's dirtiest maypole dance. At the front of the crowd, Jenny was screaming her encouragement, encouragement I did not need. What I lacked in Sadie's acrobatic skill, I made up for in enthusiasm. A delayed champagne buzz kicked in and I decided I was a natural. I was born to dance. I felt the power of all those who had gone before me coursing through my veins. This one was for Britney. And then, from the corner of my eye, I saw a group of guys, all in black suits, white shirts and black ties cheering me on. All except one of them. Tall, black hair falling over one eye, tie half undone, collar open. That one just stood there smiling, shaking his head.

'Alex!' I yelled, leaping from my pole into the crowd, pushing through the disappointed boos until I reached my man. My arms grabbed for him as soon as I was close enough not to fall over and coiled tightly around his neck.

'Tell me you didn't see? Did you see? Say you didn't see.'

'Oh, I saw,' he nodded. 'Nice work, Nomi.'

Leaving my new vocation behind without a second thought, I kissed him, not letting go until I was breathless. 'I missed you.'

'I missed you.' He pressed his lips against mine so hard that I could feel his heartbeat in the kiss. 'Come here.'

We stumbled backwards into one of the secluded booths at the side of the dance floor, Alex pulling a deep red curtain closed behind us and shaking off his suit jacket. I fell backwards on a blue velvet sofa. If it's called a sofa when it's seven feet square and doesn't have arms or a back. More picky people might call it a bed. Regardless, I felt like I hadn't seen him in months. And I felt like he hadn't touched me in even longer.

'You look amazing,' he whispered, a hand sliding up my leather-clad leg until it found warm skin. 'Vegas suits you.'

'Don't look so bad yourself,' I replied, my breath catching as his hand didn't stop. 'But I think that might be the end of my career as a professional dancer.'

My back against the cushions, my legs curled up at his waist, I grabbed hold of Alex's tie.

'I don't know, you looked kind of into it.' I felt his smile pressed against my lips. 'It's a noble profession. Or something.'

'Probably going to give writing one last shot.' I was struggling to maintain my train of thought. Hands. Hands were everywhere. 'Are you having a good time?'

'I am now,' he said, pressing his face into the curve where my neck and shoulder met and waiting for me to shiver exactly as he knew I would. His lips worked their way up my throat until they found my earlobe, while one hand ran restlessly through my hair and the other busied itself working my dress upwards. Not that there was far for it to go. I closed my eyes, letting my hands wander around a little themselves. Suddenly everything was hot and close and damp and good. Feet away from the dance floor but a world away from reality, I worked my way down to his belt buckle and unfastened quickly while I still had the ability to use my hands. He paused, swallowed, nodded and bruised my lips with his. I was having a hard time keeping control of myself, and the quicker Alex's kisses and the warmer his body became next to mine, the closer I came to giving in completely.

'Angela,' I felt him more than heard.

'Alex.'

'I love you.'

'I love you too.'

I had to whisper because I didn't trust my voice not to break. His face was too close to see clearly, but the bright green of his eyes, the white of his skin and the jet-black glossiness of his hair blurred into something magical, and it was the last thing I saw before I closed my eyes and I felt myself slip over the edge.

'We should leave.' Alex broke the sweaty silence moments, minutes or hours later. 'We should go.'

'We should go,' I agreed, tugging at the gossamer fabric of my dress. Not displaying my knickers in public was one rule I did try to live by. Tried and failed sometimes, but still, I tried. 'I should find Jenny, tell her I'm leaving.'

Alex nodded, combing my hair to one side. Thank God bed-head was the look I'd been going for. It was definitely the look I had now. Also known as 'scarecrow' or 'homeless lady'.

'I'll get a cab – meet me outside.' He kissed me

briefly on the cheek before pushing the curtain aside to leave.

I sat on the edge of the bed, swinging my legs like a little girl and waiting for the flush to leave my cheeks. Alex had vanished back onto the dance floor with slightly dishevelled hair, loosened collar and a George Clooney swagger. I was left with a fright wig, red-raw chin and matching cheeks. Hardly fair. I repaired as much of the damage as I could with my powder compact and replaced my lip gloss. There, totally presentable. I hopped up and opened the curtain to find Sadie clapping her hands in front of me.

'Oh my God, were you fucking?' She pressed her hands against her face with glee.

'No, I was not,' I said with a prim sniff, nose in the air. Not for the want of trying, but she didn't need to know that. 'Have you seen Jenny? I think I'm going to call it a night.'

'Oh my God, you were!' She flashed me a million perfect teeth. 'I saw your dude headed outside. Nice.'

If only I'd known the way to Sadie's heart was through public acts of indecency.

'So you'll tell Jenny I left?' I covered my chin as a reflex action. Stubble rash would hardly support my defence, and I didn't feel like getting into an argument. 'And you'll be OK?'

'I will be fine,' she said loudly, swigging directly from the vodka bottle I hadn't noticed in her left hand. 'I have, like, a million friends here. Thousands.'

My forehead creased with the effort of following her logic. 'But a thousand is fewer than – you know what, never mind.' I was drunk, but not that drunk. 'Please just tell Jenny I left?'

'She left an hour ago.' Second swig. 'With the Mr Blond.'

Oh bugger. She left with Ben?

'Left with to share a taxi or left with – you know?'

'She left with him the same way you're leaving with Alex. To bang his brains out.' Sadie held out the vodka bottle. 'Take a shot.'

'Very generous, but I'll pass,' I said, rubbing a ring finger under my eyes and trying to blink away the dry ice. 'I'll see you tomorrow. Get home safe.'

'Sure.' She planted a far too familiar kiss directly on my lips, drowning my subtle pinkish gloss in slashes of Russian Red. 'You be safe too.'

I was fairly certain we weren't talking about the same thing.

'There are condoms in my room.'

It was good of her to clarify.

CHAPTER THIRTEEN

The ride back to the hotel was frustratingly short, but I was sure it would be a toss-up as to who was more upset when we pulled up in front of the De Lujo – me, Alex or the cab driver. The uber-swank lobby of our hotel didn't even register with Alex as he pulled me straight into the lift and let me press the button. It was only when we tumbled straight through the open door to our suite and onto the floor that I remembered I needed to remember something.

'Jenny!' I grabbed a stray stiletto sitting on the floor beside my head.

'If you're thinking about Jenny right now, I'm doing something really wrong.' Alex sat up and settled his hand on my stomach.

'No, she left! Ben!' I waved the shoe in his face as though it would somehow make everything make sense.

'Ben?'

'Ben!' I nodded feverishly. 'She's here! I have to get her.'

'You know I think Jenny's hot, but I was really thinking this might just be me and you. Come here.'

Even though I got that speeding sensation in my

stomach when he spoke, I was full of drunken determination.

'Two minutes.' Prying his fingers from my beautiful dress, I attempted a straight line into Jenny's room. Give or take a couple of stumbles, I made it in under a minute. 'Jenny?' I stage-whispered, knocking lightly on the door. 'Jenny, are you in there?'

In my mind, I was doing a good thing. I was stopping a friend from making a big drunken mistake that she would regret in the morning. The fact that I was probably trading a night with Alex for an evening of hair-holding and silent sobbing was just part and parcel of best-friend martyrdom.

'Jenny,' I called a little louder. 'I know you're in there.'

I was her friend. And as her friend, there was no way I was going to let her throw her relationship with Sigge under a bus for the sake of a one-night-stand with an old one-night-stand. Yes, Ben was hot, but so was Sigge and he loved her. And she loved him. Jenny was impulsive and hot-headed, but she'd hate herself in the morning. She'd 'accidentally' cheated on someone she loved before and never forgiven herself. I wasn't about to let her make the same mistake again.

'*Jenny*,' I bellowed, banging on the door with my fist. 'Open this bloody door. Right. Now.'

After all the trouble she'd caused herself with Jeff, Sigge was a breeze. He was sweet, he was attentive and he knew how to make cookies. What else could a girl want? She would never throw all that away for a quick fumble on Ben if we weren't in Vegas. Probably. I heard the door click open slowly, quietly, as though not to wake a sleeping occupant, and waited impatiently. I was ready with my lecture. Ben was trouble, just like Jeff had been trouble.

But it wasn't Jenny behind the door. I looked up at the tall, completely naked blond man staring at me. Like I said, he was trouble.

'Jeff?'

'Angela.'

We stared at each other for a moment, Jeff quickly covering his manhood with his hands, me looking away, face bright red. For some reason, he was still wearing his tie and socks. It was not a sexy look.

'I, uh, Jenny?'

'She's asleep.' His face flamed scarlet, hopefully directing some blood back up to his brain. 'We're sleeping.'

Of course. Nothing going on here but a perfectly innocent, naked sleepover.

'Right then.' I tried to move but for some reason was completely glued to the spot. 'I'll let you go back to . . . sleep?'

'Yes. Sleep.' He shuffled back into Jenny's room. Through the open door I could see her, face down, passed out, completely starkers on the bed. Perfectly innocent. 'Thank you so much.'

'Of course.' I waved him away, over-politeness kicking in. You could take the girl out of England . . . 'Absolutely. Good night.'

Eventually, the humiliation fairies decided I'd done my time and released my feet, allowing me to sprint back to the lounge. Alex had done away with his jacket and tie (thank God) and was working on the third button of his shirt.

'This place is amazing.' He gestured towards the view. I couldn't even look . – the flashing lights were making me feel nauseous. At least, I wanted to blame the lights.

'It's not Ben.' Whispering was entirely unnecessary, but it felt appropriate. I paced around the room, trying to work out what to do.

'Angela, I don't know who Ben is.' Alex grabbed hold of my hand and held me still. But I didn't want to be still. I felt sick. 'Where's Jenny?'

'In bed!'

'With Ben?'

I looked to the sky for strength.

'With *Jeff*.'

'Oh. Shit.'

He sat down and sank into the couch with an air of defeat.

'Just come here.' This time, it was a completely different command. I curled up on the couch beside him, resting my head on his shoulder while he ran his fingers through my hair, or tried to. Elnett was a bastard to brush out sometimes. 'There's nothing you can do about this right now, so stop worrying about it.'

'I could go in there, slap her with a shoe and demand to know what she's thinking?'

'You could,' Alex acknowledged. 'But I think it's safe to say she isn't thinking right now. Just let it go.'

I lay against his chest for a quiet moment, trying to calm the swirling mess in my mind. Jenny, Jeff, Sigge, visa. Mew. Tired, drunk and emotional never went well with stressed, upset and exhausted. But instead of passing out, the combination left me restless and uncomfortable. Too tired to talk but too alert to sleep, I twisted and turned until I found my head in his lap and stretched my legs out over the arm of the sofa.

'Sleep?'

I shook my head and stared out of the window, letting everything blur together, waiting to feel better.

Instead, as soon as I was settled, the room started to spin on my behalf. Blee.

'Talk?'

I sighed and shook my head again, weaving my soft pale fingers through Alex's long, calloused hands and squeezing until everything settled. It took far too long. He brushed my hair away from my face while we lay in silence, rhythmically sweeping away my worries, one by one. Slowly, I began to relax. Either Alex had magic hands or I just didn't have the energy to be so tense any more. Possibly both. Either way, I was happier.

'Bed?' Alex spoke in a soft, quiet voice. I could only just hear him over the hum of the air conditioner.

'I'm not tired,' I replied with equal fragility.

'Good.' He leaned down with the gentlest, softest kiss. Right away, my mind let go of everything else and focused solely on the tingling in my lips. The insistence of the last time lingered but was tempered by the dawn that was starting to glow on the horizon. I returned his kisses lazily and shuffled along the sofa to make room for his long legs on top of mine.

'I can't believe it's only two days since I saw you,' he said with half-closed eyes. 'Feels like longer.'

'You were fine for more than a month not that long ago,' I reminded him. 'Can't have been that difficult.'

'Who says I was fine?' His hand trailed slowly down my spine. 'I managed. That's pretty much the best I can do when you're not around.'

'Liar.'

Alex pushed up off the sofa and held his hand out to me. His shirt was creased, hair all mussed up at the back. He looked adorable. 'I never lie. Not to you.'

The honesty and intimacy of the moment was just all too much. In lieu of a proper response, I pressed myself against him in another long kiss, then stood with my head tucked under his chin and listened to his heartbeat. I was a rubbish grown-up.

Alex kissed the top of my head and placed a huge hand on each of my hips.

'Bed.' He cocked his head towards the hallway. 'Now.' This time it wasn't a question.

The first thought that ran through my head eight hours later was, I wonder what's on the buffet this morning. The second was, why do I feel like shit. And the third was lost under a tumbling weight of the three thousand other things that were determined to send me mad. Rolling over, I looked for Alex to make it better, but he wasn't there. Damn giant memory-foam mattress. I took his absence as an opportunity to attempt to make myself look faintly more human, grabbing face wipes from the side of the bed and repeatedly dabbing day-old mascara away from under my eyes. Finally able to focus on the world around me, I noticed the piece of paper on my bedside table.

Headed back to the hotel. Call me later. A.

He had thoughtfully left his phone number after hearing the tale of the drowned BlackBerry, but wouldn't it have been more thoughtful if he'd, I don't know, stuck around until I woke up? For a moment I thought about being annoyed, but it seemed too much like hard work. Also, I caught a glimpse of the alarm clock and it was past twelve. He probably had plans. With Jeff.

Jeff.

Jenny.

Jenny and Jeff.

Oh cock.

As much as I did not want to, I forced myself out of bed and into the lounge. Jenny's shoes had vanished from the hallway and been replaced by Sadie's, and a room-service trolley sat quietly in the corner, pretending it wasn't there. I almost turned around and went back to bed, but an out-of-place blanket on the sofa caught my attention.

'Hi.'

The top of Jenny's head peeped out from under the covers, her rebel curls giving her away.

'Morning.'

I stood stock still, arms folded, brain quickly trying to decide what expression to adopt. Was I supposed to be mad? Sympathetic? Did I want the details? No. No, I did not want the details.

'So we have to be at the heliport thing at two.' She shuffled out from under the blanket and stretched like a dying cat. 'I cannot think of anything I would rather not do than get in a helicopter right now, but—'

'We're going in a helicopter?' I was awake. And easily distracted. 'Really?'

'I meant to tell you last night,' she nodded, rubbing her eyes far too hard for someone over thirty. 'Erin organized it as a Christmas gift.'

Lovely Erin. I was going to have to give her that scarf after all. And a hug.

'Yeah, so we need to leave in like, half an hour?'

'Jenny?'

'Angela?'

'What happened last night?'

She stood up, wrapped one arm around the opposite shoulder, showed off her best yoga stretch, then did the other, looking me in the eye with a shrug.

'Nothing.'

Well.

'Nothing?'

'Apart from you getting in touch with your inner Gaga?'

'What happened with you?'

'Nothing happened with me.' She actually laughed. 'I wasn't the one who decided to take up pole dancing then eff my boyfriend behind a curtain.'

'I didn't actually eff anyone,' I replied, desperately trying to suppress the memory of the pole dancing. That was going in the vault. But really? She was just going to pretend it didn't happen?

'Relax.' Jenny gave me a quick passing hug as she headed into the bedroom to get dressed. 'It's Vegas, it doesn't count. Crazy shit goes down.'

Colour me gobsmacked.

Apparently so, I thought. Like me pole dancing, meeting movie stars in the gents and a bit of selective amnesia.

The ride out to the heliport was more awkward than an awkward thing. Sadie, oblivious to everything as per, talked about herself and her fabulous evening dancing with James Jacobs (who she was sure wasn't really gay because of the way he kept looking at her – I just couldn't be arsed to burst her bubble) and how wonderful she felt. I suspected pharmaceutical intervention; there was no way someone could drink the way she had been drinking and still be so bloody chipper. Jenny encouraged her with the odd enthusiastic noise, but spent most of the car ride staring at the scenery, bottle of Vitamin Water permanently attached to her right hand, mobile phone to her left.

I stared at Jenny through very dark, very big sunglasses, ready to leap out of my seat at any moment and yell 'J'accuse!', but I didn't. I was mad at her for cheating on Sigge. I was mad at her for sleeping with a man who was engaged. But mostly I was mad at her for lying to me. I was hurt. My sensible voice, which weirdly often took a similar tone to Louisa's, reminded me this wasn't about me. Maybe she was genuinely hurt and confused and just wasn't ready to process what had happened out loud.

But then my more judgemental voice, which sounded not at all weirdly just like my mother, pointed out that she had lied to my face and I had every right to be angry. I didn't know what to do. Maybe Jeremy Kyle was on Twitter. He'd know. It didn't help that the righteous indignation voice was much louder and more persuasive when accompanied by a soundtrack of Sadie and an increasing headache.

I looked at Jenny and sulked. I wished I had some Vitamin Water.

After the longest car journey in the history of man, we bundled out of the car into blazing sunshine that was disturbingly cold and were led into a small boxy office, given unflattering to everyone-alive-except-for-my-two-friends jumpsuits and made to stand on a scale. As if I didn't feel bad enough.

'OK, ladies.' A young man in shorts, T-shirt and trainers stood in front of us chewing loudly and visibly. 'This is what's going down. My name is Cody. We're gonna fly out to the Canyon, circle around a little so you can take some pictures, and then we're gonna set down, take a little walk and head back. Should be about two hours. Now, concerns? Questions?'

I only had one.

I raised my hand.

'Are you the pilot?'

'Yes, ma'am,' Cody replied with a curt nod.

All of a sudden, I didn't feel terribly happy about the helicopter. Pilots were like doctors. They were supposed to be older than you and always wearing a suit. Or at least proper shoes. And they were almost certainly never called Cody. They had respectable, no-nonsense names like Peter or Brian or Colin. I bet no one called Colin ever crashed a flying vehicle. Anneka Rice never got into a helicopter with someone chewing gum. And if Anneka didn't do it, I wasn't doing it.

'I can assure you I am full-trained, ma'am.' He winked at me. Not helping. 'Eight months' professional flying and no fatalities.'

Eight months?

'Hey, as long as he's never crashed it, right?' Jenny rested a hand on my shoulder. 'It's fine.'

'I didn't say I've never crashed one, just no fatalities,' Cody said, laughing heartily. 'Now, let's get you ladies strapped in.'

Sweet Jesus, this was how I was going to die.

'Uh, Angela?' He pointed at me. I raised my hand obediently, much to Sadie's amusement. 'You were the heaviest, so you're in the back.'

Always a delight to hear.

'And then Jenny? You're in with Angela. Sadie, you're in the front with me.'

I chose to ignore his gooey expression and just hoped he was still able to keep this thing in the air with an erection. Sadie flashed him a smile and did this annoying little thing with her shoulders. It wasn't quite a shrug, it wasn't quite a shimmy, but it successfully displayed her boobs to full effect and simultaneously pissed me off.

Once we were inside, we were issued with headsets and microphones and informed this was how our pilot, bloody Cody, would communicate with us and how we would communicate with each other. I made a bet with myself as to how many pop culture references Tom Cruise would get in during the journey. I hoped for *Airplane!*, anticipated *Top Gun*. I was never terribly keen on being fastened into anything, so allowing a man who made jokes about crashing helicopters to strap me into a helicopter immediately before he flew it over a canyon did not make me feel good. I'd been so excited at the idea of the trip and then so annoyed with Jenny, I hadn't really thought about the reality of buzzing around the skies feeling like shit. I'd never been in a helicopter before. I was a good flier, after my second drink, but this was something very different. Plane plus a gin and tonic equals a happy Angela. Helicopter plus several pints of vodka the night before equals a very unhappy, incredibly nauseous Angela.

As soon as we were in the air, it became a me-against-the-world fight not to puke. And I was not going to lose. I'd done all the public puking I had any interest in doing. In fact, not vomming outside my own bathroom was going to be one of my New Year's Resolutions. Along with not being deported, getting an iPhone like the rest of the world and always having some kitchen towel. We never seemed to have kitchen towel. Something that would have come in incredibly handy at that precise second as the helicopter lurched forward, as did the contents of my stomach.

'You OK?' Jenny asked.

'Do I look OK?' I replied.

She pulled an 'ooh, handbags' face and settled back into her seat, staring out of the side of the helicopter. I tried to do the same, to gaze out onto the natural wonder of the desert, the golden crevices beneath us. But all I could think was, what a silly place to bury

Megatron, there are all these natural giants' steps he could use to escape. It was testament to just how shit I felt that my brain couldn't accept that *Transformers* was not a documentary. And so while we flew around one of the world's natural wonders in our own private helicopter, while Jenny and Sadie oohed and ahhed, while the pilot played the theme music from *Top Gun*, I closed my eyes, rested my forehead against the cool glass and patiently waited to land with my eyes closed.

It took another fifteen minutes before I had the balls to look out of the window. It really was beautiful. All the colours of a Bloomingdale's autumn catalogue – brown, gold, bronze, tan and deep, deep reds, highlighted with a little green here, a ribbon of blue there. Clearly I had been friends with Jenny for too long.

'Hey, are you OK really?'

She gave me a nudge and a concerned look. But the concern felt fake and the nudge just made me retch. Again. Right, enough was enough.

'No,' I snapped. 'I'm not OK. Are you OK?'

'I'm fine?' She looked at me as though I'd gone crazy. Charlie Sheen crazy.

'Really?'

'Yes?'

'Uh, guys, you know we can hear you, right?' Sadie's voice crackled through our headphones.

Unfortunately for Sadie and Cody, I didn't give two shits.

'Nothing you want to tell me?'

'No?'

'Really, Angela, we can hear every word.'

'Piss off, Sadie. Nothing?'

'Nuh-uh.'

'Right.'

'OK, then. Jesus.' She turned back to the view and

took her phone out of her bag to read a new message. A message I could quite clearly see was from Jeff.

'Give me that phone.' My arm shot out entirely of its own accord and grabbed for Jenny's iPhone, but she was not giving it up.

'Uh, ladies.' Cody's voice piped up in my headphones. 'It's usually best not to fight in a helicopter.'

'Get off me, you psycho.' Jenny gave as good as she got, struggling against her seatbelt to bash me on the top of the head with the phone. Double insult. Before she could get in a really good swipe, I turned away, slapping my hands in the air as though I was doing the doggie paddle. Except, instead of water, I was doing it in Jenny's face. It was only fair that she try to defend herself. It was just unfortunate that defending herself redirected my slaps into the back of Cody's head.

'Holy shit!' he yelled. 'This stops or I'm turning this bird around.'

Just like my dad on the way to Alton Towers. He'd never do it.

'What is wrong with you?' Jenny shoved her phone deep into the bottom of her bag. 'Seriously? Are you drunk right now?'

'I know you shagged Jeff,' I bellowed at the top of my voice, right into my mic. 'I know you did, all right?'

The feedback shrieked through our headsets before I'd even finished screeching: Sadie and Jenny scrambled to protect their ears. Cody visibly clenched every part of his body and the helicopter swerved and dropped ever so slightly. But ever so slightly was just enough to push my poor stomach over the edge. Before I could grab for a sick bag, before I could hold back my hair, I puked all over Jenny's shoes. Thank God they were closed-toe.

*　*　*

203

Not nearly soon enough we were on the ground, just by the edge of the Grand Canyon, and I was curled up, head on knees, happy to be on solid ground. Jenny, on the other hand, was not so happy.

'Jesus, Angela?' she yelled. 'These are Tory Burch.'

It was never a good sign when she raised her voice at me.

'Sorry,' I mumbled. I wasn't sorry. I was pissed off.

'You thought that was a good time to talk about this? In a fucking helicopter?'

'Not especially,' I admitted. 'But you didn't seem very chatty earlier when you were merrily telling me nothing was wrong.'

'So I wasn't ready to talk about it.' She threw her arms up in the air, blocking out the sun. Even her silhouette was furious. 'I don't have to tell you every-thing that happens in my life. I don't actually have to tell you shit.'

'That's nice.' My sensible voice told me she was just lashing out because she was hurt. My mean voice told me she was a right old bitch who needed a good slap. 'Thanks.'

'Don't start with that tone, seriously.' She kicked a rock over the edge of the cliff. I took it as a warning and shuffled back a little. 'Don't start judging me. I'm sorry my life isn't as perfect as yours, but sometimes things don't go according to plan.'

'Are you kidding me?' If I'd had a goat, he'd definitely have been got. 'You're telling me things don't go according to plan? As if this is news to me?'

'Whatever – you know all this shit is going to work out for you.' She was shouting far too loudly for Cody's liking. It was interfering with his staring at Sadie as if she were a chocolate-coated FA Cup trophy. 'Alex is going to ride in on his white horse at the last minute and marry your ass so he doesn't have to do his own laundry, and everything is going to be OK.'

'I don't do his laundry.' In fact, he did mine. I was scared of the laundrette. 'And you know that's not going to happen.'

'No, I know you're pretending it's not going to happen.' Jenny dropped to the floor in front of me. 'Because you're scared he's going to say no if you ask.'

I hated when your friends could read your mind. 'No, I just want to stay here on my own terms,' I lied. Well, half lied. 'I'm not saying I don't want to marry Alex. I just don't want it this way. The visa or the marriage.'

'Then have fun back in England. I'm sure it's missed you.'

'I don't think it's that bothered,' I sniffed. 'There hasn't been a Facebook campaign or anything.'

She punched me in the arm. Hard. 'Angela, stop being an asshat about this and just do it. At least you know what you want.'

And so at last we got down to it.

'And you don't?'

Jenny breathed out loudly and tucked her hands up inside the sleeves of her sweatshirt.

'Maybe not.'

I didn't quite dare hug her – we were very, very close to the edge of a cliff – so instead, I pushed my foot out until it was touching her toes. The puke damage seemed minimal, so I didn't think I was putting my Converse at risk.

'Surely you're not going to throw everything with Sigge away over a one-night-stand?'

She stared at the ground, picking up loose stones and putting them back down again. Interesting answer.

'Are things with Sigge not good?'

'Things are fine. Great.' She still didn't look at me.

'Then . . .' It took me far too long to work it out. 'It wasn't a one-night-stand?'

At first she didn't move at all. And then, very slowly, she shook her head.

'And it hasn't just been in Vegas?'

More shaking.

'Oh shit, Jenny.' No time for fear of hurtling to my death now. I pushed myself onto my knees and crawled over to my friend. Under her hair, her face was streaming with tears. 'Why didn't you tell me?'

'Because I know I'm stupid.' Her voice was raw and scratchy already. 'It's so stupid. Things are going so well, and now this. But I can't stop it. I want to but I can't. And I didn't want you to think I was awful.'

Whereas this way, I just thought I was awful.

'Jenny, you can tell me anything. All that stuff I said to you the other night? About telling you everything? That works both ways. I will never ever judge you.'

She looked up disbelievingly.

'All right, I will never, ever be anything but supportive,' I corrected myself. 'I may occasionally judge a little bit, but that's because I'm an arsehole. Judging will be silent, support will be vocal. Always. I am always here for you. Even if I'm in England. You'll just have to Skype me in.'

'I just don't know what to do.' She lay back in the dirt and stared up at the clear skies. Wrinkling my nose at the dust and muck, I did the same. Solidarity, sister. 'Sigge is awesome. He's the sweetest guy I've ever dated, and, you know, I can see a future there. We have so much fun together, and I know he's really into this, but it's just . . . Jeff. You know?'

'How did it happen?' I asked, half closing my eyes. She was actually on to something with this lying-down

206

malarkey; my stomach settled and the deafening buzz in my head quieted itself to a low hum. Except that as soon as I didn't feel sick, I realized how badly I needed a wee. 'Only if you want to talk about it.'

'Remember that time he showed up at my apartment?' she started. Of course she wanted to talk about it. 'When I'd just met Sigge?'

'That was months ago. It's been going on since then?'

'No. No, he came over to talk.' I heard the air quotes in her voice. 'But I told him to go fuck himself and was all super-proud of myself for walking away. But then about a month later, he called and said he wanted to get things in a good place with us before he got married.'

Her voice faltered a little on the last word, and I reached out to hold her hand. After an accidental boob graze, I finally found her fingers.

'And I was really happy with Sigge by then – I felt like I'd be OK. So I said sure, figured I'd get some closure and make him buy me a really nice, really expensive dinner, but I guess we never made it to dinner. It was so weird. One drink and it was just happening. I couldn't believe it.'

Having witnessed a booze-fuelled Jenny and Jeff reunion show first-hand, I could believe it.

'But as soon as it was done, I felt horrible, like I just wanted out, but he said there were still feelings, and there are still feelings, but I have feelings for Sigge too. And he hasn't cancelled the wedding. I mean, he's here on his bachelor party, for God's sake.'

I thought back to the happy times when I only had a visa to worry about.

'So, what, you thought you'd come out here and change his mind?' I asked. 'Convince him not to go through with it?'

'I don't know what I was thinking. When I saw you last week, on Bedford? I'd been at his place. Your place – God, I don't know how you didn't bust me. He said he wanted me to break up with Sigge, then he'd call off the wedding. I said if he called off the wedding, I'd break up with Sigge. So we're kind of at a stalemate.'

'Do you want him to call off the wedding?'

'I don't know,' she said. Then laughed. Then started to cry. 'I want someone else to make the decision for me. If he gets married, it's over. For good.'

Jenny rolled over, dusting my face with Fekkai-scented curls and crap from the floor, and shoved her head under my chin. Nothing like a floor-snuggle between friends.

'I miss living with you, Angie,' she whined. 'This wouldn't be happening if you were home. This stuff never happened when you were there.'

'This exact stuff happened when I was there,' I replied. 'I mean, literally this. I think you have to decide what you want. You can't let Jeff decide for you. And if things aren't right with Sigge, Jeff or no Jeff, you should break that off.'

'But they are right,' Jenny sighed. 'I know it sounds stupid, but I am in love with him. When Jeff isn't around, my brain flicks a switch and he doesn't exist. And all I want is to raise little Vikings in the suburbs with Sigge. He makes me really happy. Honestly. What do I do?'

I knew she wasn't lying, but I just didn't have an answer. I'd never been in a situation where I was in love with two people. I'd been in a situation where I was sleeping with two people, and I couldn't even cope with that. Throwing big fat feelings into the mix did not sound like fun.

'You genuinely couldn't choose between them?'

'When I think about losing Sigge, it makes me feel sick and sad. When I think about losing Jeff, it just seems impossible. Like, my brain just won't even acknowledge that it's possible. That we're inevitable.'

'But does he make you happy?'

'No.' She paused. 'But I love him.'

'Bugger.'

'Yeah.'

She sniffed loudly. 'Maybe I should just throw myself in the canyon. Oprah isn't on TV any more, I saw the last Harry Potter movie. What is there to live for?'

I tried really hard to think of something helpful. 'We still haven't seen the last *Twilight* film?'

'I read the book. They all die.'

'Really?'

'No. Dumbass.'

And then she started crying again. With nothing better to contribute, I joined in.

'So, your friends? They're like, together, right?' Cody whispered far too loudly to Sadie. 'The scene earlier – lovers' tiff?' Apparently the roar of the helicopter blades made him both deaf and stupid.

'Just dumb,' Sadie replied with reluctant affection. 'They're just real dumb.'

I faired considerably better on the return leg of the flight and spent most of it idly patting Jenny's hand, staring out at the Hoover Dam and wondering if it wouldn't just be easier if Jenny and I married each other. All to the tune of 'Take My Breath Away'. Jenny's dilemma made mine seem so much simpler. I loved someone. He loved me. I didn't want to leave, he didn't want me to leave.

'You know, if you just tell him you're all out of

options, I bet Alex will suggest the marriage thing anyway,' Jenny said, displaying worrying evidence of her mind-reading skills once again. 'I'm just saying.'

'I did say I'd see him later.' I gave her a tiny shrug. 'I suppose I do have to talk to him about what's happening. With the job and stuff. See what he says.'

'It's not a bad thing, you know,' she smiled. 'A man you love wanting to marry you. Regardless of the motivation. Anyway, would you marry someone you didn't love just because they needed a visa? I sure as hell wouldn't.'

'Probably,' I nodded back. 'I'm not very good at saying no. Terribly polite.'

Jenny laughed in agreement. 'Remind me of that the next time I need a favour.'

'Because me waitressing at your cocktail party wasn't enough fun?' I shuddered at the memory of peeling sweaty latex from cold skin.

'Actually, yeah,' Jenny said, shuddering at the memory full stop. 'We're good.'

'Thought so.'

I said goodbye to the rivers and rocks and wild horses as Cody announced we were ten minutes from landing and, more importantly, ten minutes from a toilet. All the natural majesty the earth had to offer couldn't compare with how badly I needed a wee.

CHAPTER FOURTEEN

Jenny let me use her phone to call Alex on the understanding that I was not allowed to spend the entirety of our last night in Vegas 'macking on my man'. Given that I didn't really know what macking meant, first I made the promise and then I made the call.

'Hello?' He answered on the third ring.

When a number I didn't know called me, I stared at my phone until it went away and then ignored the little voicemail icon on the screen until the number beside it was in double figures. Alex, however, had a debilitating phobia of voicemail and almost always answered his phone. Given his previous life as the village bike, this occasionally led to some very awkward conversations at three a.m. on a Saturday morning. Honestly, who keeps a booty call number in their phone for two years? Not that I'd ever had a booty call number to keep in my phone in my entire life, but still. I thought it was weird.

'Hey, it's me, I'm on Jenny's phone.' I examined my fingernails and frowned. I was in need of a manicure, desperately. This hand was not wedding-ring ready.

'Good to have her number,' Alex replied. 'That girl needs to be kept on a leash.'

'I know.' I silently reprimanded myself and shoved my hand into my jeans pocket. Horse then cart, not cart before horse. 'She says hi.'

'She's there? I won't ask what happened this morning then. Until tonight. We still on for later?'

Number three hundred and forty-two on the Reasons I Loved Alex list. He was a secret gossip. He could pretend he wasn't all day long, he could turn his nose up at as many copies of *Us Weekly* as he liked, but it didn't find its way into the bathroom on its own and I certainly didn't take it in there. Often.

'We're still on. I actually have a couple of things to talk to you about.'

Like, how much we're supposed to tip our doorman for Christmas and also, whether or not you would like to marry me. Immediately.

'Did you steal eighty million dollars?'

'No.'

'Marry Elvis?'

'No.'

'Steal Mike Tyson's tiger?'

'Yes, but that's not what I wanted to talk to you about.'

A vision of Alex in a white jumpsuit with a giant quiff popped up far too easily. He could totally rock a quiff.

'Where d'you want to go?' he asked, putting my fantasy right back in its box. 'Anywhere you're desperate to hit up?'

I went through my mental list. Sharks at Mandalay Bay. Lions at MGM. White tigers at the Mirage. The Forum shops at Caesars. The all-you-can-eat buffet anywhere. The more I thought about it, the more it seemed like my ideal vacation spot was actually the café inside the gift shop at the Bronx Zoo. Unless . . .

'The Venetian?' I suggested. Was there a better setting to propose a marriage of convenience than a casino modelled on the most romantic city in the world? A fraudulent marriage in a fraudulent Venice. Perfect. And excellent positive thinking on my part.

'Awesome. They have a great casino.' I'd forgotten about his secret love of gambling. Going crazy on the blackjack table wasn't really in my plan. 'Not that we're going to spend all night gambling,' he added quickly. 'Although I feel like you might be kind of a good luck charm.'

'Have we not met?' I ran a hand through my hair. Ew. Helicopter head. It needed washing. 'Is earlyish OK? I promised Jenny we'd go out later, what with it being the last night and everything.'

'So I'm the warm-up act – nice,' he said with a smile in his voice that I hoped would still be there after our conversation. 'Of course. The guys have some big crazy night planned and if I'm not there, I'm pretty sure his best man will hunt me down and kill me. Dude is intense.'

'So, seven-thirty? At the Venetian?'

'Done and done. Can't wait.'

'You're meeting at the Venetian?' Jenny asked when I handed the phone back. 'Awesome. We should get dinner at Bouchon once you've done the deed. Celebrate.'

Ever since she'd made her confession, Jenny had been a new woman. Honesty was good for the soul and also, it seemed, the complexion. She bounced around the lounge of our suite, pulling outfits from the samples Ben had sent over while I tried to avoid the mirror beside me. Neither Jenny's confession nor the helicopter ride had been good for my soul or my

213

complexion. I looked like death. And the racks and racks of designer ensembles made my heart hurt. Mostly because I knew we had to send them back when we left.

'You sure you don't mind?' I sighed at a floor-length black gown and silently sobbed for my butchered blue dress. 'Me seeing Alex, I mean.'

'No way.' She pulled out a hot pink body-con number that made me instinctively suck in my gut. 'I need a little time to unwind before tonight. I haven't tried to party for three nights in a row for a long time. If I don't sleep, I might die.'

'And if Jeff calls?'

'Then I'll talk to him.' She traded the pink for an emerald-green kimono thing. Mmm, roomy. Perfect Christmas dinner dress. 'Like you're going to talk to Alex. Do you know what you're going to say?'

'Nope.'

'Do you know what you're going to wear?'

At last, an important question.

'I was thinking maybe the blue one I tried on yesterday.' I flicked lovingly through the silks, satins and chiffons. So. Many. Sequins. 'It was so pretty. And I think I could eat quite a lot in it without looking too fat.'

'These are essential facts to take into account,' Jenny nodded gravely. 'But what about this?'

She pulled out what might have been the most beautiful dress I had ever laid eyes on.

'Tibi. You like?' She swished the coral-pink silk in front of me. Delicate pleats fell from an empire waistline in a sartorial sigh. I wanted to marry it. I would definitely want to marry me in it. Hopefully it would have the same effect on Alex.

214

'Sadie has some nude Choos that would go with it perfectly.' She passed it over, fiddling around in a white cotton dustbag. 'And you should wear this clutch.'

It wasn't just a clutch, it was a work of art. The bag was long and slim, lovingly made from midnight-blue velvet with a silver skull clasp. And just the right shape to use as a weapon in case I needed to beat someone to death. Something I always looked for in a handbag.

'It's McQueen,' Jenny stated, as though it explained everything. 'It is more precious than your life.'

'Ooh.' I held out my hands. 'Gimme.'

Between the dress, the bag and Sadie's shoes, that was my outfit sorted. I smiled at myself in the mirror. Just the words to worry about now. And how hard could that be? I was a writer, for God's sake. Ha.

Several hours later, I arrived at the Venetian looking as good as I'd ever looked. My hair was soft, shiny and pinned back from my face, my make-up was subtle but glowing, and my dress was incredibly pretty. The fact I couldn't really walk in Sadie's four-inch pale gold Choos took a tad of the shine off the overall effect, but as long as I didn't have to hobble far, we were all good. I was practising my best Lady Penelope walk when I heard someone wolf-whistle.

Turning as quickly as my shoes would allow, I wished I had my camera. Man alive, my boyfriend was a good-looking man. He was leaning against a marble column in a suit that would have made Don Draper have a little cry. Sharp, slim, slate grey, complete with waistcoat and pocket square. I felt weak at the knees. And a lot of other feelings that were far less ladylike.

215

'Well, hello, beautiful.' He sauntered over and kissed me on the cheek as though we always met outside Vegas hotels dressed like characters from *Mad Men*. On your average day, we met outside the bathroom dressed like characters from *Happy Days*. Acting like characters from *Happy Days*.

'Hi.' I took the arm he offered and blushed. Something about his suit and my dress was having a strange effect on my hormones. 'You look amazing.'

'Why, thank you.' He brushed imaginary fluff from his lapel. 'I bought it today.'

The sharp lines made his shoulders look broader and his waist even narrower, and when he did a slow spin for me, his arse looked really very lovely. 'Did you win big or something?'

'I'm up,' he replied mysteriously. 'We don't have to worry about the rent this month, anyway.'

'Ooh, will you buy me something pretty?' I was never one to miss an opportunity. Or a cliché. I'd always wanted to be a gangster's moll.

'Looks like you already bought yourself something pretty.' He nodded appreciatively at my dress. 'It's nearly as cute as you.'

'Whatever,' I laughed and shook my head. Beaming.

He paused, cupped my face in his hands and leaned down to kiss me properly. 'You look beautiful,' Alex whispered. 'Whether you like it or not, OK?'

'OK,' I mumbled. 'Thank you.'

Damn you, hereditary inability to take a compliment.

Once we'd established how pretty we both looked, Alex resumed position, leading me through the Venetian to I didn't know where.

'I'm not entirely sure when I'm going to wear it back in Brooklyn, but hey, it's a suit, right? There's always a reason to have a suit.'

'We'll have to go to lots of terribly fashionable cocktail bars in the city,' I suggested. 'Or we'll throw a party or something.'

'Yeah, someone will get married eventually –' He held the door open – 'and I can't turn up at another wedding in my jeans.'

The mere mention of the 'W' word was enough to quicken my pulse to double-time. My heart was pounding to the point of panic attack and we weren't even inside yet.

'I guess we're gonna have to go to Jeff's wedding, actually,' he carried on, completely unaware of my impending stroke. 'Now I'm in the wolf pack.'

'He did not call it that.'

'He did,' Alex confirmed sadly. 'One of the guys had T-shirts made, but we made an executive decision not to wear them since, you know, we're not twenty-one.'

'Boys on Tour.' I couldn't see Alex in a screen-printed stag-do T-shirt any more than I could see Jenny in a pink glittery cowgirl hat, draped in L plates, adorned with penis deeley boppers. Actually, that was a lie. She'd love that. 'They didn't mind you hanging out with me?'

'Please refer to the "we are not twenty-one" comment,' he replied. 'And yeah, the best man sulked a little, but Jeff was cool with it. He wanted a little alone time too.'

'As long as he is alone.' I thought back to Jenny's Grand Canyon meltdown. 'Things are a mess.'

'So I'm guessing it wasn't just a one-off thing?' Alex asked as we strolled through the casino. I pretended not to see his eyes darting from table to table.

'Nope, it's been going on for a while,' I said, trying hard not to be distracted myself. 'How did you know?'

'Female intuition. And Jeff kind of tried to explain this morning.'

'He did? What did he say?' I was fascinated to hear the boy's side of things. It was like listening in on a secret conversation. That hardly ever made sense.

'That they had some stuff to work out, that there's some history there. I told him I didn't need to know and we left it there.' He looked perfectly happy with this conclusion. 'The guy was clearly uncomfortable.'

'Well, yeah,' I agreed while silently sulking that he wasn't nearly nosy enough for my liking. 'We don't have to talk about it.'

'Right.'

'Right.'

As we passed through the hotel, I couldn't stop staring at the people hanging around on the casino floor. It seemed like the entire world had descended on the Venetian to get their gamble on. Row after row of shiny slot machines were manned by row after row of glassy-eyed women, one hand hovering over the shuffle button, elaborate cocktail in the other, giant cup of quarters nestled between their knees.

The tables were another story altogether. It took me a moment to work out why the outfits improved as the tables got smaller, but then it clicked. The lower-limit tables were bigger and the gamblers were squeezed more closely together, all jeans, T-shirts and bumbags. The high-roller tables were smaller and more spacious, with a clientele all suited and booted, even this early in the evening, and while there weren't too many women at the tables, there were plenty around. The general rule seemed to be, the higher the limit, the lower the neckline. Regardless of how many thousands of dollars or cents were up for grabs, the hooting and hollering was universal. It made *Planet of the Apes* look like a civilized affair. Maybe I didn't need to visit the zoo after all.

'So it's an actual affair?' Alex broke my train of thought with the word we do not use. 'He didn't really say how long it had been going on.'

Ha, I knew he would break.

'It's something.' I couldn't stand the word affair. It was just a fancied-up word for cheating, dressing up something terrible as romantic, passionate and understandable. The English language equivalent of lipstick on a pig. 'I don't think Jenny even knows.'

'So she doesn't know what's going on, but she's still sleeping with an almost married man.' Alex made a very distinct clucking noise in the back of his throat. Not unlike something my mum might do. 'Classy.'

Sometimes, just sometimes, boys could be total arseholes.

'And Jeff isn't to blame in the slightest?' I could feel my hackles rising.

'Sure he could have said no, but so could she. She's the one who chased him to Vegas.'

'She didn't chase him to Vegas.' Although she sort of did. 'She's really struggling with this, you know.'

'Then why doesn't she just stop?' he asked. 'Instead of taking advantage of his cold feet.'

I couldn't believe what I was hearing.

'So this is all Jenny's fault? The man who is actually engaged to another women but still pursued his ex, telling her he loved her, telling her he would cancel the wedding if she broke up with her boyfriend, has got nothing to do with it?' I was quite aware that my voice was very, very high and just the teensiest bit psychotic, but I did not care. This was bullshit.

'That's what she told you?' he laughed. 'You believe her?'

'Of course I believe her.' I stopped and all but stamped my little foot and almost lost a Choo in the process.

'All I'm saying is, Jeff is still getting married. I'm here for his bachelor party?' Alex turned to place reassuring hands on my shoulders but I shook them off. I didn't want to be reassured, I wanted him to apologize for being a knob. 'And Jenny is kind of a loose cannon when it comes to guys. Specifically Jeff.'

'Because you have always conducted yourself impeccably in all matters of the heart and trousers?' I slapped his arm, hard.

'Wow.' Alex took a step back, his Don Draper hair coming undone and falling in front of his pissed-off face. 'We're going there?'

There wasn't enough time to listen to all the voices in my head before I had to say something. I really didn't want to pick a fight about Jenny, about Jeff, about Alex's slutty, slutty past or anything else, but I couldn't not defend my friend. He was completely out of order.

'No.' I rubbed my forehead, trying desperately to reverse out of this cul-de-sac of bullshit. 'But you can't honestly believe that this is all so incredibly black and white? You can't actually be placing all the blame on Jenny.'

'She loves drama — you know she loves drama.' The smile was completely gone from his voice. 'What's more dramatic than some tortured affair with a married man?'

'And the fact that he's trying to emotionally blackmail her into breaking up with Sigge?' We had officially reached hands on hips stage.

'Whatever.' Alex dismissed my argument with one very annoying word. 'The guy is getting married. He's done nothing but talk about his fiancée all weekend.'

'Apart from when he's been shagging my best friend blind?' I questioned.

Alex breathed out loudly, closed his eyes and opened them again.

'Hey, here's an idea.' He took my hands from my hips and held them in his. 'We agree they're both totally dumb, we're awesome, and how about we start tonight again?'

It still wasn't an apology. It still wasn't him admitting he was bang out of order. But it was probably a good idea since I was planning to ask him to marry me. You couldn't really call someone a cock and then pull a proposal out of the bag.

'Fine.' I slapped both of his hands awkwardly and nodded towards what looked like, but I was fairly sure wasn't three hours after sunset, natural daylight. 'Shall we?'

Alex gave me his best lopsided half-smile and nodded. 'We shall.'

Almost as soon as I walked through the doors into the Grand Canal shopping mall, I lost my tiny mind. Without leaving the state of Nevada, we had been magically transported directly to Italy. The stone floor, the bright blue skies, the columns, the archways and, bugger me, the bloody canal. It probably helped that (a) I had a very strong willing suspension of disbelief and (b) I'd never been to Italy – but woah. I looked back over one shoulder. Yep, definitely still a casino. Amazing.

Wandering around, Alex seemed to be as lost for words as I was. It was incredible, as though someone had given a group of drama students an unlimited budget and a *Rough Guide to Venice* then said 'We want that. But with a Banana Republic.' But it wasn't just the shops that gave it away. I was fairly certain this version of Venice wasn't entirely accurate. For one thing, it didn't smell, and I had definitely heard that the Grand Canal was a bit ripe. Plus I was pretty sure there wasn't a Nathan's Famous Hot Dogs or a Panda Express in the original Venezia. Probably just as many tourists wearing baseball caps, but fewer human statues. I hoped. The whole effect was incredibly disconcerting, and as I was already on edge, it felt like this place was testing my sanity. So far we'd been in hotels that were super-luxe rather than themed. I was officially too scared to visit New York, New York; I could only imagine what they'd stuck in there – a Pizza Express in the middle of Central Park maybe? The only thing that soothed my troubled soul was the abundance of Christmas trees. I really couldn't verify whether or not Italy approved of a twenty-foot Douglas fir covered in ribbons, baubles and enough lights per tree to put Blackpool to shame on every single street corner, but the Venetian certainly did. And I liked it.

'This place is weird,' Alex said.

'It is,' I agreed.

'You love it, don't you?' he asked.

'I do,' I confirmed.

The Venetian was fake and flashy and wonderful. The uber-kitsch always floated my boat, and anything to do with Christmas made me want to do the Snoopy dance. We had found my spiritual home.

'There's no hope for you. You know that, right?' Alex pulled me away from a group of opera singers and walked me further down the canal. 'I should have known better than to let you into Vegas. You're gonna be one of those old women serving at the Tropicana with a cigarette hanging out of her mouth telling everyone how the city stole your soul.'

'Will I have a massive bouffant and too much blusher?' I marvelled at the massive Madame Tussauds and let Alex lead the way, trusting him not to push me into the canal.

'And you'll tell anyone who'll listen how you came for a weekend and never left.' He draped his arm around my shoulders and sighed. 'Because Vegas was the thing that had been missing all these years.'

'It completes me.'

'I am so offended.'

'Really?'

'No. It's Vegas, baby.' He kissed the top of my head, the argument seemingly forgotten. On his part. 'So you said you had something you wanted to talk to me about?'

'I did.'

Eeep. I was absolutely not ready for this conversation. I was more scared than the time I had to tell Jenny that I'd spilled red wine all down her new cashmere sweater. And also that I had borrowed her new cashmere sweater.

'So, shoot.'

Panicking, I looked around. Surely there had to be some sort of distraction? I mean, there should at least be a man offering to get us a girl to our room in twenty minutes or less. If you couldn't rely on a pimp in Vegas, what could you depend on in this world? Without hookers, I went for the next best option. Gondolas.

'If I swear I won't fall in, can we please go for a gondola ride?' I gave Alex my best puppy-dog eyes. 'When in Rome?'

'We're not in Rome,' he said. 'We're not in Venice. We're not even in Italy.'

I traded my puppy-dog eyes for the 'just do as you're told' expression I usually saved for the times I needed him to go out to buy me tampons. I was pulling out the biggest weapons in my arsenal, but we were at defcon one here. And what was more romantic than a gondola ride in Venice?

After far too many seconds of deliberation, he kissed me on the forehead and waved towards the boats.

'The things I do for you,' he moaned.

This did not bode well, considering the next favour I was going to ask. But at least I was getting my boat trip. And hopefully not a wet bottom.

Climbing aboard the boat in the middle of faux St Mark's Square, I considered the fact that I should have agreed not to start singing 'Just One Cornetto', but since the reference would have been lost on my American boy, I just made that promise to myself. Getting into a gondola in four-inch heels was tricky. Getting into a gondola in four-inch heels without flashing your knickers was impossible. With Alex guarding my modesty, I just about managed to clamber aboard while keeping both of my promises. I was as surprised as anyone.

'Welcome to the Grand Canal of Venezia. My name, it is-a Guido,' the gondolier had the worse fake accent I had ever heard. He made the cast of *Jersey Shore* sound like they'd been spending every summer in Tuscany since The Situation was nothing but A Slight Concern. 'I will give-a you a guided tour around our beautiful-a water ways-a.'

'If I give you ten bucks, can you not?' Alex held out a ten-dollar bill. I held my breath. Guido pocketed it in a heartbeat.

'*Grazie, signor.*'

He actually looked quite relieved.

'So when you're not pole dancing and Jenny isn't banging her ex, what have you guys been getting up

224

to?' Alex asked, sliding in beside me at the end of the gondola. It was not comfortable.

I considered his question for a moment and decided to ignore the Jenny comment for the time being. 'It has mostly been pole dancing and illicit sex,' I conceded, 'but I have also flown around the Grand Canyon in a helicopter, fallen in the Bellagio fountains, been shopping and eaten myself blind at the breakfast buffet.' It sounded quite exciting when I said it all out loud.

'Sounds like a good time.' He took hold of my arm and circled my wrist with his hands. 'I should handcuff myself to you so I don't have to go to another strip-club breakfast buffet.'

'Please tell me you're joking.' I covered his hand with mine. 'But it's not a bad idea. Maybe you could handcuff me to you, then when they come to deport me, they'll have to take you too.'

'Kinky.' He nuzzled my neck, momentarily knocking off my concentration. Damn him and his obscene cuteness. He did smell lovely.

'Speaking of deportation,' I started in my breeziest tone of voice, 'I have had a bit of bad news.'

'Oh?' He pulled away from the nuzzle. Proximity equalled fuzziness. Fuzziness equalled less terror. Less terror equalled easier conversation. Shit.

'Yeah.' I took a deep breath in, raised my shoulders and rolled my eyes. Totally relaxed. 'I haven't had a lot of luck with those pitches I put out. To get the media visa.'

'Just how much luck is not a lot?'

'Ooh, none?' Still breezy. Definitely breezy. More or less.

'And what does that mean?' Alex was not echoing my breezy. He was the opposite of breezy. His tone of voice was somewhere between an angry maths teacher and a youngish police officer.

'Um, I'm sort of running out of options on the old visa front.' I stared directly ahead, focusing on a teenage boy spitting off the bridge we were about to pass under. If he gobbed on this dress, so help me God, I'd give them a real reason to deport me. 'In that I don't really have any options.'

'Jesus Christ.' He leaned forward, resting his well-dressed elbows on his well-dressed knees. I noticed for the first time how shiny his shoes were. It was weird to see him out of trainers. I didn't like it. 'There must be something we can do? The whole neighbourhood is crawling with Brits.'

I gave the boy on the bridge my filthiest look. He stood up straight and shoved his hands in his pockets. Brilliant – I had wasted my powers of mind control on the wrong boy.

'Well, either they know something I don't or they are "extraordinary",' I replied, trying to remember to breathe. 'Lawrence the Lawyer says I'm not.'

'What does Lawrence the Lawyer know?' Alex placed his hand over mine. It was meant to be a reassuring gesture, but all it did was make me incredibly aware of how sweaty my palms were. Sexy times. 'We'll work this out, I promise. Just let's get Christmas out of the way, OK?'

There was so much I didn't like about that sentence. Firstly, Christmas should never be 'gotten out of the way', it should be celebrated endlessly and dragged out until you get food poisoning from the leftover turkey, somewhere around mid-January. Secondly, Alex's resumed breeziness was altogether too authentic. He was not panicking enough. He should have been wailing, thumping the bottom of the boat and screaming,

'Why, Lord, why?' at the sky. The pretty, blue, painted-on sky. He could at least tear off his tie in frustration. Or maybe punch Guido. He was totally listening in.

'The thing is, there just isn't that much time,' I said hesitantly. 'To keep waiting.'

And there wasn't. The incredibly selfish people at the INS hadn't included a Christmas card in their lovely letter, so I assumed there wasn't a birth-of-baby-Jesus amnesty on deportation. Season of goodwill, my arse. 'And I don't want to ruin Christmas for everyone.'

'Angela, no one is as excited about Christmas as you. You could not ruin it for anyone but yourself. The rest of us are just scared of accidentally revealing that Santa Claus doesn't exist. I almost rented a Santa suit just to keep you happy.'

Sadly, I had to tell seven-year-old Angela (alive and well in my subconscious) that he was probably joking about the suit before I could carry on with the conversation. I could not be distracted. I had to make him take this seriously. Without scaring him.

'Alex, I'm worried.' I wiped my palms on what I hoped was an inconspicuous bit of my skirt and rested them on his knee. 'Really worried that I might not be able to get a work visa.'

'Don't be.' He turned towards me, his hair rebelling against his slick suit by falling into his face, brushing against those high cheekbones, his eyes sleepy and sparkling all at the same time. He actually looked pretty pleased with himself. Knob. 'It's all going to work out OK.'

Right. I was out of options. I looked to the faux heavens and cashed in all my good karma chips.

'The lawyer did say there might be one other option.' Hmm. Was it possible the high, singsong voice wasn't the best way to go with this. 'Maybe.'

We sat in silence, me sweating in a manner that would be unbecoming on Bernard Manning, and Alex's happy-go-lucky expression melting away until he looked as tense as Robert Pattinson breaking down outside a *Twilight* convention. And presumably just as scared. I wondered how long we would have to sit there in silence before he put two and two together and actually said something, but as it turned out I didn't have the patience to wait.

'Wecouldgetmarried.' I blurted it out more or less as all one word – no pauses, no time for breathing, no margin for error.

Alex didn't say anything. He sat beside me, his casual slouch replaced by a posture so rigid you'd have thought someone had left the coat hanger inside his suit jacket. Silence. I counted to ten. And then to twenty. And then the verbal diarrhoea kicked in.

'It wouldn't be a real married.' When in doubt, I always thought it best to carry on waffling until someone stopped me. The fact that this tactic had never really worked terribly well for me before didn't stop me now. 'It would be visa married. Just paperwork really, just like, a favour. Not anything. Nothing would have to change. At all. It wouldn't mean anything. Not that marriage means anything these days anyway, right?'

Sometimes the person who was supposed to stop me burst out laughing. Sometimes, when that person was Jenny, they gave me a slap. And sometimes, that person just sat in absolute silence, their mouth a grim line, the fear of God in their eyes. Like now.

'And I wouldn't hold you to it, obviously.' I attempted a laugh. It was a failed attempt. 'Seriously – me, you, city hall and a piece of paper, never to be spoken of again. Just like going down the post office.'

Of course it was nothing like going to the post office. Going to the post office was one of the most soul-destroying experiences in all of the universe. And probably much more complicated than getting married, really. Did there need to be five different ways to send my mum a birthday card? Thank Christ for Moonpig. While I continued my internal rant at the postal services of America, Alex was still frozen. I tore my eyes from the middle distance and forced myself to look at him. His face was ashen. No hilarious jokes about Father Christmas now, eh, Alex? This was not a good sign.

'Really, I've thought of every other option and this is all there is.' My voice dropped to a weak whisper. 'This is the only way I can stay here.'

At this point, I just needed him to say something. And I assumed Guido was pretty invested as well, as the gondola crashed into the side of the canal.

'My bad,' he muttered in a distinctly un-Italian accent.

But the bump shook Alex's tongue loose at last, and as Guido got us back on course, Alex cleared his throat to speak.

'You want me to marry you for a visa?' he asked in a voice I didn't recognize.

'Yes?'

Gone was the easy expression. Gone was the arm around the shoulders, the hand-holding and the sparkling eyes. This was bad. I'd never seen him look like this before. Not even when I shrank his vintage Rolling Stones T-shirt in the wash. Which, incidentally, was why I wasn't allowed to do our laundry any more. For some reason it felt like I was failing a test. I wanted to jump up and down, hold his face, tell him I loved him, tell him this was the only way we could avoid a long-distance relationship that would fall apart over a tearful Skype call within a week because I would either be sent to prison for killing my mother or top myself because the UK was three weeks behind the US with *True Blood*. But instead, I took my turn at playing musical statues, too scared to breathe a word, to breathe at all.

After far too long, Alex coughed, loosened his tie and nodded.

'OK then.'

I sat back, my entire body giving in, as though I'd been carrying something incredibly heavy for the longest time and finally let it go. For one second, I was relieved. And then I felt sick. And then I started to cry. The exact chain of emotions every blushing bride-to-be went through, I was sure. I took a deep breath, trying to fill myself up with air, and wiped away the tears before Alex could see them.

'So we'll get married.' He was still nodding to himself, checking out his own shiny shoes. Admittedly they were very distracting, but I'd hoped the idea of us getting married might have been enough to put them in second place on the list of things he should be thinking about. 'It's just paperwork. Getting married doesn't mean anything to you. It's nothing.'

And there were the tears again. This time I had to look away as several renegade rivulets streamed down my cheeks before I could stop them.

'What does marriage mean anyway, right?' After such a long silence, Alex just couldn't seem to stop talking. And the more he said, the more I really wished he would. 'It's not like anyone else we know is taking it seriously. Jeff sure isn't worried.'

I didn't know what I'd been expecting. In my head I'd gone through so many different scenarios. I was ready for him to say no, I was ready for him to say yes, I was ready for him to sweep me off my feet and whisk me away to Tiffany. I just wasn't ready for him to say it meant nothing. Alex and I had talked about marriage before, in relation to our friends, as a vague, far-off thing that was sort of on the horizon but not something we really needed to think about any time soon, like a pension or a Blu-ray player, but I supposed, really, I'd been hoping he'd been thinking about it as much as I had. And not just because I needed a visa but because he wanted to marry me. But apparently, it didn't mean anything.

'We should just get it done while we're here.' He carried on talking in that strange voice. 'Less hassle. Easier than in New York. Shit, we should just do it now, while I'm wearing a suit.'

'I'm supposed to meet Jenny at ten-thirty,' I said, not really sure why.

'It's the perfect Vegas vacation.' Alex had become the human equivalent of a nodding dog. 'Gamble a little, get married and still make dinner. Perfect.'

'Alex.' I hoped my voice didn't sound as thick with tears as it felt. 'We don't have to.'

'No other option, right?' He threw his arms up in a shrug, throwing me off balance. 'This is what you want.'

'I don't want to leave.' I tried to pick my words carefully, something I probably should have done five minutes earlier. 'But if you don't want to do this, I get it. It's not like the post office. That was a stupid thing to say.'

'Not the first stupid thing you've said,' he replied too quickly. Ouch. 'Honestly, I'm flattered that you asked me and not one of Jenny's gay mafia.'

'OK, stop.' Being engaged did not suit Alex Reid. 'Forget I said it. Please.'

'I can't, can I?' he turned to look at me for the first time since I had made my romantic proposal. His eyes were not shining with love. They weren't anything. He looked . . . disappointed. 'Because you did say it. You need to get married to someone or you have to leave.'

'Not someone.' I ran the hem of my dress through my thumb and forefinger, straightening out the pleats and folding them again. 'This is all wrong, I didn't mean—'

'So we get married, we go home and we just go on with life like normal.' Alex pulled the silky material out of my hands. 'That's the deal?'

I had no words left. I'd used them all up while I was babbling about how getting married was just a bit of paperwork that wouldn't change anything. I was so incredibly stupid.

'So congratulations?' Guido broke the most excruciating silence in history as we drew to a halt. '*Si?*'

'*Si*,' Alex replied, jumping out of the gondola and letting Guido help me back onto solid ground.

'Good luck,' he said, dropping the Italiano. 'You're gonna need it.'

Face to face outside an authentic Italian Panda Express, I took Alex's hands in mine, hoping to stop feeling like something he'd trodden in. Without words, he shook his head, looked behind him, looked over my head, looked anywhere that wasn't at me before folding me up in his arms and pressing my face against his chest.

'I love you.' My voice was muffled but I used all the strength I had to make my words clear. 'I don't want to leave.'

'I know,' he replied right away, but I couldn't help

232

but hear a question in his voice. 'It's going to be fine.' And after a beat, with an air of resignation. 'I love you too.'

It was exactly what I wanted to hear, I thought, as he released me from his slightly too tight hug and took my hand in his. But I just didn't believe him.

CHAPTER FIFTEEN

Everything that happened after leaving the Venetian was a blur. Alex dragged me along behind him as we marched through the casino, back out into the marble lobby, my heels clicking across the floor like a quickened clock. I just didn't know what it was counting down towards. The evening was too cold to be outside in nothing but a little silk dress, but Alex didn't want to wait for a cab. He'd either he'd gone mad, drunk fifteen Red Bulls when I wasn't watching, or he really, really wanted to get married. There was of course another option – that he wanted to get it over with before he changed his mind – but I didn't really feel like thinking about that one.

Stunned into silence, I had used up my dialogue quota for the day by spouting such epic quantities of shit about how getting married for a visa wouldn't mean anything to me. Alex, on the other hand, must have taken a vow of silence while we'd been apart because he couldn't stop talking. My boyfriend wasn't particularly chatty at the best of times. He was definitely someone who on the whole only said something when he had something to say, but now I couldn't shut him up. Every thought that passed through his mind was vocalized, and none of them made me feel any better. According to his iPhone, if we got married at De Lujo, they gave you one hundred dollars in chips so that was something. Getting married was a great write-off for the suit. There was definitely a song in this, if not an album. Now he had something to put in his Christmas cards to his family. The list went on.

His family. I hadn't even met his family. And he hadn't met mine. What would my mum say? She would be heartbroken. And that actually made me feel bad. With every step we took towards the chapel, I was regretting this whole thing more and more. To the point where I just wanted to sit cross-legged in the street and cry.

'Welcome to the De Lujo chapel.' A very polite if slightly tired-looking woman in a smart white suit stared at us from behind a low counter not ten minutes later. 'How can I help you this evening?'

'We want to get married,' Alex replied. 'Can you hook us up?'

'Um, actually . . .' The girl didn't seem particularly phased by the fact that her happy couple was made up of a manic groom and tear-stained bride, but then I had a feeling this wasn't her first time around. 'We had a cancellation this evening. We're all ready to go with an "elegant affair" ceremony right after we finish up with the couple inside.'

She looked up and gave me her brightest smile. I wondered if she was on commission.

'If you don't mind using someone else's colour scheme, I could do you a really great deal. Otherwise I just have to throw the flowers out anyway.'

'Let's do it,' he agreed on our behalf, fishing around in his wallet for his credit card. I could feel myself getting hotter and hotter, and the room began to sway.

'Do you have a bathroom?' I whispered.

The countergirl nodded. 'The bridal salon is to your left.'

I nodded back and turned as carefully as I could. I didn't know the exact shotgun wedding etiquette on doing the deed in bare feet because your fiancé had made you run in front of cars, across the Strip, against a light because he didn't want to wait for the walk sign. Maybe he'd been trying to get me run over. Even though I didn't have health insurance, I kind of wished I had.

'I love spur-of-the-moment weddings,' the girl confided to Alex as I staggered across the hallway. 'So romantic.'

'Yeah,' I heard Alex reply. 'All my dreams come true.'

The bridal salon was beautiful. All hand-painted cream wall coverings, overstuffed chaises longues and primping stations for the bride and her entourage. Except I didn't have an entourage. Because I wasn't really a bride. I didn't need the raised dais to make sure my train was properly puffed out because I didn't have a train. I had a slightly soiled cocktail dress that wasn't in any way qualified for the upgrade it was about to receive. At least it was borrowed, just like the bag and the shoes. And my fingernails were blue from the cold. The oldest thing I had on me were my pants. Sexy. And as for something new, did this fancy first-time feeling of genuine terror count? I wasn't glowing. I was sweating. And I had mascara smudges under my eyes. This didn't feel like the most special day of my life. It felt like I was about to sit the

236

chemistry A level exam. And I didn't take chemistry A level.

'OK, Angela.' I leaned against the sink, ran the cold water and held my wrist under the tap, trying to cool down. 'Just think.'

My reflection stared out at me, smudged and sad. My sexy up-do had become a not quite so sexy down-do during the sprint to the De Lujo, but the remaining pulled-back strands did give me an oddly bridal air. And if there were going to be pictures, at least I was considerably skinnier than the last time I'd been photographed at a wedding. Two days of booze-related puking really was the perfect pre-wedding detox. If you really hated yourself. But aside from the sexy chignon, razor-sharp cheekbones and distinctly green pallor, my reflection also looked like she meant business, so I listened.

'There are two ways to look at this.' I breathed out slowly, trying to regulate my hammering heartbeat. 'Alex has agreed to do this. Yes, he's gone mad, but he's agreed. Which is a good sign. So I could just go out there, do this, forget that I'm wearing a dress with a damp arse and know that it'll all be OK at the end of the day.'

This all seemed relatively sensible and potentially do-able.

'Or you could go out there, sit Alex down and apologize for being such a selfish wanker, tell him you love him, tell him he's the reason you don't want to go back to London and of course you want to marry him, but you don't want it to be like this.'

That also sounded sensible, but this time, it was also true. Weirdly, though, it also felt like the more difficult option.

'This isn't happening like this,' I told myself, wiping

237

away the tears and standing up straight. 'None of it.' And what's more, the shoes were coming off.

Emptying my clutch out onto the countertop, I flicked through all the crap looking for my powder compact. A girl can't walk into a situation like this unarmed and shiny. It was already going to be difficult; I didn't want Alex distracted by his reflection in my nose. With a final swipe of the powder puff and a slick of lip gloss, I stared myself down and tried to remember all the wonderful, empowering things Jenny had told me over the years. But for some reason, the only advice I could seem to summon was blow-job related, and this was neither the time nor the place. Apparently my subconscious had already decided this wasn't going to go well.

'Now or never,' I muttered, ignoring every voice clamouring for attention in my head. I'd listened to everyone else's advice, I'd heard every side of every story, and where had that got me? Sobbing in the toilets. Again. Twice in one Vegas. If there was anything that was going on the 'what happens in Vegas, stays in Vegas' list, it was crying in the bogs. Probably not what the marketing team at the tourist board had in mind, but that wasn't my problem.

I scooped my make-up together and dropped it all in my bag, being careful to make sure all the lids were tightly fastened – it was my something borrowed after all. But one of these things was not like the others, in that it wasn't mine. Stashed among my prized collection of NARS neutrals was a small black bullet covered in bling. It looked like something I might have used when I was seven. Or like it belonged to Paris Hilton. Either or. I popped off the top to find a bright red lipstick that looked familiar. Where had I seen this before? Of course – it was Sadie's. Everything she owned was covered in finger-slicing Swarovskis. It was the safest bet in Vegas that she'd been first in the queue for a vajazzling. But what was it doing in my handbag? I puzzled for a moment. For Sadie's lipstick to get into my make-up, Sadie would have had to have been in my make-up. But since Sadie wasn't familiar with little things like boundaries, privacy or locks, it wasn't beyond the realms of imagination. Not that it was important at that exact second. I congratulated my brain on a well-played game of procrastination, hopped from one bare foot to the other and shook myself down.

As soon as I stepped out of the bathroom, Alex stood up quickly and, without a word, knocked the confidence right out of me. He still looked great – beautiful, really – but something was wrong. His eyes were red and he looked like he was about to tell me he'd just remembered that he'd bought me a kitten for Christmas and forgotten to put air holes in the box. It wasn't a positive look. But I had to say what I had to say, dead kitten or no dead kitten. I really hoped there wasn't a dead kitten.

'Alex, I need to talk to you.' I put the shoes on a low couch and rushed over, hands out in front of me, ready. 'This is stupid.'

'I think you should sit down.' He covered my arms with his, pushing them down by my side. 'I just—'

'No, we need to talk.' I would not be silenced. I had to tell him everything. I had to . . . sit down. Alex physically pushed me onto the low sofa and shot his own do-as-you're-told face my way. I busted mine out monthly, but I'd only seen Alex's once before, and that was at Thanksgiving, when he'd pulled rank and insisted I didn't need a fifteen-pound turkey to feed four people.

'Will you just fucking listen to me for once?' He squeezed the tops of my arms.

'Ow.'

It didn't actually hurt, but I had to prove a point. It was difficult to give a speech about how much you loved someone and wanted to be with them for ever when they were swearing at you and leaving indentations in your bingo wings.

Trying not to pout, I looked at him and bit my lip. Aside from the fact he'd clearly had something of a cry himself while I was over-emoting in the toilets, he looked so serious I couldn't bear it. I wanted to lean in and kiss him and make all of this go away, but I was frozen in place. Partly by his vice-like grip, but mostly by the paralysing fear that had struck me ever since I was pinned to the couch.

Alex looked towards the doors of the chapel and then back at me. 'I just took a look inside and . . .' He shook his head and relaxed his hands a little. Shaking his head, he made a soft laughing noise that I did not enjoy. 'Angela, I don't know what to do.'

As soon as the words were out of his mouth, I burst into tears. And as soon as I burst into tears, the doors of the chapel burst open, 'I Like It' by Enrique Iglesias blaring out at a million decibels. Interesting replacement for Mendelssohn, but each to his own. It was only when Alex let go of my arms and took my hand instead, whispering 'I'm sorry', that I got really worried. And it was only when I recognized the screeching blonde rolling out of the chapel in a white strapless dress that could have doubled as a handy compression bandage for my dicky knee and a bouquet of peonies, held up by the tall, gorgeous, blond man, that I started to panic.

'Sadie?' I let go of Alex's hand and stood up. 'Ben?'

'Angela! You got my message!' Sadie threw every single one of her ninety pounds across the room at me, knocking me right back down on the couch. 'Isn't this awesome?'

'Is it?' I blew her hair out of my mouth and looked at Alex with wide eyes. He quickly leaned backwards, trying to avoid the heavily perfumed mess that had collapsed in my lap. 'I mean, congratulations?'

'I didn't get married, you dumb shit.' She clawed her way up my front, getting a good handful of boob in along the way, and pushed off my lap until she managed a shaky upright position. 'See?'

Showing me her back, I saw the word 'bridesmaid' scrawled on her beautiful, beautiful dress in bright red lipstick. Ah-ha. And of course Sadie was wearing a painted-on white dress to someone else's wedding. But . . . oh, shit. Just which someone else were we talking about?

'Angie!'

The shriek was loud enough and high enough to break every window in the hotel. And there were a lot of windows. Jenny stumbled out of the chapel towards me in the ruffled, feathered dress. So transfixed was I for a split second that I failed to notice Jeff staggering out of the chapel behind her.

Mew.

'I saw them while you were in the bathroom – I didn't know what to do?' Alex said into my hair as Jenny and Jeff held hands and bounced up and down on the spot before pausing, staring deeply into each other's eyes and collapsing onto each other for a full-on slobbering session. It was quite possible I'd never ever seen her so drunk. And I had seen her Drunk. I'd only been gone a couple of hours. What the hell had she been doing?

'I think the traditional thing is to object,' I replied, too scared to move. A sparkly diamond ring winked at me from Jenny's left hand. So this had really happened? 'With shouting.'

'I'm not getting involved.' He pulled his phone out of his suit pocket, checked the screen and put it back. 'This is nothing to do with me.'

'It's everything to do with you.' I turned, stunned. 'Jenny's my best friend. Jeff is supposed to be your friend. You're here on his bachelor party and might I just remind you, that would be a bachelor party that was not related to this wedding.'

'Uh, yeah, she's your friend, emphasis on the your, and I was a last-minute stand-in for the bachelor shenanigans. At no point did I sign up for groom shepherding.' He shrugged, upsetting me and the line of his suit. For the first time that evening, I wished he was wearing jeans and a T-shirt. I wanted my Alex, not this fancy-dress imposter. 'I sent the best man a text. I think we should just get out of here.'

It was just all too much. Jenny and Jeff had moved onto the next sofa and the gratuitous snogging had descended into an orgy of hands. Thank God that dress was so involved – the wedding video was already something they could never show their kids. And it was also being filmed on Sadie's jewel-encrusted silver iPhone. That didn't add to the sense of occasion.

'We can't just leave.' I jumped up after Alex and followed him out of the chapel, shoes in one hand, bag snugly under my arm. 'This is ridiculous.'

'This whole night has been ridiculous.' He turned quickly, taking me by surprise. I dropped the shoes. I dropped the clutch. I stared at the angry man in the suit. 'What a surprise. You're knee-deep in Jenny's shit again.'

He walked straight out of the chapel, leaving me and the girl at the counter very confused.

'Is he coming back?' she asked, pointedly looking away from the sofa where Jenny and Jeff were mere moments away from consummating their marriage. Sadie and Ben were nowhere to be seen. I had to assume, classy gal that she was, they'd vanished into the toilets. 'Are you going ahead with the wedding?'

'I'm going to say no,' I replied, without the mental strength to think about what that meant. All I knew was that Alex was walking away from me. Whether it was for now or for ever, I had no idea. 'So sorry.'

'No worries,' she chirped. 'No shortage of weddings around these parts.'

'So I see.' I ran out into the casino, leaving my shoes and clutch where they fell. 'Alex, please.'

He stopped right by a bank of *Wizard of Oz* slot machines, giving us an audience of little old ladies with an awful lot of hair. One eye on us, one eye on the Dorothy, they nudged each other and kept pumping the quarters.

'Alex,' I yelled one more time, accompanied by a chorus of 'We're off to see the wizard'. Moments like this were supposed to be soundtracked by Adele or Beyoncé, not Judy Garland and a bunch of Munchkins.

He leaned against the side of the nearest slot, much to the chagrin of its player, until she checked out his backside and nodded at me in approval. 'I have to go figure this out. Leave it.'

'Wait.' I reached out, needing him to fill the empty space between us. It felt too permanent. But it wasn't. Alex came back to me, pushed my hair back and held my face in both of his warm hands. He leaned in to kiss me, warm and soft as always, but it didn't feel right. It felt like a sigh. And just like I knew he would, he broke away first, ran his thumbs across my cheek-bones and stroked his hands down my neck, resting on my collarbone.

'Just let me go,' he repeated. 'I'll talk to you tomorrow.'

And then he walked away.

'Don't worry, honey,' slot-machine lady yelled over the clicking and whirring. 'You're in Vegas. Plenty of fish in the sea.'

'But that's my fish,' I replied, watching him disappear around a corner. I never wanted to see that suit again.

CHAPTER SIXTEEN

Shoeless, bagless, cashless and Alexless. I slouched over to the bar and hopped up on a bar stool. At least that was easier in bare feet.

'What can I get you, miss?' the bartender leaned across the gilt surface to give me his best smile.

'Can I charge it to my room?' I asked.

'Of course,' he replied.

'Dirty martini. Big one.'

These were desperate times and desperate times called for desperate measures. And loads of gin. I'd promised myself I wouldn't get drunk tonight, that a little wine with dinner, maybe one cocktail afterwards, was more than enough. But that was before. I wanted to be wankered. The bartender was quick and the martini was strong; both things made me very happy. There was no way I could process the night's events without at least one drink in me. Not for the first time, I wondered if I had a drinking problem. No, I decided, I'm just turning into a real New Yorker. Just in time to be sent back to London, where I will be labelled a lush and sent to bed without any dinner.

'Are you going to drink that or swim in it?'

I looked up from my massive martini to see James, phone in hand, grin on his face. A sober, smiling man. It was a refreshing change. Setting the precious martini safely on the bar, I let James scoop me up in a hug.

'I've been calling you, piss-head,' he said, letting me go and ordering a whiskey and Diet Coke. 'Should have known I'd find you here.'

'I'm sorry, I lost my phone,' I explained. 'It's been one of those days.'

'Why do I feel like that's an understatement,' James asked, throwing a fifty-dollar bill on the bar without looking. Flash bastard.

'What gave it away?'

'No shoes, knackered hair, no lipstick and you've clearly been crying.' He took a sip of his drink and carried on. 'You're here on your own, you've lost your phone, and you're drowning in a martini so big it needs a life guard. Can't have been your best day.'

For some reason it was easier hearing that in a British accent.

'It wasn't my best,' I admitted, taking another glug of lovely booze. 'How was yours?'

'Got up at midday, had a massage, gave myself skin cancer at the pool, had a nap, had dinner, came here. Can't really complain.'

I gave him a level look over the top of my rapidly emptying glass.

'I hate you.'

'I know you do,' he nodded happily, his curls bouncing around his perfect face. 'Here are your options. You can tell Uncle James all about it and we can get hammered, or you can pretend none of it ever happened and we can get hammered. Your choice.'

This was going to take some serious thinking.

'My friend has been secretly shagging her ex and they just got married, even though he's engaged to someone else and was supposed to be here on his bachelor party. And I asked Alex to marry me so I could get my visa and he said yes, but then he went a bit mental and walked off and I have no idea what's going on.'

'You've been busy, then?'

I nodded. 'Quite busy.'

We sat drinking in amicable silence until both our drinks were dry. James slammed his empty glass first, I followed suit. And smashed the stem of the martini glass.

'Shit. Sorry,' I winced at the bartender.

'Happens all the time.' He swept the glass over to his side of the bar and smiled. What a pro.

'Does it really?'

'No,' he replied. 'Another?'

'Yes, please,' James answered for me. 'So what are you going to do?'

'I have no idea.' I really didn't. 'About any of it.'

'Well, there's sod all you can do about your friend, really.' He started ticking off my problems on his fingers. 'Obviously you're worried about her and you want to be there for her, but if she's being a dickhead, she's being a dickhead. You've already talked to her about all of this, yes?'

'Yes.'

'And she did it anyway?'

'Yes.'

'Then you can't do anything else but wait for her to come round. She will,' he promised. 'And she'll need you then. Until she sorts herself out, you need to worry

247

about your problems first. Starting with this visa nonsense. How come you suddenly need to get married? I thought you had a visa.'

He was ever so good. Taking a tiny sip of my second martini, I made a mental note to try harder to stay in touch this time. Clearly I was in need of gay wisdom on a regular basis. 'I did.' I put the martini down, determined not to inhale this one. 'But I lost my job at *The Look* and so I'm out on my arse.'

'And you've looked into all of the others?' James was clearly not trying to pace himself. He chugged back half his whiskey cocktail in one gulp. 'I'm a total expert in US visas. I think I've had them all.'

I filled him in on the current situation, Lawrence the Lawyer's less than optimistic feedback and the general lack of options.

'So I've got, like, a fortnight to get a job, become extraordinary or get married. I really couldn't tell you which is realistic at this point.' I pushed my hair back out of my face, almost all of it having escaped the pins by now. I don't know how, but cocktails always make your hair slippery; there has to be a scientific reason. Pantene should look into it.

'Hate to be the bearer of bad news, but I know so many people who have got married for visas in LA, and it hardly ever works out,' James said. 'And it's a tough time in the job market, I know. Are you sure you can't apply for the O-1? That's what I've got.'

'Last time I checked, I haven't been in any films. And getting papped snogging you in the back of a taxi didn't seem to be enough for my lawyer. He said I could apply, but he also said I wouldn't get it.'

'He sounds like a right ray of sunshine.' He grabbed an olive from my drink and popped it in his mouth.

My stomach rumbled loudly, reminding me I hadn't had dinner. Gin-soaked olives weren't meant to be my only sustenance. 'Was he at least hot?'

I nodded, scarfing the remaining two olives before he snatched them.

'Well, that's something, at least,' James mused. 'Let me talk to my lawyers. They might be able to see another way around it. They're good at getting people visas.'

'That would be amazing.' The rush of gratitude I felt was so strong that if I could have given him the olives back I would have. And I hated parting with food. 'Honestly, James, that would be incredible.'

'They might say the same thing,' he warned me, but raised his glass to mine at the same time. 'But it's worth asking. Now, what's going on with Alex?'

Pacing myself be damned. I swigged my drink and shook my head. 'I think I really messed up.' I closed my eyes and let the gin settle. 'And by think, I mean know.'

'I'm assuming it wasn't Alex's idea to get married for the visa?' he guessed.

I shook my head.

'But it doesn't sound like your dream come true, either.' James was so wise. If ever there was an advert for coming out of the closet, it was him. I knew it would make him happier, but I had no idea it would drastically improve his intelligence. 'Things like this are never a good idea, especially when you are actually in a relationship with someone. It only ever works when there are no emotions involved, and even then it doesn't usually work for long.'

'Where were you when I was listening to everyone else?' I moaned. 'This is all very good information that would have been useful yesterday.'

'Why were you listening to anyone but yourself?'

'Because I'm a moron?'

He let that one settle for a moment. I looked down at my feet and wrinkled my toes. Between the Vegas sprint in too-tight shoes and wandering around barefoot, my pedicure was completely destroyed. It really added to the overall look. At least no one would be mistaking me for a hooker. At least, not a good one; there was no way I could charge a hundred dollars for a blow-job in this state. Happy memories.

'I want to say it's all going to be OK . . .' James interrupted my reverie with a tap on the knee. 'But only you know if that's true. I don't know him well enough. I do know he loves the arse off you, though.'

'I don't know.' I rested my elbows on the bar and slurped my drink, no hands. Sexy. 'The more I think about it, the more I reckon asking him to marry me for a visa while repeatedly insisting that marriage means absolutely nothing to me might have been a bad idea, whether he loves the arse off me or not.'

'Especially if he loves the arse off you!' James knocked my elbows off the bar and whacked me on the arm. 'You didn't?'

'Did I not already tell you I'm a moron?' I asked, rubbing my arm. I was taking some serious abuse on this holiday, physical and emotional.

'Angela, you twat,' James groaned. 'Can you even imagine how that would feel? If someone you loved, someone you wanted to spend the rest of your life with, asked you to piss away all your hopes and dreams for a bit of paper while ranting on about the fact that marriage didn't mean anything, what would you say?'

'Yes, thank you very much for the opportunity?'

'Or?'

'Fuck off you heartless, callous, tactless bitch?'

'Yeah.'

I replaced the elbows with my face. 'Fuuuuuuuuuck.'

'Yeah.' James rubbed the back of my neck with a gentle hand. 'It's not a lost cause, don't panic. I'm sure you'll be able to talk this out.'

I made a noise that implied agreement. It was the best I could do.

'And by talk, I mean beg and plead,' he carried on. 'Probably going to have to be some bribery in there too. Have you got him a good Christmas present?'

I shook my head, rattling my forehead against the bar. Why hadn't that second martini numbed all pain yet? When you couldn't rely on gin, you couldn't rely on anything.

'We'll think of something,' James promised, still massaging my neck. 'Give him tonight to cool down, and tomorrow we'll sort it out.'

'But I really want to talk to him,' I said. 'I just want to explain. I just want him to talk to me.'

'He's a man,' he explained. 'He doesn't want to talk and you can't push him. Give him his space.'

I hated that he was right. Why couldn't men just be reasonable like women?

'And what am I supposed to do until then?'

Raising my head, I saw a third full martini glass sliding across the bar to join the second, half-empty one. He was right. There really wasn't another option.

'Right then,' I took a deep breath. 'Let's do this.'

'You're putting it in wrong,' I whined at James some hours later.

'There's only one way to put it in,' he replied, frustrated. 'It's not my fault, it's your fault.'

'How is it my fault?' I dropped to the floor and leaned back against the door to my suite. 'It's a key. How hard can it be?'

'Hard enough.' He shoved the key card into the slot as hard as possible and yanked it out quickly.

'That's what she said,' I cackled. 'Honestly, ramming it in and out like that isn't going to help.'

'That's not what your mother said last night.' He kicked me in the hip. 'I don't usually have this much trouble.'

'I've heard that before.' I closed my eyes and tipped my head back. James was ever so tall. 'Actually, I haven't.'

'Then you're a very lucky girl.' With grim determination, he slid the key card in one last time and whipped it out quickly. Unfortunately, the buzz and the click were not enough notice for me to pull myself together, and as the door opened, I fell backwards, my arms tangling themselves in James's long legs and bringing him right down on top of me.

'Angela, you only had to ask,' he said, face-first in my boobs.

Laughing so hard I was worried I might do a little wee, I looked up to see someone I didn't recognize, drink in hand, standing over us.

'You guys OK?' asked the stranger.

'Why are you in my room?' I asked, shoving James away while he mumbled something about never having this trouble with Blake.

'It's a party?' The stranger looked back into the lounge, where I saw dozens of people standing on the sofas, drinking, dancing and generally misbehaving. Of course, they had already seen me. I had made an impressive entrance.

'Angela!' It was a familiar shriek and not one I was hoping to hear. Sadie danced over to me. It spoke volumes that every pair of eyes switched to her. And if I couldn't hold a room with my legs akimbo, wrapped around a homosexual movie star, when could I?

The thing with Sadie wasn't so much that she was famous as that she was just painfully pretty. And it wasn't as though I wasn't used to hanging out with a good-looking girl. Jenny was that friend who makes every man on the street turn their head and every woman wish she'd spent five minutes more on her hair (not least me), but Sadie was something else. One look at her and you knew there was no point in trying. I couldn't begin to imagine what men went through, seeing her in the flesh. And for a split second, I wondered how it must feel for her to think that drooling and letching was an automatic reaction from everything with a penis. I collected compliments and squirrelled them away for fat days, classifying my wardrobe by colour, season and 'this is the dress that stranger on the train said was pretty'. I was still flattered by catcalling from a building site. I looked at her, still in her graffitied bridesmaid dress, and sighed. Imagine never, ever having a fat day.

'We're having a party — it's a wedding reception.' She held a hand out to help me up but let go as soon as she spotted James. 'James!'

'Have we met?' he asked, a raised eyebrow for Sadie, a wink for me.

'Uh, only about a thousand times.' She curled her arm around his neck and sat down on his knee, despite the fact he clearly didn't want to be sitting on the floor in the doorway.

'Sadie, where's Jenny?' I shuffled myself into a kneeling position. 'I need to talk to her.'

'I haven't seen her since the wedding.' Sadie fluffed her massive honey-blonde hair in James's face. He did not look impressed. 'They didn't come back here.'

'I thought you said this was a wedding reception?'

I scanned the lounge for Jenny's giant hair but found nothing.

'It is. She's just not here.' She looked at me as though I was stupid. There were plenty of things I'd said in the last twenty-four hours or so that would have warranted that expression, but that question wasn't one of them. 'They're probably screwing somewhere.'

'You do realize Jeff isn't Jenny's boyfriend?' I tried to be as clear as it was possible to be. 'And that Jenny isn't Jeff's fiancée?'

'You have no sense of adventure,' she replied. 'Where are your shoes?'

'Fuck knows.' I clambered up off the floor and pushed past her, heading towards my room. 'And they were yours anyway.'

Thankfully, the fifty or so strangers that had invaded our hotel suite hadn't made it as far as my room, and I heard myself sigh out loud as I closed the door on the madness outside.

'Sanctuary,' I breathed, checking the room phone for messages. Nothing. I didn't know whether to be relieved or not. Ignoring James's advice, even though I knew full well he was right, I tapped in Alex's number and waited for it to ring. But it didn't. Straight to voicemail.

'Hey, it's me. I just wanted to call and say . . .' Losing my mobile in the Bellagio fountains might have been a blessing. I couldn't think of a single occasion when my picking up a phone without a completely written-out script had gone well. This was no exception. 'I wanted to say goodnight. So, goodnight. Speak to you tomorrow.'

I hung up and lay back on my bed, trying to put the entire day out of my mind. The soft mattress rose up to meet me, wrapping me in and whispering that it was all going to be OK. Our original plan was to go back to the room for me to change, find shoes and then go to a party at Caesar's Palace where James was supposed to be showing his face. But now I was horizontal, I just couldn't see it happening. I heard a knock at the door and assumed he had come to get me. Maybe I could convince him to get into bed. Since I clearly wasn't trying to seduce the big gay, it might not be impossible. And it was a lovely bed.

'I'm just lying down for a second,' I shouted. 'Come in.'

'Angela, why do you hate me?'

Brilliant. It wasn't James. It was Sadie. And from the sound of it, a drunk, tired and emotional Sadie. Since I could more or less tick all three of those boxes myself, I really didn't want to have to deal with her.

'I don't hate you.' I rolled over until I was face down in the soft, soft cottony clouds of pillows that littered my bed. 'Go back to the party, Sadie.'

'You do hate me.' Her voice came closer and closer until I felt the mattress give very, very slightly. 'Jen's always telling everyone how awesome you are, but you're just such a bitch to me. It's totally obvious.'

Ahh. Lovely Jenny. I mean, Jen.

'I'm sorry, I didn't mean to be a bitch.' I realized my monotone response probably wasn't my most convincing, but I was very tired. And I did hate her. It was probably all she wanted to hear anyway.

'You don't mean that.' She jabbed me in the arm until I sat up. 'Seriously, why don't you like me?'

'Because you won't let me go to sleep?'

'I'm not leaving until you talk to me,' she said. 'So you might as well get up.'

With a huge sigh and an almost irrepressible desire to smother her with a pillow, I sat up and looked at

Sadie. Sitting on the end of my bed, a hoodie covering her unbearably tight dress and her hair all pulled back in a ponytail, she didn't look nearly as annoying as usual. In fact, she looked like a little girl. If you took away the eyelash extensions and the fake tan, she could pass for a common or garden obscenely hot college student. Which didn't really make me like her any more when I thought about it.

'You're jealous, right?' She shook the sleeves of the hoodie down over her hands. 'That's what it is?'

'Bloody hell,' I blustered. You couldn't say she was afraid to get to the point. 'How many times have you asked that?'

'Never.' She looked completely nonplussed. 'I've never had a roommate before.'

I wrinkled my forehead. 'What are you talking about?'

We stared at each other for a moment, both trying to work out what the other was on about.

'Ohhhh.' Sadie broke first, laughing loudly. 'You thought I meant jealous of me in general. No, I meant you're jealous of me and Jenny. You're pissed that you're not her roommate any more.'

'Ohhhh,' I echoed. Clearly I hadn't given her enough credit. 'Right. Yeah. I probably am a bit.' Or a lot. Or loads. Or so much, I could taste bile when I thought about it.

'I know you guys are super-close,' she said. 'Jen misses you. You're like, her best friend, you know, not just her old roommate.'

Obviously living with my bestie was rubbing off on Sadie. Here she was, hanging out in my bedroom after midnight giving me a very Jenny pep talk. Her mentor would be proud.

'And don't feel bad about the whole jealousy thing – I'm totally used to it.' She held her hand just above my ankle, as though I might snap her wrist off if she actually touched me. And for a second I thought about it. Just when I was starting to think she might not be entirely evil.

'I am sorry if I've been a bit difficult,' I offered. 'Really. It's just, I sort of felt like you didn't like me that much, to be honest.'

'Oh, no.' Sadie popped upright then bounced down beside me on the bed. So she was officially comfortable now? 'I think you're kind of awesome. I mean, Jen told me your story and everything. I'm just a huge bitch. You just have to kick my ass. Or ignore me. Everyone else does.'

I couldn't not laugh. She was so much more self-aware than I had realized.

'Who ignores you? Seriously?' I attempted to join in the gal pal extravaganza by awkwardly patting her shoulder.

'Oh, everyone.' She rolled over onto her back and waved a hand at me. She really was tiny, and now I couldn't see her perfect boobs, I almost felt compelled to give her a hug. 'That's the thing with modelling – people only talk to you when they want you to do something.'

It was difficult not to start playing air violin.

'It's not an excuse, but when no one's listening, you get used to just giving orders instead of asking questions.' The music in the lounge almost drowned out her gentle self-analysis. 'So, yeah, maybe it looks like I always get what I want, but I don't.

I didn't think she was trying to make me feel bad on purpose, but she was doing a fine job.

'I don't have that many friends, I can never make it work with a guy. I always pick the wrong one. I don't know.'

'You're not seeing anyone right now?' I hoped her tales of celebrity shagging would take the edge off the guilt trip I was enjoying so much.

'Been single since my last boyfriend.'

Bugger.

'He really messed me up.'

Double bugger.

'I mean, how screwed in the head do you have to be to only date models then spend all your time telling your girlfriend you hate her because she's a model? That was pretty confusing.'

Fine, I admitted to myself; maybe having a twenty-three-inch waist wasn't worth all this drama.

'You're so lucky to have someone like Alex. He wouldn't care what you did for a job. He loves you whatever, right? It's so obvious.' Sadie sniffed loudly and kept talking. 'I don't know, maybe I need to be on my own. Until I stop being a bitch.'

'OK, enough is enough.' I couldn't cope with any more self-deprecation from the model and it was never a fun time hearing someone tell you how lucky you were immediately after you had fucked up big time. 'You don't sound like you're particularly happy with your lot in life? What's that all about?'

Two could play at the Jenny Lopez game; I'd learned a trick or two in my time.

'I am happy,' she said slowly. 'I think. I know I'm super-lucky to do what I do. I just don't love it as much as I used to. Meeting Jenny, seeing her go off to work every morning smiling? That's crazy. And even seeing how upset you got when you didn't get those jobs, I was like, huh. When I don't get a job, I'm pissed off, but I'm not upset. I'm kind of relieved.'

'So if you weren't modelling, what would you be

doing?' I templed my fingers and channelled our very own Oprah. 'If you could do anything?'

'I'd still want to be involved with fashion somehow,' she answered, quickly this time. 'Or maybe more on the beauty side. I'd love to have my own make-up range. Or design a denim line. Or write about fashion?'

'Can you write?' I asked.

'No.' She admitted. 'But I'd like to try.'

'I'd start with the first two options then,' I replied.

It felt a bit like the time my twelve-year-old cousin told me he wanted to be an astronaut – such a pipe dream; but I tried to remember how well-connected Sadie must be. Without even knowing how well-connected she was, Jenny and Erin worked with dozens of top beauty and fashion companies. She could absolutely make this happen if it was what she really wanted. 'Life's too short to be miserable, you know?'

'I never think about things like that,' she replied. 'I guess that's why I'm such a bitch.'

'I didn't think about things like that until I met Jenny.' I gave her our first official hug. 'You're in good hands.'

'Come and have a drink with me.' Sadie leapt off the bed with all the energy of someone who hadn't technically been jilted less than twelve hours earlier.

'I'm ever so tired.' I yawned for effect. 'Maybe I'll just crash?'

'No way – it's our last night.' Sadie threw the sweater to the ground and shimmied her dress into position. 'Haven't you been listening? I always get my own way.'

'Then this will be a good learning experience for you.' I turned back onto my front and breathed face down into the pillows. Bliss. 'I've done my good deed for the day.'

With one vaguely horse-like whinny, she left my

room without even slamming the door. I smiled. A great big, half-drunk, entirely exhausted smile. It was the expression of someone who knew one of the worst days ever was almost over. When I woke up, it would be tomorrow, and honestly, how could tomorrow possibly be as bad as today?

But then I heard the door open again. I should have known she wouldn't give up that easily.

'Get your arse out of bed, Clark.'

She had returned with reinforcements in the shape of James.

'I'm not having you moping in here.' He started playing the bongo drums on my backside until I rolled over. 'Where do you think you are? This is the land of bad decisions. You can't start punishing yourself for anything that happens here until you get home. You're going to have a good time whether you like it or not.'

'Maybe being a martyr is my idea of a good time,' I grumbled. Sometimes I really was my mother's daughter.

'Damn it, woman,' James shouted. 'What is moping around in here going to achieve? Apart from nothing. You can either stay in here and ruin your holiday altogether, or you can come outside, do shots you can't stand and dance to music you hate, just like everyone else, all right? In fact, there isn't a choice. Letting me dry-hump you to Katy Perry is not optional.'

It was a beautiful image.

'But I'm tired, and it's not like I lost fifty quid on the roulette table, is it?' I tried to kick him away, but James was considerably stronger and more committed to his dream than I was.

'I once dropped a hundred grand on a party at the Palms, got coked off my tits and gave a very famous movie star who insists he is not nearly as gay as everyone thinks he is a blow-job on the ghost deck at the Palms,' he reminisced happily. 'I woke up in the middle of the desert in a convertible Mustang with three puppies in the back of the car and a crate of Cheez-Its. And I still think Vegas is a good thing.'

'Classy,' I replied, desperately wanting to ask who the movie star was.

'I woke up in Paris one time,' Sadie offered.

'Where did you start out?' James asked while trying to heave me off the bed. I let my entire body go limp, refusing to make it an easy task.

'Uh, Hard Rock?' Sadie did not attempt to assist with the heavy lifting.

James pished her attempt to black-dog him. 'That's hardly a million miles away.'

'Oh, right.' She pulled her hair out of its ponytail and shook it out. 'I meant Paris, France.'

James and I locked eyes in silence.

'Long story.' She put her hands on her hips and assumed her best Jenny pose. 'Now, Angela Clark, get your ass out of bed, take this, drink this and put this the hell on before I lose my shit.'

She really had been paying attention to her roommate.

'Fine, I'm up.' I slouched beside the bed, looking down at my pink princess dress. It was in a bad way. Like me. 'But I'm not taking anything. You do whatever you want, but really, I ate pot brownies when I was in the second year of uni and spent an entire night trying to make scrambled eggs before I had to call my mum to tell her I could feel all of my fillings. So I'm fine.'

'It's just a caffeine pill.' Sadie thrust a little brown pill into my hand, followed by a can of sugar-free Red Bull. The breakfast of champions. At one a.m. 'Jenny would kill me if I tried to roofie you.'

'I would kill you if you tried to roofie me,' I replied,

reluctantly taking the pill. 'And I am concerned by the fact you even threw it out there as an option.'

I hadn't dabbled in caffeine supplements since the third year of university. It wasn't quite as shambolic an experience as my dalliance with heavier narcotics, but at one point, Louisa did find me sitting outside the corner shop at six a.m., shaking and insisting I needed them to open because I had to have a strawberry Pop-Tart or I would die. Pharmaceuticals were not my friend. And yet, ever the victim of peer pressure, I took it anyway.

'Halfway there,' Sadie congratulated me, handing over something black and slippery. It felt like a dead seal. Sexy. 'Put this on.'

'Can't I just put my jeans on?' I asked. 'I mean, I already did the most stupid thing you asked. Surely I don't have to do stripper-at-a-funeral fancy dress as well?'

'That's my dress,' she replied in a level voice, while James dissolved into a wild cackle. 'It's Vince and it's amazing.'

I held the leather tea towel out in front of me. 'I don't think it's going to fit.' It really did feel like I was stating the obvious.

'It's got a lot of give in it.' Sadie wasn't going to give in. 'Just try it.'

Comforted by the fact that they were going to have to cut me out of this when it got stuck under my armpits, I shucked off the knackered pink Tibi and yanked the Vince over my head.

'It fits!' Sadie said, clapping her approval. 'See? It's just like Spanx.'

'I can't breathe!' Gasping for breath, I looked down, only for my own boobs to nearly poke my eyes out. 'Oh, hello.'

'That's obscene.' James shook his head. 'I love it.'

'Hi, stereotypical gay man.' I tried to hold my hand out to him, but the dress was too restrictive to allow for courtesy. The cap sleeves cut off my circulation, ensuring an evening of penguin flapping and no sitting down. 'Nice to meet you. I'm going to be your hag for the night.'

'Shut up and put some make-up on,' he said, grabbing my Red Bull and knocking it back. 'You look like shit.'

Since my make-up collection was AWOL, along with my borrowed handbag and Sadie's shoes, I borrowed a judicious amount of eyeliner from Jenny's stash and let Sadie spray so much Elnett into my hair even Dolly Parton might have thought it was a bit much. It took less than five minutes to transform me from a shop-soiled Betty Draper into a poor man's Angelina Jolie. Quite the result.

The makeshift wedding reception hadn't stopped for the want of a bride or groom. It was chaos in the lounge, my beautiful snow-white room covered in bodies bumping and grinding and God knows what else. My poor sofa.

'Do you have any idea where Jenny and Jeff went?' I shouted at Sadie over the music. 'I'm worried about her.'

'We were all at the Venetian,' she said, trying to remember. 'Then me and Ben kind of, uh, hung out on our own for a while and then she was gone. I have no idea where.'

'And where's Ben?'

'Remember how I was telling you I pick the wrong guys?' she replied. 'He's one of the wrong guys. He went, I don't know, somewhere. Hopefully far away.'

'Well, I can't stay here.' I tapped my foot in time to what was passing for music. 'Where can we go?' The Red Bull Pro Plus cocktail was kicking up a fuss in my belly and a nervous spasm in my arm. This wasn't good.

'Let's go on an adventure,' Sadie clapped. 'I'll get my passport.'

'Can we leave now, please?' I asked James. 'I cannot wake up in Paris. I don't think I'm allowed back there.'

'Oh, Angela.' He swept me up in a terrible *Dirty Dancing* lift and held me high off the floor, ignoring my yelps. 'There's no way they can send you back to the UK. New York needs you.'

'And I need the toilet,' I squealed, holding onto his wrists for dear life. 'So I'd put me down before there's an accident.'

And he did.

If only men would do as they were told without the threat of being peed on.

CHAPTER SEVENTEEN

The first thought that ran through my head was how badly I wanted a strawberry Pop-Tart.

The second, third and fourth all came to me more or less at the same time. Where am I? What am I wearing? Why does my mouth taste like I've been eating dirty cat litter and who is that in bed next to me? Not recognizing your bedmate immediately was something I had only experienced once before, and it wasn't my favourite way to induce a stroke but it was one of the most effective. And this wasn't my hotel room. It was the opposite of my hotel room. Dark, dank, mirrored ceilings and pleather everything else. I rubbed the bed sheets between my thumb and forefinger. They were absolutely not machine-washable. Vom. More worryingly, my dress had been replaced with a green velvet tunic. And, unless I was very much mistaken, I was wearing a hat. It would appear I was dressed as an elf. What kind of weirdo had a Christmas elf fetish? I mean, aside from me?

'Oh God.' I made the right shapes with my mouth to speak, but no sound came out. Someone had flicked my mute switch in the night. I hoped that was all they had flicked. My head was swimming with images of the night but not fuzzy with a hangover, more like a movie on high-speed rewind so I couldn't quite follow the plot. 'I've been Hangovered.'

'Morning, lover.' The body beside me stirred, and I was almost certain it wasn't Bradley Cooper.

Just as I was about to start screaming, my brain kicked in all at once. I had not been drugged. I had willingly taken caffeine pills. Even though I knew how they kicked my arse. Even after I'd seen what they did to Jessie on *Saved by the Bell*. I sat up and rested my head on my knees as the events of the night before came streaming back. The dancing. The phone calls. Oh dear God, the phone calls. What I wouldn't give to be hungover, curled around the toilet and having a little cry.

'I'd take your arm off for a bacon sandwich.' James stretched a red-velvet-clad arm in front of me. 'A proper, honest to God bacon sandwich. Loads of brown sauce.'

The swell of relief that came from knowing the man in bed beside me was gayer than a Kylie concert crashed over me so hard, I collapsed back onto the bed.

'And a tea. I need some tea. Do you think they've got room service here?' He sat up and looked around at our skeezy surroundings. 'Hmm. Maybe not, maybe not?'

I pressed my forearm over my eyes and let the rest of the jigsaw pieces merrily slot themselves into place.

'Why couldn't I have just got super-drunk and passed out?' I asked. 'Why did I have to take caffeine pills and remember everything?'

'Maybe you could fill me in?' James suggested. 'I'm sure I didn't leave my room dressed as Father Christmas last night.'

'No, you did not.' I pressed my fingers to my temples and willed my memory to stop rewinding. 'And you didn't get it at the Wynn, either.'

'We went to the Wynn?'

'But you wouldn't let me go in because you said I needed to give Alex his space,' I nodded. 'So we went next door instead.'

'What was next door?'

'Santa's grotto.'

'Really?'

'Santa's grotto strip club.' Catholic churches should install mirrors on the ceiling; they were wonderful for making sure you were suffering an adequate amount of shame.

'Ahh. Would that be where we got these terribly flattering outfits?'

'Happily, no.' It was an odd day when your biggest source of relief was that you hadn't swapped clothes with a stripper. 'There was a drugstore next to that. I do think it was my idea, though. Sorry.'

'You should wear green more often,' James commented, rolling up the sleeves of his Father Christmas suit, a large, cheap beard tangled up around his neck. 'Suits you.'

'It actually does.' The mirror on the ceiling was also very useful for checking out my outfit without getting out of bed.

'I can't believe we went to a strip club,' he groaned. 'I mean, there's nothing there for either of us. It's just sad.'

'Well, I think I did mention it at the time, but you insisted it was a Vegas rite of passage. After that, all I remember was my caffeine crash, and you said you had somewhere we could stay.' I looked around the room once more and tried not to cry. 'Good work.'

'I don't remember any of that.' He looked relieved. I was jealous. 'It's weird, though. I feel like I've hardly slept.'

'What time is it?' The bottoms of my feet were sore and filthy. Truly, I was disgusting. 'We're going home today.'

'It's actually only nine.' James checked the time on his phone. 'The last call was made on my phone at three. So we must have checked in about then?'

'Shouldn't worry. I'm guessing they let the room by the hour.' I tried my hardest to avoid the judgemental mirror, but since every surface in the room that wasn't wipe-down-ready was reflective, it was more or less impossible. I looked like an extra from *Kiss Saves Christmas*. Except less feminine. 'That last call – it wasn't to Alex, by any chance?'

'As an early Christmas present, I'm going to lie to you.' James threw me a handy wet-wipe from the intimacy kit he'd just popped. Ew, ew, ew, ew.

'Can I check my email on your phone?' Glutton for punishment.

'It's physically possible, yes, but I don't know if you have the manual dexterity.' I was pretty confident I would be OK with it. There were no large bodies of water within these four walls. 'Where is yours again?'

'Water-damaged,' I replied, tapping my username and password onto the screen while James went off for a wee. 'What's the bathroom like?'

He was quiet for a moment. 'If you can hold it, hold it.'

'Gotcha,' I murmured to myself. I'd been hoping Alex might have sent something, even if it was a torrent of abuse, but nope, not even a lolcat. But there was another email from my UK editor, only this time from a personal email address. Oh.

Angela, can you give me a quick call? Best to try my mobile, whenever's good.

Double oh.

I considered the boundary-crossing issue of using the phone of someone I hadn't seen in a year to make an international mobile-to-mobile phone call for approximately seven seconds before curiosity got the better of me. I wasn't a cat; I'd be fine.

'Hi, Sara?' It took me a couple of goes at the international dialling codes from a mobile, but I got there in the end. 'It's Angela. Clark.'

'Oh! Hi! What a lovely surprise!'

Sara and I didn't speak often, but when we did, she didn't usually sound like she was being bugged by the FBI.

'You said to call,' I replied hesitantly. 'Is this a bad time?'

'Noooooo.' The length of her single-word reply cost James about three quid. I quietly assumed he never actually checked his phone bills.

'Is everything all right?' It clearly wasn't.

'It's just . . .' Sara coughed, cleared her throat and sighed. 'I know we don't know each other that well, but I just wanted to check in on you. We had an email at the office, from the US.'

'Right.'

'And it said you were, um, working. As a, well. Escort?'

Just when you thought things really couldn't get any worse, life always managed to find that one extra kick in the bollocks.

'Sara – ' I almost couldn't bring myself to ask – 'did that email come from Cici Spencer?'

'Yes?'

269

'OK, well, I'm not an escort.' Which of course is exactly what an escort would say. Cunning plan, Cici. 'Really, I was waitressing.'

'Angela, I'm not having a go or anything, I was just worried about you. I know how hard life can be out there in New York, but it just seemed a bit extreme.' Sara's very British sense of acute embarrassment was in full flow. 'Sometimes it starts as waitressing in these places, but then you hear stories from the other girls, and the money is good, I know, but you're a good writer, really good.'

'Sara, let me stop you there.' A strange sense of calm settled over me. 'I'm not an escort. I'm not waitressing in a strip club. I was a cocktail waitress at a friend's event for one night only as a favour and she had all the waitresses wear these stupid outfits. I'm not shagging for money. I'm not serving overpriced drinks somewhere they do shag for money. I'm absolutely, positively not an escort.'

Although, now I had said it out loud, I wondered how much you could make as a waitress down at the Gentlemen's Club. All those cabs running around with blatantly illegal photos of Jordan on them, they must be constantly hiring.

'Oh. Really?'

Apparently I had not been emphatic enough.

'Really. Cici's a psycho. And I would be the worst escort ever.'

'True,' she laughed, relieved. I tried not to be offended. But, ooh, if they had only cancelled me because they thought I was selling it, maybe they wouldn't cancel me! 'It's a bit of a shame, though. I was going to wait for the drama to die down and then ask you to do a Belle de Jour-type thing for me.'

'So you are actually finishing me?' I asked. Bye-bye, tiny flicker of hope.

'Yeah.' She sounded sorry, even if she wasn't. 'I mean, this email thing didn't help, but it has been running for a year. The team want to freshen things up.'

'With a column written by an escort?'

'It was just an idea.'

Couldn't blame me for being a bit put-out.

'There will be something,' she promised. 'I just don't know what it is yet.'

'Sounds about right.' I nodded to James as he emerged from the bathroom looking very upset. 'Talk to you later.'

'Merry Christmas,' Sara replied. 'And if I don't talk to you before, happy new year.'

'Yeah.' My Christmas spirit was starting to jingle all the way away. 'You too.'

'Well, that was an incredibly unpleasant experience.' James couldn't seem to stop rubbing his hands together. Out, out damned spot. 'Can we just get out of here?'

And so a very hungover Santa and his worse-for-wear elf checked out of the dodgy motel at nine a.m. and squinted into the sunlight. We were clearly several miles away from the Strip, the Excalibur and Luxor winking in the distance. Still, the desert was pretty, so that was nice. James patted himself down, pausing over his chest pocket. He pulled out a key attached to a key ring from Enterprise car rental and held it up for an explanation. Being the only one in their right mind, I took it from him and pressed the unlock button. Across the car park, I heard a friendly beep and raised an eyebrow at James.

'You genius.' He gave me an appreciative slap on the arse and set off across the dusty car park. It was only in the full glare of the Nevada sun that I noticed the seams in James's Santa suit were made of Velcro. Stay classy, Las Vegas.

'I'm going to hazard a guess that you dropped me off at the motel and then went back out again?' I crossed my arms and stared at the car.

'Oh, fuck.' James stopped dead and winced with the weight of the memories flooding back. 'I didn't.'

In the back seat of the convertible were eight boxes of Cheez-Its and three adorable puppies sleeping happily inside their pet carriers. Tags on the fronts of their cages declared their names to be Jim, Sadie and Angela.

'Remember, Jim – ' I declared after a moment's consideration, walking around to the passenger seat and getting in. Puppy Jim gave a small whimper. Santa Jim followed suit – 'a dog is for life, not just for Christmas.'

It took me a few minutes to convince the concierge at the De Lujo to give me a new key for my hotel room. I didn't blame her. I wouldn't have wanted to give a key to their most opulent suite to someone who looked like a homeless elf either, but after successfully answering her security questions, she didn't have a lot of choice.

'Are there any messages?' I asked.

She shook her head. She looked scared.

'Of course not.' I waved my key successfully. 'Never mind. Thank you, I'll see that Santa puts you on the nice list.'

The concierge laughed nervously and started pressing buttons at an unseen console. Before she could have me escorted from the premises, I ducked through the thankfully quiet casino and into the lift, jabbing the PH button with a busted manicure.

Opening the door to our suite I expected to see all manner of apocalyptic destruction, but I had underestimated the power of a Las Vegas hotel cleaning crew. The place was empty. No people, no patron, no problem. The suite looked exactly as it had the day we checked in. White, shiny and full of flowers. And, just like last time, my heart sank at the sight of Sadie.

'Holy shit.' She lifted her head up from one of the couches. 'What the hell happened to you?'

She was still in her white bandage dress, but now she looked considerably more supermarket than super-model. Her hair was tucked behind her ears, matted with who knew what, and her face was pale and drawn. I wouldn't have given her ten thousand dollars to get out of bed, but I would have offered her a twenty to get back in and stay there.

'I'm an elf.' I looked down at the outfit and back up at Sadie. It was actually a nice shade of green. Very similar to the colour of her face. 'What happened here?'

'I don't know. I passed out hours ago.' She let her head drop back onto the sofa. 'I woke up and house-keeping were cleaning around me.'

'Who got rid of all the people?' My filthy feet left a train of elf prints across the carpet, but I was too exhausted to give a shit. My mother would have been mortified. Good job I wasn't planning on telling her.

'I did.'

Standing tall, all big hair and bright smiles, Jenny stood in the corridor that led off to the bedrooms, bathed in golden early morning light. She was sparkly and shiny and clean. I was dank and dirty and grim. A Tim Burton elf to her Disney princess. The cow.

'Angela, why are you dressed as Robin Hood?' she asked, descending the steps into the sunken lounge, all cream cashmere sweater and skinny jeans as though nothing was wrong.

'I'm an elf,' I repeated. 'Jenny, why are you dressed like you're about to star in an advert for settees?'

'These are my clothes?' She curled her legs underneath herself on the sofa and unscrewed a bottle of Vitamin Water. 'Really, honey, you need to go and take a shower. You would scare children. You're scaring my ovaries. Looking at you is stopping me from ovulating.'

For a moment I did think I might have gone mad, but one quick look at Sadie's expression reassured me that I had not. Her jaw was practically on the floor.

'Jenny, you do remember what you were doing the last time we saw you, yes?' I put my hands on my felt-covered hips. It was quite snug, actually.

She tilted the bottle to her lips and nodded. The sun glinted off the diamond ring she was still wearing on her wedding finger.

'You left your shoes and your handbag in the chapel,' she replied. 'They're in my room.'

Not for the first time in my life, Jenny Lopez left me speechless.

'OK, I'll say it.' Sadie sat upright on the sofa. 'Have you gone fucking crazy?'

Jenny set the bottle down on the coffee table and twisted the ring around her finger but said nothing.

'That thing isn't going to answer for you,' I said. 'Unless it's a magic ring and I saw the *Green Lantern*, and that is not the ring from the *Green Lantern*.'

'You saw that?' Sadie asked. 'No one saw that.'

'Not now, Sadie.' I was shouting now. 'Seriously?

You're just going to sit there in your lovely clean jumper and pretend everything is absolutely fine?'

'What is your issue with this sweater?' she yelled back. 'And yes, I am going to pretend everything is fine because I'm not pretending. Everything is fine.'

'And where is your lovely husband?' I held my arms out and looked around the suite. 'Popped out to get the *The New York Times* and a fucking clue?'

'Oh, snap,' Sadie said, smirking on the sofa.

'You can shut your mouth,' Jenny spat at her roommate before turning on me. 'He's not here. He's at his hotel, where we spent the night. Packing. And then we're going back to New York, where we're getting everything made legal and you're going to wish you had shut the fuck up when you had the chance.'

It was too much. I was too wired from last night's Pro Plus binge to have this conversation without saying something I was going to regret, and Jenny was clearly certifiably insane. I was never coming back to Las Vegas as long as I lived.

'I'm going to have a shower and pretend none of this has happened,' I announced, turning my back on the entire scene. 'I can't deal with this. I'm not talking to you until you stop being a moron.'

'Yeah, that fits perfectly with your "I will never judge you" bullshit speech.' Jenny's voice was high and she was on the verge of tears. I didn't need to see her face to know. 'Thanks, Angela. Thanks for being the best friend ever.'

Cockingtons. This wasn't the first time my mouth had got me into trouble, but it was the first time I felt like it could really cost me my best friend.

'Fine.' I didn't know what else to say. Too much caffeine eats away at sugar coating so I wasn't able to sweeten my words. 'You're right. I am judging you. But not for the stupid Vegas wedding. I'm pissed off that you're lying to yourself about how this is all going to be OK, that it's going to make you happy.'

'You wanted me to make a decision, I made a decision.' She kicked the coffee table hard, sending her water up into the air.

'Zomg,' Sadie commented quietly as the table hit her sofa.

'You didn't make a decision,' I rallied. 'You got shit-faced and made a mistake. There's no way this was your idea. What happened? You threatened to break it off, am I right?'

She answered me with silence and a glance at the floor. Ah-ha. Now it was my turn to play psychic.

'So you told him it was over and he proposed?' I was on a roll. 'And you thought, brilliant! Now I don't have to make any more decisions! I'll just shackle myself to this twat!'

'Because your decisions are so much better than mine?' Her voice was lower but still furious. 'Ooh, I want to stay in New York but I'm too scared to ask my boyfriend for help because he's actually an asshole who will probably say no and then I'm totally screwed because I suck at everything and I can't get a job.'

'Woah.' Sadie's head flicked from left to right as though she were at the world's bitchiest tennis match. 'She didn't mean that, Angela.'

That was it. I plucked a cushion from the sofa and hurled it across the room at miss self-righteous. And missed by a mile. But the point was made. 'Actually, I did take your advice – ' even if she wasn't, I was still shouting – 'and he said yes. But it was a huge mistake. Like your face.'

It seemed like the right thing to say at the time, but once it was out of my mouth, I had to admit it didn't really have the impact I was hoping for.

'So, you got married too?' Sadie asked from the sofa. 'Is that why you were in the chapel? Why didn't you tell me?'

'No, we didn't.' I knew the waterworks were gearing up and I didn't know how to stop them. 'And now it's all fucked up.'

'Well, that sucks,' Jenny feigned sympathy and wiped non-existent tears from her eyes. 'We could have shared a wedding anniversary.'

'You're being a complete twat.' I had never been so frustrated with another human in all my days. 'Why can't you see this is not real? This is not going to last. He has a fiancée at home. You have a boyfriend and you are going to get your heart broken.'

'How do you know?' Now she was crying for real. 'What makes you the expert?'

'*I know because you know.*' I was shouting so loud, it didn't even sound like me. '*And you're my best friend.*'

Silence.

Sadie peeped up over the back of the couch. 'Aww, you guys.'

Jenny was quiet. The defiant arch of her back faltered; her straight shoulders started to slouch. Her eyes were still locked on mine, but the anger was burning out fast, just leaving the tears.

'He loves me,' she said thickly.

'I know.' I pressed my lips together hard and swiped my own tears away. 'But I don't think he loves you enough.'

'Maybe this time will be different.' She twisted the

ring around and around on her finger, trying to screw it into place permanently. 'Maybe I can change things.'

Wiping my hands on my elvish uniform, I shook my head. 'You shouldn't have to.'

Everyone shut up for a moment; the air was full of nothing but sniffs and sighs – Jenny on one side, the sleeve of her sweater darkened with tears, me on the other, green of dress, red of face. At least it was a seasonal combo.

'I don't want to be a dick,' I mumbled. 'But I really do need to go and have a shower.'

Jenny was across the room in less than four strides and her hug knocked me onto the floor in less than four seconds.

'I'm totally getting in on this. You two are insane,' Sadie yelped, vaulting over the sofa and piling on top of the girl-hug. 'It's awesome.'

'Do they have security cameras in here?' I asked from the bottom of the hot-girl pile-up. 'Because we could make some money from this.'

'Two girls, one elf?' Jenny suggested. 'I'd watch it.' She disengaged herself from the collection of limbs on the floor. 'And if you get her into the shower pronto, we might still make our flight home.'

Staggering to my feet, I gave Jenny a quick, tight hug as Sadie crawled back to her spot on the couch, glowing with girl love. 'I'm sorry,' I said quietly, squeezing out my last couple of tears. 'Really.'

'No way.' She wiped the tears off my cheeks. 'I'm sorry. I just can't deal with the fact that you're probably right. Do you want to talk about the Alex stuff? What happened?'

'After a shower?' I was almost certain the itching was all in my head, but there was always a chance the costume had bed bugs. I wanted it off.

278

'OK, I'll get you some tea.' The ultimate peace offering. 'I really am sorry. Jesus, I say some shit to you. You must be a total masochist to hang out with me.'

I patted her hand and gave her my most understanding smile.

'Just English,' I said. 'Just English.'

CHAPTER EIGHTEEN

The huge free-standing mirror was angled right at me when I got into my room. I was sure housekeeping had set it up on purpose. Staring back at me was Bizarro Angela. Wire-wool hair, black eyes rimmed with red and a nose that would put Rudolph to shame. I wished I had my phone; Louisa needed a picture of this. A warning to my future god-daughter of the dangers of, well, being me. This it what it looked like when your life went to shit. When people were sad in films, they got a bit dewy-eyed, wore slightly baggy jeans and possibly put their hair in a ponytail, but that was reserved for the worst cases. No one ever woke up in a filthy sex motel in bed with a homosexual wearing a stripper's elf costume. Where was that movie? It was a thought that stayed with me while I took a shower and the bath filled up. This was definitely a double-dip situation. One or the other just wasn't going to be enough.

I wondered what Jenny was going to do about Jeff. I wondered what I was going to do about Alex. I wondered what James was going to do with eight boxes of Cheez-Its and three puppies. I wondered if this happened to everyone when they came to Vegas. Well into my third shampoo, I heard the room phone ringing. One of the things that marked the De Lujo out as a swanky hotel was the fact that they had phones in the toilet. For some reason I found this endlessly impressive. Swiping suds out of my eyes, I ducked out from under the water and answered.

'Hello?'

'Awesome. You're alive.'

It was a reasonable reaction, given the number of voicemails I'd left for him the night before.

'I am so sorry.' Rather than try to explain myself, I thought it would be better to just go with a constant flow of apology until he stopped me. 'So sorry. Just more sorry than you could imagine. Incredibly sorry.'

'I don't think I quite caught that?' he interrupted, and I was thankful for the small smile I could hear in his voice. 'What the hell happened to you last night?'

I sat down on the toilet still wearing my sudsy hat.

'Tequila, caffeine pills and a puppy sanctuary. It's really an in-person story. What time's your flight?'

'Oh, yeah.' His voice soothed my caffeine come-down better than the shower, the bath and two packets of minibar M&M's combined. 'We're actually staying until tomorrow.'

'We are?' Hadn't Jenny said Jeff was supposed to fly home today?

'I'll be home tomorrow. Late, though.'

Blowing errant bubbles out of my eyes, my stomach started to drop again. 'We, um, we really need to talk about what happened yesterday,' I said, suddenly very aware of the fact that I was naked on the toilet.

'We do,' Alex agreed. 'But we don't need to do it in Vegas. We can do it at home.'

'Not if you're not at home.' I was very close to wailing. All I wanted was to get on a plane, get into bed, under the covers, and never get back out again, but that wasn't going to work if Alex wasn't in there with me. 'I thought you were on the same flight back as us.'

'I changed it — don't freak out.' He was perfectly calm, the opposite of how I'd last seen him. Someone had had some thinking time. Someone hadn't been negotiating dress prices with strippers and wrangling puppies. 'I'll be home tomorrow, and on Tuesday we'll sit down and work this whole thing out. Text me when you land, OK?'

Text not call.

It was a little thing, but all I heard was that he didn't want to talk to me. I was probably overreacting. Being inappropriately naked always made me overreact.

'I'll text,' I said, quashing the gnawing feeling in my stomach. 'I love you. And I really am sorry about last night.'

'Don't,' Alex replied. 'I'll see you tomorrow.'

I was fairly certain what he meant to say was 'I love you too and am also sorry, let us never speak of it again', but I gave him the benefit of the difficult-phone-conversation doubt and said goodbye. Replacing the handset, seated on the loo completely starkers with a head covered in shampoo, I pouted into the bathroom mirror. It was not a good start to a week when this was the best you'd looked all day.

Once I'd scrubbed the top seven layers of my skin clean away, dried myself off and packed up all my worldly goods, I went into the lounge to wait for Jenny and Sadie. Who were nowhere near ready. Of course.

'I'm going to have a walk around outside,' I called

at the doorway to Jenny's room. She made an acknowledging noise and then went back to swearing at her luggage. I noticed straight away that she had taken off the diamond ring. Leaving my tiny carry-on suitcase back in the middle of the lounge, I picked up my satchel and surveyed the damage. Falling into a fountain hardly ever fell into the category of a Good Thing, but when you were a beautiful leather bag that had, in all honesty, already seen its best days, it was a complete tragedy.

'I'm so sorry,' I whispered, stroking it gently. 'I seem to be saying that an awful lot today.'

The bag groaned with sympathy as I slung it over my American Apparel stripy T and let it hang on my denim-clad hip. Every inch of me was covered. There would be no mistaking me for a stripper, a hooker, a pole dancer or anything else ever again. Hopefully.

The casino was buzzing with people, most clutching a Bloody Mary to acknowledge they were aware it was Sunday. I wished I had my phone with me so I could google the number of churches in Las Vegas. I couldn't decide whether there would most likely be more or fewer than in your average town.

It was eternal twilight in here. No time, no daylight, no weather, nothing but a constant supply of cocktails and the ching-ching-ching of a slot machine paying out. Those sparkly vampires were so stupid, Washington? I got that they were trying to atone for some perceived sin, but who hated themselves enough to constantly put themselves through puberty? Eternal high school. Jenny got upset when I voiced my issues with her very favourite saga, but it just didn't make sense. The dad worked, the kids were forced to take algebra over and over and over, but what was the mum doing all day?

They should have moved here and opened a hotel. It would have made much more sense. She could have run the roulette wheel.

I gravitated towards the slots, trying not to giggle at the ever-changing screens that declared them the loosest slots in Vegas. Perching on one of the stools, I dug around in my bag for a few quarters to pass the time and stared up at the screens situated all around me. Ooh, Snooki was going to be here for New Year. That seemed sad, I thought; New Year wasn't a time to be working. I hoped she was bringing some friends. As I'd already proven, I was not a natural gambler, but who could get a slot machine wrong?

'Honey, you're doin' it all wrong.'

I knew a New Jersey accent when I heard it, and when I looked up, I knew exactly where it was coming from. A little old lady shook her head at me so violently, I was very worried she was going to lose her wig. Man alive, that was a vibrant shade of orange. She looked like Lady Gaga after a few minutes in the microwave.

'You gotta pay attention.' She pointed at the screen in front of her. 'You can't just go around pushing buttons.'

'Well, that's just good advice in general,' I said, trying to follow what she was doing, but it was just a fevered blur of nudges, freezes and rolls to my untrained eye. I was mostly disappointed that there was no actual arm to pull on any of these machines, just little bright buttons, all lighting up in no particular order that I was able to discern.

'Get over here – these are the machines you should be playing.' She beckoned me over to the one-armed bandit, away from the giant sparkly machines promising all the joys of gambling combined with your favourite chick flick. Who wouldn't love a *Sex and the City* slot machine? But I felt like I had more to learn from my new friend than Mr Big. I'd always been more of an Aidan girl.

'You learn a lot about life playing the slots,' she replied, eyes locked on the prize. 'You press a few buttons, you twist a few arms, you hope you're gonna win. Sometimes you lose a little, sometimes you lose a lot. Some people think they know how to beat the system.' She turned to me and scoffed. 'They don't. You can't beat the slots.'

'Then why play?' I asked, watching her press the various buttons in no discernible order. Hold, shuffle, spin. It all looked very confusing.

'Because sometimes you win big.' She looked back at the machine, its lights reflecting in her bifocals. 'Everyone wins sometime, but they don't know how to quit when they're ahead. Then you end up with nothing. You get everything, and then before you know it, you got nothing again. You followin' me? You know what I'm sayin'?'

'Worryingly, I am.' A nod for my new friend, a quarter for my machine.

'I been married four times.' She held up her left hand to show me an assortment of knuckledusters. 'And four times I picked losers. They don't know when to stop. They don't know how to walk away unless they're walking away from a woman. Men, they mess up their lives and they blame their wives. They'll stick with their blackjack dealer longer than their own family, and he's the one taking their money.'

More quarters in the machine. Press some more buttons.

'You girls today, you're no better.' She paused to point a long fingernail at me, just to make sure I knew exactly who she was talking about. 'I see you on the floor. You flit from one machine to the next – oh, this one isn't paying out, so I'll try another. And another. And another. And then none of them pay out and you want to go back to the first one, but it's too late. Someone else already got the jackpot. Good things come to those who wait, doll.'

'Right.' I had no idea that gambling could be such an accurate metaphor for life. Or at least slutty girls.

'So that's it.' She turned back to her machine, pressed one more button and waited while it spat out a little white slip of paper. 'You find a machine you like, you stick with it, and you quit while you're ahead. Shuffle. Now stick.'

'So you leave your boyfriend before he leaves you?'

Three pineapples lit up my screen and my tutor nodded proudly. 'There you go.'

I was unreasonably excited. The grim spectre of a life spent dancing for pennies on a New York street corner appeared in front of me. I had absolutely no willpower.

'You're saying I should dump my boyfriend?' I looked from my gambling guru to the flashing slot machine. Did I win?'

'Who's talking about boyfriends?' She clambered off her stool and readjusted her 'hair'. 'Boyfriends in general are bad news, doll. You got to find something for yourself. You work out what makes you happy, set yourself up in that business, and if you end up with a fella, then whoop-de-do. If you don't, you're still happy. And yeah, you won. Five bucks. Don't spend it all at once.'

'Do you think you'll ever get married again?' I asked, trying to follow the same pattern she'd shown me.

My mentor rattled the chain handle of a Chanel handbag into the crook of her arm and picked up a Big Gulp cup of quarters.

'Not me, doll. I cashed out a long time ago. Pamela de Lujo,' She shook my hand with a force that almost made my wig fall off. 'This place is my husband and it's more of a bastard than either of the other four, but I can't tell you how much I love it. I hope you're enjoying your stay here. Remember what I said.'

And with that she trundled off across the floor while I gaped. A personal gambling lesson from the owner of the casino. Well, that was something.

'I bet she's a vampire,' I whispered to my slot machine and pressed the play button. It chimed its agreement. Then it kept chiming. And chiming. And chiming.

'Oh, crap,' I said out loud, pretending there weren't dozens of people staring at me. 'I've broken it.'

'Not quite, honey,' replied a passing waitress. 'I'm gonna go get you some champagne.'

Because that was what I needed right now – another drink.

An hour after we were supposed to leave, I let Jenny bundle me into a limo, dazed and buzzed. Sadie barrelled in after me, laying every inch of her five foot ten out on the bench opposite. Beautiful people had no need for seat belts. They did, however, need more luggage for one weekend than I had personal belongings. Why Sadie had three giant suitcases when none of her clothes were bigger than a legwarmer was quite the mystery. I sat quietly nursing my handbag, little blue carry-on case at my feet, not quite sure what to say, not quite sure what had just happened.

'I can't believe we're leaving already.' Sadie looked

out of the window mournfully as we pulled away from the white marble majesty of Pamela's casino resort. 'I could live at the De Lujo. It's like they made it for me.'

It made me smile to think that this super-luxe palace with its beaches, its bars and all its buff bikini babes belonged to a little old woman with orange hair from New Jersey who liked to play the slots. I couldn't imagine Sadie would be her cup of tea.

'You have work this week?' Jenny asked, rubbing Kiehl's balm into her lips. The pre-flight moisturizing saga began. 'Will you be around?'

'Actually, I'm going to be around a lot more, I think,' Sadie answered, beaming at me. 'Angela gave me some really awesome advice.'

'Did she now?' Jenny turned to face me. 'And what exactly has Angela been advising?'

It was difficult to say which was more unnerving – the full force of a living Barbie doll's biggest grin or Jenny's most threatening glare.

'Please note that anything I said over the last four days cannot be relied upon or used against me in a court of law,' I said, pulling my bag closer to set up a barricade between me and my best friend. 'I'm not in a position to be advising anyone on anything.'

'No, all that stuff you said about doing something that would make me happy,' Sadie explained. 'It made me think. I was like, if I could be doing anything, what would it be? So this morning I sent some emails and I'm going to start shadowing a few people, trying a couple of things.'

'Such as?' Jenny gave me another look, one that was mildly impressed.

'I'm talking to this girl I met at Sephora about a make-up line, and I'm gonna go into the *Belle* office for a few days, see if there's anything I could do in fashion magazines.' She perked up and batted me on the arm. 'Do you know Spencer Media? Maybe I could talk to them about having you do some stuff?'

Did I know Spencer Media?

'I don't reckon *Belle* are going to be into it.' I really didn't want to get into it. 'But you should definitely go and see how it feels.'

'*Belle* though?' Jenny didn't look convinced. 'I know they're super-fashion, but they don't feel like you. I mean, I get it every month and the fashion is awesome, but when was the last time you actually read something in *Belle*?'

I pondered for a moment. 'Apart from when I wrote for them?'

'Well, yeah, of course,' she covered. 'But it's just out of touch. *Belle* doesn't know what's happening in my life.'

'Their fashion is kind of out there,' Sadie agreed. 'I guess I don't really do that much high fashion. And I kinda hate how big the monthlies are, they're too heavy. But the weeklies make me feel gross. I don't want to work somewhere if I'll constantly be needing to shower.'

'It does make checking email difficult,' Jenny said with sympathy. 'You're right, though. The monthlies are too heavy and the weeklies suck.'

'Right?' Sadie looked relieved to get Jenny's approval.

'So then what? Websites?' I asked, curious. 'I just really love the feeling of turning the pages on a magazine – it's the ritual as much as the content.'

'I'm gonna start my own eventually,' Jenny declared. 'It's all part of the New Oprah plan. My magazine isn't out there yet.'

'Can it not weigh twenty pounds?' Sadie asked. 'Though I guess it's a good bicep workout.'

'You should still definitely do *Belle*, though,' I told her. 'It'll be a good experience. Even if it's shit.'

'Yeah, I'm actually excited.' She looked surprised. 'I do love modelling, but I know it's not for ever. I'd forgotten how much fun it can be to do something new. Like the first day of school.'

'You enjoyed school, right?' Jenny asked.

'Sure.' Sadie nodded.

'Cheerleader?'

'Uh-huh.'

'Yeah.'

'Figures.'

The traffic was nose to tail on the Strip, leaving us sitting right outside the Venetian for far too long. I stared out of the window and felt my eyes sting and my nose tingle. He was up there somewhere. I flicked my hair forward until it covered my face and breathed in the scent of my shampoo until I had composed myself.

'Did you speak to him?' Jenny asked, tucking my hair back behind my ears and brushing away my good work with one hand.

'He's staying an extra night.' There, that wasn't too hard to say. 'Did you speak to Jeff?'

She stretched her long legs out across the back of the limo and looked up at the sliding roof. 'Yeah.'

'Are you OK?'

'No.'

She still wasn't wearing the ring, but it was only when she started talking that I realized she wasn't wearing any eye make-up at all. Jenny never left the house without mascara. She even made the ambulance wait for her to put eyeliner on when she was taken in with suspected appendicitis. Clearly, we were anticipating tears.

'Are you going to be OK?'

'Yes.'

She didn't sound convinced, but at least she'd said it. Sadie looked at me with her giant Snow White eyes, clearly desperate to know more, but I shook my head slightly. She'd tell us when she was ready. Knowing Jenny it wouldn't take long.

'He's going to see what we have to do to have the wedding annulled.'

Not long at all.

'He doesn't think it's legal anyway because we didn't get a licence. And he wants to talk when we get back.' She laughed a little bit. 'He's not sure it's fair to his fiancée to call things off at the last minute.'

'Wouldn't it be less fair to make her marry an arsehole?' I asked. 'Or for him to marry someone he doesn't love?'

'But he does love her,' Jenny replied evenly. 'He loves both of us. He's very confused. Everything got out of hand because we were in Vegas. He needs time to think.'

A common theme of male guests of the Venetian. Clearly the top hotel for self-reflection. I shrugged. Jenny shook her head. Words seemed a bit redundant.

'Screw that.' Sadie thought otherwise. 'Vegas always takes the blame for a lot of dumbass people doing dumbass things,' she pointed out in another startling display of insight. 'No one holds a gun to your head and says "hey, you're in my town, you dumb shit, now do twenty-five tequila shots and fuck a donkey or I'll shoot".'

It was a good point, well made.

'I love this city,' she said, taking Jenny's lip balm out of her bag and slicking it onto her own pout. 'It's a chance to get away from reality, not an excuse to act like a dick.'

The limo started to move forwards and I said my silent goodbyes. Bye Venetian, bye Bellagio, bye great big volcano. In spite of everything, I was surprised at how sad I felt. Sadie was right. The city didn't make people do stupid things, they managed that all on their own. Vegas just provided a more colourful backdrop than usual and that seemed to encourage eccentric behaviour. Maybe it was because there was such a high concentration of tigers in one place. Tigers I had not seen. Sad face.

But I wasn't leaving empty-handed. I had enough material for a hundred blog posts, about seventeen tea bags I'd nicked from the suite and, most importantly, I had an idea. Pamela, Sadie and Jenny had sparked off something exciting in me, and while I desperately wanted to demand we stop at the Mirage so I could play Siegfried & Roy (before the accident), I couldn't wait to get home and see what it could be. So that was nice.

And then there was the fifty thousand dollars I'd just won on the slot machine. That was quite nice too.

CHAPTER NINETEEN

I didn't tell Jenny about the win until we were safely on the plane so she couldn't make the limo driver turn around and make me put it all on red. She stared at the stash of readies for a few minutes before starting a new and revised Christmas list. I tried to explain to her that as much as I loved her, the odds of me ever buying an Hermès Birkin were slim to none, regardless of my high-roller status. We were looking at a Euro Lottery rollover before I spent five grand on a handbag for anyone. Well, for Jenny. The rest of the flight was spent in comfortable silence, Sadie fast asleep, me sketching out my big plan, and Jenny intermittently pulling my handbag out from under the seat in front and staring at my money.

New York was cold, but my apartment was warm when I got home and the first thing I did was light up the Christmas tree. There. Now nothing could be wrong. It glowed reassuringly in the corner as I went through the motions of unpacking. Put the kettle on, strip off my plane clothes, plug in my phone charger, even though I didn't have a phone. It was late but I wasn't ready to go to bed. Maybe because I'd taken caffeine tablets the night before. Maybe because I had a bundle of fifty-dollar bills in my handbag that amounted to more money than I'd ever had in my entire life. Maybe because when I went to bed I would fall asleep, and when I woke up it would be Monday. Monday was one day closer to D-day. As in D for deportation. But now I had my plan. My plan and fifty thousand dollars. I was staying in this bloody country whether they liked it or not. I just hoped I still had something to stay for.

All unpacked, suitcase hidden under the bed and my dirty clothes strewn across the bathroom floor, I collapsed on the sofa in my favourite flannel PJs. Alex claimed they didn't offend him, but I tried to save them for nights he wasn't around. I'd worn a lot of button-up pyjamas in my last relationship, and that had not ended well. I stared up at a picture of the two us on the fireplace and hoped I wouldn't be wearing them too much in the near future. And by too much, I meant all the time.

Jenny had taken the photo at Erin's wedding. It was out of focus, a little bit blurry and set at a weird angle. It was my favourite. We were hiding out on a balcony overlooking the reception, and Alex was whispering something to me, his hair falling down, green eyes flashing while I pressed a hand to my face and laughed. I couldn't quite remember what we were talking about, but I was fairly certain it wasn't something to be shared with the wedding party. Le sigh. For the want of something else to do, I grabbed my laptop and opened up my blog. Might as well start getting everything down on paper while it was fresh.

Adventures of Angela

What Happens in Vegas . . .
    If there's one thing we can all agree on as a people it's that 'what happens in Vegas, stays in

Vegas' is the most stupid saying ever uttered by man. Fabulous marketing campaign, terrible idea. Believing you can behave in whatever way you see fit and suffer no consequences just because you're in Sin City has less merit than a baby covering its eyes and thinking it has become invisible.

And, having just spent four very educational days in the notorious city I'm almost certain that not only is it a silly saying, it's also very untrue. A more accurate statement would be 'what happens in Vegas comes right home with you and cocks up your entire life'. There is an argument for 'what happens in Vegas stays in Vegas as long as you're an unconscionable knobhead', but that's not nearly as catchy. I can see why my alternatives might not catch on.

Having said all this, on reflection, I did some things in Vegas that I would never have done in New York. Stepping out of your life for a moment always makes some ideas seem more permissible, just like being drunk. Before you know it, you're lashed on Las Vegas and you lose your usual frame of reference. That's when the bad decisions kick in. Like taking a handful of caffeine pills, doing tequila shots then swapping clothes with a stripper so you're dressed up as an elf. Or, you know, you might do something really stupid. In reality, most people don't do anything too crazy, they just get drunk, gamble away money they don't have or marry Britney Spears.

But that would have been too simple for me. On a scale of one to ten, I managed to find an eleven. Instead of a regular Vegas cock-up (example – putting $100 into the Dirty Dancing slot machine)

I went for a big old life-altering fuck-up. The differ-ence between a cock-up and a fuck-up is epic. A cock-up is something that happens in a Carry On film or when your dad brings the wrong thing back from the supermarket. A fuck-up, on the other hand, is what happens in a Guy Ritchie movie or when your dad brings the wrong baby home from the hospital. It invariably ends in tears, if not the loss of a limb.

As I've already explained, what happens in Vegas does not stay in Vegas. It follows you home and continually pokes you in the shoulder while you're sleeping, while you're show-ering, while you're walking down the street until you turn around and confront it. So I'm getting ready to confront my Vegas vagaries with a huge apology and possibly some sort of bribe. Because wherever you are, what happens, happens, and that's not a cliché, it's a fact.

Alex never read my blog. At least he claimed never to read my blog. I had to imagine he flicked over it from time to time. Usually it didn't make a lot of differ-ence – I never wrote about us any more; I'd learned that lesson the hard way – but this wasn't so much a blog about us as a practice acknowledgement of just how stupid I had been before I could bust out my face-to-face moves. Everything seemed very clear now I'd got Las Vegas out of my system. Sober Angela knew what a bad idea it was to ask Alex to marry her for a visa. In truth, I'd known it all along; I just hadn't known why it was such a bad idea. My motivations had been entirely selfish: I was scared he'd say no. I was scared I would end up alone. At no point had I put myself in his shoes. The look on his face during the world's

296

worst proposal was something I would have to live with for ever. He was hurt. I had hurt him. And now I had to fix it. And I would, if he wanted to let me.

The relief of waking up in my own bed the next morning was short-lived. There was too much to be done to wallow in sleepy self-doubt so I fumbled for my non-existent phone on the night stand, knocking books, a bottle of nail polish and my empty pill packet onto the floor. Our bedroom was really still Alex's bedroom – nothing had changed since the first time I'd visited. The low futon had the same white bedspread, the acoustic guitar lay by the bed, books were still stacked all around and tea lights skittered around every surface. Only now, sometimes, under Alex's patient tutelage, I played that guitar, some of those books were mine, and when they burned out, I replaced the tea lights from the giant sack of Ikea candles that we kept under the sink. It wasn't that I didn't have stuff in the apartment; I did. Closets full. But as far as this room was concerned, it was my shrine to our relationship – I'd kept it this way on purpose. Whenever I came in here, I wanted to feel the same way I had the first time. His damp, fresh-from-the-shower hair brushing against my skin. His lips on my lips. His fingers entwined with my fingers. I shivered just thinking about it.

James's telling off echoing in my mind, I got up and went through to the living room, logged onto Facebook and clicked through my messages. Hmm. Nothing knocked morning horn on the head like a missive from your mum. Was I really sure I wasn't coming for Christmas, because she was in Tesco looking at turkeys and they only had big ones or crowns, and if it was just her and dad she was going to get a crown. She'd sent it five hours earlier, at four a.m. New York time. Presumably she was high at the time. I tapped out a quick response to say I hoped she'd gone for the crown and then set to on my emails. Jenny's horror at being back in the office. Louisa's horror at her belly button popping out. The edges of my mouth quirked up in a smile as I tapped out my replies. And then on to The Plan, arch nemesis of The Letter. Today was going to be a good day. Whether it liked it or not.

As the reigning queen of procrastination, I made a list of everything I wanted to do before Alex got home. I needed to write some emails, call Lawrence the Lawyer and start putting together a presentation. I also needed to do some Christmas shopping before I spent my fifty gees on Jimmy Choo over-the-knee boots and pedigree kittens. I wasn't a total shambles – I sent my emails first before layering up to hit the shops and pulling on my boots, aka Erin's hand-me-down Haider Ackermann from last season. She wouldn't be seen dead in last year's over-the-knee boots, whereas I would happily be seen dead, alive or mid-zombie apocalypse. They were amazing.

No one had told Manhattan about my ridiculous weekend away and so business was going on as usual when I emerged from Union Square, and my heart soared at the sight of the gingerbread house stalls set up for the holiday market. Christmas in Vegas was intense. It was Slade turned up to ten with a dubstep remix. It was that guy from finance who always wears mistletoe on his belt at the office party. New York was different. It was *Miracle on 34th Street* and Bing Crosby. It was proper Christmas. Chestnuts were roasting on a licensed and approved open fire, Jack Frost was nipping at my nose and I didn't even mind.

My shopping plan was simple. Start at Urban Outfitters on Sixth, head straight down to the village to the Marc Jacobs shop, pop into Alex's favourite guitar shop on Bleecker, short stop at Manatus to refuel and then wind up at Bloomingdale's in Soho to get my last bits and pieces. Then home to finish work on my presentation and wrap everything. By the time Alex got in, whenever that might be, the house would be full of freshly baked sugar cookies, beautifully wrapped gifts and me wearing an apron and a smile. And other clothes too; I'd learned that lesson the hard way as well.

'Hello? Angela?'

'In here.'

Alex walked into the living room and dropped his bag on the floor, frozen with fear.

'What happened?'

I glanced around helplessly. I was surrounded by piles of wrapping paper, reams and reams of ribbon, tape, scissors, metallic markers and gift cards. Various hats, scarves, bottles of perfume, sweaters and boxes of reindeer-shaped chocolates punctuated the shit tip. Somewhere, my laptop was hidden, playing 'Now That's What I Call Christmas'. I couldn't find it, so I couldn't turn it off. Christmas had got the best of me. I'd been beaten. Trying not to cry, I desperately kicked at a long, black box, trying to shove it under the settee without attracting Alex's attention. I'd had a very long and involved conversation with the man in the guitar shop who had shown me a beautiful vintage sky-blue Fender that had a fantastic something I couldn't even remember and an awesome black flying V that was bedazzled with a Batman logo. The Fender was expensive. The Batman guitar was very expensive but the strap doubled as a utility belt. It had been a tough choice.

'What's in the box?'

I promptly burst into tears.

Alex skipped over the sofa in one leap with a devil-may-care level of concern for Converse on cushion covers and dropped down to the floor to hold me tightly.

'I was wrapping,' I explained tearfully. 'But I lost the scissors and then the tape dispenser ran out and I was out shopping for hours and my feet hurt and I'm so, so tired.'

'This is why people kill themselves at Christmas,' he said, rocking me gently and wiping away my tears. 'You idiot.'

He sounded and smelled and looked just like himself again. Which made me cry more. 'I love Christmas,' I sniffed.

'It's an abusive relationship,' Alex said. 'You need to walk away.'

'It only does this to me because it loves me,' I argued. Sitting there, cradled in his arms, the smell of cold air still on his coat, made everything better. If only everything was so easy. Wrapping handbags was too hard. 'What time is it?'

'A little before midnight?' He pulled his phone out of his pocket to check. 'How long have you been doing this?'

'Some time?' It was all I was prepared to commit to. 'You're going to have to go in the bedroom while I wrap yours.'

I looked up, giving him my serious face. Somewhat compromised by streaks of mascara and a bright red nose, but still, it was serious.

'Mine?' He started scanning the love song to consumerism on the living-room floor. 'Something here is for me?'

Suddenly someone wasn't quite so anti-Christmas.

'Yes, and you're not allowed to see it.' I pushed him away. 'If you see your presents before Christmas day, baby Jesus cries.'

'We've established I don't do religion?' He scooted up onto the sofa and kicked off his shoes. 'And neither do you.'

'I like to hedge my bets in December.' I peeled off a layer of jumper until I was down to my T-shirt and knickers. Wrapping presents wasn't nearly as fun as I'd remembered. I'd lost my jeans during a fit over trying to fit my dad's bong into a packing tube. I'd thought it hilarious when I was passing the smoke shop in the East Village, but now it was safely wrapped up and addressed, I was worried I was just giving him ideas. Hopefully he'd be satisfied with his packet of Peeps.

Somehow we'd fallen right back into our happy place. Me having a neurotic meltdown on the floor, Alex passed out on the sofa with a seasonal addition of Mariah Carey. But that didn't mean we didn't need to talk.

'Have you got my Christmas present yet?'

We needed to talk about something very important.

'Baby Jesus doesn't want me to tell you,' he said with closed eyes.

I looked around at all my shopping splendour and rubbed my eyes dry. If there was a baby Jesus, he would use all of his magical powers to help me look half-decent right now.

'So, you had fun last night?' And please let my voice

301

not be quite so squeaky. And please let him bring up the wedding nonsense first. All my resolve had gone out the window when he'd walked in on me crying, trying to wrap a scarf and mitten set without readily available sticky tape.

'Yeah,' he replied without moving. 'The wolf pack fell apart a little so I just played some cards. Checked out the venue at Cosmopolitan. We might play a show there.'

'Did you talk to Jeff?'

Alex blew out a long breath. 'Yeah.'

'Is he OK?'

'He's fine.'

Of course he was. Jenny was at home, sobbing into the box set of *Game of Thrones*, dodging Sigge's calls and inhaling Häagen-Dazs. Jeff was probably two doors away from me, snuggling with his fiancée and pretending everything was A-OK. I picked up a NARS gift set and started wrapping with righteous indignation. Righteous indignation gave much sharper corners.

'This is going to be a lot quicker if you just say it.' Alex rubbed a hand over his face before turning to look at me. 'Whatever it is you're thinking.'

'I wasn't thinking anything.' Lies also made baby Jesus cry.

'He didn't mention Jenny, if that's what you wanted to ask,' he said. 'He mentioned Shannon. A whole bunch of times. But no mention of Jenny.'

If I ever met a woman who claimed to understand what went on inside men's tiny minds, I would punch her in the face for lying. How was it even possible that Jeff hadn't mentioned Jenny? There was a whole chain of he-knew-I-knew-he-knew-that-Alex-knew-that-Jeff-knew-that-we-all-knew-about-everything, and it was blowing every fuse in my brain. Were men that capable of pretending difficult things hadn't happened that they just erased the entire event?

'So what do you talk about?' I asked. 'For four whole days, what do men talk about?'

Alex groaned and gave me his sleepy eyes. 'Sports. Music. Ass. Can we go to bed?'

'How could a girl resist a seduction like that?' I didn't make a move to get up.

'We can talk about kittens and rainbows and ribbons if that helps?'

'Alexander Reid.' His name wasn't actually Alexander, but I found it useful to extend it when I was giving him a telling-off. The more we didn't talk about what had happened between us two nights before, the more it was a Thing. 'Don't make me beat you up.'

'So you don't want to run down to City Hall and get married?'

I turned sharply towards the sofa. He was still laid flat out on his back, head back, eyes closed.

'I think they're probably closed.' I was careful with my tone. This was my in. Gently, gently catchee hipster. Or something. 'Look, I know I went about everything the wrong way—'

'You think?' He cut me off before I got to my fabulous apology.

'Yes, I do – that's why I'm trying to apologize.' I gave him a moment to jump in, but this time he kept schtum. 'It was a stupid idea. I was stupid. Everything about it – stupid.'

Still no reaction.

'And I'm so, so sorry. I never meant to –' gulp – 'hurt you.'

This was probably the worst time in the world for Cliff Richard, but I still couldn't find my laptop, so the scariest silence of my life was filled by 'Mistletoe and Wine', like it or not.

'What makes you think I was – ' Alex echoed my pause – 'hurt?'

Well, I wasn't expecting that. 'Um, you weren't?'

'Yes, I was.'

Oh good. We were playing games. My favourite.

'I freaked out. You actually scared me,' he continued.

Not really any better.

'All that shit you started coming out with,' he went on. 'I mean, what was that?'

I took my hair out of the attractive on-top-of-the-head-and-out-of-the-way ponytail I was working and fingered the ends. It was getting long again.

'I didn't mean it,' I said. I was going to get it right this time. And I was not going to mention the post office. 'Of course marriage is a big deal. A huge deal. Epic. I knew it was a bad idea when I was saying it, that's why I didn't suggest it before. That's why I was trying everything else.'

'So you don't want to get married?' Alex said slowly. 'You'd rather go back to the UK?'

'No! Of course not.'

Alex sat up. 'No, you don't want to get married? Or no, you don't want to go back to London?'

I stared at him staring at me. How had I managed to talk myself into this corner again? 'It wasn't even my idea.' In the dictionary, there was a picture underneath the word 'exasperated' and that picture was of me. 'I just didn't know what else to do and I panicked. I don't want to leave.'

I don't want to leave *you*, the voice in my head reminded me. I really was bad at this.

'Let me guess – it was Jenny's idea?' Alex leaned

back against the sofa and laughed. His socks didn't match. 'It's maybe dumb enough. Just.'

'What's that supposed to mean?' I asked. Why didn't his socks match? The laundrette always bundled them together. They always bundled mine together.

'Ahh, come on, Angela,' he sighed. 'Don't make me say it. I know she's your friend, but that girl does nothing but cause trouble. She's a disaster. Whatever she tells you to do, you should just do the opposite.'

'So we're going to talk about Jenny instead of talking about us?' Cliff was getting right on my tits. Where was that laptop? 'Jenny is not the problem. But for the record, she is not a disaster. If this is about Jeff, I think you'll find he's the fuck-up there.'

Another excellent use of the term 'fuck-up'. I liked that it was a verb and a noun.

'He's the one who came to her. He's the one who suggested they get married.' I was really on a roll. The little sensible and so often ignored voice in my mind tried to remind me we were supposed to be talking about us, but I couldn't help myself. I was genuinely very pissed off at Jeff. 'And then he was the one who freaked out the next day and asked her to pretend it never happened. You can't do that. Just because you've got cold feet, you can't mess around with someone who loves you. You can't mess about with someone's emotions because it suits you.'

Alex narrowed his eyes. 'What, like you did?'

Colour me stunned. I felt all the blood drain out of my face and my heart started to pound. 'What?'

'You can't sit there and kick Jeff's ass for taking advantage of someone who "loves him".' A very unwelcome use of air quotes was injected into the conversation. 'When you thought it was a good idea to ask me to marry you, to *marry you*, Angela, just to get a visa so you can stay here and keep getting into bullshit adventures with your dumb-shit girlfriend.'

'Is that what you think?' I stood up. I wasn't sure why. 'Honestly?'

'That's what you said.' He placed a lot of emphasis on the end of the sentence. In all honesty I couldn't remember exactly what I'd said, but I was fairly certain I wouldn't have mentioned bullshit adventures with my dumb-shit girlfriend. As far as I was concerned, I didn't have a dumb-shit girlfriend. I did, however, have a dumb-shit boyfriend. 'Call me crazy,' he said, 'but all I have to go on are the things you say to me. I'm not a mind reader.'

And wasn't that just half the problem? Men and women really were a different species. Jenny and I were legitimately telepathic, whether it was a life-altering crisis or just knowing when the other wanted ice cream. But Alex was just going on the actual words that had come out of my mouth? Bloody hell. No wonder he was confused.

'Can we just leave Jenny out of it for a minute?' I said, trying not to stand on an iPod Nano while making my point. It was not easy. 'Let me explain.'

'No, we can't,' Alex replied, standing up without nearly as much concern for the Christmas presents. He definitely trod on at least two Bloomingdale's Big Brown Bags. 'Because she's an asshole. And she makes you an asshole.'

'I'm an asshole now?' Fantastic. I was shouting. I was mad. We were officially having a row and I was no longer in control of my mouth in any way. 'Well thank God we didn't get married.'

'My thoughts exactly,' he shouted back and stalked into the kitchen. 'You know, all the way home on the plane I was thinking, maybe I can just pretend it didn't happen. Maybe I can just go on with the plan, but you know what, I can't. I won't be used. I'm not having this shit again.'

He opened and slammed a couple of kitchen cabinets before turning around and looking at me with an expression I had never seen before and never wanted to see again. He looked sad. He looked angry. He looked like there was nothing I could say that would change his mind. He looked heartbroken.

'Again?' I was too angry to cry but too scared to be angry. I really needed to see him smile. To see anything but that face. 'Used? Alex, this is getting out of hand. Can we calm down?'

'It got out of hand already.' His shoulders dropped and he turned to walk into the bathroom. 'I don't want to talk to you right now. I can't talk to you right now.'

The door shut hard and loud then I heard the lock click and the water run. In a complete state of shock, I stood in the middle of Christmageddon, listening to 'Last Christmas' and trying not to cry. I picked up the house phone and pressed the speed-dial.

Jenny answered on the first ring.

'What's up?' she asked through a mouthful of something.

'I need to come over,' I whispered. I didn't trust my voice with any volume. 'Now.'

'Is everything OK?' she asked, immediately alert. 'Should I come get you?'

'I'll get a cab,' I replied, never taking my eyes off the bathroom door.

'Angie, are you OK?' Jenny repeated. 'What's going on?'

'I don't know.' I felt my eyes tear up and my voice wobbled. 'But it's not OK. I'm on my way.'

Hanging up, I spotted my laptop hidden underneath a copy of *The Grinch Who Stole Christmas*, slapped it shut and picked it up. The bathroom was still locked. I rested my fingers against the light wood door and waited for a moment. I couldn't hear anything but running water. Leaving the apartment seemed so ridiculous, but staying felt impossible. I was too scared of what he might say when he came out. I couldn't lie beside him without talking it out, and I couldn't talk it out without one of us getting angry. So I did the only thing I knew to do when things were going badly.

I ran away.

CHAPTER TWENTY

'And then what did he say?'

Jenny was sitting on the sofa, combing her fingers through my hair while I sprawled on the hardwood floor, a Corona in one hand, a spoonful of New York Super Chunk in the other. To my left was the emergency bag of Monster Munch I kept at Jenny's. To my right was an open bottle of wine. Jenny had drunk all the tequila before I got there, so we were punctuating beers with shots of Sauvignon Blanc.

For the first hour, I'd done nothing but cry. Face down on the sofa, trying not to throw up. After that we moved on to senseless, tearful babbling. We had now reached the part of the evening where I tried to override my suicidal tendencies by overloading my brain with delicious food and as much booze as it took for me to pass out. Two beers and half a bottle of white was the optimum amount of break-up booze to start telling the story without breaking down at every other word. I wasn't too drunk to censor it slightly; telling Jenny the things Alex had said about her wasn't going to help here. I wanted to go home, not to his funeral, and mentioning the words 'dumb-shit' in relation to

Ms Lopez was tantamount to taking a hit out on Mr Reid.

'He said he didn't want to be used again,' I choked, pausing to regulate my breathing before knocking back the beer bottle.

Since my phone was in a bin somewhere in the De Lujo hotel, I couldn't even stare at it and wait for him to ring.

'Used again?' Jenny snatched up a crisp, popped it in her mouth then made a face. Before taking another. 'I'm confused. When was the last time you used him?'

'I don't think he meant me.'

If only beer bottles were crystal balls. And why didn't Bed, Bath and Beyond sell magic mirrors? Didn't they fall into the 'beyond' category?

'The French Bitch?' Jenny asked. She was referring to Alex's less than pleasant ex. Cici Spencer aside, I tried not to speak badly of other women, but Alex's last girlfriend? Now there was a female human being who had worked hard to deserve her given moniker. As far as I was concerned, she was going to that special circle of hell reserved for Hitler, Justin Bieber and the man who invented high-waisted jeans.

'I guess so?' My beer refused to show me what Alex was doing, no matter how hard I stared, so I drank it instead. 'Maybe I should call him. He knows I don't have a phone.'

'And he knows where you are,' Jenny replied. 'He's probably freaking out just as much as you are. You did the right thing. Hanging around after an argument like that when you're both tired and emotional? You only end up saying stupid things that you can't take back.'

'That's what I thought,' I pouted. So much for Jenny always giving bad advice, *Alex*.

'Now he has time to cool down, think about what he said. He'll realize he isn't mad at you. He'll call tomorrow.'

'He will call tomorrow,' I repeated until I was almost convinced, literally sitting on my hands to stop myself from picking up Jenny's house phone. And then I remembered the look on his face and my confidence wavered. 'He'll call.'

Three days later, Alex hadn't called.

After radio silence for the first twenty-four hours, I had called and left a voicemail. Nothing. The longer it went on, the more impossible it seemed to get in a cab, go home and talk to him. On the second day, Jenny got in a cab with me, but the apartment was empty. The glittery landfill that was my wrapping station was exactly as I'd left it, and the only evidence that Alex had been there at all was a scattering of record sleeves by the turntable, an empty pizza box and several dozen empty beer bottles. A half-full carton of fries on the coffee table had been filled up with cigarette butts. Alex never smoked unless he was incredibly stressed or in France. I really hoped he wasn't in France. Jenny's reassuring expression slipped as I tiptoed around the place, afraid I'd break something that wasn't mine.

'Do you want to stay until he comes home?' she asked. 'I'll wait with you.'

But I didn't want to stay. I was scared. Instead, I picked out some clothes, grabbed some toiletries and left, careful not to take too much. I was coming back, I told myself. I was absolutely coming back.

I'd hoped he would notice the subtle cues that said I'd been in the apartment. My moisturizer was gone from the glass shelf by the bathroom mirror. I'd taken my ever-present notebook from the bedside table. His Blondie T-shirt that I always slept in came out from under my pillow and went into my bag. I wanted him to see these things and call me, come for me. But he didn't. At four a.m. that morning, wide awake in Jenny's bed, I realized he wasn't going to call.

It had been a tough couple of days for both of us. Jenny was breaking her neck over her job and breaking her heart over Jeff. Since returning to New York, she hadn't seen Jeff or Sigge. It wasn't for the want of trying on Sigge's part, at least. He'd been calling non-stop, but so far Jenny had put him off with cries of late nights in the office and a prolonged post-Vegas migraine. He was buying it for now, but we had no idea how long it would last. Jeff, on the other hand, was a mess. With only two weeks to go until his scheduled New Year's Eve wedding, he still hadn't called it off. Jenny had seen a lawyer and confirmed their Vegas trip up the aisle wasn't legal and didn't even need annulling. Jeff had seen a bartender and confirmed nothing other than the imminent need for a liver transplant. At three a.m. we got the angry phone call. At four a.m., we got the tears. By ten a.m., I was signing for the flowers with their handwritten apology. But still he hadn't called off the wedding, and still Jenny wasn't ready to talk to him. It scared me to think Alex could ever be as mad at me as she was at Jeff.

Instead of waking up someone who was self-medicating just to get to sleep, I wandered into the front room and opened the blinds. New York was never that dark, even at four a.m. The room was lit up by the lights of Lexington Avenue, taxis racing up and down, people running in and out of the deli, stumbling out of the diner. If you lay down on the sofa and pushed yourself right back into the corner of the cushions, you could see the Chrysler Building.

When I first got here, that was enough to put a smile on my face, no matter what was happening, and I was heartbroken then, wasn't I? But this wasn't the same. The last time, I felt betrayed. It was as though everything I'd ever known had just gone away. But this was different. If I lost Alex, I wasn't losing everything I'd ever known, I was losing everything I ever wanted. He was my future, not my past. At least, I hoped he still could be.

With an uncharacteristic display of action, I picked up the phone and dialled his number. I knew it off by heart now. It rang through and I waited for the click of redirection to voicemail.

'Hello?'

He'd answered. I had no idea what to say.

'Hello?' His voice was tired but he was awake. I knew the subtle differences. I knew everything about him. Or I had thought I did.

'I'm hanging up now. Do me a favour and delete my number, OK?'

'It's me,' I said hurriedly, stretching out my toes until they tingled. 'It's me.'

He didn't say anything.

I didn't say anything.

'Where are you?' he asked eventually.

'Jenny's.' If only I could have said anywhere else in the world.

'Of course you are,' Alex replied. 'It's four a.m. Can we do this another time?'

'When?' My heart rose: he wanted to talk. My stomach sank: he didn't want to talk now.

'I'll call you,' he said calmly. 'When I can.'

He didn't hang up right away and the sound of his

breathing down the line made mine stop altogether. And then I heard the click, the dial tone, silence. The lights on the Chrysler Building blurred before me and I closed my eyes to make the tears go away. Going back to bed would mean moving, and moving would mean crying, so I rolled over, stuffed my face into the back of my old couch and let the tears seep into the cushions instead. He would call me when he could.

'So this is nice?' Jenny did not look amused. 'Is this supposed to be funny?'

'I forgot how loud it was here,' I admitted, wishing they would dial back the Beyoncé just a touch. 'It was just handy for everyone.'

Three days after the late-night phone call and I still hadn't heard from Alex. Apparently 'when I can' was some sort of symbolic answer, because I was certain he had the physical and financial ability to make a phone call whenever he damn well pleased, and yet . . . nothing. I was still crying on a daily basis – at toilet paper adverts, at little old ladies in the deli, at the ovulation kits in Duane Reade – but some righteous anger was starting to creep in. As was the need to distract myself. Luckily, I was armed with willing accomplices.

Crowded around a shiny silver table in Vynl, the gayest diner in all Manhattan, were Jenny, Erin and Mary, my editor from *The Look*. I was about to unveil The Plan. Just as soon as our waiter brought me my disco fries and Bloody Mary.

'They have Justin Timberlake dolls in the bathroom.' Sadie took her seat at the table with delight in her eyes. 'Like Justin Barbies. And they're playing 'Sexy Back'. This is the best place ever.'

'No it isn't.' Mary was never one to mince her words.

'Can we please get on with this so I can go back to work and be miserable in the comfort of my own office?'

'Yes we can, and no you can't.' I looked at the door. We were still waiting for one more person. 'I mean – well, obviously you can because it's your job, but don't you wish it wasn't?'

'I wish a lot of things,' she said. 'I wish I could win the state lottery. I wish George Clooney would stop lying to himself. I wish they would hurry up and bring my pancakes. None of these things are happening soon.'

Not the most inspiring start to my proposal, but I continued regardless.

'What if I had a new job for you?' I raised my eyebrows and waited for a reaction that didn't come. Sadie looked at me blankly. Jenny and Erin exchanged small shrugs.

'Oh, for fuck's sake.' I folded my arms and pouted. 'I want to start a new magazine and I want you all to help.'

'That's a cute idea, Angela.' Mary was the first to shoot me down. As predicted. 'But this isn't college. You can't just stick a bunch of photos together and take the whole thing down to Kinko's. Launching a magazine costs millions in marketing, and the Internet is kicking the whole industry in the ass right now. There's no way a new indie could make it in this market without huge backing.'

'Not even if you were editor-in-chief?' I asked. 'And if we had Sadie Nixon as our fashion director? And James Jacobs as our entertainment director?'

'No.' She narrowed her eyes. 'But keep talking.'

'And what if Erin Stein PR was behind us?' I looked at Erin and really hoped she was. Pregnancy had lowered her standards and she smiled beatifically, nodding along.

'It is,' she replied. 'And so are all of our clients.'

'And I could be the life coach,' Jenny jumped in. 'Can I be the life coach?'

'You can be whatever you want to be,' I said, beginning to feel a little better. 'It's your magazine, after all. Remember what we said on the way to the airport in Vegas? How there isn't a magazine for us? Well, if we feel that way, surely other women must feel that way? So why don't we start one?'

A buzz of ideas travelled around the table and I started to get excited. This was what I needed right now. This and my bloody disco fries.

'I don't want to be the one who kills this,' Mary interrupted, killing it. 'But everything I said still stands true. You'd need such a huge investment, and sure I've got experience, but you need money and a publisher, and that's not me.'

'I'm sorry I'm late.' A tall blonde of the less pneumatic variety dropped into a chair beside Sadie. 'Did you already tell them?'

Mary looked appropriately confused. 'Cici?'

'Delia.' Cici's good twin held a hand out across the table. 'You can tell us apart by the fact I'm not Satan. And I'm left-handed.'

'I did,' I confirmed.

'Did they tell you it would never work?' she asked.

'They did,' I confirmed.

'So here's the thing.' Delia was considerably more persuasive than me. As soon as she started talking, everyone perked up and leaned in to listen. Even Mary. 'My grandfather is Bob Spencer, as in Spencer Media. And while I've spent a lot of years avoiding nepotism in all of its forms, I'm ready to cash in. Angela came to me with a great idea involving a lot of great people, and I want to present this to my grandfather and have him back us. I mean, why isn't there a great weekly for women that isn't just full of celebrity gossip and crappy fashion? Other countries have made weeklies work – we can do the same.'

'So you have a business model?' Mary was clearly still having issues with the fact that this was not Sadie. 'As much enthusiasm as there is around this table, we'd still need a staff. We'd still need a sales team, a marketing team, a web team, all of it.'

'And we'll work that out,' Delia agreed. 'With you as editor-in-chief and me as publisher. And yes, Angela and I have been working on a business plan. The idea is that we'd start out as a free magazine, funded by advertising with an exclusive online component, sort of combining strong editorial with an online deal site. We'll distribute through high-end fashion retailers in New York who will benefit from the deal side of the business, then we move to LA and – stage three – we'll revisit our expansion plans across the US.'

'Delia did most of it.' I sipped my water with forced modesty. 'I just came up with the idea of the magazine.'

'You should get dumped more often.' Sadie patted me on the back and I fought the urge to take her arm and break it. 'This is awesome. When do we start?'

'We've started.' Delia looked around and smiled. 'If you're all in, I'm going to schedule a meeting with my grandfather next week.'

'And what are you going to do?' Jenny asked me. 'Because this is awesome, but it needs to get you a visa, otherwise I swear I will marry your ass.'

'That is very sweet, but I'm going to be web editor.' I patted her hand in an attempt to get the scary look out of her eyes. 'I talked to Lawrence and he thinks that will be enough to put through an application, so don't worry – that's one less wedding for you this year.'

'I knew you'd work this out,' she smiled. 'And it's a relief. I'm trying to keep it down to just one ceremony per annum. You know you're amazing, right?'

'I'm pretty good,' I laughed. 'I'd be better if I had my disco fries.' Our waiter was busy behind the bar, back to the restaurant, arse bopping along in time to Donna Summer. Clearly he had better things to do than feed his customers. Like, oh, texting. I nudged my poor, poor bag open with a booted foot and checked my new iPhone. Nothing. But just looking at the iPhone made me happy. I was such an Apple whore.

'Stop staring at your phone,' Jenny commanded. 'Every time someone swipes the screen of an iPhone, a fairy dies.'

'iPhones kill fairies?'

'iPhones will kill us all,' she said sagely. 'Cell phones suck. Phones suck. Communication sucks.'

'Has he called again?' I asked while Mary and Delia hammered out some points on the business plan and Sadie asked Erin incredibly inappropriate and personal questions about her pregnancy.

'Which one?' Jenny fiddled with the cuff of her purple silk dress. 'I feel like shit. Sigge is so sweet and I was just going to eff him over without a thought. I'm such an asshole.'

'Yeah.' I tried to sound sympathetic, but it was kind of true. Though only Jenny and I were allowed to say it. 'But you love Jeff. You weren't thinking.'

'I love Sigge too,' she replied. 'I really do. When I sat down and thought about everything, the idea of not seeing him again made me really sad.'

'And the idea of not seeing Jeff?'

'I don't have an idea about not seeing him.' Jenny's eyes burned. 'But I'm pretty sure if I saw him right now he'd be leaving this restaurant on a stretcher.'

'So call Sigge, meet him for dinner. Or brunch, maybe – less pressure,' I suggested. 'You won't know until you see him.'

She nodded slowly. 'Gonna take your own advice?'

'He said he'd call when he could.' I was not going to cry in front of my new business partners. 'And he'll call.'

Since leaving Vegas, James had become my official AA sponsor; that was Alexaholics Anonymous. Every time I wanted to call and demand he forgive me, I called James. And in return he gave me some scandalous Hollywood gossip. Win-win really. Alex got the time he needed, I got to find out who was secretly gay.

'Guys take so much longer to work stuff out – everything hits them harder,' she said simply. 'Women have so many shitty, annoying things to deal with every day. Smudging your manicure, beautiful shoes that hurt like a bitch, not fitting into your jeans – it's constant disappointments. The worst thing that happens to a guy is his sports team loses. It makes sense that they lose their shit completely when things don't go their way. They're not used to it like we are.'

My best friend was truly a genius. 'Please can you write that into an article for the magazine?'

'I can and I will. But you know, sometimes it's better to know than to wonder,' Jenny said quietly. 'What happens if he doesn't call?'

I considered her question for a moment. What would happen if he didn't call? Well, Christmas would happen; that was only a couple of days away. The New Year. Then the magazine. Then Louisa's baby. Then Erin's baby. Then Jenny would probably get married. And then I would die alone with a thousand cats.

'He'll call,' I said again and looked around the table,

taking in the excited expressions and passionate conversations that were going on. 'I know it.'

New York outdid itself with Christmas Eve. The sky was clear and pale blue, the air was crisp and cold, and we had the lightest smattering of snow that was threatening to give me the white Christmas I so badly wanted. Jenny, Erin and Sadie had also done a pretty good job of showing their goodwill to all men. Or rather women. More specifically, me. So far we'd had brunch at Sarabeth's off Central Park. We'd been to see the Radio City Music Hall Christmas Spectacular. We had fought through the crowds to see the Saks holiday window displays. We had made Jenny sit on Santa's knee. They were doing a stellar job of distracting me from the fact that my boyfriend, the love of my life, still hadn't called.

We were rounding out ten days and my faith in him was starting to waver. Jenny had stopped encouraging me to call him. Sadie had stopped tiptoeing around me in the apartment. Erin had bought me an airbed. I wondered how long it would be before they started suggesting I look for an apartment. I figured I was getting an extended Christmas grace period, but New Year and all of its promises of fresh starts would put an end to that. Who wanted to make a fresh start in January? Most days I didn't even want to put on fresh clothes it was so cold. Stupid January.

'So, ice skating next?' Jenny pushed her arm through mine, feeling through the padded parka for my hand as twilight fell on Manhattan. 'Rockefeller Center?'

'This is awesome,' I said carefully. 'But I am sort of exhausted.'

The three of them looked horrified, but there was nothing I wanted more for Christmas than to just go home and sleep. Well, aside from the obvious. Delia and I had been working every waking hour on our business plan and a mock-up of the magazine to show to Bob, and when I wasn't working, I was panicking about everything un-Alex-related as possible. What if my visa didn't go through? What if Bob refused to back us? What if he backed us but the magazine failed anyway?

'No way.' Sadie shook her head. I was starting to regret bringing her into the fold. I was constantly getting outvoted by her and Jenny. Plus she left the bathroom messy. 'We are getting our holly jollies on and you are not getting out of it that easily. Tired, my ass. It's motherfucking Christmas.'

'Indeed.' I replied. I turned to Jenny. 'Really?'

'I'll let you,' Jenny shrugged, 'as long as you're not going to go to bed and listen to his album and cry?'

'What if I am?' I sulked.

'I swear, woman, don't make me send your iPod the same way as your phone.' Jenny dragged me down Fifth Avenue against the surging stream of last-minute shoppers. Salmon were stupid. 'We're going ice skating, you're going to like it, and then we're going to, I don't know, consume a million calories in hot chocolate.'

'Fine,' I sulked. 'Ice Skating. Yay.'

I'd been doing a really good job of putting on a brave face. The public crying had subsided, and last night I'd managed to go an entire bath without sobbing once. I was still waking up breathless in the night, and I was still checking my phone fifteen times a minute, but I was trying. Trying just took up so much energy, I didn't have a lot left for Christmas, and no one was sadder about that than I was. The day the words 'dashing through the snow on a one-horse open sleigh' couldn't raise a smile from me, let alone a rousing chorus of 'horses, horses, horses, horses', was the saddest day of all.

The ice rink at Rockefeller was busy, as always, but Erin knew a girl who knew a guy who knew a more important girl and we got in right away. Playing her knocked-up card, she sat out and held handbags, officially in training for motherhood, while we swapped our boots for skates. This was not the first time today I wished Jenny had told me her plans instead of surprising me with this Christmas extravaganza. I would have worn jeans instead of a dress. And if I'd known we were going to Sarabeth's, I would have worn an elasticated waist. The gorgeous Alexander Wang wool shift Sadie had given me as an early Christmas present was beautiful, but it was not conducive to eating or skating. I skittered onto the ice looking like Bambi on his way to a very fashionable funeral. I doubted he had worn Wang to see off his mum almost as much as I doubted I would be spending the next thirty minutes upright.

Of course, Jenny was a skating pro. She whirled and spun around the ice while Sadie clung to the side and waited for hot single dads to come and chat her up. And come they did. Determined to live out my Christmas in New York fantasy, I put one foot in front of the other and slid out further onto the rink. I'd been good at this when I was fifteen. Louisa and I used to go skating every week. But then I'd also been good at braiding friendship bracelets and crimping my hair, and neither of those things happened terribly often these days. Hampered by a tight hemline and the wind resistance of my parka, I was not having fun. I wasn't having fun in general. I'd done such a good job at faking it, pretending to smile and laugh and have a good time, that I'd forgotten to actually enjoy myself. I'd forgotten *how* to enjoy myself.

And now it was Christmas Eve.

Right in the middle of the Rockefeller Center ice rink, I stopped. I looked up at the giant tree covered in colourful lights and froze. He hadn't called.

It was Christmas Eve and he hadn't called.

That was it. Something inside me snapped, something that needed to shout before it cried. He was not going to ruin bloody Christmas. But it wasn't a good idea to be angry on ice skates: I'd seen *Dancing on Ice*; I knew what could happen. Enough was enough, I decided, determined to get off the ice or die trying. I was going to get out of these skates, into my boots, get on a train, sit patiently for fifteen minutes, get on another train, sit slightly less patiently for fifteen more minutes and then march straight into my apartment and kick his arse. Of course it would have been far easier to commit to this plan if I hadn't immediately fallen flat on my face.

'Shit, Angie, are you OK?' Jenny was by my side in a moment, but it was too late. My palms stung and my knees ached and I couldn't quite catch my breath. Cue the tears.

'I'm fine,' I panted between sobs. 'It just hurts.'

Most of New York's skaters had the decency not to stare at the grown woman sobbing like a toddler as she was escorted from the ice. Dropping hard onto the bench, I yanked at my laces, angry at Alex, angry at myself, angry at whoever had told me I needed to tie a double bow in my skate laces fifteen years ago.

'You need a hand?'

'No, I don't need a—' I looked up with a glare that would put the Grinch out of business and stopped dead.

There he was. Alex.

For a moment I wondered if I had actually fallen and bumped my head, but one look to my left showed

323

Jenny, Sadie and Erin sidling away, small smiles on their faces.

'About time,' Jenny said, just loud enough to hear. 'I thought the asshole was never going to show.'

'Let me help you.' Alex knelt down and went to work on my ice skates. 'Jesus, do you have these tied up tight enough?'

I still didn't have any words. He was there, right in front of me. His hair covered his face as he bent down but I could see his long, slim fingers working the knots in my laces, the tips turning red against the cold.

'I was coming to see you,' I said.

'It's cold, but it's not that cold,' Alex replied, still busy with the skates. 'The East River didn't freeze.'

'And I didn't hear anything about mobile phone networks crashing either,' I replied. This was so confusing. I wanted to hug him and apologize and feel his skin on my skin and never, ever let him go. But I also wanted him to get my skates off as quickly as possible so I could bludgeon him to death with them. Until I made a decision which one of those I was going to go for, I sat still.

Alex looked up at me with rosy cheeks. Dear God, I wanted to pinch them so badly. Then slap them. Hard.

'I don't have an excuse. I went away for a few days, went to visit my folks, did a lot of thinking,' he started. 'But I should have called you. I kept dialling, but I just didn't know what to say.'

'But you know now?' It was better to know, I told myself. It was better to know than to wonder.

He nodded and pulled the sleeves of his jumper down over the tips of his fingers.

'I'm sorry.'

Oh. Oh.

'Everything I said, it was out of order. About you, about Jenny, about all of it. I didn't even mean the stuff I was saying, especially about Jenny. I was just so mad, I didn't know where to put it. I don't do angry too well.'

'I didn't tell her what you said about her.' I fought off the desire to start singing and dancing. At least until I'd got the skates off. 'That's why you're still alive, in case you were wondering.'

'So that's why she got so pissed off when I apologized.' Alex paused to face palm. 'Shit.'

'When did you apologize?' It was not a small part of me that wanted to know why Jenny had heard the words 'I'm sorry' before I had.

'When she called me last night.' He went back to work on the knots. 'She rang. She kicked my ass. I deserved it.'

I looked across the rink, but she was nowhere to be seen. The minx.

'Alex, *I'm* sorry.' I stopped his hands with mine and bent down until our foreheads were almost touching. He was really here. 'All those things I said, I just couldn't get it out right. I do want to stay in New York more than anything and there are a million reasons why, but you're the most important one. I was just too scared to say it before.'

'Scared?' He wrapped his fingers around mine until our hands were completely entwined. It felt spectacular.

'Of what you would say.' I shook my head, embarrassed. 'That you would freak out. Mostly, that it was true.'

'You were scared that you want to stay here with me?' His voice was so low, the nosy cow sitting to the side of me was really struggling to listen in. 'Why?'

'Because.'

'That's not actually an answer, dumbass.' Alex punched me gently in the knee. 'Because what?'

'Because that's out of my hands, isn't it?' I mumbled, wriggling my fingers free and setting to on the knots again. 'If I was staying for a job or for my friends or even just because I didn't want to go back, that's all something I can control a bit. Admitting I wanted to stay for you, that puts it all in your hands. Hence the scary. And I thought . . .'

'You thought I might not want you to stay?' Alex finished my sentence. 'You thought I might not want you to stay in the country and the best way to deal with that was to ask me to marry you?'

'I didn't say my logic was sound,' I answered. 'But that's why I said all those incredibly stupid things about marriage not being important and that it was just paperwork. I didn't mean it. I just . . . I was thinking about it in the way I thought you would be thinking about it.'

'But that's not how I was thinking about it at all.' He successfully unfastened one knot as I finally loosened the other. 'And you really made me think you believed all that stuff you said.'

'I didn't, though,' I protested. Who could have known I was such a good actress? 'I was just trying to protect myself and find a way to stay. And I just felt a bit like you weren't taking the whole visa thing that seriously. Every time I brought it up you kept telling me to wait until Christmas, and I didn't want to wait until Christmas – I was freaking out.'

'Yeah, I got that.' He helped me with the final knot. 'You just can't let a guy have a plan, can you?'

'I've already told Jenny.' I tried a little smile and it almost stuck. 'You can't ask Santa for a visa. He doesn't have any pull with immigration.'

'She tells me you don't need any help any more.' He was still kneeling in front of me, still close enough to kiss. 'This whole magazine thing sounds amazing. I'm so proud of you.'

'Yeah, I think it's going to work,' I said. It was too weird that something so epic had happened in my life and he didn't know about it. 'And they're going to sponsor my new visa, so you're totally off the hook.'

Alex took a deep breath and held my hand again. 'What if I don't want to be off the hook?'

I smiled. This time it was a real one. 'Well, you're not getting rid of me that easily. As much as I've enjoyed sleeping on an air mattress at Jenny's, I would really like to come home.'

'Yeah, but what if you didn't just come home?' Alex shuffled around until he was on one knee. On one knee and holding my hand.

'You don't want me to come home?' I was suddenly very confused. And the woman at the side of me was getting very excited.

'OK, how about I give you this and you understand what I'm talking about?' He reached inside his jacket pocket and pulled out a small black velvet box.

My eyes widened to the approximate size of the moon and I instinctively slapped his arm. Quite hard.

'Not entirely the reaction I was looking for.' He pressed his lips together, cleared his throat and looked up at me. I had suddenly been overcome by a severe case of acute Tourettes and concentrated on trying to keep my mouth shut. 'Angela Clark, since I met you, you've been nothing but trouble. Within a week of having you in my life your friend threw up on my couch, you didn't put out for, like, ever, and every time you leave the state it's one drama after another.'

I slapped him again. 'I hope you're going somewhere better with this.'

'And you're a total wife beater.' He rubbed his injuries. 'But I've also heard that you won a ton of money on the slots in Vegas, so that cancels that out.'

'Phew.' I looked up at the Christmas tree behind us and back down at Alex, wrinkling my nose to try to keep my tears at bay. 'Go on. Say nice things now.'

'And I know you won't believe me now you're some super-important publishing-type person with all of Vegas's riches at your fingertips, but I've been thinking about this for a while.' He handed me the box and nodded. 'In my family, we get to open one present each on Christmas Eve.'

'God, I hate when people do that.' I really did. 'It ruins Christmas morning, it—'

'Will you please just shut up and open it?' Alex said with some frustration. 'It's very cold and my knee hurts.'

'You old romantic,' I muttered, flipping open the box. For the first time that day, I was happy I wasn't wearing an elasticated waist. Things like this did not happen to someone wearing pyjama jeans. I gasped. Inside the tiny velvet box was a beautiful emerald ring. A cushion-shaped solitaire set in a white band studded with tiny diamonds. All the lights of the Rockefeller Christmas tree reflected in them, making a rainbow. 'Bloody hell.'

'Yeah,' Alex agreed. 'Right?'

I finally managed to tear my eyes away from the ring and looked at him.

'You can't possibly expect me to wear this and not lose it?' I was entirely serious.

'I do expect you to wear it and I kind of expect you to lose it,' he shrugged. 'I had it insured.' Alex slipped the ring out of the box and took my left hand in his and slid the ring onto my finger. Woah. So this was why Jenny had made me have a manicure. That sneaky cow.

'I got it in Japan. We were walking around this vintage store and they had a bunch of really old jewellery. I saw this and I just knew. I saw it and I saw you and I saw me and I saw everything,' he explained. 'And I did my homework. Emeralds are associated with stability and balance as well as love, creativity and communication. So it seemed like the right way to go.'

'You've had this since Japan?' I asked. It was beautiful. Everything was so beautiful.

'Yep.' He curled my fingers closed and kissed my hand. 'So, how do you feel about opening your Christmas present early?'

'I don't have yours.' There was no point trying to stop the tears now, so I let them come.

'I found the guitar under the sofa,' Alex admitted. 'I totally looked.'

'Did you like it?'

'It has Batman on it.'

I paused, breath bated.

'I loved it.'

I knew it. Truly, we were soulmates. 'In that case, I accept my present.'

Alex smiled. I smiled. He nudged himself closer and pressed his forehead against mine. 'Angela Clark,' he whispered. 'Will you marry me?'

'Yes,' I replied, kissing him hard. Alex wrapped his hands in my hair and I rubbed my fingers over my new ring, PDA Nazis be damned. Behind Alex, the lights of the Christmas tree blurred with my tears and somewhere I could hear a choir singing. OK, so it was a hip-hop reinterpretation of 'Frosty the Snowman' and not choirs of angels, but this was New York. I felt his lips curving happily against mine and I knew this was how it was meant to be.

'Now go and get my boots back from Erin – my feet are freezing.'

'Jesus, woman.' He pulled my hair and kissed me again. 'Are you going to be this difficult once we're married?'

I think we both knew the answer to that.

Angela's
Guide
to Vegas

HOTELS

The Cosmopolitan

This is a super new, super swanky rock and roll hotel. And I do mean rock and roll – loads of bands play at The Cosmopolitan and the rooms are tricked out with amazing hot tubs and super-luxe balconies with gorgeous views. If I had to live in a hotel, it would be this one.

Palms

Palms is set a little way back from The Strip which means it's a little cheaper and a little calmer. As well as cool bars, clubs and a huge pool, it has an awesome spa with an outdoor hot tub. Go midweek, book yourself in and try not to cry about how happy you are when you have the whole place to yourself.

Caesar's Palace

To me, Caesar's is proper Vegas. It is fully committed to its theme, the mall has an amazing animatronic battle of the gods type thing with a massively unsafe fire hazard. I love it. And Celine sings here. What more Vegas could you want?

Imperial Palace

OK, so it's not fancy but it's a great location and they have a 24-hour-café that will serve you buckets of tea when you're in need. Proper tea. If you're looking for Vegas on a budget, this is a pretty decent option. But again, it is not fancy. No fanciness here.

RESTAURANTS

Nine @ Palms

This is one of Vegas' more fancy-schmancy steakhouses. It's at the Palms so again, off the Strip, but if you're not staying here, you could do a lot worse than dinner at Nine, drinks at Ghostbar and dancing at Moon. Celebs do it. And isn't that what Vegas is all about?

Bouchon @ The Venetian

Touted as one of the poshest spots in all of Vegas, Thomas Keller's flagship French dining spot at the Venetian is the perfect place for an uber celebration . . . like a wedding reception? Or simply if you want to eat more butter than it would take the average cow a year to produce. And they have cheese as a category on the menu. This pleases me.

Bellagio buffet

Everyone says the Bellagio buffet is the best buffet in Vegas and I'm inclined to agree. It sounds stupid but there is literally anything you can think of, from pizza to curry to eggs Benedict to fruit salad and chicken fried steak. Yeah, you heard me, chicken fried steak. Do it.

The Striphouse @ Planet Hollywood

The Striphouse is a great option if you want old-school glamour without leaving the Strip. Tucked away inside Planet Hollywood, it's all dark wood and framed pin-up photos. Very sexy. Giant hunk of cow? Also very sexy. Possibly I'm a little odd.

BARS AND CLUBS

Ghostbar
Back out at Palms. Ghostbar sits on top of the hotel and has a huge glass platform so you can enjoy your cocktails, floating in thin air. It's very swanky and the views are unsurpassable, bring your best heels ladies. Fellas, bring your best lines, the ladies are pretty intense.

Marquee
Super cool new club at The Cosmopolitan with a pool. Yes. A pool. For swimming. While clubbing. Even though it hasn't been open that long, they've already pulled some of the biggest name DJs in the world – which would mean more to me if I knew anything about DJs. But I do know it's cool. Because someone told me.

Tryst
The nightclub at the Wynn is every bit as fancy as you would expect. Velvet ropes and pricey old drinks but it's worth every penny. Where else can you dance in the open air next to a waterfall? A great dance party with a great atmosphere, definitely one for the to-do list.

MUST SEES

Lion King

I love a musical. I love Disney movies. Should you choose to combine the two, add several frozen Dreamsicle cocktails and throw the whole lot into a Vegas blender, you get the most magical experience of all time. And if you're very lucky, someone will shout 'No Mufasa, don't die!' really loudly. And that someone will be me.

Helicopter ride over the Grand Canyon

The Grand Canyon is an amazing sight at the best of times, but from a helicopter, it's just stunning. Compared to the constant visual assault of Vegas, it's a complete mindfuck. You must do this, it will be something you remember forever. Just don't turn up hungover. For reals.

Stratosphere rides

Please take a moment to imagine the best rollercoaster you've ever been on and put it on the top of a hotel. That's it. Honest. This place is absolutely worth the trek down to the 'old end' of the Strip if you're a thrill seeker. And you're in Vegas so surely you are?

Aquarium at Mandalay Bay

Aside from musicals, Disney movies and rides on various things (get your mind out of the gutter), I love aquariums. I know that's weird but I do. I'm scared of the ocean and terrified of big fish but I do like going to see them in their tanks. There's something awesome about being face to face with a shark when it can't eat said face. Ta-da!

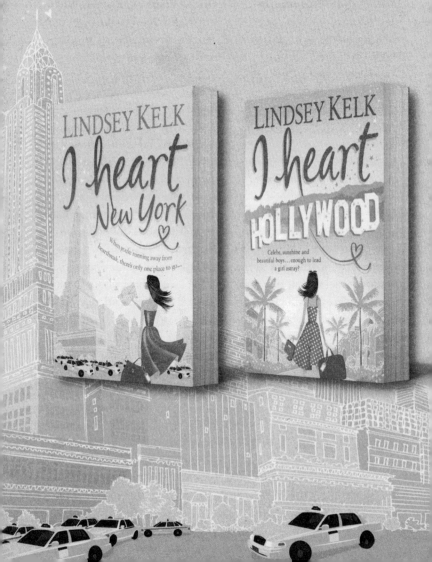

THE REST OF THE SERIES!

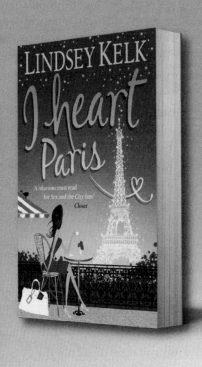

Log onto
iheartvegas.co.uk
to find out
more about all the
I heart titles.

You'll also have a chance to enter competitions, keep up-to-date with Angela's adventures through her blog, read top tips for where to eat, drink, shop and sleep in Vegas, and much much more!

The Single Girl's To-Do List

Newly heartbroken Rachel Summers must complete a Top Ten list compiled by her best friends to kick-start her fabulous, new single life – but nothing can prepare her for the adventures that unfold…

'Laugh-out-loud'
Heat

'Very entertaining'
Sun

'Fab'
Star Magazine

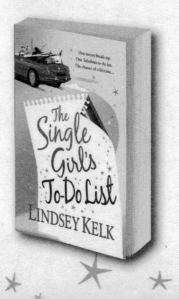